KISS THE WALLFLOWER

Books 1-3

TAMARA GILL

COPYRIGHT

A MIDSUMMER KISS

Kiss the Wallflower, Book 1

Orphaned at a tender age, Miss Louise Grant spent her life in servitude to care for her younger siblings. Now, no longer needed as a duchess' companion, Louise has procured employment in York. But on her last night in London, her reputation is shattered when the drunk and disorderly Marquess mistakes Louise's room for his lover's.

Luke, the Marquess Graham is determined to never torment himself again by daring to love. Stumbling into Miss Louise Grant's room destroys his days of bachelorhood when he is pressured into marrying her. However, the cold and distant Marquess knows they'll never have a happy marriage; his new and fetching wife will never crack the protective barrier around his heart.

Trying to make the best of a bad marriage Louise attempts to break through the icy visage of the Marquess. But when misfortune strikes and Luke reverts to his cold, distant former self, Louise is not willing to give up on the possibility of love. After all, ice will melt when surrounded by warmth.

CHAPTER 1

Miss Louise Grant folded the last of her unmentionables and placed them into the leather traveling case that her closest friend and confidante the Duchess of Carlton—Mary to her close friends—had given to her as a parting gift. Louise slumped onto the bed, staring at the case, and fought the prickling of tears that threatened.

There was little she could do. Mary was married now and no longer in need of a companion. But it would certainly be very hard to part ways. They'd been in each other's company since Louise was eight years of age, and was sent to be a friend and companion for the young Lady Mary Dalton as she was then in Derbyshire.

The room she'd been given in the duchess's London home was now bare of trinkets and pictures she'd drawn over the years, all packed away in her trunks to be soon shipped north to a family in York. Six children awaited her there, in need of teaching and guidance and she just hoped she did well with the new position. She needed to ensure it was so since her own siblings relied on her income.

Surely it should not be so very hard to go from a lady's companion to a nursemaid and tutor. With any luck, perhaps if they were happy with her work, when Sir Daxton's eldest daughter came of age for her first Season, perchance they may employ her as a companion once more.

Certainly, she needed the stability of employment and would do everything in her power to ensure she remained with Sir Daxton's family. With two siblings to care for at her aunt's cottage in Sandbach, Cheshire, it was paramount she made a success of her new employ.

Mary bustled into the room and stopped when she spied the packed trunks. Her shoulders slumped. "Louise, you do not need to leave. Please reconsider. Married or not, you're my friend and I do not want to see you anywhere else but here."

Louise smiled, reaching out a hand to Mary. "You do not need me hanging about your skirts. You're married now, a wife, and I'm sure the duke wants you all to himself."

A blush stole over Mary's cheeks, but still she persisted, shaking her head. "You're wrong. Dale wants you to stay as much as I. Your brother and sister are well cared for by your aunt. Please do not leave us all."

Louise patted her hand, standing. As much as Louise loved her friend, Mary did not know that her aunt relied heavily on the money she made here as her companion. That without such funds their life would be a lot different than it was now. "I must leave. Sir Daxton is expecting me, so I must go." Even if the thought of leaving all that she'd known frightened her and left the pit of her stomach churning. Mary may wish her to stay, but there was nothing left for her here. Not really. Her siblings were settled, happily going to the village school and improving themselves. Sir Daxton's six children were in need of guidance and teaching and she could not let him or his wife down. They had offered to pay her handsomely, and with the few extra funds she would procure from the employment, she hoped in time to have her siblings move closer than they now were. A place that no one could rip from under them or force them to be parted again.

The memory of the bailiffs dragging her parents onto the street...her mother screaming and begging for them to give them more time. Even now she could hear her mother's wailing as they threw all their meager belongings onto the street, the townspeople simply looking on, staring and smirking at a family that had fallen low.

None of them had offered to help, and with nowhere else to go, they had moved in with her mother's sister, a widow with no children in Cheshire. The blow to the family was one that her parents could not tolerate or accept and her father took his own life, her mother only days later. Their aunt had said she had died of a broken heart, but Louise often wondered if she'd injured herself just as her papa had done.

Within days of losing her parents, Louise had been placed in a carriage and transported to Derbyshire to the Earl of Lancaster's estate. Having once worked there, her aunt still knew the housekeeper and had procured her a position through that means.

She owed a great deal to the earl's family, and her aunt. She would be forever grateful for the education, love and care they had bestowed upon her, but they had done their part in helping her. It was time she helped herself and started off in a new direction, just as Mary had done after marrying the Duke of Carlton.

"Very well." Mary's eyes glinted with unshed tears and Louise pulled her into a hug.

"We will see each other again and I will write to you every month, to tell you what is happening and how I am faring."

Mary wiped at her cheek, sniffing. "Please do. You're my best friend. A sister to me in all ways except blood. I would hate to lose you."

Louise picked up her valise and placed it on top of one of her many trunks. "Now, should we not get ready for your first London ball this evening? As the newly minted Duchess of Carlton, you must look simply perfect."

"And you too, dearest." Mary strode to the bell pull and rang for a maid. "You're going to look like a duchess as well this evening. I have not lost hope that some gentleman will fall instantly in love with you as soon as he sees you and you will never have to think of York or Sir Daxton and his six children ever again."

Louise laughed. How she would miss her friend and her never-ending hope that someone would marry her. But the chances of such a boon occurring were practically zero. She was a lady's companion, no nobility in her blood or dowry. Perhaps she would find a gentleman's son in York, a man who would love her for the small means that she did possess—a good education and friends in high places. A man who would welcome her two siblings and their impoverished state and support them as she was trying to do.

"One can only hope," she said, humoring her. "I will certainly try, if not for my own sake, then definitely for yours, Your Grace."

Mary beamed. "That is just what I like to hear. Now, what should we do with your hair…"

CHAPTER 2

The first balls of the London Season had been taking place all week, and the Duke and Duchess of Carlton's was one of them. An event for the senses, with hothouse flowers upon every surface the ballroom could tolerate. Hundreds of candles blazed in the four chandeliers that ran the length of the room. The floor was so highly polished that one could see their own reflection in it. Nothing was spared to make Mary's debut in town as successful as the new Duchess of Carlton.

The ball was a crush, which was just what one wanted when hosting such a party. Louise stood to the side of the room, a little behind Mary, and watched as her friend and the duke stood greeting those who attended, the duke's hand never leaving the arch of her friend's back.

She smiled at their love and turned to watch the *ton* at play. As much as she had to think of her future, her brother's and sister's future and security, she would admit that she would miss this life. Being a companion did have its advantages, and she rarely did menial work that would normally be required of the position. Mary would not have it.

When she reached York she doubted she would ever have a moment's peace with six children underfoot. But, if that was the price she had to pay for keeping her own family safe, fed and clothed, then that is what she would do.

The strings of the first waltz sounded and the duke took Mary's hand, leading her onto the floor. Louise stepped forward, taking Mary's champagne. "Enjoy," she said to her friends, content to simply watch.

A tittering flittered through the bystanders and Louise turned to see the Marquess Graham, the Duke of Carlton's closest friend, bow to Lady Clara Quinton, eldest and only daughter to the Duke of Law. The young debutante waved her silk fan with a floral design before her face, her eyes coy as she pretended to make up her mind to dance with him or not.

Louise rolled her eyes. There were few who would not dance with the marquess, herself included. The man was beyond handsome, he was almost too pretty in fact for her palate. If such a thing were possible. His dark hair was unfashionably long, set atop his shoulders on the few odd occasions he wore it down. Tonight it was tied back with a little black ribbon and her fingers itched to pull the thread, watch it fall so she too could feel if it was as soft as she'd always imagined it.

Lady Clara gave in and placed her hand atop his, stepping out to join the waltz.

Louise watched as he pulled the young woman into his arms with expertise and in the scandalous way that had the *ton* tittering that he was going to ask for the woman's hand in marriage. They were certainly very comfortable with each other and Lady Clara was unquestionably a catch. An heiress with breeding that went back five hundred years, or so she'd been told numerous times by her ladyship's own companion at events such as these.

She sighed. How delightful it would be if there were men who looked like the marquess in York. It would indeed improve the outlook of her life if she could at least dream of one day marrying such a handsome man and be happy.

Due to the maddening crush, two women standing beside her shuffled closer to Louise. They both turned to glare at the offending people who were the cause of their annoyance. Their conversation drifted to Louise and for a moment she broke her own set of rules and listened. It was her last night in London after all, what harm would it do to eavesdrop for a moment or two?

She cast a furtive glance their way and recognized the widow, Lady Margaret Scarboro and her friend whose name escaped Louise at present. Her ladyship's tone was seething, low and trembling as she spoke of Lady Clara who danced with the marquess.

Her ladyship's friend bestowed on the dancing couple a cold stare and it stood to reason that she too disliked the marquess's choice of dance partner as much as her ladyship did. Louise wondered over it a moment. Lady Scarboro was a widow, and so it could be surmised that she'd harbored a tendre toward Lord Graham. Certainly if her ladyship's verbal assault was any indication, his lordship should not waste his time with such feeble and innocent women who'd likely bore him to death within a month of marriage.

Heat bloomed on Louise's cheeks at the insinuation of such speech. She flipped open her fan, idly cooling herself. Although she was unsure of the exact particulars Lady Scarboro spoke of, it was not hard to surmise what her words had meant. Louise stepped away, distancing herself lest anyone think she was part of such conversation.

She didn't need anything to stand in her way of leaving for York in the morning, and she certainly didn't need to leave London with the *ton* gossiping that she'd taken part in the blighting of one their brightest stars. Lady Clara smiled up at the marquess, an amused glint to her blue eyes. The young woman was in love with him, it was obvious to all who chanced a look in their direction. Certainly the gossip must be true. It would only be a matter of time before they were wed and she wished them well in their endeavors.

CHAPTER 3

Luke Ashby, Marquess Graham stumbled along the corridor of the Duke of Carlton's London home, counting the doors as he went. His eyes watered from too much whisky, and the passage swam like a pendulum in a clock. He halted, clasping the wall for support as the world threatened to turn topsy and fell him on his ass.

He took a deep breath, the thought of the delectable widow Lady Scarboro who awaited him in a room keeping him on his feet. All night she'd teased and touched him, the heat in her eyes enough to singe his skin at times. The candescent touches on his person left him with little doubt as to what she wanted. Her one good, hard stroke of his cock as they were seated at supper, hidden by the table top, even now made him throb.

Luke took a calming breath, forcing himself to feel up to the challenge of making her ladyship's introduction into his bed one that she'd remember for years to come, and possibly therefore allow him to do it again.

He smiled at the thought, walking on and thankfully, coming to the fifth door from the stairs, just as she'd instructed him. He glanced up and down the passage, hoping no one would miss him from the ball that was still in full swing downstairs.

A small twitch of conscience plagued him at the thought of bedding a woman in one of his friend's bedrooms, but the thought of her wrapped about him, taking him into her willing, hot body expelled such doubts.

Without knocking, he entered the designated room, and closing the door, stood at the threshold a moment, willing his eyes to focus in the dark space. He could faintly make out the shape on the bed, a dark presence in the room. No candle burned to light his way, nor was the fire stoked high enough to allow him to see clearly.

Damn it, he'd break his neck walking to the bed.

"Margaret," he whispered, creeping closer with caution. "Margaret," he said again, louder this time. Luke ran a hand through his hair. "Do not tell me she's fallen asleep," he mumbled. If that were the case his reputation for a libertine would be shot to hell and he'd never be able to face his friends at Whites ever again.

To have a woman fall to sleep on him was scandalous!

"Are you asleep? I thought we had other plans." He dipped his voice, shuffling out of his superfine coat and throwing it aside. Quickly he rid himself of his waistcoat and reaching behind his head, pulled his shirt from his person.

He reached out, grappling for the bed, and finally feeling the soft textures of the blankets, he climbed atop it. His lips quirked and his cock swelled at the slight form, lying in wait beneath him. He ran his hand along her leg, squeezing it a little and enjoying the long lines of her body.

Margaret rolled onto her back, a delectable little sigh escaping from her lips.

"I'm here, darling. Do wake up, we have games to

play." Luke crawled over her fully, feeling his way to kiss her.

The moment his lips touched hers—the softest lips he'd ever felt in his life—his alcohol-confused mind recognized that something was wrong. Dreadfully not right.

The woman beneath him stilled, her lips puckered tight without an ounce of give in them. He frowned, pulling back. "Do not tell me you've changed your mind."

A scream rent the air, piercing in its intensity. He stilled, shocked at the deafening sound and lifted himself back, trying to make out who the woman screaming bloody murder was underneath him.

Luke scrambled backward, unable to get off her quickly enough. The door flew open, slamming against the wall with its force and he swore. The light from the hall beyond threw visibility into the room. The duke and duchess stared at him in abject horror and to Luke's dismay, disappointment clouded his friend's eyes.

"There has been a mistake." He held up his hand, halting Carlton's step toward him. "Dale," Luke said, bending to pick up his waistcoat and shirt. "I thought it was Margaret in the bed," he whispered, cringing as more onlookers started to build in the doorway.

He grimaced, looking back toward the bed, frowning as he tried to place the woman who glared at him, her fierce blue eyes brimming with fire. Luke slipped on his shirt, hastily throwing on his waistcoat and tying up the buttons.

"Would you look at that," a feminine voice purred from the doorway. "The Marquess Graham's breeches are open. Why sir, you are most indecent for those who can see you." Luke's fingers flew to his pants and he tied up his front falls, the hole in which he found himself growing wider and deeper by the minute.

Dear God, how would he get himself out of this mess?

The duchess entered the room, walking over to the woman. "Are you well, Louise? We heard you scream."

The woman cast him a dismissing glance. "I'm well, Mary," she said, shuffling out of bed. "I do not know what any of this is about. I was asleep and the next thing I know there is a terrible weight above me that reeked of sweat and spirits."

Luke scoffed. "I do not smell, madam." A voice cleared and Luke met the raised brow of his friend.

"I think that is not the point, Graham."

Shit. Luke glanced at the ceiling, anywhere but the many faces watching what was at play from the door. The duke walked over to everyone. "Do go back to the ball. We will join you all shortly."

Margaret, Lady Scarboro, stepped forward, blocking the duke from shutting them out. "I hope the marquess is going to do what's right and offer for the girl. To ruin someone so callously, an innocent with siblings to consider." Margaret shook her head and Luke fisted his hands at his sides. *How dare she.* It was her that he was supposed to meet, and now she was playing the honest and honorable card. That was rich coming from a woman renowned for cuckholding her husband during their marriage.

Those about her ladyship mumbled their agreement, staring at him as if waiting for him to do just that, kneel down and propose. He would not! Luke glanced at the duchess who had placed a dressing robe over the woman beside her. The girl wasn't a debutante, and although he'd seen her before he could not remember where.

The duke shut the door with a resounding bang, but he didn't avert his attention from the duchess or her companion who spoke in hushed, rapid tones.

"Lady Scarboro did not seem to know that you were

meeting her. If I can trust what she'd just stated at the door about you." The duke walked over to the hearth and sat in the wingback chair. "But I would believe you over her ladyship. Her history of being deceitful leads to such a surmising. Even so, you and Miss Grant have been found in bed together, with your front falls open, no less. Tongues are wagging as we speak and if we're to limit the damage to Miss Grant, there is only one solution that I can see."

"I will not marry her."

"I will not marry him."

Both their words merged into one refusal and Luke heaved a sigh of relief that he wasn't about to be hitched to a woman he did not know, or had ever heard about within the circles that he graced.

He shuddered at the idea of marrying, of having a wife and possibly children in the future. Having been orphaned at an early age, he no longer needed such support and had grown up relying on himself for most things. His grandmother was always there, hovering like a ghoul, but she too was gone now and he was on his own.

Just as he preferred it to be.

Marriage did not fit in with his plans.

The duke stared at him, unmoved, and panic clawed across his skin. "You know I never plan to marry, Carlton. We will explain that I simply entered the wrong bedchamber and be done with this mess."

"You will not be done, though, will you, Graham? The *ton*, at this very moment, will be spreading across town what they saw here tonight. My wife's friend's reputation will be ruined."

Luke spied his coat jacket and, picking it up, shuffled into it. The young woman's face was pale, her dark-blue eyes wide with the announcement that her reputation was lost. Guilt assailed him, but he forced it aside. He should never had agreed to come upstairs to have some fun and games with Lady Scarboro.

Her ladyship's smugness flashed before his eyes and his own narrowed. Had she planned this for him? Had she schemed to force his hand with a woman who was far removed from him in his social standing?

"You're suggesting that I marry her." Luke took a calming breath. This could not be happening.

"If you do not, Miss Grant will be ruined." The duke came over to the fire, holding his gaze. "You're better than this, Luke," he said, using his given name. "You must do the honorable thing."

He swallowed the bile that rose in his throat. The room closed in around him, his skin prickled before a cold sweat ran down his spine. He'd never wanted to marry. Such a road led to heartache and despair and he would not put himself through that emotion again.

The duchess and Miss Grant spoke quietly beside the bed, Miss Grant glaring at him with any opportunity that was afforded her. He stared down at his feet, cringing. Whatever would he tell his cousin? They had made a promise, a pact that the title would go to his relative, his heir upon Luke's death. A wife meant the possibility of children, of a family of his own.

He ran a hand through his hair. The idea repulsed him. If indeed he did find out that he was tricked into this scheme by Lady Scarboro he would ensure she was ostracized by the *ton*.

"Miss Grant, it seems that my error has led to us being placed into a position of matrimony. I will marry you and I apologize for any trouble this may have caused you. It was not my intent."

He cast a glance at Miss Grant, watching as the duchess spoke into the young woman's ear. The woman was not unfortunate in appearance, her hair was a pretty deep-russet brown color and her eyes were large and round, perfectly shaped brows arched over them. Her full lips were set into a displeased line, but even that position revealed two dimples on either side of her cheeks.

No, Miss Grant wasn't so very bad in relation to her looks, but her breeding, her non-existent dowry. Well, that was another matter entirely.

He would never live down this mistake.

She sighed. "Very well," she said, raising her chin. "I will marry you, but only because I'm being given no other choice. Do not expect anything from me."

Luke raised one brow. The word *prickly* floating through his mind. "Good, because you should not expect anything from me either."

The duke clapped his hands, drawing Luke's attention back to him. "It is done then. You are betrothed."

CHAPTER 4

Aweek passed and still the marquess had not returned to marry her. He'd left a missive for the duke telling him he'd gone to Doctors Commons in London to procure a special license from the Archbishop of Canterbury. A procedure that may take some time and a hefty amount of guineas if what Mary had told her was true. Even so, a week did seem overly prolonged, even to Louise.

She sat alone in the duke and duchess's drawing room. A book lay closed and unread in her lap, her ability to do anything other than think about the Marquess Graham impossible.

At this very moment she should be in York, starting her new life and ensuring the safety of herself and her siblings. She sighed, placing the book on a nearby table and standing. Her letters to her family should have reached Sandbach by now and they would know their situation had changed.

Over the past week Louise had ample time to think about her change in circumstance and a small part of her, the common sense part was happy that marriage was imminent. Her brother and sister would return to town to live with her, and she could possibly secure them a better future than she could've given them before. Give them the life that their parents had not been able to. A life where one did not need to worry about whether they would eat dinner that evening or not. If they were able to order a new winter coat or boots.

It had been better for them all from the moment her aunt had procured her the position with the Earl of Lancaster, but still, Louise had always wished for more for them. They were good people and deserved only the best.

Her mind wandered to the marquess. A marriage to such a powerful man within the *ton* had never been her goal. A simple country gentleman would've suited her very well. He was so very well-regarded in the higher echelons of Society, even if he did have a wicked reputation when it came to women. She shivered, unsure if she would be able to meet his standards both within Society and in his bed.

As a companion she was always there and yet excluded. Not part of the set or seen, rarely spoken to and mostly ignored by the society in which she circulated. Of course, Mary had never treated her in such a way, had always tried to include her and ensure she was happy, but Mary's friends had not, and it had been easier to meld into the silk wallpapers than to cause raised brows when she imparted information or an opinion on a subject that they did not see her fit to know about.

A footman in bottle-green livery knocked and entered the room. "A letter has arrived for you, Miss Grant."

She took the missive, recognizing the seal to be Sir Daxton's. Louise broke the seal and read the missive quickly.

. . .

Miss Grant,

We have received word that you were found in a compromising situation with the Marquess Graham. Please take this letter as termination to our agreement for you to travel and work for my family. As a Christian man I shall take this opportunity to express that your sins will not be forgiven by God and I suggest you repent such behavior and seek forgiveness before your soul is doomed for eternal damnation.

Sir Daxton

"Well," she said aloud, reading the note again to ensure she understood what she read. She had written to Sir Daxton, explained her situation had changed, but obviously he'd heard the scandalous part of her betrothal. The marquess had sent out a notification in the paper that they were to be married. Obviously not soon enough if she was to receive such missives from people in York of all places. Was the whole of England in possession of her downfall?

Damn the marquess and his inability to keep from sampling the female flesh for one evening.

Had his lordship actually ruined her then she could understand such reactions from people, but to be accused, shamed for an event that was none of her doing was unacceptable. She was still a maid for heaven's sake.

Mary strode into the room, male voices accompanying her. Louise turned to watch as the duke and Marquess Graham entered close on Mary's heels. Glancing past them all, she spied an elderly man with thin graying hair brushed flat on his head with the help of some sort of pomade to hold it in place. His lined face had seen many years, and he waddled into the room with a decided limp.

"Prepare yourself, Miss Grant. We're about to be married." The marquess came up to her, looking her over as if she were some horseflesh he was inspecting for his stable. "Not the finest gown, but under such circumstances, that will have to do."

"Graham," the duchess chided, taking Louise's hand and squeezing it a little. "Don't be so blunt. If you've not forgotten the whole reason my friend is in this predicament is because you could not behave yourself for one night."

Louise sniffed, lifting her chin. "I was thinking the same thing before you joined me."

The marquess took her hand, placing it on his arm, and walked her over to where the priest waited for them before the fire. Louise looked down at her hand atop his arm. Her fingers were gloveless, her having not thought she'd need them in the drawing room today. Had her mother been here she would've been so terribly aghast that she hadn't worn gloves on her wedding day.

Fear shot through her at the realization. This was her wedding. She was marrying the Marquess Graham, which meant tonight would be her wedding night. She swallowed, her heartbeat loud in her ears and drowning out the priest's words.

The priest mumbled through the ceremony, and Louise, as if hearing herself from a far-off distance, answered when required. It all happened very quickly and soon enough the priest was pronouncing them husband and wife. The marquess stared down at her and she raised her chin, ignoring the fact that she would not have been the type of woman he would've ever married under normal circumstances.

She may not be a diamond of the *ton*, a woman of wealth and good bloodlines, but she was also not to blame. They were in this position because of the rogue before her, and it was his fault that he'd had to marry a woman of no rank or anything else.

Her breath lodged in her throat and for a moment she

thought he might lean down and kiss her. Instead he turned, shaking the duke's hand and accepting a kiss on the cheek from Mary. That his smile was lackluster should not hurt, but it did. She'd told him herself not to expect anything from her, and he should not.

Still, to be so undesirable was not what a bride, no matter the circumstances, wished to feel on her wedding day.

"I think champagne is in order to toast to the new Marquess and Marchioness Graham," the duke said, turning to a footman nearby and requesting the beverages.

The footman did as he was bade and within minutes a crystal flute was handed to each of them. Mary held up her glass, smiling. "To the happy couple. May you only have bliss and," Mary pinned the marquess with her gaze, "may you know what a gift you've been given this day."

Heat rose on Louise's cheeks and she glanced down at her shoes, anywhere but the marquess or the duke whom she had no doubt was willing his wife to behave. Louise almost snorted at the idea. Mary was not one to be told what to do.

The champagne was cool, fruity and refreshing and the nicest thing that had happened to her so far this day. She furtively took in the marquess. He wore a day suit of royal blue. His cravat drew the eye to his lordship's neck, and the wide shoulders that followed. He was a tall gentleman, a man without fault some would say, but he did have a fault.

And it was her. His marriage to her.

Louise finished her drink. "Am I to stay here, Lord Graham or am I to move to your townhouse today?" There was little point in not discussing the elephant in the room. Her and her sleeping arrangements. She would of course prefer to be traveling to York instead of being married to such an ogre. This was not the type of marriage she'd thought to have for herself. Even if she'd only married a man of little means, she'd always hoped there would be affection between them. No amount of money in the world—and the marquess had quite a lot of it from all accounts—could make anyone happy.

His eyes widened and it wasn't hard to tell he'd not thought that far ahead when he'd decided today was the day they would marry.

She raised her brow. "Should I have my trunks sent over or would you prefer another night as a betrothed and not a husband?"

Mary chuckled and turned it into a discreet cough. The duke glanced at his wife, shaking his head.

"You shall return with me, of course. Mary will have your things sent over directly. I have already hired a lady's maid for you and she'll attend you upon arrival."

It was Louise's turn to be surprised, but she schooled her features, not wanting him to know she'd not thought it possible of him thinking of anyone else but himself. "Very good."

The marquess glanced between them all and Louise felt very little inclined to help him fill in the awkward silence that had fallen between them. The situation was not ideal and as no one was particularly happy about what took place not a half hour ago, one was not inclined to celebrate.

"Well then, I suppose we should be off," he said, placing his champagne glass on the table.

Louise nodded, turning to Mary and the duke. "Thank you for all you've done for me over the years, Mary. I will always be grateful."

Mary waved her thanks aside, pulling her into her arms. "None of that. We've always been sisters and we shall continue to be so even after our marriages."

Louise returned the embrace, blinking to stem the tears that threatened at having to leave her friend, her home and a place where she'd always felt welcome and respected. To leave and travel with Lord Graham, enter a home where the servants no doubt knew the dubious start to their union would be humiliating. They probably thought she'd trapped and tricked the marquess.

"Remember, Louise, to be true to yourself and the marquess will soon see that he has married a rare gem among the paste littering the *ton*."

Louise chuckled. "We shall see I suppose, but in any case, I shall make the most of the marriage and try my best."

Mary let her go and they started toward the door where the duke and marquess had already walked through. "I know you will and I hope with all my heart that you find happiness. I know this is not what you wanted, and I'm sorry this has happened, but also another side of me, a selfish side I suppose, cannot help but be thankful that I'll have you in town. A neighbor across the park in fact."

"That close?" Louise said as they made the front steps.

Mary pointed across Grosvenor Square to the row of townhouses across the green. "The marquess lives in that large property with the black door, so we shall see each other regularly and I do want to see you as often as possible."

Louise smiled. "I know, and thank you. I shall call on you later this week and we shall have tea."

LUKE STUDIED MISS LOUISE GRANT, now Louise Ashby, Marchioness Graham who sat across from him in the carriage, her attention fixed somewhere outside the window. He had thought over the day, their wedding and ultimate marriage he'd be stuck with until his death and he'd come up with a plan that would suit all those involved. Even Louise he was sure.

He would take her out to his country estate in Kent, settle her in the Graham family seat and return to town, finish up the Season, his parliamentary duties and return to Ashby House in the fall. The carriage rocked around the corner, heading for the southern road out of London and he spied the moment she questioned their direction.

"Mary said that your home was across the park. Are we not returning there, my lord?"

He tore his gaze away from her, disliking the fact she looked quite pretty in her day gown, her eyes wide and bright with query.

"We're traveling to Kent this evening, not far from Maidstone in fact. My estate is not far from London, four hours by coach. Your luggage will arrive tomorrow."

Her brow furrowed. "But Mary said... That is to say I thought I was going to be living with you. In London."

He chuckled dismissively and she flinched. He ignored the pinch of conscience that he'd hurt her feelings yet again and strove to ignore his emotions. What did Louise expect, after all? He'd told her that he would give very little in the marriage and she had too. This was no love match, or even a mild affection match. They were simply two people who had been forced to wed due to his own error of judgement and Society's narrowminded views.

He rubbed a hand over his jaw. To be forced to wed simply because he'd entered the wrong bedchamber was absurd. That he was married at all, a bona fide bachelor of the *ton*. It was well known among his friends that he never wished to marry, or beget heirs. He had his cousin set to fill those shoes and responsibilities.

His father, god rest his soul, would not be pleased by his decision in life, but he simply could not find it within himself to long for such things. Not that he wasn't fond of children—several of his friends had married and produced offspring—but to think they could be taken away within a moment of time, due to illness or an accident... He shuddered.

No. He did not want to experience such heartache.

Losing his parents and sister had been enough pain for one lifetime. He did not want to go through that again.

"She was mistaken. We're to travel to Ashby House and that is where you'll stay. Of course I shall not impose myself on you this evening, even though consummation is recommended, but we have time for such matters. You need not fear me on that score." His gaze traveled once again over her delectable, womanly curves, her delicate hands that rested in her lap without gloves. He would have to ensure that she was properly attired. He would have the best modiste sent from London to make up a new wardrobe for her. No wife of his would be shabby and without fashion sense.

Her eyes flashed fire. "I'm not afraid of you, my lord. You may sleep with me or you may not, it makes little difference to me."

He turned his full attention to her. A light, rosy hue kissed her cheeks. He bit back a smile. She may speak forward and without shame, but her words had embarrassed her a little.

"Do you wish for me to come to you tonight? I will of course, but not without your approval. It would be no chore, I can assure you, and I promise to make it worth your while."

She shifted on her seat, giving him a dismissing sniff. "I

shall pass, my lord. But thank you for your kind offer in any case."

They rode along in quiet for a moment, the sound of the wheels on the dusty gravel road along with the coachman who spoke to the horses every now and then the only sound to break the silence. "Well, do let me know if you change your mind."

CHAPTER 5

The Marquess Graham's estate was too pretty for words, just like its master. Louise stood outside the mammoth front door. The windows flickering with the reflection of the afternoon sun was blinding. Not to mention the size of the home was, in her common opinion, simply ridiculous. Who needed homes as large as this? She took her newly minted husband's arm as he led her indoors and was sure upon entering the hall that the entire village of Sandbach's population could fit under its roof.

"Your home is very grand, my lord. Very beautiful." Her eyes darted everywhere, unable to comprehend that she was now mistress of such a grand estate. Gold-lined paintings of the marquess's family hung on the walls, delicate furniture sat in corners and before windows. The curtains hung the full length of those windows, billowing upon the marble floor. Opulence was everywhere she glanced about, trepidation running through her that she'd fallen into the role of wife and caretaker of all these fine things left no small amount of fear.

The staff lined up before the staircase and his lordship

introduced her to everyone in a matter of minutes. Louise tried to remember who was whom, but with so many of them it would take her many weeks before she would be able to memorize each of them.

"And this is our housekeeper, Mrs. Dunn. She'll ensure you know your way about and what is required of you as mistress of the house."

Louise clasped the older woman's hand. "It's lovely to meet you, Mrs. Dunn. I think I shall rely on you quite a lot after seeing the marquess's home."

The housekeeper's eyes widened and darted between her and the marquess. "Shall we go upstairs? I will show you to the marchioness's rooms if you like."

Luke gestured for them to go, before he turned and started for the door. "Are you not coming with us?" Louise asked, halting her steps.

He took his time in turning around to face her. "Apologies, my dear, but I have business in town. Mrs. Dunn will ensure you're settled and well cared for. I shall be back when I'm able to get away from London."

Louise kept her attention on the marquess as he turned about and left, closing the door with a decided bang and seemingly putting an end to their newly minted marriage also. She gritted her teeth. How dare he do such a thing to her? It was not her fault they were in such a predicament. If he'd only been able to keep his desires in check both of them would be living the life they both wanted.

A little voice taunted that this life was a lot better than the one she was going to have in York. To be nursemaid and tutor to six children would have been taxing for anyone. Not to mention being away from Mary and her siblings would've also been trying. At least married to a marquess gave her freedom to better care for those she loved.

"Come, my lady. I think you should see your rooms. When we received word that the marquess was marrying, he instructed us to prepare your rooms. He ordered new curtains and linens for the bed. No expense spared and I must admit to thinking the room is quite the prettiest in all the house."

Louise pushed all thought of the marquess—Luke—from her mind and followed the housekeeper. The upstairs to the home was no less extravagant than the downstairs, and the staff bustled about, lighting and changing candles, placing hot-house flowers in vases, some swept and dusted the many pieces of furniture the marquess owned. The house was a hive of activity, a place of employment for many it would seem.

"How many staff does the marquess have at this estate, Mrs. Dunn?"

"This is the largest estate of the marquess and he has eighty-five at last count. But bear in mind that includes gardeners, stable hands, gamekeeper, those types of trades. It's not all house staff I should mention."

Louise mulled over the number. If there were eighty-five people here, how many people across all his estates did his lordship have? And now she too was responsible for these workers, and in turn, their families who relied on them. "Please be assured that if there is any issue with anything that any of the staff have, any concern at all, do not hesitate to come to me. I will always be available to them."

Mrs. Dunn stared at her a moment, before she nodded, a small upturned twist to her lips. "Thank you, my lady. I shall endeavor to do so."

They came to a stop before a set of double doors. Mrs. Dunn turned the handle and pushed them open, revealing the room. Louise gasped, stepping into the great space, at a loss for words. For there were no words to describe such a beautiful space. The marquess had not spared expense with redecorating her suite, as Mrs. Dunn had mentioned. Pastel colors covered the chairs, the bedding and curtains. It was as if summer had kissed the room and left it blooming. Flowers of the same soft color palette sat atop her mantle, and a small, round table with two small chairs sat beside the large bank of windows. A pretty place to write letters perhaps.

Louise walked over to the windows and looked out on the vast property beyond. Lawns for as far as the eye could see spread out before her, a river, flickering under the summer sun ran between the trees beyond and she sighed, a feeling of peace, contentment and happiness overflowing her. This was her home now. She was a marchioness.

Oh, the wonderful things she could do with that position.

"Mrs. Dunn. I have two siblings who live with my aunt in Sandbach, Cheshire. Please have two more rooms cleaned and prepared for their arrival. They'll be here within the week."

"You have siblings, my lady?" Mrs. Dunn beamed at the news. "Oh, it's been many years since we've had more than his lordship under this roof. To have a wife and her siblings. Well, that is wonderful, my lady."

"My brother and sister are both fifteen, almost sixteen. They've been living with my aunt for some years. I'm sure you've probably heard already that I was the Duchess of Carlton's companion prior to marrying the marquess." Louise saw little point in trying to hide who she was, she had nothing to be ashamed about in any case. "I could not have my siblings with me then, but I certainly can now. I know my aunt would like to travel and has not been able to due to her commitments with my siblings. But that can change now and if I'm to be here at Ashby House without the marquess, I shall have my siblings here instead."

"So they shall live here permanently?" Mrs. Dunn asked, her eyes bright.

"Yes, they will." And if the marquess had any issue with her inviting her family to stay, he could come out to Kent and tell her himself. Louise untied her bonnet and slipped it off, placing it on a nearby chair. "What I've seen of the house so far is simply beautiful. Will you show more of it to me before dinner?"

Mrs. Dunn bobbed a quick curtsy, gesturing toward the door. "Of course, my lady. Please follow me."

Louise stepped out of the room, no longer Miss Louise Grant, a lady's companion. Instead, she was the Marchioness Graham. And if she could not have the affection of her husband, she would at least gain the affection of his staff.

LUKE RODE HARD atop his mount toward London, needing to distance himself from his bride. A woman whom he had every right to lay claim to, to take into his bed and bed her good. Instead, he hauled back to London as if the devil himself were after him.

And perhaps he was. At least the female version of the archangel.

Town was not so very far away, and within a few hours the outskirts of London started to pass him by. He was thankful for it. Tonight he had the Clinton ball that he'd been looking forward to attending. Even if he were only married hours ago, that did not mean that his life should alter or stop simply because of a woman.

He cursed the mistake that led him down this path. If

he happened upon Lady Scarboro this evening, he would demand she own up to her part of his downfall. For he had fallen. He shook his head. *Married.* Not only married but married to a woman with no rank or lineage. A lady's companion.

It wasn't to be borne.

But somehow he must. Luke pushed his mount on, determined to continue with his life as was, and be damned the weight that now hung about his neck. With Louise settled at Ashby House she would be well cared for and happy, as he shall be in town.

She expected nothing and he in turn wanted nothing. Of all the marriages he could have had, at least in this respect it was tolerable.

CHAPTER 6

One month later

Louise sat in the drawing room and read for the second time the latest missive from Mary. Her friend was decidedly annoyed and put out at the marquess, who she reported went about town as if he'd not married at all. Mary begged her to return, to take up her place as his wife at his London home and put to rest the rumors that the marquess had continued his life of carelessness as if he were still a bachelor.

"I think the duchess is right," her sister Sophie said, staring at her with an annoyed air. "Who does this new husband of yours think he is? He cannot go about town just as he did before. His life has changed. He has a wife."

Louise sighed, folding the missive and slipping it into the small pocket on her gown. Sophie was right of course and so was Mary. The marquess from all reports was making a farce of their marriage. And as poor as she was, as low as she'd been on the social sphere, she was now a marchioness and that at least gave her a voice. A voice to stick up for herself and the future she wanted.

"You ought to march into London and show the marquess you'll not put up with such treatment," her brother Stephen said, striding into the room. He wore a newly purchased riding jacket and pants and his knee-high boots gave him an air of a country gentleman.

Within a week of being at Ashby House, Louise had her siblings brought to stay, and over the past month all of them had transformed somewhat to the people the world expected them to be. At least outwardly they suited the accommodations they now called home, even if Louise felt like an interloper every minute of every day.

Hence why she'd not traveled to town when Mary wrote to her asking where she'd disappeared to. To enter the *ton*, walk side by side with the very people she once worked for, a companion, an invisible woman behind a one of means, was not something that Louise thought she could do.

Nerves twisted in her stomach at the thought of being so bold and she stood, coming to join Sophie on the settee before the unlit hearth.

"The marriage is not one in the truest sense. I did not expect anything from the marquess and he in turn did not want anything from me."

"So what?" Sophie said, raising her brows. "Things change and what...you're expected to rusticate here in Kent for the rest of your young life, alone and without the prospect of children because the marquess cannot give up his wayward lifestyle?"

"Sophie, lower your voice, the staff will hear you," she chided.

"Let them hear us," her brother cut in. "We ought to

pack you up and leave. We'll come with you, Louise. The marquess needs to know that he's no longer a bachelor. That he has a wife, my sister, and I'll not let him treat you in such a way." Her brother stared into the dark hearth, his fingers tapping idly on the marble mantle. "I thought these toffs had honor. Your husband doesn't seem to have any."

Louise let all that her siblings were telling her sink in. Over the last few days they had stated this exact plan multiple times. They were angry with the marquess, she could understand that, but to travel to town, to invite themselves into his home felt wrong somehow. "What if we travel to town and he refuses to let us stay?"

Stephen threw up his hands. "Let him try. You're his wife, not some wench off the street. And if he does treat you with so little respect, I shall call him out and put a bullet through his cold heart."

Louise stood, coming over to her brother and taking his hand. "When did you become so honorable and sweet? You're a good man. Do not ever change."

He leaned down and kissed her cheek. "I shall never change, but as for your husband, he certainly needs to before he loses the wonderful gift that is our sister."

Sophie came over and hugged her about the waist. "If you go to town, we shall come too. We shall support you in winning the respect of the *ton* and their lofty prejudices. The marquess has a wife, and so he now needs to act like a husband."

She smiled at her siblings. How she had missed them and their encouragement. If her marriage was a disaster, at least it had enabled her to have her siblings back under her roof. To be able to feed and clothe them without the worry that circumstances may change that could jeopardize that.

"I have no wardrobe for town. I know the marquess sent a modiste to us here in Kent, but she only gave me a few gowns to get about the house and estate. I have nothing suitable for a London Season. However will I afford such a thing?"

Sophie smirked, seating herself back down on the settee. "You charge everything to your husband of course, silly. He'll pay for everything. And if you don't, I certainly will make sure everything that you purchase is of the highest quality and the most expensive item in the store. We will shock him out of his bachelorhood that way if we must."

Louise wasn't so sure such an idea would be a good one. What would the marquess say when he started to receive such bills? He had not wanted her as his wife and so now to have to pay for her gowns could be a bitter pill to swallow.

"I doubt the marquess would like that," Louise said.

"Good," her brother declared, ringing the bell pull and ordering tea. "I hope he does not. After his treatment of you this past month, sending you away as if you're a dirty little secret, I hope the bills from London's best modiste, boot makers and milliners pricks his conscience that he's been a dreadful bore and ungentlemanly in his treatment of you."

Louise clasped her roiling stomach. Could she do this? Could she return to town and be the woman worthy of the title of marchioness? She was educated, well-versed in how people were to behave in polite Society. Her best friend was the Duchess of Carlton for heaven's sake.

She nodded as fire singed away the nerves in her stomach. "Very well. We'll return to town and I'll enter the Season. It's my right, after all. And if the marquess does not like it, I'll simply ask Mary if we may stay at her house until Season's end."

Sophie clapped, her long, golden locks giving her the

air of an angel, although her soul was as strong and determined as a fallen one. "We'll leave as soon as we can organize ourselves, no more than two days I should think. And then, my lady, you shall show that husband of yours that to treat a Grant in such a lowly manner is not recommended."

"No, it's not," her brother piped in, thanking the footman who brought in a tray of tea. "He'll soon learn that you're not to be tossed aside as if you're worthless. It's his fault you've had to marry him. The Grants are fighters and if you want more from your marriage, even if that more is only children, then you deserve that happiness. Do not let this little hiccup at the beginning ruin your future."

Louise stared at her siblings. When had they grown up and become so knowledgeable and supportive? She nodded, determination thrumming through her veins. "You are both correct. I'll inform the staff we're to travel to town. Let us see if we can make a splash big enough to be noticed."

Sophie laughed. "Oh, you'll make a splash all right, and it'll be big enough to drown the marquess."

If only... At least, Louise would certainly try.

⚜

THEY ARRIVED in town three days later and thankfully settled themselves into the Marquess Graham's London townhouse without incident. In fact, upon arrival they were told that the marquess was not in residence, was in fact staying at his flat that was closer to his gentlemen's club, Whites.

It should not have surprised Louise that he would opt for a smaller residence. Even so, her fear of being so bold as to come to London had well and truly been replaced with annoyance that her husband would treat her in such a way.

The staff at their London home seemed as pleased as those at Ashby House to have someone to attend to. After the housekeeper Mrs. Ellis had shown them the house, and introduced the staff, Louise had opted for tea in the front parlor, wanting a moment alone. She sat down at the ladies' writing desk and pulled out a piece of parchment, quickly writing a missive to Mary that she'd arrived in town. She invited her friend to attend her outing tomorrow and begged her for assistance to help her with her first foray into the *ton* as the Marchioness Graham.

She rang for a footman using the little golden bell on her desk. He entered within a moment, bowing. "You rang, my lady?"

"Please have this letter sent directly over to the Duchess of Carlton's home. Also, I need a carriage tomorrow morning. We're going shopping and I'll need its services most of the morning and possibly the afternoon."

"Of course, my lady." The young man dipped into a curtsy and left, the soft click of the door loud in the sizeable room. Louise took a calming breath. She could do this. She was not an interloper or unwelcome here. She was the Marchioness Graham and no matter what her husband thought of that detail, she would show him that she was here to stay and that no one made a fool of her.

Especially when none of this was her fault.

THEIR SHOPPING EXPEDITION was unlike any Louise had ever experienced in her life. The shop assistants went above and beyond to help her and the duchess in choosing the full wardrobe of evening gowns, day gowns, morning and riding ensembles. Colors that suited her dark hair and fair skin. Nothing that left her washed out or looking sickly. When holding up the deep reds and greens, she had almost looked like a different woman. Gone was the lady's companion, and in her place stood a marchioness. A woman who in her own right had power within the *ton*, whether the Society she now graced liked it or not. She was here to stay and she would not let anyone, not even her husband, look down on her and her common beginnings.

Had she not had such a humble start in life, she would not be the generous, caring woman she was. Which, in her estimation, was a lot better than those born to wealth that cared nothing for the common man or his struggles.

After her gowns, hats, caps and bonnets were ordered from the modiste and promised within a fortnight, they had gone on to purchase a riding hat from a gentlemen's hat maker. They visited shoemakers and ordered slippers and evening shoes. Reticules, gloves, muffs and shawls were ordered, all to suit the different gowns and outings she'd attend.

To celebrate their afternoon of shopping, of fun and plenty of laughter, they had traveled to Gunthers and tasted sweetmeats, pastries and fruit ices. The outing together had given Louise a chance to catch up with the duchess, whom she'd not seen since her marriage to the marquess. And allowed the duchess to get to know Louise's sister Sophie who accompanied them.

"You're going to look beautiful at the Kirby ball next week," Mary declared, smiling. "Madame Devy has assured you the sapphire embroidered gown will be delivered by then. As much as I care for Lord Graham, his treatment of you is intolerable and I'm looking forward to seeing him eat humble pie."

Louise took a sip of her tea, enjoying its rejuvenating qualities. "I'm sure I'll see him before the ball. The accounts he's to receive in the coming days will no doubt alert him to my arrival in town. The size of the bills may ensure I see him sooner rather than later."

Mary and Sophie chuckled. "You may be underestimating how much you're worth now, my dear. The Marquess Graham's estate is one of the richest in the country. I believe Cavendish is on equal bearing with your husband's wealth." Her friend threw her a mischievous grin. "The accounts may alert him to you being in town, if your staff has not notified him of this fact already, but I do not think this is what will bring him to your door. He'll be more interested in why you've returned to London when he'd decidedly relocated you to Kent."

Louise bit her lip, the thought of facing her husband for the first time in a month making her skin prickle. He would not be pleased she'd ignored his decree and returned to London. He'd likely demand she return to Ashby House and forget about the Season altogether.

"Well, I won't be going back to the country. Not until after the Season ends at least," she said, determination cloaking her words. "I may be his wife, but I'll not be sent back to Kent like an embarrassing little secret. I cannot help but be disappointed that he's not put a stop to the talk about town about our marriage. I know he never wished to marry me, but now that he has, all due to his own tomfooleries, he should squash any talk about us. My arrival in town at least should put to rest that he'd sent me off to the country never to be seen again. Now I have to try and gain some respect within the *ton*. Not that I care what they think, but I'll not be laughed at. Not by any of them."

"I shall be right beside you too, and the duke also. The marquess and the *ton* will not stand a chance of bringing you down." Mary plopped a pastry into her mouth with a determined nod.

Louise liked the sound of that and hoped it would be so. This was her life now, no matter if she'd imagined different. She was married and the sphere in which she now circulated was exalted. That did not mean that she would lose who she was, for nothing could change her principles, but she would not let those who sought to tarnish her name to continue. The Marchioness Graham was in London, and she would not be looked down upon by anyone. Not even her husband. The marquess and the *ton* would not stand a chance in bringing her down.

CHAPTER 7

Luke had heard the rumors over the last week. His wife was back in London. The stiff-rumped chit had gone against his orders and returned to town. Not that he'd expressively demanded her to stay in the country, but he'd not thought she would leave their country estate for the viperish world of the *ton*.

Which, in fact, had turned out to be exactly what she'd done. And if the accounts he'd received over the past week were any indication, she was spending his money like water on a wardrobe fit for the Season.

He sat in his carriage and took a decidedly calming breath. The Kirby ball was one event they would both attend. The Duke and Duchess of Carlton had demanded his presence in support of their mutual friend Viscount Kirby who had just inherited his title. Of course he would've attended in any case, whether his wife was present or not, for he would never leave Christopher alone to face the horde of young ladies who would no doubt be looking to capture his attention. The lad was only one and twenty, too young for marriage and he would not have him become prey to the matrons of the *ton*. No matter how well they thought the young lord would suit their charges.

That his wife would also be present was merely a complication or annoyance depending on his mood. Over the last few weeks he'd pushed aside the hurt he'd registered on her face when she'd realized he was leaving her in Kent. It was his fault, after all, that they were married, she didn't deserve to be treated with his wrath. He was more angry with himself than with her. He'd placed them into this position. His selfish need for pleasure had outweighed his common sense that night and now they would both pay for his sins.

The mistake had caused ripples throughout the *ton* and of course with his cousin, whom Luke had promised the title would revert to upon his death. His relative had taken the news of his marriage reasonably well, even so, Luke had assured him that the union would not bear children and so the title would be his cousin's one day.

Luke tapped on the roof and the carriage door opened. He strode into Lord Kirby's Mayfair residence and shook his hand at the doors to the ballroom. His young friend seemed uncommonly nervous, and he supposed stepping into the new shoes of viscount and being so very young was want for some anxiety. A few whiskys would put him right.

He strode into the ballroom, the crush of people almost as oppressing as the smell of perfume and sweat. His nose twitched and he started toward the windows where at least some fresh air may venture indoors and save his senses.

Luke spotted Carlton, who seemed to have his very idea of being near a window and he made his way over to him. "Evening. Looks like Kirby had a good turnout this evening."

Carlton, thankfully on his own, his duchess nowhere to be seen, nodded. "A successful ball for his first." The duke took in his appearance before turning back to watch the dancers. "Good to see you here. I had wondered if you would stay away."

Luke took a crystal flute of champagne from a passing footman, taking a much-needed sip. "I suppose you're implying that because my wife is to attend that I would not." He glanced at his friend. "I promised Kirby I would be here tonight and I am. My wife had no bearing on the matter."

Well, a very little bearing. He was interested to see how she had fared all this time without him. How she took to the sphere in which she now circulated. Luke schooled his features as he studied those about him. He did not see Louise among the faces.

"She's not here yet. Mary is bringing her tonight, but they had a small dinner party to attend to first at Lady Scott's. A woman both the duchess and marchioness have known for some time."

Luke ignored the fact that Carlton assumed he'd been searching for Louise, he didn't want anyone to see that he was curious to see her again. Instead, he mulled over Lady Scott and tried to put a face to the familiar name. "Was she not married to a Scottish viscount? He passed away, did he not?"

Carlton smirked. "Died under his mistress for all accounts, although the family will never state such a thing publicly. You may wish to watch what Lady Scott says to the marchioness. She's not a supporter of infidelity."

People would assume, based on Luke's past behavior, that he *was* a supporter of infidelity. They couldn't be more wrong. When one was married, one ought to take their vows seriously. It was a conversation that he needed to have with his wife. He didn't want children, and she certainly did not wish for him to be her husband, so some sort of agreement would need to take place between them. He could not go the rest of his life without sleeping with a woman, so his wife would ultimately have to be his bedpartner, slake his needs, but they would have to be careful. Louise had said for him not to expect anything from her, and such a proposition suited him to a point.

Luke finished his champagne, placing the glass on the window ledge behind him.

"Have you seen the marchioness since her return to town?" Carlton asked, his attention fixed on something near the ballroom doors.

"I have not," he answered, unable to remove the indifferent tone from his voice. "I do know she's been spending a small fortune at the dressmaker's, but otherwise, no, I have not called on her."

Carlton's smirk deepened and Luke frowned. "What is it? Is there something I should know?"

The duke nodded toward the door and Luke glanced through the crowd and the breath in his lungs seized. He felt his mouth pop open and he closed it just as quickly, not willing to let anyone know that the sight of his wife left him…stunned.

The duke cleared his throat. "Who knew Miss Grant was so very beautiful."

Luke frowned, the compliment on his wife not as welcome as he thought it might be. To hear another man say such a complimentary thing didn't sit well and he adjusted his stance, schooling his features.

How was it that the young woman he'd interrupted from sleep was this dark-haired beauty, with striking blue eyes and tempting mouth. Companion or not, how had he not seen her before…

Because you were not looking close enough.

Luke pushed the thought aside, smiling a little in welcome as the duke of Carlton and his wife came to stand before them. The duchess went straight to the duke, wrapping her arm in his. Louise came and stood at Luke's side. Even from here he could feel her pulsating with anger, with annoyance at his presence. He took her hand and placed it on his arm, turning toward her.

"You look beautiful, my lady." Legally that was exactly what she was. His lady, and yet, from the hard set of her lips, her stance against him, her not being a willing participant to this farce of a marriage was obvious.

Out of his peripheral vision he took in her sapphire gown with the billowing silk skirt that did little to hide her bountiful figure or slim waist. She was nothing like he remembered, not that it changed their circumstances or his thoughts on their marriage, but at least she now looked the part of marchioness. That was something, he supposed.

A footman bowed before her, and she took a glass of wine. "How very fortunate to run into you here, my lord. How have you been, *husband?*"

Her use of the term husband startled him and he tore his gaze back to her, not missing the amused grin on her lips. "I think I'm as well as you are, *wife*." His reply merely garnered him a chuckle that ran over his skin and felt like feathers, enticing and soft.

Lord Stopford bowed before the marchioness, barely giving Luke a second look. "Would you care to dance, Lady Graham? I see that your husband has not done the right thing by you and asked, and so I thought to remedy the dissatisfaction."

She let go of his arm and stepped out with his lordship. "I would love to, thank you."

Luke smiled at their parting, and yet anger thrummed

along his spine. Their marriage was not wanted by either of them, and yet the idea that she may take a lover, cuckhold him, made his stomach roil.

It should not. Only a moment ago he himself recognized the need for them to speak about what would occur in their marriage. But the marchioness could not have a child that was not his, should the worst happen and she fell pregnant. He would never allow another man's son to inherit his title, so where did that leave them?

He watched as Louise laughed and danced with the exceedingly handsome earl. Grudgingly he had to admit that she looked beautiful in the man's arms, more so than he'd ever known. As a lady's companion he'd always known her to be about the duchess, a friend in need if required, but he'd never glanced beyond Mary's shoulder to look at who stood in the shadows.

A failing on his behalf, but he was a marquess. A man of his stature and rank within the *ton* was expected to make a marriage worthy of the title. In his case Society at large did not know he intended never to tick that box.

But now that he had, and seeing his wife dancing in the arms of another man, well, now he didn't know what the hell he was feeling at all.

"Troubled?" the duke asked, leaning close to ensure privacy. "He is but one of many who've noted your absence from the marchioness's life and seem set on remedying the situation."

He clenched his jaw, his teeth aching. "The marchioness has been making a spectacle of herself?" Not a fair question, even he would admit, but it would force Carlton to tell him the truth of the situation without looking as desperate for information as he was.

"The marchioness has been beyond reproach, and we have escorted her everywhere, and returned her home at the end of the night," the duchess inserted, her cool gaze dismissing him before she looked back toward the dance floor.

"Louise is not whom you should be worrying about. There is a rumor about London, as you're probably already aware, that you do not intend to have a true marriage. That you were overheard at Whites as stating the union was in name only." Carlton narrowed his eyes on him and Luke felt as small as a bee. "The gentlemen who have no interest in a bride have taken that, along with your continual attachment to your bachelor residence in Mayfair, as confirmation that you do not care one whit what the marchioness does or with whom."

The duke's words rang with dread and Luke stared about the room, noticing for the first time this night that the guests glanced his way, small, secretive smiles on their lips and laughter in their eyes. Was this what people were thinking?

He sighed, adjusting his cravat. He ought not kid himself. It was his fault they were gossiping about him, his marriage and what kind of life he was willing to have with his wife.

No life at all.

Luke mulled over the complexity of the situation. The thought of having a child with Louise, while not wholly awful, left dread to churn in his stomach.

Damn the *ton* and its stipulations, its rules and censure.

"I suppose that means that I'll have to change that opinion and soon."

The duchess raised her brow, giving her husband a secretive smile that Luke did not appreciate.

"I suppose it does, and if I were you, I would do it sooner rather than later. Tomorrow would suffice."

Luke followed the marchioness's progress as she

stepped off the dance floor, walking with Lord Stopford until they came to another group of gentlemen and some ladies. They welcomed her into their circle and spoke amicably.

His hands fisted at his sides as his lordship's hand sat upon her back, too familiar and too damn close. Lord Stopford laughed at something someone in the set said, and glanced Luke's way. If he registered that Luke didn't appreciate his hands upon his wife he did not show it, he merely kept his hands upon her person.

What the blasted hell was Louise thinking to allow him such liberties? She was a lady's companion, she knew the rules of what was correct and incorrect. And yet, from what he knew of the duke and duchess's courtship, maybe the woman knew when to be lax in her rules and what was appropriate for a lady in such a situation. Louise had certainly granted her charge—now the Duchess of Carlton —liberties she should not have been allowed.

Before he knew what he was doing his feet took him across the room. He charged across the dance floor, ignoring the startled *yips* and *excuse mes* as he went directly across to where Louise stood with her group of tactile *friends*.

Where were these people when she was nothing but a lady's companion? Certainly, nowhere he'd ever seen them. They had not wanted or bothered to know who the duchess's companion was and Louise should not be such a fool to be taken in by their pretty words and false friendships.

Lord Stopford raised his brow as he came up to them, and his refusal to let go of his wife sent hot anger coursing through his blood. He came about the back of Louise, taking his lordship's hand and twisting it away as he came to stand beside his wife.

Lord Stopford stepped back, his eyes narrowing, but without a word.

Good. Hopefully the bastard understood that he would not, nor would he ever allow Louise to take a lover.

"If you'll excuse us. My wife promised me this next dance," he said, smiling at the ladies. They tittered and gushed at him, as they always did, but their fawning was lost on him. His chest felt tight, and a small sweat broke out on his skin.

Luke took a calming breath, unsure why he was reacting in such a way. He'd almost committed violence against a man for actions that he himself had partaken in only a month past.

The thought shamed him. Now, with the shoe on the other foot, to see someone else take a pointed interest in what was essentially his did not sit well and he silently begged for all the husbands whom he'd given sleepless nights to forgive him.

Louise walked beside him as if nothing was amiss, and he wanted to break that icy shell she'd erected about herself. When he pulled her into his arms, there was no wilting wallflower, no hurt registering in her eyes. No anger or fear. Nothing.

He didn't want nothing. He wanted to know what the hell sort of game she was playing.

"Enjoying yourself with Lord Stopford's paws all over you? Or maybe I should ask how long you've been shagging him. You've been in London a month now, plenty of time to have a gentleman of the *ton* warm your bed."

She smiled up at him and he cursed. When the hell had she become so alluring? Had he been blind all the times he'd stood with the duke and duchess? He supposed he had been. His fixation had been on Lady Scarboro and the pretty little debutante Lady Clara, whom he liked to play and tease. Not that he would have ever married her, but it was amusing and a pleasant way to pass the time.

This woman in his arms, his wife, was punishment for all his wrongdoings. God was punishing him for being a cad.

You are a cad and you deserve everything you get.

He dismissed the voice, pinning her with his gaze. "Answer me."

"I have to have someone to warm my bed. My husband has made it abundantly clear that he will not."

He shut his mouth with a snap, pulling her close as they turned within the waltz. The music was loud in his ears and his nape pricked with awareness that all eyes were upon them. Watching and wondering what they were discussing.

If only they knew...

"You better tease, madam." His voice vibrated with temper that he did not recognize within himself. What did he care who his wife flirted with? He should not. He was not emotionally involved with this woman. Their union was a mistake. One of his making. To be so territorial with her was confounding and he growled.

"If you ventured to live with your wife, you would know. I cannot be expected to be alone for the rest of my life. I must carve out my own little bit of happiness if you shall not supply it for me."

He shook his head, pulling her closer. "You said that I should expect nothing from you. Are you a liar as well as an unfaithful wench?"

His words broke through the defensive wall a little and her eyes flared, anger making the deep blue of her irises like a fathomless, swirling sea. "I was angry and upset when I said that. You ruined me in front of the whole *ton* and then demanded marriage as if I should be grateful. Of course I said what I did. Anyone would."

The feel of her in his arms, all womanly curves, pulled at a part of him who longed for a woman in his bed. No matter what the *ton* may think, he'd not taken a woman into his bed since the night he'd walked into Miss Grant's room.

Lady Scarboro had of course tried, and failed. He was certain her ladyship was the sole reason he was married at all and he'd never take her into his bed again.

So what the hell was he going to do? Take Louise into his bed, which inevitably led to children. A family. No matter how careful one was, if a child was meant to be, it would happen.

Damn it all to hell. It wasn't to be borne.

"You want a true marriage. A family. With me."

She focused on something over his shoulder and he wanted her to look at him. Not some unseen thing behind his head. *Him.*

"I cannot have it with anyone else, can I? I'm married to you, so who else can I have such a future with?"

The scent of jasmine wafted from her skin and he breathed deeply, having always loved that fragrance above any other. She was too tempting, too sweet for him. He was a rogue. A selfish, obstinate lord who was used to getting his own way.

However was he going to deal with her?

Her statement clanged about in his head like a death knell. How indeed...

CHAPTER 8

The following morning Louise stood in the foyer of the marquess's London home as trunk after trunk was carried through and up the stairs.

Her sister came to stand beside her, her eyes full of amusement. Louise, on the other hand, felt as though she were having an out-of-body experience. The marquess was moving in, that was obvious, but what was not so obvious was whether he would give her the marriage she longed for.

They had been without a family for so long. With her siblings having been separated from her, she wanted them to be part of her new future. That the marquess was here was at least one small step in making a go at their marriage. Surely he wished for a child. An heir. From what Mary had told her, he'd also been without his parents for many years. Could he be as lonely as she'd been at times?

She clutched her fingers before her, her hands cold and clammy. "I cannot wait to meet the marquess. Is he handsome?" Sophie asked, almost bouncing in her excitement.

"He's very handsome, but he's yet to arrive. Come,"

she said, pulling her toward the front parlor that she'd taken to using the most during the day. It gathered the afternoon sun and was warm, no matter the English weather.

They sat and had tea, the clock on the mantel clicking the minutes away, winding Louise up more and more with every passing second. Would the marquess be amenable or surly? Would he show his dislike of their situation by making her life here with him uncomfortable? Louise watched as her sister flicked through the latest fashion plates, while Louise's attention was wholly focused on the front door and of any new arrivals.

What seemed like hours passed by and then, finally, the muffled male voice and the clipped steps of someone heading toward them sounded outside the door.

Nerves pooled in her stomach and Louise stood, adjusting her dark-pink morning gown and ensuring all was in order. Her sister continued to read, oblivious to the turmoil that wracked her body.

The door flung open and in strode the marquess. He'd removed his gloves and hat, both clasped in one hand at his side. He took in the room, his blue eyes stopping on her sister. "Friend of yours?" he asked, his eyes narrowing with inspection of her.

"Lord Graham, may I introduce you to my sister, Miss Sophie Grant. Sophie, this is Luke Ashby, Marquess Graham."

Sophie's eyes widened and she stood, dipping into a pretty curtsy. "Very pleased to meet you at last, my lord."

His lordship placed his gloves and hat on a nearby table, coming to stand before the fire. "A sister," he said, turning his attention back to Louise. "Anything else that I should be aware of?"

Louise clasped her fingers before her, unsure how to tell

him that she also had a brother who lived here. From the displeased line of his brow and unsmiling lips, the news of a sister was not welcome either. This was not the best start to their married life under one roof, but then, the start of their marriage was not good to begin with.

She straightened her back. "Yes. My brother is also living here. You ought to know that as well."

LUKE SHUT his mouth with a snap and wondered for a moment if he'd stepped into another world. Who were these people who lived here? Of course Louise had stated they were her siblings, but how had he never known such a thing about her, especially now that she was his wife?

"Would you please leave us for a moment, Miss Sophie?" he asked, smiling to buffer the annoyance he felt running through his veins. His wife, uncommonly pretty today in her dark-pink muslin morning gown, sat on a nearby settee and waited for him to speak.

No longer the wilting wallflower, it would seem.

"How did I not know that you had siblings? Or that they were living here?" Under his roof for who knows how long. He schooled his features. He was married now, the life of bachelor that he'd enjoyed so very much was over. Still, it rankled that it was the case or that he now seemed to have an instant family.

One that he'd never wanted.

"They've been living with my aunt due to our limited means. Upon our marriage, I had them travel to Ashby House to be with me. When the duchess asked me to return to town, I had them come along."

Did you now… "How old are you siblings?" he asked, curious despite himself.

"Almost sixteen, my lord. Sophie and Stephen are twins, you see."

He turned to face the fire, wanting to remove her from his vision. After their dance last evening, he'd dreamed of her. The dream had not been one that allowed sleep-inducing refreshment. Instead, he'd dreamed of stripping her sapphire gown from her body, unveiling the hidden gems beneath all that silk and taking his fill.

The morning gown she wore today seemed uncommonly fetching and not what he needed to see if he was to keep his hands off her. Ensure that they both understood what type of marriage they had and what was expected of them and what wasn't.

The image of Lord Stopford dancing with her the night before, his hands low on her back, his words close to her ear flittered through his mind and he fisted his hand on the marble mantel.

"I suppose since they are your family I'm unable to deny the request of them staying here with us. Even so, it would have been nice to have been asked."

Her eyes flared and she stood, coming over to him. "I would've asked, of course, but I did not think to see you again until the end of the Season and well, I knew my aunt wanted to travel, so I requested them to come to me. I did not mean to overstep my mark."

Luke drank her in, tall and proud before him. Her eyes were bright and clear, and uncommonly lovely. If he were to choose a woman for himself to marry he supposed someone as fetching as Miss Grant would have suited him very well. Her figure was perfectly proportioned and curvy, her gowns accentuated all the correct places one's gown ought. Her nose was small and straight and her lips...

His attention snapped to that part of her person and he stilled when her sweet, pink tongue flicked out to moisten them. Luke blinked, bringing back his thoughts from the dangerous territory where they'd wandered. He straightened his spine.

"What is done is done and if they're your siblings, I will not deny them your company." Not that he needed to be responsible for any more people, but he supposed, as the siblings were almost sixteen, they would not be long under his roof before they too sought their own paths in life. He could accommodate that. It was not so very much to ask.

"Now," he said, waiting for her to meet his gaze. "Regarding our marriage and what I expect from you."

She nodded without words and he ignored the hope he read in her blue orbs. Did she expect a true marriage? Surely not. Not after how their nuptials came to be in the first place. "We will keep to our rooms and not share a bed, for now at least." At least until he could procure a French letter to use while making a beast with two backs. "I also expect absolute fidelity from you. I will not condone you sharing a bed with any other gentleman of the *ton*. Especially Lord Stopford whom you seem to favor so very much."

His wife scoffed and he flinched. "You find such a request preposterous, my lady?"

Her lips thinned into a tight line and she watched him like a genius watched a fool. He wasn't anyone's fool. "And while I'm remaining the vestal virgin, how are you conducting yourself about town, my lord? Are you taking an oath of chastity or am I expected to turn the other way and ignore your indiscretions?"

Luke had never had a woman speak to him in such a forward manner, and bugger him if it wasn't a little amusing to see that his wife had some spark to her blood. A small backbone after all. "As a marquess and gentleman what I do is none of your concern, madam."

He stepped past her and he stilled when she gripped his upper arm, stalling him. A shock ran through his arm, echoing throughout his body and he stilled.

What the hell was that?

"I'll not be made a fool of twice, Lord Graham. You've already bundled me into this marriage through a situation not of my making. I'll not then stand by and watch as you sleep your way through the women whom I have to entertain." She let go of his arm, attempting to throw him a little as she did so.

He didn't move an inch. "I will be discreet." The lie almost choked him and he swallowed. He would not be told what to do by a woman, certainly not a woman he did not want. Who did this chit think she was?

She raised her chin, a perfect rosy hue spreading across her dimpled cheeks. Sweet mercy, she was pretty. Prettier than he'd ever realized. His body, typically male, had a typical male response. Louise's attention drifted over him as if she sensed his train of thought and she stepped back. "No."

He followed her. "No?" he said, menace in his tone. "You do not have a choice." And she did not, as unfair as that was. An image of his parents flittered through his mind, happy and loving, his little sister playing at their feet before a roaring fire as they sat together, arms entwined, enjoying a night in watching their children play.

So long ago now since they'd left him.

"Of course I do. I will not allow you to go on with your life as you once did, my lord. I'm here, a marchioness because of you, and if I want affection in my life and my husband is unwilling to secure that for me, I will seek it elsewhere."

He clasped her upper arms, wanting to shake some sense into her. Instead, his mind diverted to how very small she was, how with very little effort he could break her. Not that he ever would, but being so near to her he once again was reminded that she was his now. If he so chose, he could seek his husbandly rights this evening and have her.

Dear God, that was tempting.

She glared up at him, all fire and ire, her eyes blazing with anger. Good, he wanted her angry at him. Anger meant she would not push him, seek him out and demand things he was not willing to give her. Such a road led to disaster and broken hearts.

He knew that better than anyone.

"No you will not."

Her breasts rose with each of her labored breaths and he fought not to glance at her bodice. "You must sleep with me. The marriage must be consummated, otherwise I see very little point in continuing this charade. An annulment would be better than this."

His fingers slid about her arms, slipping down to her elbows. His body hardened at the idea of bedding her. If she was as passionate in bed as she was when arguing with him, bedding her was not a good idea. He could get used to heat between his sheets. But she did make a good point. He had to consummate the marriage if he were to keep her.

He thought over her demand, knowing he had little option. She was his wife. He must at least sleep with her once. Nothing would come of it, he would make sure of that.

"Very well. I'll come to your room this evening."

Her mouth popped open on a small gasp and he tore himself away, striding from the room before he took her blasted delicious mouth and lay claim to her. There would be minimal kissing, no affectionate pets or words. He would keep her at a distance. Distance meant safety. She would not wheedle her way into his heart. She may have everything else that she desired—her siblings, clothing, food and jewels—but not him.

Never him.

CHAPTER 9

Louise bathed and dressed in one of the new silk shifts that Mary had helped her pick out the other day while shopping. She sat at her dressing table, dabbing a small amount of jasmine scent on the underside of her jaw.

She caught herself in the mirror, her eyes uncommonly large and startled almost. The thought that tonight she would sleep with Lord Graham was almost too unbelievable to believe. He was London's most coveted rake. An unpardonable flirt. And he was her husband.

However was she going to be enough for him?

The idea that after tonight there would be no more nights was not acceptable. After her parents had passed away, leaving her to care for her siblings, she'd wanted to give them the family they craved. Now she could do that. Help them find their future paths, whatever that may be, become a mother herself and love unconditionally.

She'd silently hoped that her move to York may prove to be the stepping stone to such a life. To be the mistress of her own home, beholden to no one. In a way she was that now, although where she'd hoped for love, and respect in her marriage, she'd received a hasty wedding to a man who could not be in the same room with her longer than ten minutes.

Louise rose from her chair and went over to her bed, staring at the linen that had been pulled down for her in preparation for sleep. She climbed in, settling the blanket about her waist and stared at the door that led to the marquess's room. Not one sound came from the chamber and she chewed her lip, wondering if he was preparing himself. Was as nervous as she was.

Never in her life had she ever been so intimate with a man, and although Mary did tell her of some of the things that happened between a husband and wife, a lot of the time her friend had simply looked dreamy and declared that Louise would enjoy it. She would see.

At a time like this, doubts plagued her. To enjoy such a thing seemed an odd thing to do, and yet, Mary had insisted all would be well.

The door opened and the breath in her lungs seized. His skin was darker than she'd thought it would be, sun kissed and warm looking in the candlelit room. Her eyes devoured him, took their fill as he stood still and unmoving at the door.

Corded muscles flexed as he stepped toward the bed, his breeches the only article on his person and she remembered to breathe lest she gasp.

"Are you ready?" he asked, his tone business-like and cold. It wasn't a tone she wanted to hear and Louise steeled herself to change his mind about them, about their marriage. Although she was unsure why he pushed her away—the idea of a family and life—she would find out the reasons and she would battle against his walls.

This was their life now whether they wished it or not

and she would do everything in her power to make it as best as could be. There may never be love between them, but there would be respect and affection.

She would have nothing less.

❧

LUKE BIT BACK the curse upon seeing Louise lying in wait upon her bed. Her large eyes ran over him and he stilled, feeling her inspection of him as if her fingers had slid over his body. Touching every ounce of his flesh.

He strode over to her with a determined stride that was by far the opposite of how he was feeling. Louise was a pretty little thing, and tempted him to take his time with her, to touch, and kiss, taste and explore more than he'd planned.

But no. He would not. Such a path would only lead to pain and he'd suffered enough of that emotion to last him two lifetimes.

The candle beside the bed flickered and he reached out, snuffing it with his thumb and forefinger. The fire bathed the room in golden light, and since this was Louise's first time with a man, the shadows may help in relaxing her. Not to mention, the less he could see of her the better for him.

He leaned down and, taking her face in his hands, kissed her. He wasn't a brute after all, and he didn't want her to suffer any more pain than was necessary. And yet, the moment his lips touched hers he'd known it for the mistake it was.

Her mouth mimicked his and shot fire through his blood. Her hands, tentative at first, but then more bold slid up his chest to clasp his shoulders. Luke came over her, pinning her onto the bed and kissed her deeper still. Slid his tongue into her mouth and lost himself for a moment to the sweet taste that was his wife.

He'd silently hoped she would've balked at his touch. Demand that she wasn't ready and that he should leave. His head spun at her soft, needy gasp and returned kisses. She wanted this. She wanted him. More than he'd bargained for.

The softness of her breasts brushed his naked chest, and frustration rode him. He needed to feel her skin. Taste and savor it for this one night. He clasped the hem of her nightdress, sliding it up her body. She sat up a little as he wrenched it over her head, breaking the kiss only a moment as he came back down onto her.

This was not what was supposed to happen. She was not supposed to respond to him. *He was not supposed to respond to her...*

Luke groaned, giving up his fight against his own desire for the woman beneath him. One night of mutual pleasure would satisfy his duty to her as her husband. After that, they could continue as husband and wife in name only.

His response to her was the same as all his responses to women whom he lay with. A small voice mocked him on his thought.

No it was not.

৩৵৶

LOUISE KISSED her husband back with as much passion as she knew how. Her fingers dug into his shoulders, slipping around to clasp his nape, hold him against her as he continued to kiss her as if she were the only woman in the world he wanted.

It was a sweet dream, and one she wasn't silly enough to believe. Not yet at least. But she would change his mind about them. A marriage, even if the couple did not come together in the traditional way, still stood a chance of happiness.

Surely he must see that.

They were certainly getting along well enough in this area if she were to think so boldly. Louise gasped, pushing herself into his hands as his palm molded her breast, his finger sliding over her nipple and spiking liquid heat to pool at her core.

Oh yes, she liked that very much.

Never before had she thought being with a man in such a way could be this intoxicating. His clever touch made her shivery and achy in places she'd not known could shiver and ache and it only left her wanting more.

Even her nakedness did not frighten her as she thought it would. His hand slid down her ribs, across her stomach and then lower still. With a wantonness borne out of years of yearning for what so many about her had—a husband, a lover—she parted her legs and let him touch her where she ached most.

His fingers slid over her most private of places and she moaned, pushing and lifting herself against him. Her body shook, a kaleidoscope of feeling and over-sensitized nerves that longed for something just out of her grasp. He teased her toward it, led her near and then took it away and she wanted it back. Craved it like a bee craves nectar.

"Luke," she gasped as he slid a finger into her body. She should be shocked at her response to him, but how could she be when it felt so right? So delicious, warm and tempting.

His kisses, hot and wet skimmed her cheek, her neck until he reached her shoulder. "You're so tight, Louise," he whispered against her neck, the warmth of his breath teasing her further until she wasn't sure what to do with herself.

"I want you," she admitted. For years she'd watched the gentlemen of the ton from afar, longing to be the woman they asked to dance, to court and flirt with. Instead, she'd been the invisible lady's companion, a wall-flower never to be plucked.

Not anymore.

Of course to have fallen into marriage with him had not been ideal, his dislike of her was palpable at times, but now that she was married to him, she would seize the opportunity to make him see her finally.

See past his lofty title to the woman he married. Make him see that although she was common, without any monetary value for his family, she was priceless, just as anyone was, no matter their background.

The security marrying the marquess had given her and her family was a gift she'd not thought to ever have. And she would not squander it. She would nurture and protect it as much as she could. Try and regain their lives without living under the possibility of poverty if something disas-trous happened. Give her siblings the stable future they'd always deserved.

Luke moved and settled between her legs, lifting one to rest about his hip. He rocked against her, her core embar-rassingly wet and throbbing. She mewled in protest when he removed his hand from there and replaced it with his body. The rigid mass of his penis pressing against her brought forth another new and delicious need to coil through her blood.

Louise lifted her other leg, hooking them both about his back. He groaned and seized her mouth in a punishing kiss, his hands fumbling between them and ripping at his breeches.

And then he was pushing into her. Breaching her body and conquering her as was his right. As was her wish. A stinging pain, quick and sharp, took place as he moved into her and then there was only pleasure. Delicious, wonderful pleasure.

He rocked into her, filling her and pushing her toward more of what she craved. With each stroke he hit some special little nubbin inside of her that ached and longed for more. Louise ground herself against him, wanting more, quicker, deeper, faster.

"Damn, Louise," he growled against her lips. "So good," he gasped.

She clung to him, their movements frantic and hard. Her fingers scored down his back, helping him to take her, wanting him to finish whatever it was that he was doing to her.

And then it happened. Her core convulsed into spasm after spasm of pleasure. Louise cried out, throwing her head back against the bedding and arched her back, allowing the marvelous feelings he evoked in her to overcome her senses, fill and enflame her.

Luke stilled above her, her name spilling from his lips before he pulled out. He pumped his shaft upon her stomach and she watched, entranced, at his body's reaction to her.

Louise lay back onto the bed, spent and satisfied, her bones like liquid beneath her skin.

He came to lay beside her, his face turned toward hers and she reached out, unable not to touch him. Would it always be like this between them? She never knew couples could find such pleasure, and now that she'd tasted what Luke could do to her, well, it left her wanting more.

His hand came over hers, holding it against his cheek, before he frowned, removing it. He sat up and slid across the bed, quickly donning his breeches and walking back toward his room.

"You're leaving?" she asked, sitting up, heedless of her nakedness. After what he'd just done to her, how he'd made her feel, she would walk about naked every day so long as he did such a delicious thing again.

Make love to her…

"Goodnight," he said, pausing at the door.

She watched him, hoping he'd turn and look at her. Change his mind and come back and do more of the same. They were married after all. There was nothing wrong with a husband and wife taking pleasure from each other.

Giving and receiving.

He wrenched the door open and quickly stepping through to his room, slammed it shut, the sound of the key turning the bolt home loud in the quiet night.

Louise sighed, a shiver of disappointment stealing over her skin. What they had done was a start, she reminded herself. The first step in moving forward as man and wife. Luke had not wished to marry, and it would take time and patience for her to win him over.

But she would and she would not scuttle off to the country to hide and disappear from his side. No. Being in London would give her the opportunities to show him he could be happy with her. If only he'd allow himself to be.

And he would be. One day.

CHAPTER 10

Over the next week Luke had gone out of his way to avoid Louise. His wife. The demure lady's companion who had turned into a hellion the moment he touched her. He sat at his desk in his room, twisting the quill between his fingers and wondering how the hell he'd lost all control the night they'd consummated the marriage.

The memory of her welcoming body, her bold kiss and reactions to his touch shot heat to his cock. It twitched, ached, and had damn well been quite the nuisance this last week. Whenever he'd smelled jasmine he'd looked to see if she was near.

If he heard her laughter in the halls of his home, he'd wanted to seek her out and see what was so funny.

He was damn well turning into a fool who was being led by a woman. Their nights out on the town had been pleasant, for her at least. He'd merely accompanied her and then done all he could to bury himself in the gentlemen's card games and stay well away from her touch.

The last thing he needed was to dance with her. If he touched her again, there was no chance that it would end with such a simple embrace. He'd be tempted to carry her from the room over his shoulder like a Viking and take her up against a wall somewhere in the house.

The thought of doing just that had him adjusting his seat.

He swore and stood, striding to the window. He clasped the wood surrounds and stared at the manicured grounds, the flowerbeds in full bloom and green, leafy trees. He willed his body to get a damn grip upon itself.

A delectable figure in deep green came into view and his body stilled. Louise kicked off her slippers and walked the few steps off the terrace and onto the lawn. She strolled about the yard, leaning down to smell the lavender and rosemary. He watched her for a moment and jumped when a light knock sounded on his door.

"Come in," he said.

The door opened and Stephen's blond locks popped around the door. "My lord," he said, an anxious tone to his words. "May I come in?"

Luke gestured for him to enter. "Of course, come in, Stephen." Luke sat back at the desk in his room and nodded for the young man to seat himself on the vacant chair across from him.

Louise's brother glanced about the room, taking in the furnishings before glancing back at him. He looked like his sister, more so than Sophie did. Luke smiled, taking pity on the lad who wrung his hands in his lap as if he were in some sort of trouble.

"What can I help you with?" Luke asked.

Stephen settled himself and turned his attention to Luke. "I was hoping, my lord, that you would teach me how to ride a horse. I've never learned before, you see. We did not have the means for such animals. Although Auntie did have a cat, but, well, you know what I mean."

Luke chuckled at his ramblings. "I understand." He leaned back in his chair, contemplating the request. "Have you ever ridden any horses before?"

The young lad shook his head. "No, never. I've been in a carriage and cart obviously, but I've never ridden a horse. With you married to Louise I don't ever want to let her down or embarrass her, you see, and what brother to a marchioness does not know how to handle a mount?"

"You love your sister?" The young man's face filled with affection or adoration, Luke wasn't sure which, possibly both. The image of his own sweet sister filled his mind and he knew that it was both emotions.

"Sophie and I owe her everything. She was sent away from us when she was only eight years old. If it weren't for her sending money back to Auntie we would've ended up in a poorhouse. She is the kindest, most hard-working woman I know."

Luke rubbed his jaw, thinking over Louise and her unshakable loyalty to those she loved. She certainly loved her siblings and the Duchess of Carlton. Even in a marriage that she did not care for, she was trying her best to please him. Make him happy when she knew he didn't want the union any more than she did.

"No more titles between us. You may call me Luke and I'd be honored to show you how to ride a horse."

The young man brightened and sat up straight. "Thank you, my lord. I mean," he paused, "Luke. Thank you, Luke."

Luke stood, glad of the distraction of Stephen's sister who strolled the gardens still. "Come then. No time like the present to learn. We'll go down to Hyde Park and start today."

Stephen stood, following close on his heels. "Really? Oh, that would be wonderful. Thank you. I'm keen to become the gentleman that Louise always thought me to be."

Luke clapped him on the back, a sense of pride filling him at being able to help the young man. "You're fifteen, is that correct?" he asked.

"Yes, sixteen in a month or so," he replied, eagerly.

"Well then, we have plenty of time to get you up to speed and fully competent by the time you attend your first Season."

Luke wasn't sure where the thought came from, but having met the young man, his eagerness to learn from him, his gratitude for Luke's help, humbled him. He'd not been given the chance to guide and help his sister, having lost her so young. Hell, he'd never had parents. Only a grandmother who raised him and then promptly passed away when he was old enough to look after himself. Having this young man to guide, to help, was akin to what he imagined having a brother would feel like.

He'd not had a family for twenty years, nor did he wish for one, his opinion on that had not changed, but he could see the draw of it, certainly. To care for people other than yourself was a new occurrence and one to contemplate. What he could say on the matter was that it did not frighten him as much as he thought it would.

And that in itself was scary.

THEY RETURNED from their ride some hours later and Luke could not remember a time when he'd enjoyed himself more. Dinner would be served soon and they were scheduled to head out to a musical night at Lord and Lady Elliot's home, and yet Luke did not feel the slightest inclination to go.

Stephen had been the best student. He had listened, taken advice, cared for the mount. A few times Luke had caught him petting the mare as if she would break, speaking in soft tones to win the horse's affection.

Luke had watched on, amused by the whole experience and was ashamed that he'd felt annoyance when he'd first heard of their arrival in town. Sometimes he really could be an ass.

"You're back." Louise stood from the settee before the fire in the drawing room upon their arrival, coming over to inspect her brother. No doubt ensuring that Luke had not injured him in any way.

"Did you learn anything, Stephen? Mrs. Ellis said you were going to ask for assistance with your riding. I hope you've studied well today."

"Stephen learned exceptionally well and picked up all that was required on the first lesson." Luke smiled at the boy, nodding his approval.

Stephen's eyes glowed with enthusiasm. "You will teach me more, my lord?"

"Luke, remember?" he said. Louise's gaze shot to his and he knew she was wondering why he was being so familiar with her brother. Luke could not answer that question himself, but what he did know was that he'd never had a more pleasant afternoon in years. Stephen was not a foolish, headstrong boy, quite the opposite in fact. He supposed being brought up poor, he was thankful for anything that came his way. Opportunities would've been limited indeed in Sandbach. "Of course I will. We will ride out again tomorrow if you like," he said, already looking forward to the outing.

"I would love that. Thank you."

Louise stared at him and the pit of his stomach twisted. The more time he spent in her presence the more he liked what he saw. She too was steady of mind, not tarnished by greed and privilege. It was a welcome change from what he was used to.

"May I learn also, my lord?" Sophie asked, turning in her chair to be part of the conversation.

Louise glanced at him, uncertainty flicking within her blue orbs. He didn't like that she was unsure of him in such a way. He may not have wanted a marriage, but he wasn't a total ogre. And after this afternoon with her brother, he had to admit that he'd enjoyed teaching Stephen how to ride a horse. If Sophie wished to learn also, then he would teach her as well.

"Of course you're more than welcome to join us. We'll go after luncheon tomorrow."

Louise watched him a moment and he could not read what she was thinking, although if he were to take a guess, she was thinking of what had happened to the man she married who wanted no part of any of them. Was only too happy to scuttle them away in Kent and leave them there forever.

☙❦❧

THE FOLLOWING afternoon Louise decided to join Luke and her siblings on their ride to the park. It had been quite some weeks since she'd been on horseback, and she and Mary had always enjoyed such outings before Mary married the duke.

She started toward the mews, her bottle-green riding gown, newly delivered by Madame Devy only yesterday, fit her like a glove. It was everything a well-made and comfortable gown ought to be. Louise could not stop feeling the soft, velvet fabric and she could not remember the last time she'd actually felt attractive.

Their outing today to instruct her siblings how to ride a horse was something she'd not been able to afford as a lady's companion. For all the luxuries that were afforded her in Mary's home, both before her marriage and afterwards, it did not give her the monetary means to gift horse riding lessons to Stephen and Sophie.

They all had missed out on so much due to their financial situation. Her aunt had done all she could to ensure Louise's funds went as far as they could, but she had to admit that now being married to a marquess, to have unlimited means was a pleasant change.

If she ensured her siblings never had to worry about money, or how to keep a roof over their heads, she was at least grateful in that way that the marquess had stumbled into her room and nearly ruined her.

Using a mounting block, she climbed up onto the back of her mount before they started toward Hyde Park. Louise took the time to watch Luke with her brother and sister. He rode between them, a groom on either side of them as well, keeping a close watch on both her siblings' horses and that no harm would come to them.

He sat well atop his horse, his straight back and ease was obvious to any who looked at him. The saddle seemed like a second home to his lordship. Her siblings gifted him with multiple questions, and never once did he sigh in exasperation or annoyance. Instead, he answered each query with an intelligent and patient reply and she couldn't help but like him a little more.

The park was a hive of activity, and they rode down toward Rotten Row to keep away from the carriages and people strolling the paths of the park.

Luke stopped his mount before the row, instructing her brother and sister to try to trot before them, explaining how to lift from the saddle using their legs and stirrups, to get into sync with the horse's stride. All the while keeping a firm, but not harsh, grip on the reins.

"Thank you for taking the time to teach them. I think you've made my brother a life-long admirer of yours."

The marquess laughed, his eyes bright with amusement as he watched her siblings ride on the sandy track. "I do not mind. In fact, I've quite enjoyed the last two days instructing him. He's an asset to you."

She tore her gaze away from his too-handsome face that only grew in good looks when he smiled. He'd not returned to her bed since he'd consummated the marriage, and when she saw him like he was now, carefree, relaxed and seemingly enjoying himself, she couldn't help but long for him to be her husband in the truest sense.

"They're both so very good. I'm fortunate to have them as my siblings."

He nodded, his eyes clouding somewhat at her words. She held his inspection of her, willing him to think she too could be an asset to him if only he would give her a chance. Let her show him that marriage did not have to be a life sentence of torture and despair.

"Good afternoon, Lord Graham. How very providential to meet you here."

Louise stilled at the sound of Lady Clara's voice and she turned a little to see the young woman riding toward them, a groom following close on her horse's hooves.

Luke bowed a little from his seat and Louise smiled in welcome, no matter her dislike of the woman she would not be rude. She took in the young debutante's riding gown of blue velvet and gold buttons, a small top hat sitting atop her golden curls. She was so very pretty, rich and from a titled family. Everything Lord Graham ought to have married, and here she was, a lady's companion who'd gained the title through nefarious means.

Unease shivered down her spine and she lifted her chin to try to dispel the doubt running through her. "Hello, Lady Clara. Are you enjoying the park today?" she asked.

Lady Clara glanced at her and dismissed her just as quickly. "Oh, Lady Graham," she said, watching the marquess and not sparing her a moment more of her time. "I did not see you there."

Louise raised her brow, heat scoring her cheeks at the comment.

"Is your eyesight failing you, Lady Clara?" her brother asked, a contemplative tilt to his head as he stopped his horse before the small party.

"No," her ladyship said, staring down her nose at her brother. He merely pursed his lips in thought.

"Oh, I thought the fact that you could not see my sister meant that you may be going blind. She is sitting practically in front of you."

Lady Clara's mouth gaped before she raised her chin. She laughed a tinkling sound that echoed with condescension. "Oh, so you're Miss Grant's brother I've heard about town. I don't believe I've ever met a lady's companion's sibling before. I would certainly not wish to meet my own servants' family. How lowering of one's position."

Her brother glared. "Rudeness is also a form of crassness and can often show a person's true character, not the face they portray to the public."

Sophie chuckled, covering her mouth with her glove to hide her amusement. Louise tore her gaze to the marquess who looked as shocked as she felt.

Lady Clara glared at her brother before she turned back to Luke all smiles and sweetness again. "Tell me, my lord. Where does your new wife hail from, before she worked for the Duchess of Carlton, of course?"

Louise went to answer before Luke had a chance to, but her brother beat her to it.

"Sandbach, in Cheshire. We lived in a cottage with our aunt if you must know, Lady Clara. Are you satisfied now? Have you insulted my family and my sister enough do you think for one afternoon, or would you like to continue your mocking visit on our riding party?"

The young woman gasped, turning her horse roughly about, but not before catching Lord Graham's eye. "Are you going to let that little nobody speak to me in such a way?"

All eyes turned to the marquess and he glanced back at Louise and then her brother. "Apologize to Lady Clara, Stephen. What you said was unkind."

Louise pushed her horse to come between her brother and Lady Clara. "Stephen will not apologize for anything that he said here today. He was just replying to her lady-ship's rudeness toward our family. Come, Stephen and Sophie, we shall leave Lord Graham and Lady Clara to catch up on their own. We certainly would not wish to sully their stature in the *ton* with our lowly bloodlines."

Louise turned and her siblings came abreast of her. She took deep, calming breaths and used the anger that thrummed through her veins to stem the tears that threatened. She bit her lip, refusing to give way to emotion. Refused to break over the fact that her husband had not stuck up for them. Had merely sat by and allowed Lady Clara to mock and ridicule her family. *His family.*

But then, he'd not wanted a family, so it ought not surprise her that he would stand idly by and allow such words to be spoken.

She swore and her brother reached over and squeezed her hand.

"I'm sorry, Louise, but I could not allow that woman to

treat you in such a way. I suppose that will end my lessons from the marquess."

She patted his hand, her anger not at him but her husband. At herself for allowing Lady Clara to pick at her as if she were still a companion. She was a marchioness now, and it was not her fault that the young debutante had missed her chance with Lord Graham. If only the little dimwit knew that the night he stumbled into her room, he was in fact supposed to be meeting Lady Scarboro, a widow he'd been rumored to be sleeping with.

The thought made her stomach churn and she could not reach home soon enough. For a day that had started out so well, it had ended terribly. And tonight she was to attend Lord and Lady Conyngham's soirée.

The torture didn't seem to want to end.

CHAPTER 11

The ride to Lord and Lady Conyngham's soirée was a quiet affair. Luke sat across from her, staring out the window, his jaw locked into a hard line, his eyes narrowed in contemplation. He was angry, he all but thrummed with the emotion, and her stomach roiled at the idea that he would yell at her. She hated confrontation, but nor would she allow him or his lofty friends to degrade her when she'd done nothing to deserve it. If anyone deserved a set-down, it was Luke for putting her in this position in the first place.

Thankful upon arriving at the soirée, she easily sought out Mary, the duke nowhere to be seen. It suited Louise perfectly for if she did not speak to someone soon about what had happened at the park this afternoon, she might scream.

Scream at her spineless husband who had taken the side of a venomous spider instead of his wife.

What was wrong with the man?

Mary kissed both her cheeks in welcome and Louise took her first relieved breath for the day. "I'm so happy to see you, Mary. I need your opinion and I really do not know which way to turn."

Her friend frowned, taking her arm and walking her to a pair of chairs nearby. They sat and Mary took her hand, concern etched on her features. "Of course you may confide in me. I'm here always. You know that."

She nodded, swallowing the lump in her throat. It had wedged there since Luke had sat silent and still on his horse, voiceless when he ought to have said something. "I don't think my marriage to the marquess is going to work. He hates us I'm sure. Thinks we're beneath him, which even I'll admit that we are when it comes to Society's standards... Even so, his actions today have made it almost impossible for me to forgive him."

The duchess's eyes widened and she held her hand tighter. "What did he do, Louise?" she asked. "Surely, it cannot be as bad as this sounds."

Louise shook her head, wishing that were true. "It is bad and I'm at a loss as to what I can do." Louise explained to the duchess what had transpired between them and Lady Clara. Her brother's set-down to her ladyship, which Mary clapped and congratulated him for, and the marquess's response. As for her husband's inability to speak except to censure her brother, well, the duchess had a completely different reaction.

"Well, Lord Graham needs a good set-down and you ought to be the one to give it to him. You're a marchioness now. His wife. How dare he take the side of Lady Clara."

As if speaking of the debutante brought her forth, she stopped before them, smiling as if butter wouldn't melt in her vicious little viperish mouth.

"Your Grace, Lady Graham, so lovely to see you here this evening. You must be pleased to see her ladyship again, your grace. If you have trouble with your gown or need help throughout the night, at least you have your servant close at hand."

The ladies that accompanied Lady Clara giggled at her insult and the duchess stood. Taller than Lady Clara, the young woman had to take a step back and look up at her grace. The duchess laughed. "Oh dear, you're so very funny, but you know who is really laughing, don't you, my dear?" Her voice dripped sarcasm. The young woman not willing to lose an argument merely raised her brow questioningly.

"I'm sure you're more than willing to tell me, your grace."

Louise stood as well, and was happy to see that she too was taller than Lady Clara. At least in that she was the victor.

"Oh I am." The duchess grinned. "You do realize that Lord Graham was never going to marry you, don't you?"

The young woman blanched and her friends' eyes widened, the two glancing at each other, suddenly unsure where this little tête-à-tête was going.

"You would not know such things. Not when she," Lady Clara said, pointing at Louise, "tricked him into coming to her room so he was forced to act the gentleman and marry her."

The duchess smiled at Louise before turning back to the young woman, who like her friends, seemed quite interested to find out the answer. "Oh no, Louise was nothing but innocent in that situation, but the marquess not so much. You're nothing but a little debutante, a girl in his eyes. He may have played with you before the *ton*, but he would never marry you. Not ever." The duchess reached out, patting the young woman's shoulder condescendingly. "Guard your heart in the future. I would hate to hear gossip about you being so very put out at the marquess's marriage. Very cross behavior if I were to give an opinion on the subject."

Louise's stomach churned at the duchess's words. She knew her friend was only trying to set this chit into her place, but by doing so if left her vulnerable to gossip, more so than she already was. Lady Clara's eyes darted between them, but there was no fear in them, only anger and Louise prayed this little incident would not occur again.

"You mock me, your grace. You're not so very much older than myself and it has not escaped my notice that your marriage too eventuated by nefarious means. And you stand there and give me advice. How very amusing you are."

"I think you ought to go," Louise said, clasping Mary's arm when she stilled beside her. "You've said enough to me and my friends today."

Lady Clara raised her brow. "Where is your husband, Lady Graham?" She glanced about the room. "I do not see him near your person. Perhaps I ought to seek him out and demand another apology. Tell your brother that your husband and I are expecting one."

With that she flounced off, her gaggle of friends close on her heels.

The duchess turned to Louise, her eyes burning in temper. "How dare she. How dare Lord Graham. There is only one thing to do for this horrible behavior."

"There is?" Louise asked, at a loss. She'd never been in so many arguments in her life as she had since marrying the marquess. And never had she thought the women of the *ton* would turn against her, blame her for his lordship's behavior.

"If he isn't going to defend you against those who seek to injure you, then you must hurt him in turn. From tonight onward you are to flirt, laugh and be merry as much as you can within our social sphere. I shall help you with this. If the marquess does not want you for himself, then he will see that others do and are not so judgmental. And then we shall see what he will do."

Louise bit her lip, unsure if she had it in her to do such a thing. Of course she'd been told her looks were tolerable by her aunt, but she wasn't a fool to think she was a rare beauty, a diamond of the *ton* such as Lady Clara was.

But if the marquess was not interested in her, perhaps she ought to show him that there were gentlemen who were. He deserved a little payback after his treatment of her family this afternoon. "Very well, we'll try it for a week or so and see what happens."

"Good," the duchess said, leading her into the fray. "Let us begin."

LUKE WASN'T sure what was afoot, but all that he did know was that his wife had become the most fashionable, most sought-after woman in London. After the altercation at the park with Lady Clara, Louise had pulled away from him completely.

No longer did she accompany him with her siblings on their riding lessons. He'd been surprised when her brother had been open to continuing the lessons, and it humbled him a little that he was able to forgive his lapse in sticking up for the boy's family.

He glanced across the room at those who were listening to the famous soprano, Elizabeth Billington. His wife was seated near the front with the Duchess of Carlton whom he'd also noticed was keeping well away from him these days. Her friendship had cooled, and he hated that his error had caused a rift between them all.

What was worse, now his wife attended events without him, going so far as to not even notify him that she was heading out and the talk at his club was that the rogues and libertines had noticed his inattention once again toward her and were sniffing about her skirts.

His eyes narrowed on his wife as she leaned over to the duchess, saying something before they both chuckled. Lord Stopford sat beside her, up to his old tricks again it would seem. The gentleman's arm sat across the back of his wife's chair and made the blood in Luke's veins simmer.

What did he think he was about, seating himself so close to his wife? He had one of his own at home, why did he not go pay court to her?

Viscount Anson sidled up to him, a wine in his hand. Graham nodded in welcome, before turning his attention back to his wife.

"I should congratulate you in your recent nuptials with the lovely Miss Grant. I must admit to being uncommonly stupid and blind to her loveliness prior to her marriage. You're a lucky man, Graham."

Luke glanced sharply at him. Did the man have a death wish? Not that he'd said anything overly crude, but the implication was there that he'd seen her now and his interest was piqued.

"Thank you," he said, keeping his reply as short as possible. "And how is Lady Anson, may I ask?"

A grin quirked his lordship's lips, but his attention did not move from Louise.

Cad!

"She is well, and Lady Graham is also very beautiful, with a quick wit about her I like. But I suppose you know that already."

Luke ground his teeth. No, he bloody well didn't know that and he ought to be horse-whipped for not getting to know his wife more. But to get to know her meant caring more than he wanted to. Showing an interest when he didn't want to be interested at all. He didn't want a family, one that could be ripped out from under him at any moment. If he kept them all at arm's length, when disaster did strike, as it always did in his estimation, he would not be as devastated as he had been upon losing his mother, father and little sister.

"Of course," he lied. He didn't speak for a moment, annoyed at Lord Anson and himself for his lack of attention when it came to Louise. He should know that she was funny, what made her laugh. What she was interested in. Instead, his fear of growing attached to her had made her a stranger to him.

He would try to make an effort while also keeping guard of his heart. It wasn't impossible to do. He'd never been a man to lose his head over a chit, there was little reason why he would with his wife. One could be present, know all the facets of one's spouse while keeping one's emotions out of the mix. Surely this was possible.

Luke turned his attention back on his wife and stilled when Lord Stopford's thumb brushed her bare shoulder. A red haze dropped over his vision when she didn't make an effort to remove his hand from her person, merely turned to him, talking as if nothing was amiss.

The hell there wasn't anything amiss.

The opera singer came to the end of her song and the gathered crowd clapped, standing and dispersing about the room. Luke didn't move, and Lord Anson moved away, thankfully, to a group of people who actually wanted to talk to him.

His wife turned in his direction, smiling, and he watched as that pretty smile faded when she spotted him. The duchess glanced in his direction also, dismissing him no sooner as she'd spotted him. As for Lord Stopford, he merely grinned, the amusement in his eyes telling Luke all he needed to know about the fiend and what he was up to. It hadn't been the first time his lordship had seduced a fellow peer's wife, but hell would freeze over before he'd allow Louise to be one of them.

He didn't move, simply watched to see what Louise would do and an emotion very similar to relief poured through him when she excused herself and made her way over to him.

As she came nearer, he leaned down and kissed her cheek, unsure where the show of affection came from, but not sorry that he'd done so. She was his wife, and she was under his protection. He ought to remember that more often when troublesome debutantes sought to insult her in front of him and the *ton*.

She glanced at him in surprise before taking his arm and standing beside him. "I did not know you were going to attend tonight. We could've shared a carriage if that were the case."

He placed his hand over hers on his arm, holding it there. "Your maid told me of plans for this evening, and I've always enjoyed a soprano and thought to attend also. We will return home together if you're in agreement."

She nodded, contemplating him and he could only imagine what was going through her mind. What was he up to? Which wasn't much different from his own muddled thoughts. It was no secret that he'd not wanted to marry the woman beside him, or any woman for that matter, but now that he had, well, she was quite lovely, in temperament and looks, and who could not be a little proud to have such a woman on his arm?

"I would like that."

They stood in silence a moment before Luke broached

the subject that had been plaguing him for days. "I owe you an apology, Louise."

"You do?"

He wasn't sure if that were a question or answer and he glanced down at her, his lips twitching at the amusement he read in her twinkling blue eyes.

"I do. For not telling Lady Clara the other day in the park to go to Hades. I should never have asked your brother to apologize, and I should have demanded her ladyship leave. It will not happen again." And it would not. Never would he allow another to insult his wife. He'd been a bastard to have allowed it in the first place.

She smiled at him and something in his chest tightened. "Thank you, Luke. And may I say, that from this moment on, we start afresh."

"I would like that also."

The evening passed pleasantly after that, and even the Duchess of Carlton was warmer to him, similar to how it used to be between them prior to his marriage to her friend. Their hosts offered supper for those who wished to stay.

Luke sat with Louise and the Duke and Duchess of Carlton and listened to their escapades during their childhood. That Louise had been sent away to be the duchess's companion at such a young age didn't sit well with Luke. She'd only been a child. Thrown into a world that was unknown to her and without the support of family. Much like himself. A marquess before the age of eight and thrown into a world that no longer housed his parents or sister.

"Did you miss Sandbach when you left? Eight is very young for one to be taken from those they love."

Louise glanced at him, shrugging a little, but in her eyes he could see the pain of that day lingering in the shadows. She may have been accepted well and loved in the duchess's childhood home, but it was still not her family. No matter how much she may have tried to make it so.

"Of course. I was sent away only weeks after mama and papa had passed away. Sophie and Stephen were only babies really, and I will admit to feeling very lost and unwanted for a time by my aunt. I thought that I had done something wrong. But Mary," she said, reaching for her friend's hand, "helped me laugh again, and I'll forever be grateful for that. I did go home when I could to visit my siblings, and I wrote to them every week. I wanted them to know me, you see. To not forget me. I cannot tell you how pleasant, how very satisfying it is that they're with me now. I suppose I have you to thank for that," she said, chuckling a little.

"Me?" he asked? "How so?"

Louise took a sip of her wine, grinning. "Well, if you hadn't stumbled into my room, I would be in York and my siblings would still be in Cheshire."

Heat rose on Luke's cheeks, but despite himself, he found himself laughing. "I suppose I owe you an apology for that lapse as well."

"Apology accepted." She wrapped her arm about his and he didn't pull away from the contact. In fact, he realized with no amount of shock that he liked having her be tactile with him.

He liked her.

Luke watched as their little party continued to talk and laugh. She had the sweetest laugh and smile when animated and happy. He wanted to see more of her in this way. The thought a few weeks ago would've been preposterous, scary even, but all he felt right at this moment was happy.

LOUISE TOOK Luke's hand as he helped her into the carriage. The blinds had been drawn in the equipage due to the night having a decided chill. Heat bricks had been placed on the floor for them and once they were on their way, it was a cozy place to spend the next few minutes before they reached home.

She pulled her cloak tight about her shoulders, the warmth from the heat brick soothing under her slippers, just as the evening had been also. Tonight Luke had been attentive, amusing and willing to be by her side, act the husband that he now was. After the terrible situation at the park she'd not thought there was much hope for their marriage, but after tonight she wasn't so certain that was the case.

He had tried and that was better than nothing.

He watched her from the seat across from hers, their knees touching every so often with the movement of the carriage. Her mind pulled up memories of the one and only night he'd come to her bed. Of how at least there they had fumbled along very well indeed.

Other parts of her warmed at the thought and glancing at him, his cutting jaw, perfect nose and dark, hungry gaze left her breathless. What was he thinking right at this moment? If it were anything like her own wayward thoughts all she could imagine was what it would be like to be taken in his arms again.

Her week of playing up to the attention gentlemen of their set had bestowed upon her seemed to have worked. Tonight, certainly, Luke had looked like he'd been ready to kill Lord Stopford when he'd seen her with him. That his lordship had played into her little plan of making him jealous, to make him take notice of her, his wife, couldn't have been more perfect if she'd actually asked him to play a part.

"Lord Stopford was very familiar with you this evening."

His deep voice thrummed through her and she met Luke's dark eyes. Lord Stopford was the last person she wished to be speaking about. "Was he? I didn't notice."

His eyes stole over her, and Louise shivered as if he'd physically run his hands over her person. Her body ached to have his touch once more, to have his clever hands trace her breasts, to feel his mouth and tongue.

She shifted on the seat, unable to look away from him.

"I don't want anyone touching you again. You're mine, and I do not share, my lady."

Louise bit her lip, wondering where this change of heart had come from. Only a few weeks ago he'd not wanted a marriage at all. Certainly he'd not wanted her even under the same roof as his lordship. And now he was being all possessive. She could only hope that it would mean he was willing to make their marriage work.

"I did not think you'd mind a caress here or there. There was nothing sinister in it." She was baiting him, she knew it, but she could not help herself. He'd maintained his distance from her for so long, that if he did not show some sort of emotion, she would scream. He guarded his heart like it was cast in iron—an impossible fortress to breach.

"No one touches you."

She scoffed, glancing out the window. "Someone has to. You certainly do not."

The marquess reached out and clasped her arm, hoisting her onto his lap. She sat across his legs, and his arm came about her back, clasping her waist and pinning her against him. "You want to be touched, Louise?"

Heat pooled at her core at his words. She found herself nodding in reply, unable to form words at present. His dark orbs glinted with a promise of something naughty and she bit her lip, wanting more than anything for him to touch her just as he said.

He kept his eyes locked with hers as his hand slid down her leg, clasping the hem of her gown and sliding it up towards her waist. Air kissed her stockinged legs, and she sighed when he pushed her knees apart a little. Still, his hand slid farther up her thigh until he touched her, *there*...

Oh yes, this was what she wanted. She wanted love, to feel wanted and needed. Not only in life, but during these moments as well. Private moments between a married couple. His finger slid over her mons, flicking the little nub with his thumb as his fingers delved farther, stroking and teasing. Louise reached up and clasped his shoulders, turning herself a little in his arms.

"I want you," she gasped as he circled her nubbin. "Please."

⚜

LUKE GROANED AND KISSED HER. Hard. Her sweet mouth opened to him and so too did her legs. They lay open, exposing her sweet heat. He pushed two fingers inside her, wanting to see her come apart in his arms. But he didn't want to take her here, he would find his own pleasure when they were home, in bed where he could savor the time alone.

He picked her up and placed her on the seat she'd just vacated. She made a little sound of protest that made his cock as hard as stone. Damn it, when had she become so damn delicious?

He pushed up her skirts, needing to taste her. Have her

come apart on his face. She didn't shy away from his actions and it only made his need for her stronger. He kissed his way up her leg, biting her stocking-clad thigh. Her legs slipped over his shoulders, and ripping open her pantalettes he paused at the delectable view of her mons before him.

She was wet and ready and he kissed her there. Her fingers spiked into his hair as she relaxed into his ministrations. Damn she tasted sweet and he laved at her, flicking her little nubbin with practiced perfection.

She mewled, pushing against him and taking her pleasure against his tongue. He ached with need of her, and he contemplated fucking her. Having her here as well as in his bed later tonight.

Luke pushed two fingers into her heat and she gasped, rocking on his hand and mimicking sex. It was too much and he pulled away, ripping open his front falls. He wrenched her to the edge of the seat and sheathed himself inside of her in one thrust.

A half gasp, half moan escaped them both. He clasped her about her lower back, and the top of the seat, holding her as he pumped into her tight core.

"Damn it, Louise. You'll undo me."

She moaned, a small satisfied smile upon her lips. "Don't stop."

There was little chance of that. He thrust deeper, his need overriding the fact he was taking his wife in the back of a carriage, like a common strumpet, and yet never had it ever felt so right. He wanted to bring her pleasure, to be the only one who did, today and every day going forward.

She clutched at his hips, her eyes bright with need. He knew the feeling well.

"Let go," he said, lifting her a little to go deeper, to stroke her well.

Her eyes widened and she threw her head back as she came apart in his arms. Spasm after spasm clutched and pulled against his cock and he was powerless not to follow her into bliss. He came hard, let her milk him of every last drop of his seed. He took a calming breath as he slid from her, flopping to sit next to her on the squabs.

She curled into his side and he held her close. Her breath was as ragged as his, and he stared at the ceiling of the carriage, wondering where the hell that overwhelming need to make her his, to ensure him she was his and no one else's came from.

That complexity he'd think on another time. Right now, he couldn't think straight if he tried. He glanced down at her flushed face, a satisfied smile upon her lips and he couldn't regret being with her. Couldn't regret that he'd married her.

But what did that all mean? He reached down and adjusted her gown, settling the skirt back about her legs before buttoning up his own breeches. The carriage rocked to a halt before their townhouse and he helped her down, following her into the house.

He needed to think, and yet he couldn't seem to think straight when he was around Louise. There was something about her that disarmed him. Her compassionate nature by far was one of the best things about her, not to mention they rubbed along well enough when alone.

But he didn't want a wife, right? Or perhaps he'd just not met the right woman. Until now.

He followed her up the stairs and instead of letting her go into her room, he pulled her along into his and shut the door on the world. Shut the door on his muddled thoughts and simply allowed himself to be with her. Enjoy her, and push down the fear that if he allowed himself to grow attached to his wife, it would rip his heart out. That she would always be safe.

Alive.

He kissed her hard and tumbled them both onto the bed. No time like the present to lose himself in her and ignore his fears.

Which was starting to be a fear of losing.

Her.

The following morning Louise all but floated down the stairs to the breakfast table. She entered the room, hoping to find Luke breaking his fast. Instead she found it empty of everyone. She turned to a nearby footman. "Where is everyone this morning?"

She sat at the table and requested tea, toast and bacon.

"His lordship along with Miss Sophie and Mr. Stephen have gone for a ride, your ladyship. They said they would be back to join you at breakfast."

Louise took a sip of tea, sighing at its sweetness just as the door opened and the marquess walked in with her siblings. All of them were flushed, hair askew from riding. They looked refreshed and happy and her heart twisted at knowing her siblings were safe and content.

She met the marquess's gaze and her stomach clutched with need. He was so very handsome and he was hers. Hers to have whenever she wanted. The thought made her cheeks burn and she turned back to her toast and bacon, hoping he'd not guessed her wayward thoughts. She was turning into a wanton.

"You're up?" he said, coming to sit at the table to her right. "You look well today, my lady."

Her gaze tore to him. He grinned, ordering coffee before picking up *The Times* beside him. "Sophie and Stephen are becoming quite the riders, Louise. You would be proud of them."

"We are, Louise. I even had a try of cantering today. I didn't fall off, so one would assume that in itself would be quite the accomplishment."

Stephen laughed. "You did bounce about though, Sophie. I thought you would break your poor pony's back a time or two."

Sophie swiped at their brother's arm, laughing. "I confess I need to learn to sit solidly in the saddle, but his lordship said that will come with practice. And I'm determined to be a great horsewoman."

"I'm sure you will be," Luke said, turning the page on his paper and throwing Louise a grin. "We are going to do a turnabout the park this afternoon in the carriage. All of us," he declared.

Sophie clapped, all but bouncing in her chair at the news.

"We are?" Louise asked, wondering at his change of heart. Had he altered his mind about having a wife and was willing to do things with her? To be dedicated to their marriage as she hoped? After last night, hope had bloomed inside her there could be more between them than she first thought. There was little doubt in her mind that when alone, the air all but thrummed with a delicious tension. Surely they could build on that, work to make their marriage one that was satisfying to them both.

"You're my wife. Your siblings are now my responsibility. A ride in the park as a family is not outrageous."

Louise studied Luke a moment as she'd never heard

him use that term before. She reached out and clasped his hand, squeezing it a little. "A ride in the park would be lovely."

Over the next few weeks they did multiple trips to the park, along with the museum, Vauxhall and Richmond Park. Little by little she learned more about her husband, what his likes and dislikes were. They laughed at gossip, and at balls and parties he was always by her side, a protector and husband.

The night he'd put little Lady Clara in her place before Louise had been an exceptionally high point in their relationship.

Louise stood beside Luke at the Cavendish ball, waiting for the waltz that she'd promised to her husband. She held his arm, enjoying the warmth that his person afforded her, being so close. He glanced down at her and she sighed, swallowing the lump wedged in her throat.

Somewhere over the last few weeks she'd fallen utterly in love with the man. They laughed and played through the days, enjoying their newly formed family, going on excursions and Luke had showed them many sights of London she'd never known of. At night they had come together, their passions set free. Not one evening since he'd pulled her into his room after the delicious carriage ride home had she slept in her bed. Always in his, always waking up in a tangle of arms and legs.

It was heavenly and she'd been powerless to stop her heart from tumbling head first into love with him. She loved him more than she ever thought a person could be loved. He was everything to her. The question was, did he love her in return?

"You look beautiful tonight, my lady," he said, leaning down, his whispered words against her ear sending a shiver of delight down her spine.

"You look good enough to eat, my lord," she teased. His eyes burned with desire and she clutched his arm harder, liking the fact that the action pushed her breast, her nipple against him and teased her.

"And you wish to eat me here, my lady?" He started moving them toward a nearby door. Louise grinned, following without question.

"Are you not going to dance with me?" she asked, as the first strains of the waltz sounded.

"No, we have other dances to take part in." Luke pulled her through multiple rooms, all deserted and closed off for the ball.

"You know this house very well," she stated, not totally at ease by the fact.

He chuckled. "I've known the family all my life and therefore the house as well. There is nothing more to it than that." He pulled her into a small room moderately furnished. The curtains were drawn, but with a moonlit night, the glow seeped through the fabric and bathed the room in enough light so that they could see.

Luke clasped her hand, walking her slowly to a nearby settee. He sat, looking up at her, and she didn't move. He was so very handsome, with his superfine suit, his groomed hair and perfectly tied cravat. She wanted to muss him all over. Send him spiraling into mayhem as much as he always did to her.

Louise kneeled before him, and his eyes widened.

"What are you doing?" he asked, although not in the least attempting to shift her from her knees.

She reached out and, holding his gaze, slipped free each button on his breeches. His eyes burned with need and heat pooled at her core. Who knew that giving pleasure, which she was utterly about to try, could give pleasure in turn?

"I've wanted to attempt this for some time now. Let me," she said, reaching between the flap of his breeches and clasping his rigid member.

He leaned back on the settee, a willing participant, and wickedness thrummed through her veins. Louise pushed his knees farther apart and shuffled closer to the settee. She ran her hand up his thighs, the strong, corded muscles beneath her palms flexing at her touch.

"This is very wicked of you, my lady."

"Hmmm," she said, pulling him free. She bit her lip, having never seen his penis so close before, she'd wondered a moment how on earth she took him inside of her with ease. He was so large, so solid and hard and yet the skin about his phallus was the softest thing she'd ever felt. Utterly amazing.

He groaned, pushing into her hand and she looked up and caught his gaze. His breath was ragged and she tightened her grip, pumping his cock a couple of times to tease him more.

"You're a vixen."

Louise leaned over him and kissed the tip of his penis. It jerked at the touch and she smiled, sticking out her tongue a little to lick the droplet of moisture that sat there. He gasped her name, clasping the nape of her neck, but not urging her down, simply accepting whatever she wanted to do to him. And she wanted to do so much.

Licking her lips, she placed them over his manhood, sliding down his engorged penis, running her tongue along the base of his phallus, teasing the vein that ran there. She sucked, increasing her speed when she noticed that doing so only seemed to give him greater pleasure.

He was delicious as she'd always thought he would be.

LUKE WAS sure he saw stars. To have Louise on her knees before him, taking him into her mouth and sucking with an expert precision left him speechless. His body thrummed with need, his balls swelled and ached for release. The base side of him wanted to spill in her mouth, and yet he wouldn't. Not here. Not tonight.

He leaned back in the chair, clasping the nape of her neck as she slid up and down over his cock. He wanted to come, he wanted to fuck her in every which way he could. Over the last weeks she'd weakened his defenses and the walls he'd put up about his heart had slowly cracked away.

His chest ached when he spied her about the house, when she laughed he smiled. Silly and odd things such as these happened all the time, and for the first time since he was a boy, he enjoyed the sound of people in his home.

Somehow Louise had shown him what it meant to have a family again. She had brought him into their fold of three and made them a fold of four and his heart had moved.

Unable to take a moment more of her ministrations, he wrenched her onto his lap, grasping at her skirts to lift them to her waist and sheathed himself fully into her tight core.

They moaned in unison before she lifted on him, kissing him as she took her own pleasure upon his cock.

"You feel so good," he said, kissing her back and tasting himself upon her lips.

She mumbled her agreement as she increased her pace, her little mews of satisfaction keeping him from coming too soon. Her core suckled his cock, warm and tempting as sin. She shook in his arms and he knew she was close. She rode him, knew how to bring pleasure to herself when atop him like this and he sat there, holding her and letting her have her fill.

"You're so beautiful," he gasped. Louise murmured his name against his lips as the first contractions of her climax spiraled through her. Luke let go, allowed her core to drag him along and he moaned her name as his seed shot into her again and again.

He kissed her deep and long, and the final stone about his heart crumbled away and he accepted it for what it was.

He'd fallen in love with his wife.

CHAPTER 13

A letter arrived two days later from a woman who claimed to be nursing their aunt who'd grown ill during her visit to Bath. The woman requested Louise and her siblings come to Sandbach as soon as possible.

Louise set the letter in her lap, looking over to Luke who sat at his desk, watching her.

"Is something the matter?" he asked. He stood, coming over to her. "Who was the letter from?"

Louise handed it to him, before standing and ringing the bell. "We'll have to go straightaway. I'll have the maids pack a valise for each of us."

Luke looked up from the missive, understanding clear in his eyes. "Of course. I'll have a carriage readied for you. I will follow you in a day or two. I have a parliamentary session tomorrow that I cannot miss."

He stood and pulled her into his arms. She wrapped her hands about his back as tears pricked her eyes. Her aunt had been there for all of them for so many years. Upon her marriage, she'd sent some of her pin money to help her with her travels, and her aunt had wasted no time going about England and Scotland on her tours.

That she had fallen ill in Bath and that it did not sound good was so unfair. "Just when she was enjoying herself, having a little time for herself, and this happens."

Luke rubbed her back, kissing her temple and hair. "Maybe it's just a passing virus and she'll soon get better. Before you panic, wait and see what she is like when you get there."

Louise nodded. He was right of course, but her stomach churned at the idea of losing her. She was the last person they had in the world. Their only living blood relative.

"I will try," she said, just as the door opened and a footman entered.

"Ready the traveling coach and have her ladyship's maid pack a valise for her and her siblings. Straightaway," Luke said.

The young footman bowed. "Of course, my lord," he said, closing the door softly behind him.

Luke leaned down and kissed her. "It will all be well. I promise."

She hugged him again, hoping that were so.

❧

THE CARRIAGE RIDE to Sandbach was a long and arduous one. They had forgone staying overnight at the Inn at Northampton, and had instead simply changed horses, ate dinner and continued toward Cheshire. Louise stared out the window, the night closing in fast. The inn had given them heated bricks and in this part of England it looked like they had suffered some summer storms, the road muddy with water, laying over it in places.

She glanced back at her siblings, both of them sound asleep and each of them leaning up against the side of the carriage. She took in their fine clothes, their fuller cheeks and smiled that she'd been able to finally give them security. The chance of a life just a little easier than their prospects were before.

A large crack sounded and Louise clasped the squabs as the carriage tipped alarmingly to one side. The sound of screaming horses and that of her siblings merged with her own as they rolled off the road and down an embankment. Grass and rock broke into the carriage, wood splintered and Louise gasped as something solid smashed into her forehead. The world blurred before her, all of them flaying about like dolls being tossed in the air, before everything went quiet and thankfully, peacefully, black.

ONE WEEK LATER, Luke sat beside the bed where Louise lay, still and injured after their accident. Having heard of the carriage accident, he had ordered her and her siblings to be moved to Lord Buxton's estate, a friend of his for many years and who was more than willing to help. Luke had demanded his doctor from London travel to them and attend her posthaste.

Unfortunately, Louise would never get to say goodbye to her aunt, who passed away the day of the carriage accident. His heart hurt for her that she would wake and find out such news, news that would break her heart.

He ran a hand over her face, pushing aside a lock of hair that had slipped over her eyes. Her forehead sported a large, deep gash that the doctor had stitched, but it would leave a scar. Possibly leave her with a scar far deeper than the skin.

The doctor had warned them that she may never be of sound mind again.

That she had not woken at all, not even when they had placed smelling salts beneath her nose was not a favorable sign, or so the doctor had stated. Luke spoke to her daily, just as he was told to do, and yet she continued to lay still, not even a flicker of an eyelid or twitch of her finger.

Nothing.

He sat back, running his hand over his jaw as the sight of her brought back a deluge of memories. Of his mother and father, little sister lying on their beds, cold and dead. Never to laugh and smile again.

He couldn't do it again. He should never have allowed himself to care. Nothing good ever came out of caring for others. Louise, lying in this bed, lifeless and pale. Her stillness was the thing that haunted his dreams, a nightmare come true to life. It was not what he'd ever wanted to partake in again.

The door to the room opened and her brother hobbled inside, the walking stick helping him about. He too had been hurt, a severe sprained ankle, multiple cuts and bruises. Surprisingly, Sophie had fared the best of the three. She had sustained cuts and bruises, but had managed to miss most objects that would cause her harm and had been the one who waved down help for her siblings when she'd climbed up the embankment and sought assistance.

The driver was found dead, and the doctor had come to the conclusion he'd had some medical event prior to losing control of the carriage. Both carriage horses had to be put down. When Luke had inspected the carriage at the nearby town, he'd been amazed anyone had survived such an accident.

Thank God they had, but there was a lesson in this for

him. He'd let his guard down, let himself feel and care for someone again only to have that possibly ripped from under him. If his life had taught him anything, it should have been that perhaps he wasn't meant to love. Perhaps he wasn't worthy of the emotion.

"Any change, my lord?" Stephen asked, seating himself at the other side of the bed.

"No." Luke stood and strode to the window, needing to see anything other than his wife in such a condition. "I have to return to London. I'm not sure when I'll be back."

Stephen glanced at him, his face ashen. "You cannot leave. Not with Louise in such a state."

His words tore at his conscience and he pushed it away. He'd almost lost this young man as well. A boy on the brink of manhood that he'd grown to care for. To think that all of them could've been torn away, just like his own sweet sister. His stomach churned at the thought. He couldn't do it.

Panic seized him and he leaned against the window-pane for support, breathing deeply lest he cast up his accounts over the Aubusson rug at his feet. If he left now, before she worsened, then he could distance himself from the situation. Allow others to deal with the issue and be done with it. To stay, to see Louise worsen, wither away and die before him was not to be borne. He'd seen enough dead bodies to last him a lifetime, he would not stay and see another. Not if he could help it.

"I must go," he said, unable to meet Louise's brother's disapproving eyes. Yet he didn't need to look at the young man to feel the loathing aimed at his back.

"If you care for my sister at all, even the smallest amount, you will stay. Help us bring her back."

Luke cringed. Damn it, the urge to bolt coursed through him, yet his feet remained lodged firmly on the floor. His mind screaming to leave and another part of him, a part he'd not thought to use ever again ached to stay. To be strong and face the worst head on.

❧

"LUKE?" Louise fought against the fog that clouded her mind. Her mind was awash with images of her rolling, of flying about in the carriage as they tumbled down the embankment. The sound echoed in her ears and she opened her eyes, wanting to rid herself of it all.

She focused on the ceiling sporting images of cherubs on clouds. She tried to remember where she was heading and why. She took in the four-poster bed and couldn't place it.

Where was she?

"Luke?"

A warm, comforting hand clasped hers and she shut her eyes. "I'm here, Louise."

"Stephen. Sophie? Where are—"

"We're both well, sister," her brother said, taking her other hand and clasping it tight. He leaned over it and she heard the sob that broke through his composure. "We're a little bruised and sore just as yourself, but we will heal."

Relief poured through her like a balm and she couldn't hold back the tears that ran down her face. They survived. That's all that mattered.

"What happened?" she asked, looking to Luke who sat beside her. She reached out and touched his cheek and stilled when he pulled away from her.

"Your driver had a turn, the doctor thinks he may have suffered a heart spasm that killed him. He lost control of the carriage and it toppled down an embankment, taking the horses with it. It's a miracle that any of you survived."

Her head thumped and she reached up, gasping when she felt the bandage on her forehead. "What happened to my face?" She tried to feel the injury, but could not due to all the bandaging.

"Something hit you in the forehead. Possibly a heating brick from inside the carriage when it toppled over. You were cut very badly and will have a scar," Luke replied, all business-like and cold.

Her brother smiled at her. "You will still be as pretty as ever."

Louise chuckled and then cringed as the action made her head pound. She gasped. "Auntie. We need to go. We're supposed be at her bedside."

"I'm sorry, Louise," her husband cut in, pushing her back down on the bed. "Your auntie passed away the same day of your accident." Remorse tinged his tone. "You've been asleep for a week. There was nothing that could be done."

She clutched at Stephen's hand and her brother held her tight in turn. "We never got to say goodbye to her. After all that she'd done for us."

"You know Auntie was happy for us all, you especially. She's no longer in pain, Louise. The doctor said that he suspected her to be ill for quite some time but never told any of us. She is in a better place now."

Louise tried to allow her brother's words to soothe her, but they did not. They should have been there. They should have held her hand as she passed away.

"Can you give me a minute with his lordship, please, Stephen?"

He nodded, standing. "Of course. I'll tell Sophie you're awake and that she can visit you in a little while."

"Thank you," she said.

Luke turned toward the door. "Stephen, have a missive

sent to doctor that her ladyship is awake and that he must come immediately."

"Of course, my lord," he said, closing the door behind him.

Louise leaned forward, needing to sit up more. "Can you please place some cushions behind me? I'm tired of lying down." Luke helped her to sit upright and she sighed in pleasure at the new position. She needed that above anything else.

"How are you feeling?" He sat back in his chair, watching her, and she frowned, assessing herself from within. "I'm sore and have a headache, but otherwise I feel well enough. I would love a cup of tea."

The marquess stood and rang the bell. "If the doctor approves it, we'll return to London as soon as you're able."

She nodded, unsure how she felt about going back to town. Right at this moment all she longed for was a quiet country setting, away from the bustle of the Season where she may read to her heart's content and explore her new home some more. Take the time to grieve her aunt.

"I'm sorry about the carriage. About all this trouble." She glanced about the room. It was very beautiful and well kept, but it wasn't as nice as her room in town, or her suite at their country estate.

He waved her concerns away. "You have nothing to be sorry about. I'm just sorry that all of this happened. I thought that you may never wake up."

His words were that of a man who had worried and cared over the past few days, and yet his tone remained cold and aloof. A shiver stole down her spine and she couldn't shift it. "Have you been here all this time?" She hoped he had been. To think that he cared enough to be by her side until she woke would surely show that he cared.

"I have, yes, but I must leave today, unfortunately. I

have business to attend to in town that cannot wait. Now that you're awake, I feel no reason to dally any longer."

"Can it not wait?" She reached for his hand and this time he pulled it back, linking both in his lap. He glanced down at his fingers, anywhere it would seem but her. What was going on? Prior to her leaving for her auntie's they had been getting along so very well. They had been becoming close, or so she thought. What had changed?

"It cannot. I'm sorry, but I must leave for London tonight."

Louise sat up, clasping the bed as the room spun. "Please don't go, Luke."

He glanced at her but a moment before he stood and started for the door. "I'm sorry, Louise, but I must."

"Luke," she said again as he walked from the room. She stared after the empty space for a long moment. Even when her sister came into the room, gushed and thanked the Lord that she was awake, still she could not concentrate on what her sibling was saying.

Why had Luke left? What could be more important than being together at such a time? She slumped back on the bedding, allowing her sister to fuss over her while her mind whirled in thought.

She would get better and then she would return home. Maybe it was the shock that she'd woken up. Maybe he really did need to return to town and there was no nice way of telling her that he'd have to leave her. Either way, she would be back in London soon enough and then they would talk. All would be well.

She hoped.

CHAPTER 14

Louise had been back in town a month before she'd been well enough to attend a small soirée that the Duchess of Carlton was hosting. Her husband over the last few weeks had gone out of his way to avoid her. No longer did he attend balls and parties with her, and he'd also stopped coming to her room, stating that she wasn't well enough. That she needed rest, not him.

How little did he know.

She did need him and it was Luke whom she wanted. Tonight was a rare treat and he had accompanied her, and she was determined to reach him. Have them return to how they once were, and to have him not be this cold, aloof man he'd become since her accident.

Louise studied him in the carriage as he stared out the window. "I'm so glad that I've been able to come out to Mary's party. Thank you for coming with me."

He threw her a small smile, but that was all. "Of course," he said, looking back out the window. "We could not let them down."

Louise wrung her hands in her lap, not sure what to say to reach him. "Is everything well, Luke? Since my accident I've hardly seen you."

He raised his brow, but still refused to glance her way. What was going on?

"I'm sorry you're feeling ignored, but as the wife of a marquess, that is sometimes part of the deal I'm afraid."

She frowned, anger replacing the confusion in her veins. "You did not ignore me prior to my accident, in fact we were together most days. What has changed?" He'd been so attentive, loving toward hers and her siblings. He'd purchased her brother and sister a new horse each and gifted Louise the family jewels. The man who sat across from her, dismissive and cutting, was not the man she'd fallen in love with.

He shrugged, his countenance one of disinterest. "Nothing has changed."

She shook her head, having heard enough. "That, my lord is utter cow dung," she said, sitting forward. "You've been avoiding me. I only get one-word answers from you. You never come to my room any longer. Have I sprouted snakes out of my skull since the accident? Will you turn to stone if you dare look my way?"

He did look at her then and the shadows that lingered in his gaze sent chills down her spine. "I'm looking at you now."

She shook her head, unable to take much more of his treatment. If this was how he was going to be—hot one moment and as cold as ice the next—she didn't want to be a part of this charade. It was not what she wanted. She wanted him to love her as much as she loved him. That he'd not been there for her during her weeks of recuperation should have warned her to expect less from him.

Foolishly she'd hoped it had merely been a scare he'd suffered and he'd soon be back to rights. Just as she was. Her hopes had been dashed during the weeks she'd been back in town and he'd slowly, gradually disappeared from her life altogether.

"Is this the kind of marriage you want? Do you want to be strangers? A husband and wife in name only? Tell me now, because if that is so I want no part of it."

He scoffed at her words and she flinched. "It is a little late for that, my lady. You married me, did you not? Knowing full well I never wished to be saddled with a wife. This is the price you have to pay to have my name. I'm sorry you feel disappointed, but it is what it is. I suggest you move on and make the best of the bad situation."

Louise nodded, her eyes burned with unshed tears. "I suppose you're right. I will do as you ask."

The muscle at his jaw flexed and he stared at her a long moment, before he moved toward the door as the carriage slowed. "We're here. Come," he said reaching for her hand when he stepped out onto the footpath.

Louise didn't move. "I have a sudden headache. Please give my apologies to Mary and the duke."

He gestured for her to follow him. "Come, Louise. You must attend."

She shook her head, wrapping her cloak about her shoulders, needing its warmth after the sudden chill running through her veins. "No. Please notify the driver to return me home. Thank you."

He closed the carriage door, the muscle in his jaw flexing, before he said, "Return Lady Graham home, thank you," he said to the driver and without a backward glance, started for the townhouse doors. Louise sat back in the squabs, rubbing her thumping forehead. "Goodbye, Luke," she whispered as he disappeared from view just as the carriage lurched forward and they went in their different directions.

To start different lives.

CHAPTER 15

Louise sat on an outdoor reclining chair, a woolen blanket about her knees as she looked out on the grounds of her home. Or Lord Graham's estate in Kent at least.

She'd been here several weeks now, and still he'd not come. She'd hoped when he'd found her gone from their London home after the duke and duchess' soirée that he would've come to his senses and followed her.

He had not and now, out of pure stubbornness, she would not return to town and seek him out. She'd asked for him to tell her what was wrong. Asked him to return to the way they were, and instead of explaining his actions, he'd thrown at her coldness, aloofness. Dismissed her wants and needs and instead demanded a marriage like the one he'd wanted prior to growing close to her.

But what about what she wanted in a marriage? Did he not care for her feelings at all?

Sophie sat on the chair beside her, laying a book on her lap as she stared out on the lawns. "I saw that the mail had come today. Anything from the marquess?" her sister asked, opening her book to where she'd finished reading last.

Louise shook her head. "Only a letter from Mary and Auntie's solicitor. The cottage in Sandbach has been sold and the funds are being placed into investments to hopefully give you and Stephen some funds upon your marriage."

Sophie reached out her hand, clasping hers. "You're always so good to us. Thank you for caring for us so very much. You are the best sister anyone could ever wish for."

Louise patted her hand, fighting back tears. She'd been crying a lot lately, and at the oddest things. Not to mention her stomach had been very unstable. The two facts ought to bring her joy for she knew what they meant, but they did not. Not as it should in any case.

She wanted to share her news with her husband, with her siblings, but she could not. Not yet at least. When she had control of her emotions, had closed her heart off from the man she'd married who had made it abundantly clear that he cared very little for her, then she would tell him and her family.

She clutched at her stomach. No matter what happened between her and the marquess she would love this child with all her heart. Never allow the child to feel unwanted or unloved as she was feeling right at this moment. Stupid of her to be so attached to a man who had told her he'd never wanted to marry her, but her heart had other ideas and she'd been powerless to not fall heedlessly in love with him.

Little good that did for her.

"Are you going to tell the marquess?"

Louise glanced sharply at her sister, frowning. "What do you mean?" she asked, hoping she meant something entirely different.

Sophie gestured toward her stomach. "The baby? Are you going to tell him about the baby?"

Louise took a calming breath, her stomach roiling in dread. "How did you know?"

Her sister scoffed, picking up her book. "You vomit each morning, sleep in the middle of the day and cry when you lose at chess. I think it's pretty obvious that you're pregnant."

At her sister's words she laughed, the first time in an age and she could not regret her amusement. She'd not found many things funny these past few weeks, but somehow her brother and sister always managed to cheer her up.

"Does he deserve to know?" she said, regretting her words as soon as she'd said them. Of course he deserved to know, but did he want to? The thought that he would scorn their child as much as he'd scorned her filled her with panic and not a small amount of anger. She would not allow him to treat their child such. Over her dead body would she allow him to disregard their son or daughter.

"You need to tell him, Louise." Her sister sighed, shaking her head. "His actions of late make no sense. When you were injured, he was beside your bed every day and night. Refused to leave the room unless forced. For him to up and leave, almost panic when you woke makes no sense."

Louise frowned, thinking on her sister's observations. "I asked him in London what was troubling him and he would not say. He was so cold and aloof, very disinterested in me and so very different than how he was prior to my accident."

Their brother came out on the terrace, only a small limp remaining from his injured ankle. "I think I know what happened to the marquess."

"You do?" both Louise and Sophie said in unison. "What?" Louise asked.

"He never told me exactly what occurred, but he did lose his family when he was young, right?"

Louise nodded. "That's right. He wasn't with them when the accident occurred, and he'd been orphaned."

Her brother nodded, a contemplative look on his face. "It was a carriage accident, wasn't it? I'm sure I heard the staff at Lord Buxton's estate talking about it. They mentioned how very unlucky the marquess was that he'd almost lost his wife and her family in the same way he'd lost his own."

Louise stared at her siblings in shock. How had she not realized that fact herself? She thought back over everything she'd known of the marquess, before and after their marriage and although she'd known of his family's death, she'd never asked him how it had occurred.

A carriage accident.

Poor Luke. Her own accident had no doubt brought forth terrible memories and fears he'd sooner forget and so instead of holding her close, being thankful for her survival, he'd pushed her away.

He'd protected his heart.

"I have to return to London." At her words a footman stepped out onto the terrace. "My lady, the Marquess Graham has arrived."

CHAPTER 16

A month after Louise had left London Luke had crumbled and gone to Whites, unwilling to stay at home another day. He'd declined all invitations to events about town, and had instead thrown himself into estate business, going so far as to visit his estates in Sussex and Cornwall. All the while he knew that Louise was staying at Ashby House in Kent. He'd fought with himself not to go to her. To beg for forgiveness. For her to understand.

But what would he say? There was not a lot he could say to fix the error that he'd made, but how?

The leather chair crunched across from him and he glanced up to see Carlton sitting before him. A glass of brandy swirling in his friend's hands.

"We've now turned to drinking, have we?"

Luke feigned ignorance and took another sip, his head spinning a little since he'd had many a glass before this one. "I don't know what you mean."

The duke raised a disbelieving brow. "Why don't you just admit that you miss her, you stubborn fool?"

He leaned farther back in his chair, feeling less than

inclined to listen to reason when spoken to in such a way. But then what did he expect? He'd acted an ass and the duke knew it. Hell, all of London knew it.

"I doubt she'll want to speak to me even if I did seek her out. She left me, remember?"

The duke scoffed. "You forced her hand. What did you expect? I saw the way you watched her at balls and parties after her accident. You love her and yet you pushed her aside. You need to go to Kent and fix this problem you've created. You need to tell her you love her and that you're sorry for being scared."

Luke placed his empty glass on the table before him, running a hand over his jaw, surprised to feel stubble there. Hell, he'd let a lot of things slide over the last few weeks. Even his own appearance.

Carlton was right. He was scared. Scared to death of loving Louise so fiercely that the thought of losing her chilled his soul. But he could no longer live with that fear. He'd let it control him long enough, taint his life and haunt his dreams.

He swore and stood. "I leave early tomorrow morning." The decision lifted a weight that had been pressing on his shoulders for years and with it he felt free. No longer would he live a half life. Now was time to live. It would be what his parents wished. What little Isabella would want for her big brother.

The duke stood, draping his arm about his shoulders and walking him toward the upstairs smoking room doors. "Good man. Give our love to Louise and good luck, my friend, even though I'm sure you will not need it."

He nodded, hoping that were true. "See you next Season."

Luke left Whites and made his way home, giving orders upon his arrival of his intention to leave first thing in the morning to Ashby House. His staff went straight to work in preparing for his departure. Luke headed upstairs, needing to work on his own hygiene before he saw Louise again. His world had turned to shite, along with his appearance, but he didn't need her to see it also. He would hide that from her at least outwardly, for heavens knew, he was a mess inside and his only cure was his wife.

Louise.

CHAPTER 17

L uke handed the footman his missive to give to the marchioness and started toward the old elm tree that overlooked the valley on the western side of the estate. He stared down at his parents' graves, and his little sister's. Forever young at only six years of age.

He shut his eyes a moment, stemming his tears before he looked down at the three headstones, always the same emotion washing over him when he visited them.

Guilt.

Guilt that he'd refused to go on the outing that day. He'd wanted to stay at the estate and play with his toy soldiers. He'd always wondered if he'd been there that maybe he could have saved her. Maybe being in the carriage may have changed all their fates.

A twig snapped behind him and he turned to find Louise standing before him. She was the sweetest thing that had ever come into his life. A woman so full of love that she'd wanted to give it to him too, even when he'd not wanted a bar of it. Still she persisted and eventually had worn him down. Won his heart.

Only for him to turn her away at the first sign of difficulty. He was an ass, but hopefully, she would forgive him his stupidity.

"Louise, this is my family," he said, stepping aside and showing her the graves beyond.

She walked past him, kneeling to read each one, before she stood, her dark-blue eyes full of questions and hurt. Damn it. He'd put that emotion there and he ought to be horsewhipped for doing so. He'd never wanted to hurt her. Not intentionally.

"They died when I was eight. Heading for a picnic in which I refused to go on. I didn't want to leave my toys, you see, and so being the selfish little ass that I was, I got to play with my toys while they died not two miles from here."

"Oh, no, Luke." She reached out to him, taking his hand. He shook his head at her ability to care, even after all he'd done to her. He played with her fingers a moment, needing the time to compose himself, the lump in his throat awfully large.

"The horses were spooked and the carriage rolled. They all died and they never returned home that night. The house was shut up and I was bundled away to Sussex to live with my grandmother. A woman who tolerated me, taught me how to be a marquess, but little else. I forgot, you see."

Her eyes held his and he could see the unshed tears in her eyes. "What did you forget, Luke?" she asked.

"I forgot what it was like to have a family. A caring and a joyful family to come home to. I forgot what it was like to be responsible for others and care for them. To want the best for them now and for their future." He stepped closer to her, taking both her hands. "When you were hurt I couldn't see straight. The fear that you would never wake up, just as my family had never woken up...I couldn't do that again and I panicked because I'd already gone too far."

"Too far?" She frowned, stepping closer. "How?"

He glanced at the sky, praying for strength lest he lose his composure completely. "I love you, you see. The thought that I would lose you, that you could be taken away from me within a moment of time. I couldn't stand the thought."

She reached up, clasping his jaw. "So you pushed me away to protect yourself." Louise lifted herself and wrapped her arms about his neck, holding him close. "I'm here, Luke. I didn't die. I survived. This time, you didn't lose everything."

He wrapped his arms about her back, feeling the warmth of her skin, her scent of jasmine, the expansion of her chest with each breath she took. So unlike his family who had been cold, gray, and still as death.

He clutched at her, the memory bombarding him and he gasped, and for the first time since he was a child, he cried. Cried for the loss of his parents, for the loss of a sister who had so much to give to the world and had never had the chance. For the loss of his childhood and his ability to love. But not anymore. Louise had broken down his walls, had showed him that to love was to live and he wanted nothing more than to love and be with her forever and a day.

"I'm so sorry, my darling," he said, kissing her neck. "I will never push you away again. Ever."

Louise rubbed his back, a comforting gesture that he remembered from his own mother. "I'm sorry too. I didn't know, Luke and I should have asked. When we lost our parents, we were thrown into our auntie's home, and although she loved us, we were so poor. I too was sent away at eight, but having my siblings to love and care for made me only want to protect them, keep them safe always."

She paused, pulling back to look at him. "I intended to travel to York for work, but I did hope to marry one day to a man I loved who could support me and my siblings. When you stumbled into my room that night I thought all of my dreams had been crushed. That you had ripped that future away from me, but you had not. You only made my dreams come true."

She reached up, rubbing away the tears drying on his cheeks.

"I did?"

She nodded. "You did." She smiled, leaning up to kiss him. "I love you too and I promise, it will take a lot more than a carriage accident to tear me away from you. You have my word on that."

He tried to smile, but his lips merely wobbled. "Promise?"

She wrapped her arms about him again. "I promise."

EPILOGUE

Seven months later

Louise pushed as pain ripped through her body, threatening to tear her in two. The midwife kneeled between her legs, telling her to push, that she could see the baby's head, but she'd had enough. She just wanted it all to end. For the pain to stop.

She tried to close her legs and the midwife *tsked tsked* her, pushing her knees apart. "Come on, my lady. Push hard. We're nearly there."

Luke lifted her higher on his chest and held her hands. "Come, my love. Push as hard as you can. We're almost there."

A baby cried in the hands of Sophie who stood beside the bed, her sister's tears dripping onto the newly born babe and Louise wanted to tell her to stop dribbling on the baby, before another contraction hit and she bore down. The only time she felt a little relief was when she pushed.

"That's it, my lady." Louise flopped back on Luke,

panting. "The head is out now, my lady. One more push for the shoulders and we'll be there."

"It better be so," Louise said, ignoring Luke's chuckle at her ear. The contraction came fast and hard and she pushed with all her might, wanting the child out and the pain finished.

Please, God, let it be done.

She screamed as the babe pushed through and out into the world, its squeaking cry loud in the room, starting off the other baby her sister held.

"It's a boy, my lord, my lady. You have both a girl and boy."

Luke shook behind her and she patted his arms, knowing that her husband was emotional over the news. The midwife handed off the child to her maid and Louise looked back at Luke, smiling. He leaned down, kissing her softly. "Thank you, my darling for giving me such a wonderful gift." He glanced up at the babies, pride over-flowing from him and making her smile. "I cannot believe it. Twins."

"Well, they do run in the family, need I remind you, Luke," her sister said, pointing at herself.

Louise laughed and the midwife declared her well enough to lay back on the bed. Luke moved from behind her and helped settle her on a bed of pillows at her back and then she gestured for the babies to be handed to them.

Sophie placed the little girl in Louise's arms and Luke, having taken their boy from the maid, came to sit on the bed beside her. They stared and played with the babies for a time as the midwife went about cleaning the room and giving instructions to the staff.

"I shall be back after dinner and will sleep here this evening, just to be sure all is well through the night."

Luke glanced up and nodded. "Thank you, Mrs. Turner. That is most welcome."

Sophie walked the midwife to the door. "We'll leave you alone for a little while. I'll bring Stephen in a little bit to meet his new nephew and niece."

"Thank you, Sophie for today. You were wonderful." Her sister nodded and left, closing the door softy behind her.

Louise looked between the babies, sweet and innocent and her heart filled even more than she'd ever thought it possible. "We have a little family," she said, running her finger over her daughter's golden hair that was only just visible atop her head.

Luke leaned over and kissed Louise on the temple. "We were already a family, now we're merely a bigger one."

She chuckled, supposing that were true. Her son fussed in his father's arms and Luke cooed to him and he soon settled again. "He likes you." Louise reached out and touched her son's cheek, so soft and new. So perfect.

"May I ask something of you, darling?" Luke met her gaze, before looking down at his daughter.

"Of course, anything."

He took a breath, quiet a moment before he said, "I would like to name her after my sister. I think Isabella suits her pretty little face."

Louise looked back at her daughter, nodding. "I think she looks like an Isabella as well." She lifted her daughter, kissing her cheek. "Hello, Isabella. It's lovely to meet you."

Luke lifted their son and kissed him in turn. "And what about this strapping young man? What shall we call him?"

"How about we name him after his father. I've always had a love for that name."

Luke glanced at her quickly. "After me?"

Louise nodded, turning back to her son, not quite

believing she'd just given birth to two babies and had lived to name them at all. Certainly, throughout the ordeal there were times where she'd thought she would absolutely die.

"Yes, after you. Luke, Viscount Tomlinson, future Marquess Graham. I think it suits him very well."

Luke caught her gaze, and she read all the love that he had for them in his eyes, for they no doubt matched hers. He leaned down and kissed her again, lingering a little this time. "Thank you, my darling. Have I said today how much I love you?"

She grinned, nodding. "You have. Multiple times, but you may say it again if you want. I like hearing it."

"I love you. I love you. I love you," he repeated.

She chuckled. "And I adore you too."

Forever.

A KISS AT MISTLETOE

Kiss the Wallflower, Book 2

Lady Mary Dalton fills her time with anything she pleases—and she pleases to do as she likes. With no interest in a husband, Lady Mary is perfectly content to remain in Derbyshire for the rest of her days. However, Mary's parents have other ideas.

For the Christmas festivities at Bran Manor, Mary's brother brings home the Duke of Carlton, an infamous man known for his many improprieties, as well as for his distaste in matrimony. Despite his rakish ways, Mary is drawn to him in the most vexing and exasperating way.

But when Mary stumbles into the Duke of Carlton's arms one snowy eve, an undeniable attraction is set into motion. Suddenly, marriage no longer seems so horrific—for either of them.

CHAPTER 1

Lady Mary Dalton, eldest daughter to the Earl of Lancaster jiggled her fishing pole, having felt a rapid jerk of her line. Too slow to catch the fish, she left her line in the water hoping to feel another little nibble and possibly reel in a nice-sized carp or bream for Cook to prepare for dinner tomorrow.

The snow relentlessly fell outside as she sat wrapped up in furs and wool on the family's frozen lake in Derbyshire. The ice house her father had the servants move onto the lake each year was a welcome retreat from her mother's complaints. Mama didn't think ladies should fish, particularly in the middle of winter. Women should be wives. Women should have husbands. Women should have children. Her daughter should be married by now…

Blah, blah, blah, she'd heard the words too many times to count.

It was practically the countess's motto. Unfortunately, what her mama wished for was the opposite of what Mary wanted. She'd never been like her friends, had never loved shopping in London in the weeks leading up to their first

Season. She cared very little if the men of the *ton* thought her a worthy, profitable or pretty ornament for their arm.

The outdoors had always been her passion and some days she'd wished she'd been born a man, or even into a family that were not titled and rich. Just an ordinary, working family that could do as they pleased. At least, that was what she'd always thought everyone else had since her own life had been so orchestrated.

Mary jiggled her line a little and sighed. At least she was home at present, thanks to her mama falling ill with a cold that she could not possibly stay in Town to endure since someone might see her red nose.

With any luck, her mother would decide to stay in Derbyshire and not travel back to Town to finish up the Little Season before Christmas. Thankfully, spring and summer would soon return and she was looking forward to those months. When the snow melted away and rivers ran and she was able to go outdoors again not just to fish on the ice but to walk the surrounding hills and forests and climb the rocky outcrops that scattered her magnificent county.

The door to the icebox opened and her father entered. He was rugged up in a fur coat, a hood covered his head and most of his brow. A thick woolen scarf wrapped about his mouth and nose, and he looked like an Eskimo. Mary chuckled as he came in and shut the door, before sitting on the little wooden stool across from her. He picked up the spare fishing rod, placing bait on the small hook and dropped the line into the water, dangling it just as she had.

"Mary, there is something we need to discuss, my dear," he said.

His downcast tone didn't bode well for them to remain in the country and she prepared herself for the disappointing news that was undoubtedly to come.

"My dearest girl is to be three and twenty in few days, and it is time for us to have you settled and married before the end of the next Season. We thought our annual Mistletoe Ball would be the perfect opportunity to invite our neighbors and their guests to celebrate Yuletide. It would also act as a reintroduction for you into society and to show those present that you're most definitely seeking a husband next year and are open to courtship."

The thought sent revulsion through her and she stared at her father a moment, wondering if he'd lost his mind. It was one thing to return to London, but using their Christmas ball as a means to showcase her assets was mortifying. "Must we go back to London at all? You know I do not do well in Town. I am not like the other girls. I don't take pleasure in grand balls and parties. I'm much more comfortable here in my ice fishing box, swimming in our lake or walking the beautiful park with Louise. I'll be miserable if you make me endure another Season. Even you said how much you loathe London and the backstabbing *ton* who live there."

Her father half laughed, jiggling his line. "You're right I do abhor it, but you need a husband, to be given a secure future and happy marriage. Just as your mama and I have had."

That was true, her parents had a very happy and loving relationship, but that didn't mean such a path was the one she wanted to tread. What was wrong with being a wallflower that wilted into an old, unmarried maid? Nothing in Mary's estimation. To be married meant she would have to conform to society, be a lady all the time, host teas and balls. Live in Town most of the year and submit to a husband's whims. Such a life would not be so bad if she found a man to marry whom she loved, and who loved her. A gentleman who liked the country life over that of

London and allowed her the freedom which she was used to. But after numerous failed Seasons already, *that* was unlikely to occur.

Her heart twisted in her chest. "I do not want to return. Please don't make me, Papa."

"We must, but with Christmas upon us, we'll have more time here at Bran Manor, plenty of time for you to enjoy the last few months of being an unmarried woman."

Her father looked at her as if such news would make everything well. It did not.

He cleared his throat. "We want to see you happily married and settled. I would love nothing better than to welcome a titled gentleman, worthy of an earl's daughter into our family. You never know, you may find a man who loves the hobbies that you do, admires and appreciates your exuberance for life and country walks."

Or she might find no one of the kind, make a terrible mistake that she would be stuck with for the rest of her life. "What if I don't find anyone with such qualities, Papa? Last Season, certainly I never did. All the gentlemen were self-absorbed dandies who inspected mirrors more than they interacted with the women surrounding them."

Her father chuckled, tugging sharply on his line and pulling out a good-sized trout.

Mary despaired at the sight of his catch. She'd sat here for hours and hadn't caught a thing and here was her papa, not here five minutes and he'd caught the largest fish she'd seen all winter.

She shook her head at him. "You're no longer invited into my ice hut. You cheat," she said jokingly, smiling at her papa.

He grinned, looking down at his catch. "I'll have Cook prepare this for tomorrow night. It will be a feast."

"You know, Papa, I'm an heiress and financially independent no matter whom I marry, thanks to you, Mama, and Grandmother Lancaster. Why should I marry at all? It's not like the family needs funds, and I will never be considered an old, poor maid not worthy of society's company. Your title and wealth prohibit such ostracism. So is it really necessary that we go? There may be a young man in Derbyshire who is looking for a wife and would be perfect for me. I could have the love of my life right beneath my very nose, and miss him by going to London, looking for the wrong man."

Her father paused from putting the fish in a nearby basket, before he said, "I must remember to give your tutor a better letter of recommendation due to the fact you're able to negotiate and barter as well as those in the House of Lords." Her father threw her a consoling smile. "But, alas, we do not live in a time where young women of means and of family can live independently without a husband. I will not allow you to be placed on a shelf to have dust settle on your head, nor will I allow you to live an unfulfilled life without a husband and children of your own. You would be an asset to anyone's family you married into, and I want to see you happy."

Anger thrummed through her at the narrow-minded idea that she needed a man to make all her dreams come true. She did not need a husband to be happy, and the sooner her father and the men hunting her fortune realized this, the better.

Mary yanked up her fishing line, placing her rod against the wall. "I don't see why I have to marry anybody. This is 1800! A new century, please tell me that gentlemen of society and England will come out of the dark ages and see that women are worth more than what they can bring to a marriage, or how large a dowry they have, or how wide their hips are for breeding!"

Her father raised his brow, clearly shocked. "Hush now! I'll hear no more protest from you. I would never force you into a marriage you did not want with your whole heart. We want you to be happy, to find a gentleman who allows you the freedom to which you've grown accustomed. But you *will* marry, my child, and you will continue to have Seasons in Town until you do."

Mary couldn't believe her father. It was as if he were only half listening to her. "I will not find someone. I know this to be true." She crossed her arms, hating the idea of going back to London. "You know as well as anyone that I'm terrible around people. I get nervous at balls and parties so that I'll say something out of line, or not be fashionable enough. I stutter when asked direct questions, and my face tends to turn a terrible, unflattering shade of red during all those things. Please do not do this to me, Papa. *Please*," she begged him.

Her father stood, seemingly having enough fishing for one day. "You are going and for your mother's sake, you will enjoy the Season or at least make a show of enjoyment while in public. Do not fret, my dear," he said, his tone turning cajoling. "We will be there with you. To hold your hand and not let you fail."

She blinked back the tears that threatened. Her first Season had been miserable. Her mother, even with a fortune at her disposal had not procured her a fashionable modiste and so she'd been dressed in frills and ribbons that made her look like a decoration instead of a debutante. Her gowns had clashed against her olive-toned skin and dark hair and not a lot had improved regarding her wardrobe since that time.

Even despite her father being titled, with multiple properties about England and her dowry being more than anyone could spend in two lifetimes, no one had befriended her or took her under their wing other than her dearest companion Louise, of course. Mary sighed, knowing it was not entirely everyone else's fault that she was ostracized in Town. She'd gone above and beyond to distance herself from girls her own age, and had been cold and aloof to the gentlemen who had paid court to her.

At three and twenty, what was left open to her but to be standoffish. To marry at such a young age would mean her lifestyle, her love of the outdoors and pursuits indulged in only by those of the opposite sex would end. Would have to end because her new husband would demand it of her. Demand she acted as the earl's daughter she was born and as his wife.

Mary met her father's gaze and read the concern in his eyes and a little part of her disobedience crumbled. She hated to disappoint her parents, and of course she wanted them to not worry about her, but how could she marry and remain the woman she was?

She narrowed her eyes, thinking of possibilities. "If I'm being forced to go, Papa, and I do wish to state that I am in no way agreeable about traveling to London. But if I do have to go, smile, dance and play the pretty debutante, there are some rules that I wish to instruct you and Mama of."

Her father stopped adjusting his fur coat and gave her his full attention "What is it that you want, Mary? We're open to negotiation."

"I will choose whom I marry. I will not be swayed otherwise. The man I marry will suit me in all ways and I will not be pressured to choose if one does not materialize next Season." Mary raised her chin, waiting for her father's response, but when he did nothing but stare at her patiently, she continued. "I want a new wardrobe for the Season. And I'd like a lady's maid of my own, not Mama's.

She has a habit of putting my hair up in styles like Mother's and it makes me look…" Mary fought for words that wouldn't hurt her father's feelings when discussing his wife.

"A woman of mature years?" he said, smiling a little.

"Yes." She nodded empathically, "That is exactly what I mean."

Her father regarded her for a moment before he came over to her, placing his arm about her shoulder. "That does not seem like it's too much to ask. I will speak to your mama and ensure she will not stand in your way."

"Thank you, Papa." Mary busied herself putting her gloves on while she pushed down the guilt her request brought forth. Had she wanted to, she could've asked for a new modiste and maid years ago and her parents would never have stood in her way. But her determination to remain an unmarried maid had made her hold her tongue. Being unfashionable in Town had meant very few wished to be around her, or be seen on the dance floor with her, and that had suited her very well. But she could not remain so forever, not if her parents were so determined to see her as a wife. If she had to embark on this side of life, at least it would be under her terms and with any luck she'd find a gentleman who'd enjoy the outdoors as much as she did and not wish to clip her wings. To find such a man she supposed she would have to mingle more and actually bother to get to know them this Season.

"Come, let us get this fish back home. I'm sure the dinner gong will sound very soon."

Mary let her father shuffle her out the door, before they started back toward the house. In the dissipating light, the estate was a beacon of warmth and much preferred than where they currently were. Mary resigned herself to the fact that they would return to London in the spring, but at least she would have control of her gowns and there was Christmas here in Derbyshire to enjoy.

Her elder brother always brought friends to stay, and so this year would be just as merry as every other. A little calm before the storm that was the Season.

CHAPTER 2

November 1800

Dale Ramsay, the Duke of Carlton stood to the side of the room, watching the gathering throng in his closest friend, the Viscount Kensley, the future Earl of Lancaster's drawing room waiting for the dinner gong to sound so they could eat.

They had traveled all day, and Dale had to admit that if they did not get some food into him soon, he would either tumble over from too much wine, or his stomach would growl so loudly that the women present would think him a bear.

Mistletoe hung from every possible location in the room, from doorways to the candelabras. Lady Lancaster had even placed little cuttings of it and located them on sideboards, mantles, anywhere there was a spare spot. Was the lady looking for the few young women and men that were here present to steal a kiss or two?

Not that Dale would mind stealing a kiss if one was

available. There were certainly some very fetching young women in attendance.

The drawing room door opened and taking a sip of wine, he coughed, choking a little on his drink at the sight he beheld. What a monstrosity, or better yet, who was the young woman who was dressed like someone who'd stepped out of the mid-eighteenth century?

He took out his handkerchief, wiped at his mouth, and watched as Peter went up to the young woman, pulling her into a fierce hug and kissing her soundly on the cheek.

Dale observed the young woman was not completely unfortunate, even though she was wearing spectacles. Was the poor woman also blind? It would certainly explain the lack of knowledge regarding her gown. You could not fix what you could not see.

Peter started toward him and Dale schooled his features to one of polite interest. As his friend neared the young woman, he took in her appearance more. Her dark long locks were tied back into a design that Lady Lancaster also sported, but it did not compliment the young woman. Nor did the mustard-colored gown she suffered to wear since it made her look washed out and even a little ill.

"Carlton, may I introduce to you my sister, Lady Mary. Mary, this is my good friend, the Duke of Carlton."

She bobbed a neat curtsy, and stared up at him with the widest green eyes he'd ever beheld. Her gown was of little advantage and Dale had an overwhelming urge to send her to his ex-mistresses' modiste in London, who was one of the most sought after and finest seamstresses in the city.

Dale bowed slightly. "Lady Mary, it is a pleasure to meet you at last. Your brother has spoken of you often."

She threw him a doubtful look but smiled. She did have a very pretty smile. "I'm sure you lie, your grace, but thank you, in any case. I shall take your charming words and believe them."

Peter chuckled. "Mary, do not tease the duke. He will think you mean what you say."

Her eyes skimmed him from top to toe, and Dale had the oddest sensation run through him. Her inspection wasn't at all what he thought a young unmarried woman ought to do to a peer, and yet this country miss, an earl's daughter no less, whom he'd never met in his life before seemed to think it appropriate.

"Perhaps I do not tease, Brother." She grinned mischievously, and Dale found himself smiling.

He schooled his features once more. "On the contrary, my lady. Your brother has spoken highly of you and I'm pleased to make your acquaintance."

"And I you, your grace." She studied him with shrewd eyes, and he met her boldness by raising his brow. "You spend most of your time in Town I assume?"

"I do," he said, glad she'd stopped inspecting him like an insect that needed stomping on. He was sure that she did not approve his answer.

She glanced about, her disinterest in their conversation obvious. "I dislike London and I'm not looking forward to going back, but alas, as a female I have little choice. Isn't that right, Brother?"

Peter shook his head at his sister. "Mary, let us not quarrel in front of our guests. You know I'm looking forward to having you in Town next year."

She sighed, plucking a glass of wine from a passing footman and taking a sip. "I should imagine you love the Season, your grace? Enjoy the nights out about Town, the horse rides in the park among other things."

Dale clamped his mouth shut. *Other things...* what on earth did that mean? Did she allude to the many gambling hells he attended, nights at Vauxhall or the many women who sought his companionship? He glanced down at her, her fierce green eyes full of mirth stared back without a by-your-leave.

He marveled at her boldness. "I do enjoy all the delicacies that Town affords. So many entertainments to appreciate, it is like one big feast that I cannot get enough of."

Mary's cheeks turned a delightful shade of rose, and he grinned.

Peter cleared his throat. "I see Miss Grant has arrived, Mary."

She glanced behind her and bobbing a quick curtsy excused herself, leaving Dale to watch after her as she joined the woman who looked a similar age to her by the window.

"Is your sister out, Peter?" he asked, watching her still. Now with her friend, Lady Mary seemed to brighten even more when having a conversation with someone she liked.

"She had her coming out five years ago, but nothing came of it or any subsequent Seasons. Our parents are hoping to gain her a match with the forthcoming Season, much to Mary's distaste."

Dale raised his brow, taking a sip of his wine. "Oh, she does not wish for marriage?" It wasn't often any young woman of Lady Mary's age would not want such a thing. Certainly, Dale had never met such a woman before in his life, and he had five years on Mary if he correctly estimated her age.

"How old is your sister?" Dale asked, unable to tear his eyes from her as she moved about the room. The idea that he found the Lady Mary interesting enough to do such a thing pulled him up short and he shifted his gaze from her.

Peter's eyes met his over the top of his wine glass and

the steely edge to his friend's gaze gave him pause. "Why so much interest in Mary?"

Dale raised one hand. "I was merely making conversation. I'm not interested in your sister as anything other than a friend. I did not see her in Town last year and was merely curious as to her age." And part of what he said was indeed true, he was curious about the woman who seemed to have a voice, despite that her gown stated otherwise, and she was without fear of him. Being a duke there were few who could boast such a thing. Other than his friend Peter that is.

"Mary has just turned three and twenty." Peter glanced about the room. "Lady Hectorville is here, I see. That should make you happy, Carlton."

Dale fought not to cringe at the mention of the late earl's wife. "Not particularly. I had one liaison with the woman, when I was in my cups and she was hiding her appearance at the time and I did not know it was her."

"Much to her despair. Look, my friend, she is observing you and seems quite forlorn that you have not said hello."

His friend laughed and Dale threw him a quelling glance. "That night was a mistake and one I shall not make again. I have apologized to her, even though she did not want to hear it, but either way, what is done is done and she's since moved on with another of our set."

"Maybe you ought to tell her that she needs to move on from you, because from where I stand it certainly does not seem that way."

Dale looked to where Peter had glanced and he ground his teeth. Damn it, he'd never thought her ladyship would be here of all places. How was it that the woman was even invited? She stood beside Lady Lancaster and her determined interest in Dale must be obvious to any who bothered to notice.

"How is your family acquainted with Lady Hectorville?"

"She is one of my mother's closest friends. They have known each other for many years, even though there is a fifteen-year age gap between them. When they're together you would not know that was the case."

Fabulous, that was all Dale needed. A meddling Lady Hectorville who sometimes still sent him love notes begging for him to call, or Peter's mother who undoubtedly knew he'd tumbled one of her closest friends. He cringed.

"So, my friend, what are we going to do now that I have you up here in Derbyshire. We may go riding tomorrow if you like. There are some very fine locations to visit about the property, and I wish to show you the hunting lodge. Could be a thought to bring up a group of friends in the summer and make use of it. What say you?"

Dale lifted his wine glass in mock salute. "I think that sounds like a wonderful idea on both counts. Shall we say we'll meet at the stables at nine in the morning to scout it out?"

Peter clinked his glass against Dale's. "I shall see you then."

CHAPTER 3

The following afternoon Mary took the air outside, determined to be outdoors every day no matter the weather. Her mind wandered from thought to thought, or if more truthful, one thought that is. The duke.

Mary wasn't sure what to make of her brother's friend. Of course she'd heard he was a duke well before his arrival at their estate. Peter seemed to get along with him very well, even though the man was a much sought-after gentleman in Town and held a lot of sway within the House of Lords. If her mother's unending information about the duke was to be believed. But there was something about the fellow that gave her pause, a niggling annoyance that she could not place. Something that had troubled her the moment his steely eyes and unflinching inspection of her occurred in the drawing room last evening.

Her friend and companion, Louise, came up beside her as they walked about the grounds; bundled up in fur coats they both appeared three sizes larger than they were. But, when there was snow underfoot and one was stuck indoors, such clothing had to be worn, no matter how bulky. No-one wished to be stuck inside all the time.

"It's so cold, Mary. Can we return indoors now?" Her friend pulled her coat closed further and Mary smiled. Louise had always preferred the warmer months and hated any season other than spring or summer.

"We'll just finish going around the house and then we'll go back inside. It's so refreshing though, don't you think, to be outdoors? With Peter home with his friend, and Mama with her guests, inside is becoming a little crowded."

Louise's eyes glistened with amusement. "What do you think of the duke? I don't think I've ever seen a more handsome fellow in all my life."

"Well, our life has been cosseted here most of the time in Derbyshire. I'm sure when we return to London next year, Town life will offer you more diversion and interest than the Duke of Carlton. It's simply we've been out in the country so long and only ever meet the same people. Anything new and shiny always sparkles brighter."

Her friend snorted. "Are you being sarcastic, dear Mary? I don't think there are many who would not continually be distracted by such a man."

Mary conceded the point. The duke was exceedingly handsome, with his dark locks that had a slight waviness and curl to them. His straight nose and cheekbones made his profile devastatingly lovely and made her stomach flutter each time she chanced a look at him.

Her body was becoming a traitor to her. She didn't want to feel anything other than bored amusement that he was present. Mary certainly didn't want images and thoughts bombarding her mind as to what he might be like to kiss. Was he so very wicked as all the gossips had painted him these past days? There was a rumor that he'd once bedded Lady Hectorville, and if her ladyship's glances toward the duke when she assumed no one was looking were anything to go by, Mary certainly could believe that tidbit of information as fact.

"Very well, I shall agree with you on that, but even so, he is just a man who'll eventually marry a woman to warm his bed and fill his nursery with heirs for his great title. Whomever the duke marries it'll be a monetary and status alliance, not a love match."

"And to be a power in the *ton*. A duchess that all other women strive to imitate, do not forget," Louise added.

Mary stumbled to a halt. Louise gasped as the duke, whom they'd not seen sitting on the steps of the terrace stood, and bowed before them.

Heat bloomed on Mary's cheeks and her stomach did that stupid little fluttering again. She glared at him. What was wrong with her?

She cleared her throat, clasping her hands tight within her fur muff. "Your grace, we did not see you there."

One ducal eyebrow rose in agreement. "No, you did not. I can only assume that had you known I was sitting here you wouldn't have said such things about my character."

Mary chanced a glance at Louise and sighed at her friend's abject horror of them being caught. If her friend's eyes went any wider her eyeballs would pop out.

She smiled the sweetest smile she could muster for someone who was obviously used to no one talking about him at all. Certainly not to his face. "You would be mistaken, your grace. I never shy away from what I believe in or think. If I have an opinion on a subject or person, whatever it may be, you can always be assured I'll speak the truth."

His too-intelligent eyes inspected her, and Mary shivered. How was it that his mere gaze could make her react so? She fought not to roll her eyes at her own idiocy. Maybe a trip to Town for another Season wasn't such a bad idea after all. This shivering and fluttering whenever she was about the duke would never do. If she had to marry as her parents ordained, then it would be to a man she respected and loved, not to mention a man who allowed her to carry on with all the hobbies she currently enjoyed. She eyed the duke. *What kind of man are you?*

"Perhaps it's the spectacles that make you so forward with your opinion." The duke reached out and slid them off her face. His buckskin-gloved fingers touched her temples and she gasped at his presumption.

"Excuse me, your grace, but just what do you think you're doing?"

She looked up at him, and although she could see perfectly well without glasses, they did help her see objects that were at a distance.

He stared at her for the oddest time before he said, "just seeing what you look like behind your spectacles."

"And do you always do what you want, your grace?" Mary asked, suspecting that he did. The man oozed authority and she doubted there wasn't much that he did not get his way with.

"Always," he said, before turning on his heel and striding toward the terrace doors.

"Well, how odd," Mary said. Louise sighed, a dreamy expression on her face as she watched the duke head back indoors. He closed the terrace doors with a decided click, leaving them alone once again.

Louise caught Mary's gaze. "He still has your spectacles."

After his odd departure Mary had completely forgotten the fact that he'd walked off with her spectacles. She ground her teeth, not wanting to seek him out to get them back again. She huffed out an annoyed breath, supposing she would have to. And after that, it was probably best that she did not seek him out again while he was here. Her body needed to learn that the Duke of Carlton, no matter his attractiveness, was not for her. She had a Season to find a gentleman who would suit her and she would not allow a pretty face to steer her off-course.

❧

DALE SHUT the terrace doors and leaned against the wooden frame a moment. Feeling something in his hand he looked down and cursed. What the devil was he still doing with Lady Mary's spectacles? And why in hell had he taken them off of her in the first place?

The moment he'd seen her glance up at him, her eyes wide and clear and the prettiest green he'd ever beheld he knew he was in trouble. He didn't need to think her eyes pretty, or anything about her appealing. She was his best friend's sister. A woman who spoke her mind without restraint and obviously was so very used to doing as she pleased. She was certainly not duchess material. Not the type of obedient and placid woman he was looking for.

His mother had been opinionated, often arguing differences of opinion with his father. He didn't want a wife with similar characteristics. He wanted only peace in his marriage, something that he never enjoyed as a child.

Her rebuttal that she would only ever speak the truth whether the person was present or not was proof of that. Even if the *ton* was full of lies and deceit, her frankness was not a character trait he wanted in a wife. There were plenty of gentlemen who did not care if their wives were opinionated. Dale was not one of them.

That she'd not shied away from his sometimes overbearing self, had been welcome however. But then his friend Peter had never been scared off by his title either, and it was one of the reasons they were friends. He could tell Peter anything and know he would give him the absolute truth in his opinions.

Not just agree with him all the time simply because he was a duke.

Lady Hectorville sidled next to him and placed her arm around his own. He smiled down at her out of politeness while swearing inwardly at her affront. "Lady Hectorville, are you enjoying the gathering here in Derbyshire?" The question was benign, and he hoped soon enough she would find more amusing sports. Her reported lover was present so why she was hanging off his arm was beyond him.

"Oh, indeed I am. Lord and Lady Lancaster have been the most wonderful hosts these past few days and I'm looking very much toward the coming month here, and Christmas of course. Are you staying for the festivities, the Mistletoe Ball, your grace?"

He had thought of staying, but with her ladyship's presence the entire time, maybe Dale would have to rethink his decision. "My obligations are not fixed on any one place in particular. I did say I would stay for a time, but I'm unsure if that will incorporate Christmas."

Lady Hectorville pouted and he turned his attention to the few guests that were taking tea in the parlor. "And your sister, Lady Georgianna? Where is she to spend Christmas this year?"

Dale smiled at the mention of his sibling. He missed the chit and hoped she would be home soon. "She's spending Christmas in Spain with our aunt who's traveling abroad. She'll return to Town in the spring."

"Oh, Spain. How diverting. The warm Spanish sun,

the hot nights and even hotter days. Sounds positively divine," she cooed up at him.

He nodded, not entirely sure that the direction in which her ladyship spoke didn't have an altogether different meaning to that of the weather. The terrace doors behind him opened and Lady Mary and her friend, Miss Grant, entered the room. Dale watched their progress as they joined Peter near the pianoforte.

Her ladyship lent out a long-suffering sigh. "Poor Lady Mary, I do worry for her. She's so very bookish and the spectacles she's often sporting do nothing to improve her appearance. I worry that she'll remain a spinster, be placed up on the shelf to collect dust like an unwanted ornament."

Dale bit his tongue in reminding Lady Hectorville that to speak about someone in such a manner was not befitting of her ladyship's status. He thanked a footman for a glass of wine and took a fortifying sip to cool his ire. "Really? Do enlighten me?" he asked, his curiosity to see just how far her ladyship was willing to go further to cast doubt on Mary who was the daughter of a supposedly close friend of hers.

"Well, she does not draw or paint or take any time in needlework from all accounts. Instead she's a dab hand at fishing. Fishing! Of all things and is a better shot than her brother from what Lady Lancaster tells me. The young woman will never make a match with such qualities."

Stranger and stranger. Dale's attention strayed to where Lady Mary stood and he took in her gown, her features and demeanor. She was quite animated and loud, but then she was in her own home and among friends, so one did tend to let their guard down.

Her ebony hair shone as dark as the midnight sky, even when tied up in a severe knot. But with her spectacles missing, one could see the promise of an emerging beauty if one looked hard enough. Her green eyes were certainly one of her best features, and upon meeting her had given a hint to a woman of intelligence.

"I'm sure in time Lady Mary will marry. No matter how society views her as possibly lacking in refinement. There are other qualities that recommend her." Dale shut his mouth with a snap, not knowing why he was defending the woman. Probably because she was Peter's sibling and Peter was his closest friend.

Lady Hectorville clasped her chest. "Oh, I do hope you don't think I meant any slight against Lady Mary. I love her as if she were my own child, but I do like to think that if I were a mother, I too could see the faults in my own children. No matter how disappointing such a thing may be."

"Of course," he said bowing. "If you'll excuse me, Lady Hectorville." He started toward Lady Mary and coming up to Peter, pulled the spectacles from his waistcoat pocket.

"Lady Mary, I do believe these belong to you." He handed them to her and she cast a quick glance at her brother who stood silent, watching them with a warning glint in his eyes.

Dale straightened and clasped his hands behind his back.

"Thank you, your grace."

"What is Carlton doing with your spectacles, Mary?" Peter asked, his tone one of suspicion.

"Lady Mary had been taking the air with Miss Grant and had misplaced the spectacles on the terrace railing. I was merely returning them." Total bollocks, but he didn't need Peter to imagine that there was anything at all between him and his sister for there was not, nor ever would be. She was much too independent, and he had a sneaking suspicion she was a bluestocking as well as a wall-flower. His wife would be a demure, quiet type of woman, suited to the role of duchess and all the responsibilities that came with it.

Not to mention he would never jeopardize his friend-ship with Peter. They had shared many a night out on the town in London, and he doubted Peter would want his sister marrying a man known for his rakish ways.

Peter clasped him on the back, smiling. "Well then, you're a good man. Thank you for giving them back to Mary. She's often doing that, leaving them here and there. Aren't you Mary?" Peter said, turning to her.

"I'm terribly forgetful with those sorts of matters. Thank you, your grace, for returning them to me," she said, before she touched her friend's hand. "Shall we head upstairs, Louise. I wish to read for a time before dinner."

Both ladies left without another word and Peter smiled after them. "What do you think about Miss Grant? She's grown most pretty since I've been away at school. She is Mary's companion and been with us since she was a child."

Dale took another glass of wine from a passing footman thinking over Miss Grant. "Do you care for her? Remember that marriage is a lifelong commitment. I doubt there would be anything worse in the world than to be partnered with a woman who after six months of marriage turned into a shrew and stopped all wifely duties once you'd begotten an heir."

Peter's eyes widened. "Hold up old boy. I only asked what you thought of her. I'm not planning to marry at all at present."

Dale chuckled to break the small tension between them. "You know my thoughts on marriage. It is a decision to be thought over with great care. My parents' match was not a union I would wish upon anyone else, and so I simply do not wish for you to make the same mistake.

The memory of his parents arguing could still, to this day, make his blood run cold. Both were high-handed and never at fault. When both parties refused to give way, let a disagreement go, fireworks were often what resulted. Although Dale never witnessed any physical injury, he had his suspicions that such had taken place behind closed doors.

"Your parents however seem to have a happy and affectionate marriage. Let them guide you and I'm sure they'll do you no wrong."

Peter mumbled something under his breath and Dale thought about what Lady Hectorville had said about staying. Perhaps he ought to return to his own estate before the snow became too thick underfoot for travel. But he did enjoy being with Peter and his family who were jovial and welcoming, even his sister, as odd as she was.

He would think on it some more.

"You missed the announcement at breakfast about our annual Mistletoe Ball; it is to be held again this year. Although really it's just a guise to try and advertise that my sister is still open to marriage and courting if anyone should be interested. Even so, it's always good, jolly fun. What say you?"

"When is this to take place?" Dale asked, not entirely sure he wished to be part of such entertainment. He would have enough of society, all the balls and trappings next year in Town.

"A few days before Christmas. Do say you'll attend. My parents will be sorely disappointed if you leave. Just like myself, we do not wish for you to be alone at Christmas."

That was true, Dale also didn't wish to be alone at such

a festive time. Not really. With Georgianna away in Spain, Carlton Hall was large and very empty, almost like a crypt. Not a place to enjoy the holiday season when alone.

"Very well, I shall stay until after Christmas as planned. I suppose I shall be able to stomach a ball well enough."

"Excellent," Peter said. "Now come, let's go play some billiards. I think we've done the pretty by my mother and given the guests here today enough fodder to keep them happy for an afternoon or so."

Dale liked the thought of that. "Lead the way." Escaping the afternoon at home sounded right up his alley.

Just then the door to the parlor opened and in walked Henry Ryley, Lord Weston. New to the title of Viscount, the young buck had made a debutante cry during her first ball. He was as obnoxious as he was stupid. Dale sighed, wondering why in the hell Lord Lancaster had invited such a dandy.

The viscount strolled into the room, greeting his hosts and looking about as if he owned the place. He was all blond, his golden locks and height made him most agreeable to the ladies present if their tittering and simpering smiles were anything to go by.

Dale looked about the room and fought not to roll his eyes as some of the younger women giggled and blushed.

"Weston," Peter yelled out, catching the young man's attention. He strolled over.

"Kensley," his lordship said, shaking Peter's hand. "It's good to see you. How have you been? I've not seen you in Town of late."

"No," Peter said, smiling. "I've been traveling in the country for some weeks." Peter turned to Dale. "Your grace, this is Viscount Weston. Lord Weston, this is his grace, the Duke of Carlton."

Dale bowed slightly.

"Pleasure, your grace. In fact, I've just come from the stables and been admiring your gray stallion. Beautiful beast if ever there was one," Lord Weston said jovially.

Dale narrowed his eyes. "He's a good horse," was all he was able to manage while also trying to remember what debutante it was that this popinjay insulted and what that insult had been about.

"Is Mary home? I should like to see her again. I've been so busy in Town this past Season that I did not get to see her much."

Peter smiled at the mention of his sister. Dale arched a brow. Lord Weston was on a first-name basis with Lady Mary? He studied the man with a disinterested air. As little as he knew Lady Mary, it would be a shame indeed if she set her cap for someone like Lord Weston.

"She's gone upstairs to read before dinner, but you'll see her later. She'll be so excited to see you again too. I know how close you were as children."

"You've known the family for some time then, Lord Weston?" Dale asked, curiosity getting the better of him.

The young viscount glanced at Dale with annoyance and there was something in his gaze that gave Dale pause. If he were a betting man, he would lay money on the fact that his lordship had a nasty streak in his blood. He'd seen glances like the one his lordship just bestowed on him, his father had thrown them often toward his mother before all hell broke loose. Here, Dale supposed he could not cause any mischief, even if the question had annoyed the gentleman.

"Lord Weston and our family are neighbors, your grace," Peter said, answering the question quickly.

He took a sip of his wine, glad to hear this was how they were acquainted, not by some other means such as Weston's courtship of Lady Mary. "Are you staying or merely visiting, Lord Weston?" Dale asked. Normally a good judge of character, there was something about this man that he didn't like. Finally, the memory came back to him as to why he disapproved of the viscount. The young debutante he'd made cry had been courted by his lordship for weeks, so much so that the family had expected an offer of marriage. Instead, he'd ceased all contact with the chit and refused to stand up with her at balls and parties. She became the target of censure and amusement for her friends. The young woman had returned to the country and Dale wondered if she would return next year and try again. Something told him she would not.

"I'm staying," the gentleman said, raising his brow and holding Dale's gaze.

Dale narrowed his eyes. "I see."

The young viscount spied another guest he wished to speak to, and he made his farewells.

"Shall we?" Peter said, gesturing toward the door.

Dale nodded. "Yes, let's go."

CHAPTER 4

Mary came downstairs later that evening and found Lord Weston present. She had not expected him to arrive since when she had seen him last Season in Town he'd been less than pleased to greet her. His slight, even if not noticed by the *ton* had hurt more than she'd been willing to admit even to her parents and she had eventually talked herself into believing that it was all in her mind.

And so it seemed to be if his animation and pleasure at seeing her again was anything to go by.

"Lord Weston. Henry," she said, using his given name, "it is so very good to see you." She came up to him and laughed when he pulled her into an embrace. Her parents smiled at their familiarity, and didn't seem inclined to chastise her over their conduct.

"It is good to see you again too, Mary and Miss Grant as well. I'm sorry I'm late to arrive. I've only just returned from London."

Mary smiled at his lordship who seemed very happy indeed to be back in Derbyshire and talking to her. For years she'd harbored a little infatuation for his lordship.

How could one not be with his golden locks and sinful gaze that made him look like a fallen angel? Mary might be somewhat skewed against marriage, but she was not blind.

She supposed she had gravitated toward him so often because she'd known him since childhood and deep down knew he'd never look to her as a wife, and so he was a safe option to be amusing with.

"Well, you're here now and that's all that matters. Mama has invited quite a few families from Town so you should feel quite at home."

"I'm sure I shall," he said, smiling down at her.

Mary's stomach flipped a little and she had to force herself to glance away from all his grandeur. How handsome he was. His perfect nose and lovely clear blue eyes that set him apart from most men.

Mary's gaze slid to the Duke of Carlton's, surprised to find his eyes narrowed in contemplation as he watched them. She turned her attention back to Lord Weston. The duke was too good-looking for his own good as well, and probably well aware of it.

The dinner gong sounded and forgoing formalities, her parents led everyone into the dining room. The dinner was five courses of fish and game, turtle soup and winter vegetables. No expense was spared for their guests and Mary would commend their cook on her dinner later that evening. The dinner lasted some hours, all of them enjoyable, full of conversation and laughter. Just as this festive time of year ought to be.

Mistletoe ran along the center of the table with cuttings of holly to add a little color to the decoration. With the fires burning in every room, their mammoth home was transformed into a wonderland of Yuletide and cheer.

After dinner Mary sat near the edge of the drawing

room, watching those in attendance. She sipped her mulled wine and listened while Louise played a Christmas tune on the pianoforte.

Her stomach fluttered as Lord Weston made his way toward her, his smile as wicked as ever. She'd known him most of her life, and there was something about him that she'd always been drawn to. Perhaps it was the fact he was in reality unattainable. She was no elegant, ethereal-looking beauty, she was dark of hair, and eyes a plain, unremarkable green. Her skin looked kissed by the sun.

And he was simply too perfect to ever look at her. They were as opposite as night and day.

"All alone, Mary? We're missing your company and so I've come to drag you back into the fray."

She smiled, inwardly sighing at his beauty. For a moment her gaze slid to his lips, pulled back to show perfectly straight white teeth. He had lovely lips too. In all honesty there wasn't much about him that wasn't faultless.

"A moment's peace I assure you, but I shall mingle in a little while. We have missed you these past months. Have you enjoyed Town this Season?"

He leaned back in his chair, sliding his arm to sit along the back of her own and she started when his thumb reached out and circled the bare skin on her shoulder. "I did, but I would prefer a stroll outdoors with you in its stead? I know it's cold, but I remember that such a thing never bothered you before."

Mary jumped up, not sure her heart could take any more of his touch. "I'm not sure that is wise…"

His lordship stood, mischief in his gaze. "Come, it's only a stroll. We're old friends, and have walked outdoors numerous times. No harm will come to you, I promise."

Mary glanced at her mother and seeing her nod of

approval, relented. "Very well, my lord. Let me grab my shawl."

Only minutes later they made their way out onto the terrace which had earlier today been shoveled free of snow. A light dusting covered the flagstones still, and the chill was beyond what she expected. Their outing would be of short duration.

The glow from the windows lit their way as they strolled slowly along. Mary glanced out into the gardens, not sure what Lord Weston wanted to discuss with her, if anything.

"We have always been friends, have we not, Mary?"

He said, pulling her to a stop. Her elbow burned from his touch and her heart thumped loud in her chest. More so than it ever had before.

"Of course. Why do you ask?" She glanced up at him, a tentative smile on her lips. Was Lord Weston looking to court her? Mary thought over the possibility a moment. He would certainly suit her character and most importantly he was their neighbor here in Derbyshire. She would not have to leave the lands that she'd grown up on. She could remain close to her parents and her brother when he decided to marry.

She'd not thought of the viscount as an option before, but all night he'd made certain to remain close to her. His lordship knew of her love for the outdoors, for fishing and hunting and was only ever supportive of it. He would not try and change her ways, or make her conform to society...

His attention snapped to her lips and all thought flew out of her brain.

"Have you ev—"

Mary lunged at his head, kissing him before he could finish what he was about to say. Their teeth cracked together and horrified Mary felt blood across her tongue as she slid back to earth. She stepped back, heat suffusing her body at the bumbling fool she'd just been.

"I'm sorry, my lord. I do not know…"

He stared at her, his visage one of shock and pity and if the earth could swallow her she hoped it would do so right at this moment.

He cleared his throat, pulling out his handkerchief and dabbing at his lip that horrifyingly was bleeding. "I think you should return indoors, Mary. I need to ice my lip and will return to the drawing room soon."

She nodded, feeling all kinds of stupid. No refined gentleman such as Lord Weston would look at her with anything other than sympathy and she was a fool to think he harbored ideas of them marrying.

Mary glanced down at her gown of lace and ribbons, absurd bows that were not the least fashionable on anyone over the age of five. "I apologize, Lord Weston. It will not happen again."

She ran, heedless of everything about her, and instead of returning to the drawing room, she entered another door further along that opened into a corridor toward the conservatory.

Mary stifled back a sob as the prickling of tears stung her eyes. Her past five Seasons had been all disasters, and now, after trying to kiss one of her oldest friends she would prefer to die of mortification than have to face him again.

She rounded a corner that led into the conservatory and clashed straight into a wall of muscle. Strong arms came out about her, but her near run had too much momentum and she took him down, landing with a thump on top of him.

"Oh, I'm terribly sorry."

Mary went to roll off him and heard a rip near her

breast. Looking down she spied one of the gentleman's buttons on his superfine coat was hooked onto one of her lace ribbons.

"I'm stuck," she mumbled, placing her legs on either side of him so to free her hands and try and unhook herself from the gentleman. His own hands came around her and he sat up, bringing her with him. She gasped, forgetting the button and ribbon as she glanced up and died a second time that night of mortification.

"Your grace, I did not know...that is to say," she fumbled for words. "I do apologize for this."

He stared at her with dark hooded eyes, his mouth set in a thin displeased line. He was angry at her. She expected no less after tackling him just now.

"Here let me." His fingers joined with hers as they both fumbled to remove the button from the lace. Their heads bent close Mary caught a whiff of his scent, sandalwood and something else, something sweet and delicious that made one want cake.

The duke mumbled something unintelligible, and unable to help herself she looked at him instead of concentrating on trying to remove herself from his lap. Up close he was as handsome as any she'd seen, even Lord Weston who was pretty where the duke was like a replica of a chiseled god.

Certainly the duke's shoulders were wider than Lord Weston's, and his legs seemed quite muscular between her own. The thought brought awareness as to how they were sitting. She on top of his lap, her skirts hiked up about her waist and a...what was that hard bulge near her inner thigh?

She gasped and their gazes locked. Mumbling a curse, one she heard as clear as day, the duke ripped them apart, the lace ribbon now an ornament upon his own button before he picked her up and deposited her on the floor beside him.

He stood, his back to her as he adjusted his clothing. Mary could do little but stare at his back, the view from down on the floor giving her the perfect location to study the duke's other assets, like his bottom.

His Grace turned, the muscle in his jaw flexing when he caught her ogling his person. Instead of turning from her in disgust, he reached out a hand to help her up. "In a rush, Lady Mary?"

All thoughts of Lord Weston fled from her mind after being entwined with the duke, and she gaped at him a moment trying to remember what her flight into the conservatory was about.

And then she remembered. Her first kiss. Or, perhaps she ought to remember it by the first bloody lip she'd given a gentleman with her own mouth.

"I apologize again, your grace. I needed to be alone and didn't expect to find anyone in this part of the house."

He studied her, his brow furrowed. "Is something amiss? You look as if you've been crying."

She swallowed, shame washing over her in spades. Mary looked down at her feet, working her hands before her. "I made a mistake that I cannot take back and now I'll never be able to face a certain person ever again." Very well, it may have been a little over-dramatic, but the thought of what she'd done, of how Lord Weston had reacted, it certainly felt as though her life would never be the same. If only she'd not tried to kiss him. What had she been thinking!

His warm hand clasped her elbow and he led her into the conservatory. "Come and sit. I know we do not know each other well, and maybe that will make it easier to unburden yourself."

She sat on the cold marble seat and went to pull her shawl about her arms, only to find it missing. She looked back out into the hall where she had collided with the duke and spied it on the floor.

"Are you sure you wish to hear about my antics, your grace?" she said, huddling a little into herself, the room chilly in the night air. The duke shuffled off his coat and slipped it about her shoulders. His heat engulfed her, settling about her a notion of calm.

"Of course I'll listen to you. Whatever you have to say."

Mary bit her lip, reminded of what had happened with Lord Weston. The words spilled from her over what she'd done and how his lordship had reacted. Why she was telling his grace this information she did not know or understand, but his offering to hear her concerns were kindly meant and he was Peter's friend after all. Peter would never be close with anyone if they did not have his trust. And heaven helped her, she desperately wanted to tell someone about what happened. "Lord Weston looked at me as if I'd grown two heads," she continued. "I know I'm not as fashionable as other women in Town." She gestured to her dress and the duke looked her over, pity entering his gray orbs. "I'm opinionated and perhaps a little wild. I ran into you and entangled myself in your buttons. But my parents are adamant I marry, and I worry that I'll make the wrong choice. I do not wish to be trapped in an unhappy union." She looked up at him and held his gaze. "Please tell me not all gentlemen are looking for simpering debutantes with no voice."

DALE STARED AT LADY MARY, utterly enthralled by her zest to make men see women, women such as herself more than the fripperies their mamas dressed them up in. To admire women who were educated and opinionated. Dale could admit that he might be a little biased against such features. He could only assume because his mother had been such a woman, and it had always brought out the worst in his father.

Dale sighed, patting her hand in comfort. "Unfortunately, Lady Mary, men are not always that bright of mind." *He certainly was not.* "Having a sister of my own, I've come to realize that the female sex is more often than not more calm and thoughtful toward others. Of course you get some degree to all sexes that are not so, and you're not different."

She threw him a cautious smile and he noticed her dark, long eyelashes. Not to mention in the scuffle in the hall, her hair had come loose of some of the pins and cascaded over her delicate shoulders. His gaze shifted lower at he drank in the bountiful breasts that sat hidden beneath the ribbons and lace.

That he knew what she felt like in his arms also did not help his constitution.

"How will I ever face him again? I'm mortified."

Dale placed his arm about her shoulders, rubbing her arm in comfort. "You will face him like you would anyone. You will raise your chin and think no more of it. We've all made mistakes such as the one you made today. Laugh it off and forget about it. It was only a kiss after all."

He looked over to a potted rose across from them, but all he could smell was Lady Mary and the sweet scent of jasmine.

"He's so very well received in Town. He'll never speak

to me again, he'll probably laugh at me and call me a silly child who needs to grow up."

"Are you?" Dale asked, meeting her gaze when she glanced at him.

"Am I what?" she asked, her eyes bright with unshed tears.

"A silly chit who needs to grow up?"

She pulled back a little, clearly affronted. "Of course not!"

He shrugged. "Well then, you have nothing to worry about."

She sighed, her breasts rising at the action. He tore his gaze away, concentrating on the plants about him. "I don't know how to be fashionable and worldly. I'm simply too rough about the edges to ever change, I believe. I don't particularly want a husband, but if I do have to marry, Lord Weston does suit my requirements. He's our neighbor and we've known him for years, so he knows me very well. Knows that I'm too set in my ways now to change. You see, your grace," she said, sitting back. "I like to experience all things. To be well versed in life. We must read, love, laugh and play. Swim, fish, dance and…"

Dale removed his arm and watched her patiently. "Kiss," he ventured, inexplicably entranced by her. He watched her, the line of her neck as she glanced up at the glass roof, looking at the stars beyond.

"And kiss," she whispered, longing echoing in her voice.

Her eyes met his and a heady, dark emotion swirled inside Dale. This girl, woman, he should amend was dangerous to men like him. Such little temptresses made them want things they would otherwise steer clear of.

He sighed, studying her a moment. As much as he disliked Lord Weston, if that was whom Lady Mary thought would suit her temperament and character, who was he to naysay her? "I'll tell you what, Lady Mary. Do you want me to help you regain your Lord Weston and have him eating out of your hand like a puppy for the remainder of this house party?"

Her eyes brightened, making her more beautiful than he thought possible. Damn it all to hell he didn't need to think of her in such a way. He cleared his throat. "I will give you one piece of advice, and you must follow it. To the letter." Dale paused, looking down his nose at her. "Are we in agreement."

"Oh yes." She nodded eagerly, which jiggled her breasts in his peripheral vision. *Dear Lord in heaven he was in hell.*

"I would suggest you be honest with Lord Weston. If you think he suits you, then let him know that you're open to courtship. Be flirty, charming, and honest with him. Forget about the kiss, his reaction, all of it. Lift that pretty face of yours and look him in the eyes, be bold and forthright. Talk of more than the weather, discuss what you enjoy, what you love to do, and if he is not a fool, he will fall at your feet. I promise you that."

"Is that what you like, your grace?" she asked.

Dale started at her question before he stood, needing to distance himself. "I respect honesty above everything else."

"Thank you, your grace," she said, standing. "My brother normally has good sense and I see he had the good sense to befriend you. You're an honorable man." She held out her gloved hand and he reached for it, bringing it to his lips and bowing over it slightly.

"Good luck, Lady Mary and may the man who deserves you win."

She threw him a dazzling smile, striding to where they had clashed, swooping up her shawl, she glanced back at him one last time before she was gone. He smiled after her, shaking his head in amusement. This country retreat had just become more interesting. Now he could sit back and watch the games unfold. Or at least, the one Lady Mary was playing.

CHAPTER 5

M ary spent the following day adjusting all her gowns. She would not wait until next Season as discussed with her father, she would alter the dresses she wore now to suit her better. Mary tore at lace and ribbons, lowered her necklines and removed any sort of frippery that decorated her dresses. Underneath all the accessories, her dresses were handsome enough and would do before she could order a new wardrobe next Season.

Mary assessed her handiwork, unable to fathom why she'd allowed the hideous adornments for so long.

Tonight she would put into place the recommendation the Duke of Carlton had suggested to her. She would be feminine but intelligent with conversations that were worthy of discussion amongst the opposite sex. She would laugh in a sultry manner, but remain ladylike, show interest in the opposite sex, instead of indifference like she'd always done before. That, along with her own modifications, namely her clothing and hair would give her an idea of how she would go when back in London. Mary had also gone as far as to ask her mother's lady's maid to style her hair in a more modern style, some tendrils falling softly about her face and making her look more worldly than a country lady. All that was left for her to do was dress.

There was a quick knock on the door before her friend Louise bustled into the room. Louise was already dressed for dinner and she looked lovely as usual with her petite frame and pretty smile.

Louise stopped inside the door, shutting it behind her. "Oh, Mary, your hair looks marvelous. So much more elegant and suitable for your age."

Her maid blushed, clearly pleased with herself and Mary smiled. "I cannot thank you both enough for helping me today with everything that I asked. I should have acted before now regarding my gowns instead of thinking of mother's feelings. I wasn't actively seeking a husband before though, and so didn't see the point. But if I am to marry as my father has stated, I need to be more amenable and willing to talk to gentlemen, open and honestly. If I am more willing, maybe I will find someone who will suit my character better." The more Mary thought about this, the more it made sense to her. Instead of dismissing, but engaging, she might find a gentleman who would allow her pursuits to continue and the marriage would be a happy one for both involved.

Louise nodded. "It is certainly worth a try. There are marriages made within the *ton* which are grand love matches all the time. There is no reason why yours will not be."

"Like who?" Mary asked, lifting her arms so her maid could help her into her gown.

Louise blinked, biting her lip. "Well...I cannot remember at the moment, but I'm sure there are such couples."

Mary stifled a laugh. "In any case, we had better finish getting dressed for dinner, there is still much to be done."

After much cutting and re-stitching, the dress Mary wore tonight was the most revealing she'd ever worn. The sapphire silk set off her dark hair and sun-kissed skin. There were no bows or ribbons, no gaudy lace or high necklines, this gown was simple yet fashionable. Simply perfect for her first night in proving that although she might like the outdoors, fishing, and shooting, swimming in the summer, that did not mean she could not also be a lady.

She stood before the cheval mirror, taking in her appearance. To finish off her ensemble her maid placed a small sapphire that hung from a delicate gold chain about her neck. The final piece of her transformation. Mary smiled, not recognizing the woman staring back at her. She looked completely different and yet the girl gazing back was also the same. And she liked what she saw.

"You look beautiful," Louise said, coming up behind her and catching her eye in the mirror.

Nerves fluttered in Mary's stomach and nodded, raising her chin, ready to face her future. "I think this will do well enough."

⚜

DALE STOOD CONVERSING with Lady Hectorville who had cornered him the moment he came downstairs. Her whispered words and sultry tone had worked on him once, on a night he had been in his cups and not himself. Her seduction that evening had worked, but not this night. Not ever again.

Why her ladyship continued to seek him out for bed

sport baffled him, and in truth had started to become a nuisance.

Did she not have better things to do with her time? The woman really needed a hobby. If she didn't find something other than men to occupy her time, she'd soon end up with syphilis.

The door to the front reception room where everyone was gathered before dinner opened, and Dale glanced toward the new arrivals. Taking a sip of his whisky, he coughed, choking on his drink at the sight of Lady Mary. Lady Hectorville glanced at him sharply and he cleared his throat, schooling his features into a mask of indifference.

But boredom was the least of his emotions at that moment. Like a moth to a flame, so too was Dale's attention riveted on her. Lady Mary greeted her mama, curtsying and smiling as her mother gushed over her daughter's stunning appearance. Minus the lace and bows that normally adorned her gowns, but something else was different too. Her hair had been styled to better suit her age, and gave one the opportunity to admire her lovely neck.

"She is very beautiful tonight. I did say to Lady Lancaster that she should allow Mary to wear clothes that were more fashionable and popular among the young set, but my friend is so set in her ways. But la, look at Mary now. A woman, not a young girl in braids anymore," Lady Hectorville said.

That was certainly true. The bountiful décolletage was proof of that. And she was only five years younger than himself, not an old maid at all. If she were to attend London next year wearing such gowns she would find a husband soon enough.

The thought left him cold and he took a sip of his whisky, tearing his regard from the delectable little morsel.

A hot, and urgent need sat heavy in his gut and he took a few calming breaths. *Remember she is not for you.* And while he knew it, Dale still allowed his gaze to return to her and to bask in the idea, just for a moment, what it would be like to kiss her...and perhaps have her lips curve in that pretty smile just for him. To date he'd yet to find a lady who made him want to give up his more sensual pursuits and settle into domesticity. But the desire coursing through his veins now made him really look at Lady Mary. Dale frowned. She was fire...and fire with fire was never a good combination. No...for whenever he decided to take the plunge into matrimony, it must be a lady of cool demureness. With admirable willpower he tore his stare from her.

HUFFING OUT A DISGRUNTLED BREATH, Lady Hectorville flounced off. He glanced to his side as the sweet scent of roses caught his attention and his lips twitched into a grin. "Good evening, Lady Mary. You look very fetching tonight, although I think you're already aware of that."

She grinned mischievously, taking a glass of wine from a footman who bowed before her. "I am being more practical in my choosing of a husband and will take heed of your advice and be more personable, more interested, but I also needed to make a few changes myself." She glanced down at her gown and drew his attention there also. "I shall have Mama purchase a new wardrobe next year, but the alterations to my gowns I have made today will do well enough until then."

His gaze moved over her, taking in the narrowing of her waist beneath the silk dress. She was very fetching in it. The empire cut suited her body shape, and Dale couldn't help but wonder if her hips were as bountiful as her breasts.

Dale took another sip of his whisky and mortifyingly found it empty. She chuckled and he knew she'd seen his lapse in concentration.

"Let me get you another." She waved a footman over.

"Thank you," he said, heat flaming his cheeks. He cleared his throat. "So, you're going to take heed of some of my recommendations. I do hope you find them beneficial."

She bit her lip and he ground his teeth. A woman who was utterly clueless that she was charming was nothing short of dangerous. "Well, I think what you said made sense. If I can hold an intelligent conversation with a man perhaps I'll like him enough to allow him to court me. As much as I'd love to keep escaping the marriage trap, I know I cannot do so forever," she whispered, leaning close to him and giving him a good view of her bust and the white chemise that sat against her skin.

Damn she was the sweetest thing he wanted to taste, savor and enjoy every ounce of her.

"Lord Weston has not brought up my lapse in conduct since it occurred. I'm glad we've been able to get along just as we ever have."

Dale narrowed his eyes at her tone that although determined, did hold an edge of longing to it. "Is Lord Weston a gentleman whom you would consider a possible suitor?" Dale turned and watched the viscount, dismissing him as a scoundrel and a vain one at that. Certainly not worthy of a free spirit like the intelligent Lady Mary.

She lifted her face and gave him her profile as she glanced across the room to where Lord Weston stood talking to Lady Hectorville. Her ladyship all but hanging off the young lord's every word. His lordship eating up the attention like a glutton.

"Father and mama would certainly approve, and as I said, he's our neighbor. I would not have to move out of the county and I would be close to home. But I promise I will not rush into anything that I'm not certain of. After five Seasons in Town, you must believe that of me, if nothing else."

A light blush rose on her cheeks at the mention of it and he wanted to reach out and see if her skin was as heated as it looked. "Are you ashamed?"

One delicate shoulder lifted in a shrug. Dale tore his gaze away from her person. In all seriousness, did she have to keep reminding him of what lay beneath her gown? It was bad enough that he knew he could never have her. Not in the way he'd like to.

The idea of her beneath him, her hair mussed from bed sport, her lips swollen and red from his kisses, her body marked from where he'd dragged his lips from the tops of her nipples to the core of herself. She'd never think of the washed out popinjay Lord Weston again if he did act on his desires.

A clap on his shoulder startled him and his whisky spilled over his coat sleeve.

Peter laughed. "Ho there, my friend. I did not mean to startle you so."

Dale placed the tumbler aside, pulling out his handkerchief to dab at his jacket. "I did not see you come over, that is all."

"Brother," Lady Mary said, looking less than pleased that her sibling had decided to join them.

"Mary," Peter said in return in just as bored a tone. "Should you not be talking to the eligible gentlemen here instead of boring my friend with your nonsense? To mingle will be good practice for next Season."

She sighed, rolling her eyes. "Charming. And I should hope I wasn't boring you, your grace. I think I can say with honesty that we're friends and can speak plainly."

Dale caught Peter's eye and didn't miss the flicker of contemplation in his friend's orbs. "Of course we're friends, Lady Mary." When he didn't venture to say anything further, she made her excuses and left to sit beside her friend on a nearby settee.

"I do apologize, Carlton. My sister is a little eccentric and straightforward to the point of being blunt. If she's said anything inappropriate, I shall speak to her about it."

Dale shook his head, dismissing the idea. He actually liked the fact that Lady Mary spoke her mind. The *ton* was full of lies and intrigues and quite rightly, he never enjoyed that side of society.

"She did not bother me."

"Huh," his friend said. "Well, let me know if she does. Even if you are a duke and a good prospect for many beautiful women, my sister is not one of them. She needs to understand that."

Dale frowned, not for the first time feeling as though Peter thought him unworthy of his sister. "Why would you say that? Am I not suitable for your sister?" The question was asked before he could rip it back. What was he saying?

Peter's eyes widened. "Oh, you're a good enough catch and suitable for her of course, but we're friends and she's my sister. Do not forget I know how much of a rogue you are, and have shared in your wild nights in London. She would not do for you."

Something about Peter's tone put him on edge and he bit back an impertinent retort. Instead, he said, "From what you stated yourself we would make a good match, so do explain why we would not." Dale knew what he was saying. It was because of his antics in Town, how he lived. The hard way in which he existed. Nights out at gambling dens, endless balls and parties, women who fell at his feet willing to warm his bed. That Peter knew and had partaken in his lifestyle was reason enough his friend would push his sister away from his orbit, even so, it rankled.

"Mary will marry for love or not at all. If there is one thing that I know about my sister it is that," Peter said, smiling a little to try and dispel the tension that had risen between them.

Dale stared at his friend, hating the fact that Peter thought so little of him. "And she could not love me?"

Peter glanced at him, wide-eyed. "Could you love her enough to change your ways? To stop your nights of debauchery, of gambling, of flirting with every beautiful woman who crosses your path? You my friend are a wild one, and I daresay only a very biddable wife would condone your rakehell ways. That woman is not my sister and the sparks that would fly would be quite terrifying."

Dale turned his attention back to the gathered guests, not sure he could answer such a question at this time. He would be a good catch for any eligible woman, even Peter's sister, but he would not pursue her. Not because it was obvious Peter did not think he was suited to her, or her needs, but because Dale didn't want to marry just yet. A marriage, to him, was something toxic, a partnership that put people at odds and made them do emotionally damaging things to one another. If he ever married, his wife would be a quiet, biddable woman. She would know her role as duchess better than anything else, and therefore they would never come to odds. Lady Mary was not that woman. To imagine a life with Mary made him envision confrontations, arguments and debates. His gut churned at the memory of his parents' disagreements.

"I could not," he said, agreeing with Peter. "I hope the next Season has a happier ending for Lady Mary than the last."

At that moment the dinner gong sounded somewhere in the depth of the home, and they made their way into the dining room. The night passed well enough, but being seated across from Lady Mary, Dale couldn't help but listen to her conversation with Lord Fairchild, an eligible Marquess from Kent. They spoke of geography and touched on the geology of certain areas about England. The types of fish that his lordship's lakes boasted and that his lordship would enjoy a spot of ice fishing while at Bran Manor. Her carefree laugh, free from restraint or what was expected of a woman of her rank made him smile. Somehow Lady Mary made him yearn for a life he'd never thought to have. Of a marriage where intelligent conversation was to be had, not just about gossip or gowns, or who had a new paramour, but real things. Things that impacted their life, like politics, family, wants and needs. It seemed Lord Fairchild was also thinking the same.

Dale glared at the fellow, tearing his gaze away to look further along the table. He caught Peter's regard, the hardened line of his jaw letting Dale know he'd caught him watching his sister.

He turned back to his meal and Miss Grant, his dinner companion seated to his left, determined to put out of his mind Lady Mary. If not for her sake, then at least for the sake of his friendship with Peter.

CHAPTER 6

Since her transformation Mary had started to enjoy the country house party, and even didn't mind the fact that she could not go outdoors as much as she'd like. Lord Weston plus a flurry of other young gentlemen had been most attentive since she'd updated her gowns to be more fashionable. Allowed herself to be more open to the concept of courtship and Mary found not all of the men were unlikable. Lord Fairchild loved his country estate and spent many months there instead of in Town.

Perhaps finding a husband who suited her was not such an impossibility as she'd thought.

This morning however she would leave the guests and go for a well-deserved ride, having sent word to the stables earlier to have her mare Pegasus saddled. The air was crisp, cutting even, as she started toward the stables, but with her bottle-green riding habit, leather kid gloves, fur cap and scarf, her short ride would not be too taxing. And she needed to get outdoors, to feel the air on her face, be alone to think and relax and not have to be the person that society wished her to be. A woman who stitched before the fire and played piano instead of going outdoors in inclement weather. A woman who was demure and without opinions of her own, everything that she was not.

She started over the northern hill at the back of the property taking Pegasus at a slower pace than usual. With the snow underfoot, not too thick to stop all riding thankfully, but even so, it was thick enough to miss something in the undergrowth, to cause her horse to misstep and possibly hurt itself.

This side of the property was left to grow as nature intended and with very little maintenance from their gardening staff. It made for better hunting seasons and always ensured the sport was good when the gentlemen came up for shooting parties. Mary made her way to the shooting lodge, a sanctuary for herself when not in use. That the lodge also had a stable, always well kept no matter what the time of year, which meant she could place Pegasus in a stall and wile away the day reading, strolling the nearby woods, or simply enjoying her own company.

She rode Pegasus up to the stable door and frowned when she spied it slightly ajar. Had she left it open when she'd been here last? That was a month or so ago, or had one of the groundskeepers accidentally forgotten to lock up when checking on the place. Mary slid off looking about to see if she could see anyone else about.

She walked up to the door and peering inside saw a horse munching hay in one of the stalls, the saddle laying over the stall door and bridle too. Relief ran through her followed by confusion. Whose horse was that?

She turned about, searching, but couldn't see anyone. Was the intruder inside the lodge? Was he living there without the family knowing? Not letting Pegasus go, she walked over to the lodge and peered through a window, her stomach turning into knots as she recognized the man lazing away on a settee beside a window. Without a care in the world, his boots sat up on the chair arm, his arm casually resting behind his head while the other held a book.

In this relaxed stance the Duke of Carlton looked even more devastatingly handsome than he did in a ballroom. Or across the dinner table watching her all night.

Mary turned back to the stable and settled Pegasus before entering the lodge without knocking. This was her lodge after all, or at least her family's and she had more right than the duke to be here. The thought boosted her courage that he might be annoyed at being interrupted.

He started, dropped his book on his lap, and partly sat up when she entered. Realizing it was only her, he chuckled in evident pleasure, and her treasonous body fluttered at the sight of him.

"You scared me, Lady Mary. I did not think anyone would find me hidden away out here at this time of year."

Mary pulled off her fur cap and laid it on a nearby table. She went to stand beside the fire, which was burning fiercely and warming the room. "You have found my sanctuary, your grace. I often come out here to do exactly as you're doing. Today I needed a little peace, the guests have been locked away inside for some days now, and I think some are getting a little sick of the indoors." And she was getting sick of some of them.

He cocked his eyebrow. "You more than most, I assume?"

She nodded once. "You assume correctly, but," she said, gesturing to his book, "I'm more than willing to leave you in peace and come back tomorrow. I do not want to intrude." Even though this was her hunting lodge, the duke was here first and she was unchaperoned.

He sat up, placing the book beside him. The action brought home once again how broad he was across the shoulders, his muscular thighs and large hands. The memory of him holding her after she'd run into him floated through her mind, bringing with it other thoughts. Of his hands running over her body, pulling her close, teasing her every nerve and making her shiver.

"Please, stay. You're shivering and obviously cold. Let me fetch some water and we shall make some tea."

Mary didn't correct his assumption about her shivers. She glanced down, pulling off her gloves, controlling herself not to gawk at him as he stood. He collected the old metal kettle from a nearby bench and started for the door. As much as she tried, her gaze sought him out through her lashes and she admired the view of him from behind as he went out the door.

Upon being left alone, she sighed. Whoever married the duke would be a very lucky woman. The idea of being ravished by him was almost enough to drive all thoughts of anyone else out of her head. Certainly Lord Weston didn't bring forth the ideas and imaginings that the duke did. Nor Lord Fairchild for that matter.

She contemplated that point before he returned and placed the water on the little grill that sat over the flames. He returned to his chair, and folding his legs he asked, "What else do you like to do, Lady Mary, other than sneaking away to hunting lodges when no one is looking?"

His lazy smile made her blood warm. Mary sat, pulling her legs up under her and clasping a nearby pillow to lean against. "Do you really wish to know, your grace?" Not many gentlemen ever cared to know how women passed their time, but then nothing the duke had done since she'd met him had actually made any sense and so she was willing to give him the benefit of her doubts if he really wished to know.

He threw her a half smile. "I would not have asked if I were not interested."

The duke was becoming more interesting by the minute. "I'm especially fond of fishing both in the winter and summer months. I love to swim and I've been practicing rock climbing of late. As you know we have some very good peaks here in Derbyshire."

A small furrow appeared between his brows. "You like to climb rocky outcrops? Is that not dangerous? Do your parents know you take part in such a sport?"

He looked at her as if she'd lost half her mind.

Mary shrugged. "Do not tell my parents, they do not know. And I have taken precautions and secured some ropes. It's all perfectly safe, so long as they hold."

He contemplated her for a long moment, and she fought not to fidget in her chair. How was he able to make her feel all warm and fuzzy every time she was around him? He made her want other things so very different to how her life was at present. Her own home, a marriage, children, all things she'd not had longed for before. She frowned, the thought was as perplexing as it was frightening.

"You should not be climbing rocks by yourself, Lady Mary. What if you fell? It could be days, weeks even, before anyone found you in these parts. You could be long expired by then."

All true, and nothing she'd not thought about herself, but all her hobbies were an escape of duty and she would be loath to have to stop. It was who she was after all, to pretend to be anyone else was impossible to imagine.

"I never climb overly high, but I like the thrill of it." She sighed, smiling at the thought that next year would be her last opportunity to be so carefree. Unless she found a husband who allowed her to continue her passions. "It's such a rush when I reach the peak, makes me simply want to do it again and again."

The duke shifted in his chair and cleared his throat. "Tea, I think."

☙❧

DALE DIDN'T MOVE from his chair. He knew he ought to get up and help Lady Mary with the teacups, sugar and teapot, but he simply could not move. Not yet at least. After her little chat about rock climbing, reaching peaks and wanting to do it again and again, all he could think about was what she would look like beneath him, giving and gaining pleasure.

The hardness in his pants would be obvious to even a blind person, and so he sat, trying to imagine anything other than the little minx before him, writhing, gasping, biting that sweet bottom lip of hers as he brought them both to climax.

He groaned, flopping his head back to look up at the ceiling. He was a veritable ass. A blaggard who could think of nothing but plucking this sweet rose before him and putting her in his coat pocket.

Mary sat the tea in front of him, setting out the cups and saucers while they waited for the kettle to boil over the flames. "Is everything well, your grace. You look a little flushed."

He sat forward, in part to try and disguise his groin, which thankfully was starting to behave itself, but also because he wanted to be closer to her. "I am well, I assure you. Just enjoying my unexpected company."

She smiled at him. The gesture was genuine, and laughter lurked in her eyes. Peter's sister was, if he were to summarize her at all, a jovial, happy kind of woman. She certainly spoke to their guests as if all of them were her friends, and she liked to laugh at jokes, even when Dale didn't find all of those being told by Lord Weston overly amusing.

Dale decided he liked her very much and would like to see her settled and happy and with a gentleman who allowed her to do as she pleased, including rock climbing.

"I am too. When I heard Peter was bringing a duke home this year, I did have a rather unfortunate notion as to what you would be like."

"Really," he said, interested to know what her thoughts may have been. His, upon seeing her the first time, were less than complimentary, and he was ashamed of what he had thought of her that night. A disaster with very little fashion sense. The woman who sat before him had taken charge of her life, and was unrecognizable to the woman he'd first seen. "Do tell me your thoughts."

Lady Mary grinned, her eyes dancing with mischief. "I actually thought you would be a prig. All lofty airs and looking down your nose at all of us. Even though my father is an earl and Peter is your friend, I couldn't help but wonder if you'd find such house parties, festive and merry to be too tame for you?"

"Ahh," he said, leaning back in his chair and running a hand through his hair. "So you've heard the rumors?"

Her grin increased and Dale found himself smiling. "Are they rumors or statements of fact?" She schooled her features and threw him a penetrating gaze. "Are you really as wild as they say you are? Or is the *ton* mistaken in judging you so wrong?"

Dale wished they were judging him incorrectly, but it wasn't so. So how would he answer such a question without looking like the established rake that, in truth, he was. "The *ton* is not wholly incorrect." He couldn't say more, as it was this conversation was highly inappropriate. To tell Peter's sister that he'd had multiple bed partners, sometimes at the same time, was not what this, this…

"Your brother tells me you're three and twenty."

"That is correct." She stood and going over to the fire, picked up a cloth that sat on the mantle and then took the kettle off the boil. She poured the hot water into the tea pot, jiggling it a little before letting it sit to brew.

"How old are you?" she asked in return, meeting his gaze.

"Eight and twenty. Old enough to know that our conversation subject is not appropriate."

She chuckled, deep and teasing and the sound warmed his blood. He shouldn't like her this much or her company. He'd certainly never had this reaction to anyone else before. "Then it is lucky that I'm not appropriate. You only need to ask my family just how inappropriate I can be at times. I'm certainly a little too rough about the edges for most people. As well you've found out."

"I like your rough edges." Dale shut his mouth with a snap. What was he saying! She was his best friend's sister. And from the looks that Peter had thrown at him the other night at dinner he did not want Dale going anywhere near her. Not to mention Lady Mary's family expecting her to make a fine match next Season. He hoped she would not consider him in her pursuit of marriage. He would make a terrible husband for her. With both their independent natures, their life would never be calm and sedate, and she did not possess the biddable nature he'd always wanted in a bride and marriage.

God knows Dale would never tolerate being managed by a bluestocking.

"I daresay we shall be friends, your grace?"

Her statement pulled him from his musings and he nodded. "Of course. I would like to think so."

She leaned forward and poured two cups of tea. "Sugar? Milk?"

"Both please," he replied, having always had a sweet tooth, even when it came to his hot beverages.

Lady Mary passed him the cup, a small delicate saucer beneath the fine china and Dale took the opportunity to touch her gloveless fingers. They were warm, soft and did odd things to his stomach.

"Thank you," he said, leaning back in his chair and taking a well-needed sip.

"If we're to be friends, may I call you by your given name. I would like you to call me Mary."

A little warning voice in his mind told him this famil-iarity was wrong. That he shouldn't be so lax in manners with such a woman, let alone on a first-name basis, but ignoring his own counsel, he found himself saying, "I would like that. You in turn may call me Dale, or Carlton."

Pleased with herself, she settled back onto her seat, once again tucking her legs beneath her on the chair. "Good, because now that we're familiar friends and you're worldly, I'd like some more advice."

Oh damn it. What had he got himself into now? "It depends on what you ask," he said, caution shadowing his tone.

"I'd like some advice on Lord Weston. I've known him, you see, most of my life, he's our neighbor after all, and since he spends so much time in Town, if I were to marry him, I'd be free to stay here in Derbyshire, close to home and all my favorite places in the world to explore."

A cold hard rock lodged in his gut at the thought of Mary marrying Lord Popinjay who was, in Dale's estima-tion, worse than himself when it came to his philandering about town. Unlike Dale, Lord Weston did not care what happened to his conquests after he'd had his way. He simply turned his back and moved on. That gentleman loved the chase, loved being the center of attention, and Dale knew right down to his core that he'd never be faithful to Mary.

"On further reflection, I do not believe Lord Weston is suitable after all." He took a sip of his tea, not missing the flash of annoyance in Mary's eyes. "He's not looking for a wife. He told Peter and myself that only days ago. You should look to Lord Fairchild. He is better suited to your nature."

"Even so," she said, biting her bottom lip. "I'm sure that if I managed to kiss his lordship, he would see that we would suit. And that I'd be no trouble in the marriage."

Dale only just stopped himself from cursing. To marry Lord Weston would mean a marriage possibly worse than his parents' had been. Mary would demand loyalty, respect and freedom. All of those things would be lacking if she married Lord Weston. It would only be a matter of time before she'd realize her mistake that unfortunately she'd have to live with for years to come.

"You will not be kissing Lord Weston or marrying him. He's not for you."

She raised her brow, peering at him with interest. "He's the best situated. His estate is right across the fields, for heaven's sake. And you're wrong also. I will kiss his lordship, if I want. No matter if you think I cannot claim one."

Dale placed his cup of tea on the table before them, leaning forward. "I think he would be a fool if he kissed you. It would give you false hope. If his lordship did kiss you it would only be for his own selfish reasons to dally with you."

She stood, an indignant huff escaping her mouth. "You don't think I'm kissable."

Oh hell no, that was not what he was thinking, especially now that she was all fire and brimstone. If only she knew right at this moment, he wanted to claim her mouth. Kiss her hard and deep, pull her close and have her for himself. "Of course not, but young women such as yourself, an innocent—"

"Oh please, spare me the lecture," she said, cutting him off. "I will prove it to you. Before this house party is over I shall kiss Lord Weston properly and I'm going to tell you all about it, and then you will know what you can do with your thoughts on my age and innocence."

Before he could reply, she flounced out of the lodge, slamming the door behind her. "Bloody hell," he swore. Now he'd gone and pricked her pride. And now he would have to watch her like a hawk so she didn't make a fool of herself with Lord Weston. Who, just like a cat, played with its victim before consuming them. And he was determined Lady Mary would not be anyone's feast.

CHAPTER 7

Mary kept away from the Duke over the next couple of days, even though his gaze was on her every second of every day. He was shadowing her, she was sure, ensuring she didn't follow through on her threat to kiss Lord Weston. Not that she'd had a chance to even get close to his lordship since her mama's friend, Lady Hectorville had taken a liking to the young viscount.

Tonight, her Mama had set up a card night for all her guests to enjoy. Mary sat beside Louise at the whist table, and contemplated her cards, all the while aware of the scowling duke who sat beside her. But unlike herself, he was scowling at her not the cards he held in his hand.

Was he so very mad at her for telling him that she would kiss Lord Weston? Why it bothered him she couldn't fathom. Probably a brotherly affection he felt honored to have due to his friendship with Peter. She studied him, trying to make him out. He glanced up from his cards, his dark hooded gaze full of determination and something else lurked in his eyes. What though she couldn't fathom. Her skin prickled with awareness and she glanced back down at the table, feeling unsettled of a sudden.

Louise dealt the last round, and going through the play, luck was on Mary's side and she won the last trick with an ace of hearts, beating the duke's king of hearts. Mary laughed, clapping at her good fortune. She smiled at the duke feeling quite the conqueror. His grace leaned back in his chair, throwing his cards on the table

"Well done, Lady Mary. You've beaten us all."

"Of course, I always get what I want, your grace," she said, wanting him to know she didn't just mean at a game of cards. She glanced about the room, noting that Lord Weston was no longer present. Where had he gone? He had been watching them play.

"Another game, Mary?" Louise asked, shuffling the deck to the best of her ability.

"Not just at the moment, Louise." Mary stood. "If you'll excuse me for a minute."

She started for the door with the plan of saying, should anyone ask, that she was intending to use the retiring room her mama had set up downstairs. Mary came out into the hall and turned toward where the room was located. Her parents' country house was one of the largest in the county, and as a young girl she'd lost count when trying to tally how many rooms there were.

The hall had multiple sconces lighting her way, along with candelabras, the smell of beeswax permeating the air. The Aubusson runner beneath her feet cushioned her every step and she smiled, greeting a couple of ladies that she passed on her way. Arriving at the retiring room door, she continued on. Lord Weston had taken a liking to her father's billiard room and it was possible he was spending some time there.

She came up to the room, and peeked through the

door. Candelabras were alight, a well-tended fire burning in the grate, but the room itself was empty. Frowning, she turned about wondering where else he would be. Mary continued on and searched the conservatory, the terrace and all were without a soul.

Maybe he'd returned to the card room. She headed back and taking a short cut, she went through her father's library, and the small office that he used when in need of peace and privacy. This area had not been lit, but knowing the room well she crossed the space toward the other door that led onto a corridor with little trouble.

That's when she heard it. A feminine chuckle followed by a male gasp and heavy panting.

Mary stilled, having never heard such a noise before. She looked into the dark recesses of the room, but with her father's desk sitting paramount in the space, Mary could not see beyond.

Another male gasp. "Yes, just like that. Suck it."

Mary slapped a hand over her mouth to hide her gasp. Why in the world would a man be saying such a thing? And who was he saying it to? With the whispered voices she'd not been able to make out which of her parents' guests were ensconced behind the desk, but certainly two were.

She tiptoed up to the desk and peered over. Mary stumbled back, knocking the chair over that was behind her and with a loud thump, she landed on her bottom.

A muffling curse came from the other side of the room, but Mary didn't bother to wait for them to stand and see her there. She bolted for the door into the library, slamming her father's office door firmly behind her as she ran as fast as she could in silk slippers and a gown that was not made to assist with such physical activity.

Mary left the library, coming into her mama's private parlor and slammed head long into the duke of Carlton.

Again...

His arms wrapped about her and for a second time, they went down, Mary landing on top of him. The duke made an *oomph* sound as he took the brunt of the fall.

This time Mary shuffled off him as fast as she could, determined to leave, to get away from everyone and go to her room. Tears stung her eyes at what a silly little dupe she'd been the past few days. Thinking that Lord Weston might actually be a candidate for marriage. To like what he saw in her and be the first and last man to kiss her properly. Shame washed through her at not trusting herself, at not listening to the duke and allowing the little bit of attention he afforded her these past days to give rise to hopes that marriage to a man who suited her character was a possibility.

She was a fool.

"Mary wait," the duke said, catching up to her and pulling her to a stop. "You're upset. What has happened."

At that very moment Lord Weston and Lady Hectorville ran into her father's library, both Mary and the duke turned to look at them. They were still disheveled but at least dressed. Heat bloomed on Mary's cheeks, and she turned her back on them. She could hear Lord Weston start toward them, but the duke moved away, slamming the parlor room door closed and cutting them both off. The snip of the lock echoed in the room before a comforting arm came about her shoulder, leading her toward a nearby chair.

"You need not tell me what you saw, I only needed to look at them to know what has happened. Do you wish for me to tell your parents of Lord Weston's and her ladyship's actions?"

Mary shook her head, shamed that a part of her, the other part of her that was not affronted or shocked by what she saw, was also a little curious. Jealous even. Were men and women able to do such things to each other? If they were, she'd never known of it.

"No, your grace, that won't be necessary." She stood, throwing him a small smile. He continued to sit, glancing up at her and blast it all he was so handsome. With his strong jaw and chiseled cheekbones, he was an English Adonis.

Before her sat one of the most sought-after gentlemen in England, and just like the rest of them, Mary was always the good-natured friend, always to be sidelined as the dependable, intelligent sister to the future Earl of Lancaster. Never a lady to seek out, to court, and possibly steal a kiss or two from. Oh no, she was too much of a wallflower, a bluestocking to be seen as anything else than that. "Thank you for your concern, but I think I shall retire to my room. I do not feel like socializing any longer today."

Mary left without another word, and just as she expected the duke did not try and stop her. And why would he? He didn't look at her as anything but a friend. A woman to respect but little else.

It seemed to be the story of her life and she was sick of it.

❦

THE EVE of the Mistletoe Ball arrived with a deluge of snow, but even with the chill of the outdoors, it could not dampen the excitement from the house guests over the festive ball.

Dale stood at the side of Lord and Lady Lancaster's ballroom and watched Lord Weston flounce about like the little peacock that he was. The bastard having been caught with Lady Hectorville, his front falls still gaping from being open, left little imagination as to what he'd been doing with her ladyship. Dale didn't even need to ask Mary what she'd seen.

That the poor girl had harbored feelings toward Lord Weston was unfortunate. The man wouldn't give the chit a second glance. Too opinionated and if Dale was correct, Mary would be too intelligent for such a prick, and the gentleman was too thick to know it. With his own self-importance, that was one trait Dale knew Lord Weston wouldn't tolerate in a bride.

Still, Mary didn't deserve to be taught this lesson in the way that she had been, and he would ensure he sought her out tonight and danced with her.

A little tittering went through the sea of guests and Dale cast his eye across the room, trying to see what everyone was in a little fuss about.

He felt his mouth gape and he closed it with a snap. "Damnation," he muttered, remembering to breathe. His eyes feasted on Lady Mary as she walked into the room. How had she remained hidden for so long when there was such a beauty under all those atrocious gowns her mother had made her wear? More worrying perhaps, was how on earth he'd missed seeing such a prize.

Tonight Mary sparkled like a rare diamond amongst paste.

Arm in arm with her closest friend Louise, she walked through the guests, welcoming and smiling as was her nature. Dale watched as she passed Lord Weston and Lady Hectorville, pleased to see she refused to be lured into conversation, even though the prig Lord Weston still tried, even after his shameful actions that she had happened upon.

The thought made Dale hate him even more and under no circumstances would he allow his lordship to touch one hair on her dark, pretty head.

The man who won Lady Mary's heart would be worthy of her affections. As her brother's best friend, he would ensure that was so, and guarantee that Peter too followed this rule. A rarity such as Mary should not marry anyone who did not deserve her.

Dale narrowed his eyes, the thought of her married to someone else, laughing and enjoying herself as she now was, did not fill him with pleasure. If anything, it soured his mood. He rubbed a hand across his jaw, unsure of why it unsettled him so.

"My sister is a success, it would seem," Peter said, coming up to Dale and pulling his gaze from her.

He nodded, schooling his features. "It would seem she is. I would warn you to keep her from Lord Weston however. I think his lordship has other ideas when it comes to marriage."

They glanced toward the gentleman in question and Dale was glad Peter saw Lady Hectorville slide her hand along Lord Weston's arm, their level of acquaintance obvious to anyone who'd enjoyed such house party games themselves.

"I see," Peter said. "I will mention my concern to father, but as for Mary, well, she doesn't seem to know that his lordship is even here." Peter nodded toward the ballroom floor. "What are your thoughts on Lord Fairchild? He would certainly make a good husband for her. He's titled, a good sort of fellow who doesn't partake in anything notorious, and he has a Scottish hunting lodge even though he hails from Kent. Good game in the highlands."

Dale turned his attention back to Mary who danced a

minuet with Lord Fairchild. Her smile lit up the room and their ease of enjoyment together was clear. Mary's face as she looked up at his lordship with something akin to enthrallment and his lordship's was similarly pleased.

A cold knot lodged in his gut. "I know little of him, but I've not heard anything that would cause concern either," Dale said, knowing if he darkened the gentleman's name Peter would listen and would not allow his sister to be courted by him. But Dale could not act with such dishonor. He made a point of relaxing, unfisting his hands at his side. "He looks rather smitten if I'm honest," Dale said instead. "Lady Mary may not need another Season after all."

Peter nodded, then clapped him on the back. "I'm ashamed to say a few days ago I acted atrociously toward you."

"In what way?" Dale thought over their conversations and couldn't remember anything offensive.

"I practically warned you off my sister, albeit not directly, but I feel that you may have believed that to be the case. I hope I have not offended you. Blame it on sibling protectiveness, and know that I believe my concern to be an absurd notion."

Dale glanced at Peter sharply. "Why was it an absurd notion?"

Peter raised his brow, his eyes full of mirth. "Because you would never look at Mary in such a way. She's not your usual type for a start and well, she may have scrubbed up better than any time before this evening, but by tomorrow she'll be back to her normal bluestocking, wall-flower self and all this will be forgotten."

Dale turned back to watch the dancers, one in partic-ular whose infectious laughter made his lips twitch. If only that were true. Dale had come to realize that for several days now, even before if he were honest with himself, his attention often lingered on Mary. He was keenly aware whenever she entered a room or when he saw her somewhere in the house, busy with her own pursuits.

Of all the guests here for the Christmas celebrations, Mary was by far the most interesting. And now with her newly found fashion sense, she was blossoming into a beautiful woman, comfortable with who she was, no matter whom she conversed with. She now allowed gentlemen admirers to court her and not be so cold and aloof and it made the little rough pebble she once was, sparkle into a diamond.

Not that Peter needed to know his thoughts. If their friendship was to survive, he would have to get over his growing admiration of his friend's sister and find another lady to occupy his time and attentions.

"Of course you are right. When it comes to your sister, she is quite safe with me." Unable to tear his eyes away from her, he drank in the vision of perfection she was. As if sensing his scrutiny, she glanced up and their eyes met. Held.

A tremor of awareness ran over him, as if she'd recognized the lie he'd just told and was calling him out on it. Within a moment she turned her attention back to Lord Fairchild and he clenched his fist at his side before excusing himself and leaving the ballroom.

He could not want Lady Mary. He ground his teeth, heading for the card room set up in Lord Lancaster's library for the evening, in need of a small respite. He needed to get a grip on his attraction for the chit who he reminded himself, was not what he wanted.

He'd spent his whole childhood on tenterhooks with his parents arguing, he would not have a marriage where the woman might question his decisions and argue with him. Not that he could ever be violent toward a woman, but in the heat of an argument, he also knew he'd not had the best role models on how to go about such matters. The risk was too high.

He stood at the Faro table with Lord Lancaster and two other gentlemen he'd never met before, ready to lose blunt if it meant he'd forget the jewel out on the dance floor.

He would take out his frustrations here instead of with Lady Mary, where if he were able, he'd give her the first proper kiss she craved, and enjoy every blasted moment of it too.

CHAPTER 8

M ary left the ballroom after dancing with as many gentlemen as the time allowed before supper was called. With everyone taking repast in the dining room, she took the opportunity to leave for a moment's peace.

While she'd enjoyed the gentlemen who paid court to her this evening, Lord Fairchild in particular, the very one whom she'd hoped to dance with most had been absent.

She walked past the library and glancing inside could not see the Duke of Carlton anywhere. So where was he? He'd not come back into the ballroom after she'd seen him during her first dance, and after settling her mama down in the dining room for supper she knew he hadn't crept in there either.

Mary checked the usual haunts that gentlemen ventured to during such balls and parties, but the billiard room was empty and so too was the conservatory, so he wasn't having a midnight tryst with anyone.

The idea made the pit of her stomach clench. She pushed the image aside, not wanting to imagine the duke with anyone. She paused at the threshold of a small parlor that was rarely used during the winter months due to its position and lack of sunlight throughout the day.

At least in here she could have a moment alone and regain her composure and remind herself that if she had set her cap for the duke it was only because he'd been so kind to her after finding her in distress over Lord Weston.

A gentleman such as he would never look at a woman such as herself. He was her friend, yes, but she was deluding herself if she thought anything further could come of that friendship.

Mary pushed open the door and the slither of light from the passage illuminated the lone figure sitting on the chaise staring at the unlit hearth before him.

"Your grace," she said, coming into the room and closing the door. "Is everything well? You're sitting in here in the dark."

He turned and watched her; his dark hooded eyes hard to read in the shadowy room that was only somewhat illuminated by the moonlight coming in through the windows.

"You should not be in here alone with me, Mary."

His voice sounded annoyed and she bit her lip. Maybe they were not friends after all, and she'd imagined wrong when she thought they were.

"Apologies, your grace. I shall leave you." She turned for the door, hating the fact that her eyes smarted with rejection.

"Wait," he said as her hand clasped the door handle.

Mary turned but didn't venture to speak.

He stood, watching her with an intensity that sent a shiver of awareness down her spine. Just as it did when she was dancing earlier with Lord Fairchild and she'd caught the duke watching her. He looked displeased seeing her then and she couldn't help but wonder at it. Couldn't help but hope that it might mean he didn't like seeing her dance with anyone but himself.

The duke ran a hand over his jaw, seemingly struggling with some inner turmoil.

"Have you received your proper kiss yet?"

She started, having not expected him to voice such a question to her. "Would you care or even wish to know if I had, your grace? Do you not have other concerns more taxing on your mind than whether I've been kissed or not?"

"It ought to not concern me," he said, with a disgruntled air. "But it does."

What did that mean? Mary walked slowly toward the duke. She couldn't gauge his mood, but the way he stood before her, as if he were almost scared of her and would take flight at any moment, made her bolder than she'd normally be.

"To answer your question, no, I have not kissed anyone, but the night is young, and I seem to have caught the attention of a few eligible gentlemen this evening. Maybe my luck is changing," she teased.

His grace frowned.

"You would throw yourself at anyone?"

Mary gasped. "Excuse me?" she said, shocked that he'd say such a thing to her. She wasn't a wanton hussy. "Jealousy does not suit you, your grace." The moment the words left her lips she regretted them. Of course he wasn't jealous, he was merely looking out for his friend's sister. Didn't wish for her to make a spectacle or fool of herself.

He stepped closer and his chest brushed hers. Mary licked her lips, liking the feel of him touching her there. Perhaps there was a part of her that wanted to act a little wild, rail against the cage of conformity that she was obliged to abide in life.

Her love of the outdoors, doing things only men would normally take part in and should not exclude the fairer sex. Why should women always do as they're told, toe the line and behave? Not cause a scandal. Why couldn't her husband love her with a passion that suited her spirit?

"If I were to kiss you, Lady Mary, I fear that I should ruin all future kisses you should receive from other suitors, or even that of your future husband."

His words spiked her temper and boldly she lifted her hand, running it down the lapel of his coat. The superfine material was soft to the touch, and yet beneath it lay a bed of hardness, a beating heart that even she could feel was racing beneath her palm.

"Perhaps it will be I who'll ruin all future kisses for you, your grace. I may be an untried miss, but I'm a quick study."

ॐ

DALE STARED down at the little hellion before him, her sweet face beguiled, tempting him like no other had before and he ground his teeth, wondering if he should kiss her and damn well prove his point that she'd never have a better instruction in the art with anyone else. He leaned down, but a feather separating their lips. This close she smelled as divine as she looked, a tempting little morsel just waiting to be gobbled up.

"Would you like me to kiss you, Mary?" He used her given name and didn't miss the pleasure that flooded her face.

Her hand, that was still lodged firmly on his chest, slid up over his shoulder to wrap about his neck. The action brought her up hard against his chest, and through the thin silk of her gown all her delectable womanly assets pressed against him.

Her action robbed him of the opportunity to shock her a little, make her turn and run out of here. Instead, she'd met his taunt and upped the stake with a move that left him reeling.

Dale instinctively wrapped his arm about her waist, settling her snug against him and catching her gaze, now heavy with need and expectation, there was little left in him to refuse her wish.

He sealed his lips against hers, but she didn't kiss him back, and her innocence in taking part in such pastimes should've been like a dose of cold water, that had him setting away and keeping her safe.

She was a maid after all. Untried and his best friend's sister. A woman who should've been well and truly off limits.

His wits however, had other ideas.

Instead, he clasped her jaw, tilting her face to meet his kiss better and tempted her with small, soft brushes of his lips against hers. She opened on a sigh and he took the opportunity to delve between her lips, touching her tongue with his.

A sound of utter pleasure emanated from her and he groaned as she mimicked his actions, her own tentative tongue sliding against his.

"Damn it, Mary," he muttered, clasping her jaw with both hands. He stared at her, beseeching her to run. She licked her bottom lip and all sense fled. Muffling a curse, he took her lips again and kissed her. Hard. She met his onslaught head-on, a quick study she certainly was, and her ability to take charge, turn the tables on him and send him reeling when she nipped his lip with a teasing air coiled heat through his veins.

And then she was gone, wrenching herself out of his arms and staring at him with confusion. Her eyes were large and round, her breasts heaving with each breath. Dale glanced at her lips, bruised and swollen from their kiss and his need doubled. She was a temptress and he wanted her. So. Damn. Much.

He wasn't sure what was going through her mind, but whatever it was sent her packing and she ran from the room. Dale swore, running a hand through his hair. He'd overstepped his mark, perhaps even insulted her. As for what Peter would say to him if he found out...

"Shit," he muttered, striding to the door.

Dale returned to the ball, and keeping to the edges of the room, he spied Mary with her friend, both of them chatting amicably within a small group of men and women both. He studied her a moment, relieved to see she'd not fallen into a fit of the vapors, if anything, she seemed alight with color, her cheeks reddened and her lips still a little swollen from their kiss.

He let out a relieved sigh. He would ask her to dance and ensure she wasn't upset with him and to confirm she was well. After all, they had become somewhat friends the past few days and he would hate his lapse in gentlemanly behavior to sever that.

"How fetching Lady Mary is this evening. What say you, old boy," Lord Weston said, siding up to him, his gaze fixed on Mary.

"Lady Mary always looks well no matter what day it is." Dale didn't like the fact that the man was so vain that his eye was only turned when a woman was up to his standards. Not that Dale was totally innocent of that charge either, he'd certainly thought Mary's wardrobe could do with a little updating.

Lord Weston threw him a curious glance before saying,

"I wanted to apologize for the other day how you and Lady Mary found me and Lady Hectorville in a certain state of *déshabillé*. Not my finest moment, but, well, she is a vixen as you well know."

Dale understood what he was saying about her ladyship and her bed sport, but the simple fact that she often shared her bed with many and was never tied to one man soon made it clear to Dale that he could not carry on a liaison with her. He didn't share well, never had, not even as a child.

"It is probably wise that you cease such activity under Lord Lancaster's roof. I don't believe he'd be pleased if he heard Lady Mary was submitted to such an education."

Lord Weston paled at Dale's words and he inwardly laughed. Good. He wanted the fop to feel uneasy. He'd certainly made Mary so.

"Mary won't say anything, she's in love with me, you know. Tried to kiss me the other evening." Lord Weston glanced at Mary now dancing with Lord Fairchild again, and his eyes narrowed in thought. "Maybe I should let her try again and see where it takes us."

Dale fisted his hands at his side. A cold chill swept down his spine and he turned to face the little snot. "You meddle with her and I'll meddle with you. Do you understand?" His voice brooked no argument and was laced with deadly promise.

"What is it to you what I do with Lady Mary?" Lord Weston smirked. "It's not like you wish to court her. Hell, no one has these past five Seasons. She doesn't know this, but we dubbed her Ribbon Rebellion, being so fond of such adornments on her gown and that she's a bit of an unorthodox chit when it comes to society's expectations for her sex. What a laugh we had of it and she was never the wiser. Even Peter had no idea and we even mentioned the name right under his nose." His lordship laughed.

Dale clocked him one in the nose and watched with great satisfaction as he fell like an old, rotten oak, landing on his arse on the parquetry floor. The music stopped and guests standing nearby gasped as Lord Weston tumbled to the ground, blood spurting from his nose and dripping down onto his perfectly tied cravat and waistcoat.

"What the hell do you think you're doing, Carlton?" he said, his voice muffled behind his hands.

Dale leaned over him, pulling out his handkerchief and dropping it on Lord Weston's chest. "Knocking you on your arse just as you deserve. Speak again in front of me, or anywhere else about Lady Mary," he said, lowering his voice, "and you'll get another one."

He walked off, heading for the terrace where he needed to cool off. Five minutes out in the crisp, winter air was just what he needed. Distantly he heard Peter call out for the music to commence and looking over his shoulder he watched as Lady Hectorville helped Lord Weston to his feet, even if the blaggard threw off her support once he stood.

What an ass.

Dale reached the end of the terrace and looked out over the gardens covered in snow, a smile spreading across his face. What fun that was, and not a more deserving bastard was ever on the receiving end of such a blow. It would certainly give the gossips some fodder during the break in the Season and possibly into the new one. Unless another scandal broke before that.

He started when a small gloved hand wrapped about his. He didn't need to turn to know who was beside him.

MARY CLASPED the duke's hand and came to stand before him. He was upset, that was obvious. One only had to look at Lord Weston's swelling nose to know the punch the duke had afforded him had been no light touch.

"What happened?" she asked, not wanting to bother with small talk. She'd seen the duke and Lord Weston talking as she danced and had not missed Lord Weston's amused smirk at her as he talked with his grace. Something told her his lordship's bloody nose had something to do with her.

He stared down at her, and a ripple of heat, not due to the brisk outside air, stole across her skin at his intense gaze. Instead of answering her, he clasped her jaw and took her lips in a searing kiss.

She melted into him, having thought of nothing else from the moment she'd left him earlier in the night. To stay, to kiss the duke was all that she'd wanted to do, but by doing so she courted scandal. Her parents expected her to always show decorum, but she'd never been very good at that, so a stolen kiss or two couldn't hurt surely.

And it did not. It didn't hurt at all. The kiss went on, his mouth hot and insistent against hers, the slight roughness from the stubble on his face marking her skin. Mary wanted to feel more of him. She reached around, wrapping her hands on the inside of his coat, the corded muscles on his back, flexing as he held her close.

She gasped as a hardness pushed against her abdomen. Her stomach clenched. Mary stood on her tiptoes and pressed against him to where she ached most, undulated her hips to feel him better. The duke moaned, hoisting her higher, one hand reaching down to lift her leg around his hip. The cold stone of the balustrade met her bottom as he angled her over the railing, using its support to press harder against her core.

Relentlessly he rubbed against her and it was too much and yet not enough. Liquid heat pooled between her legs and she gasped through the kiss as his actions teased and taunted her toward a pinnacle she could not reach.

A loud, barking laugh from inside made them start and the duke stepped back, looking over his shoulder to ensure they were still alone. They were, and Mary wanted nothing more than to be there. To be alone with the duke and see where that delectable little action would eventually lead.

"Apologies, Lady Mary. I'm heartily ashamed of myself."

Mary couldn't stop her lips from twitching at his embarrassment. She wasn't embarrassed at all. Curious and aching yes, but embarrassed, absolutely not.

She came up to him, running one hand across his jaw. "I'm not," she said, walking back toward the terrace doors and leaving the duke shocked and still behind her.

The words that she wanted to kiss the duke again should shock her, but all she felt right at this moment was expectation. She liked him, more than she'd thought she would and ever since she'd run into him in the conservatory in all truthfulness, she'd hardly thought about Lord Weston.

Oh yes, she may have told the duke she wanted his lordship to kiss her, but that was really only because the duke didn't wish her to. Only one gentleman occupied her mind and he was on the terrace where she'd left him. She'd not thought to meet a man that not only showed interest in her life, the things she loved to do, but also listened, not just nodding and agreeing for propriety's sake.

Oh no, now that she'd had a small taste of what his grace could do to her, he wasn't going to escape that easily. And with a few days left of the house party, she would have to come up with a plan to make him lose such steadfast control about her again and kiss her some more. The idea flittered through her mind that the duke might ask for her hand and nerves pooled in her belly. She bit her lip, not wanting to give rise to hope when realistically a few stolen kisses did not mean he would offer marriage. Even so, the thought of spending more time with his grace, of kissing him yet again made excitement thrum through her veins. What a wonderful thought indeed.

CHAPTER 9

O ver the next few days Dale fought to keep his
distance from Lady Mary, but everywhere he
turned she seemed to be there. Her newfound popularity
ensured a bevy of gentlemen guests always surrounded her.
Her smile and intelligent conversations about politics,
horses or fishing, had kept them coming back for more,
and there was little doubt in his mind that come next
Season she would be snatched off the marriage mart
merry-go-round that so many got stuck on.

He sat on a chaise longue, reading the latest news from
London. The snow was falling heavily and it was
Christmas Eve meaning everyone was indoors, keeping
themselves occupied with cards or music. Earlier that day
Dale had played a game of billiards with Peter, but the
arrival of Lord Weston, his nose still bruised from the
other evening, soon meant he'd excused himself.

The little popinjay had not taken his warning to heart
and continued to seek out Lady Mary at any opportunity.
No doubt just to vex Dale, and vexing him, it most
certainly was.

Dale looked over the top of his paper and watched Lord Weston enter the front parlor. Mary was busy reading a book in a nearby chair. It was only the two of them, and she'd tucked her legs beneath her gown like she had done in the hunting lodge. A relaxed pose that he would assume a married couple might have if relaxed within each other's company.

Lord Weston sat across from her, and Dale watched as she settled herself in a more appropriate fashion, talking politely to his lordship, but if Dale was any judge of character, he would guess her interest had cooled toward his lordship.

She glanced at him and his suspicions were confirmed. The heat and determination he read in her eyes were all for him, and not the dandy sprouting on about waistcoats before her.

If Lord Weston noticed her inattention he didn't seem to say, just continued to speak as if he had a captive audience.

Dale's lips twitched. How wrong he was.

Not for anything could he tear his gaze away. The more he looked, the more he wanted to see of her, not just across the room, but elsewhere too. Someplace quiet, private and alone. Asleep on his bed would also do very well.

Peter stood before him, cutting off his view. Dale started and looked up, schooling his features. His friend stared down at him with something akin to annoyance and Dale gritted his teeth. "Morning Peter," he said, folding his paper and setting it on his lap.

"We need to talk."

His friend's concerned tone made him frown. "Sit and tell me what is troubling you."

Peter did as Dale asked and he gave his friend his full

attention. "Lord Weston has asked Father if he may court Mary."

Dale sat up, fury spiking through him at the audacity of the man after he'd told him to stay the hell away from her.

"I have not forgotten your warning about him, and I told my parents of your concern, but they're adamant that Lord Weston is genuine and whatever you saw his lordship and Lady Hectorville doing was wholly innocent."

Dale swore. "Peter, your sister caught them in a compromising position, not I. I merely was the messenger. She cannot marry him; he'll never be faithful to her and she deserves so much more than that."

Peter's mouth pulled into a thin, disapproving line. "I agree. We must help her find a gentleman who is suitable." His friend turned to him. "Do you have any ideas?"

Dale pulled at his cravat, the warmth of the room making him sweat. "No-one present. I think she needs to have her Season next year and see if there are any more suitable gentlemen who pay court to her." He paused, glancing at her. Lord Weston had shuffled closer to her person. If he moved any closer, he'd be sitting on Mary's lap.

"If your parents will not listen, we'll have to ensure Lord Weston gets the message loud and clear to stay away. He'll end up giving her a disease."

Peter's eyes flew wide and he gasped. "Surely you jest."

Dale shrugged, partly wondering why he was so set on Lady Mary not being married to such a bastard. What was it to him whom she married? So long as she was happy with her choice, he really didn't have much say in the matter. But to think of her married to another, to share her bed, to have her bestow delectable kisses to anyone but him… He glared at Lord Weston, not appreciating the thought.

"I do not. With the amount of bed-fellows he's had, it'll only be matter of time before she has the pox."

Peter stood, and Dale watched as Mary's brother marched up to Lord Weston asking him to a game of billiards. Dale picked up his newspaper, feigning reading as he listened to the conversation. That Peter had surmised that if he kept Lord Weston away from Mary that would ensure the chap would not court her.

It was basic in concept, but could work, especially if Dale helped him with that endeavor. He smiled knowing he'd enjoy hindering Lord Popinjay from being able to pay court to Mary.

A lone finger pulled his paper down and Dale looked up to see Mary standing before him. Her gown had a pretty light green floral pattern over it. It was summery in appearance, but with the long sleeves and green shawl it was suitable for the cold time of year.

"Lady Mary," he drawled, his body alerting to the fact that she was so close to him. Her hand picked up his paper and tossed it on the seat beside him. She leaned down, placing her hands on either side of his head, pushing him back into the cushion.

"What are you and my brother up to? Lord Weston was trying to court me and you should know I was enjoying it very much."

"As if you could marry such a man."

She raised one brow, a small grin on her lips. "No, of course not, but I was enjoying watching you dislike his courting. That, your grace, was worth the few minutes in his presence."

Dale reached out, running a finger down the small hollow at the front of her throat, tracing it down between her breasts, which at this angle, spilled a little over the front of her gown. He bit back a groan, itching to spread his hand over her soft silken skin, tease the sweet nipples to hardened peaks beneath her dress.

"Don't push me, Lady Mary. You may not like the outcome."

She chuckled, leaning down further to kiss him softly on the lips. He didn't move for fear of ripping her down on the seat beside him and finishing what they'd started the other night. The memory of her pliant body, willing and enjoying him on the terrace filled his mind and his body hardened. They were in the front parlor damn it; anyone could come in at any moment. He glanced quickly toward the door and clenched his hands at his side when he realized it was open.

"Maybe I'd like the outcome," she said, running a finger over his bottom lip before standing up and severing all contact. The instant she was gone he missed her touch. He swallowed, completely at a loss as to how he was to handle the little vixen. Never had he met a woman who threw the rules of society aside to walk her own special path through life.

He was utterly beguiled.

Giving him another saucy smile at the door, she turned and left the room. He stared after her, his heart racing in his chest as if he'd been taking part in strenuous exercise.

If only he were, and with Lady Mary, now that would make an enjoyable afternoon.

☙❧

LATER THAT NIGHT Mary stood speaking with Louise in the upstairs drawing room, a sprig of mistletoe in her hand. She would not normally be so bold as to carry around the little plant that would allow her to kiss anyone she choose, but she was determined to further acquaint herself with the duke.

He was simply too irresistible to ignore, and she wanted to feel all that he made her feel the other night.

"If your mama finds out that you're wishing to steal a kiss from the Duke of Carlton she'll have your head on a platter and serve it for supper. You know they're already irritable with you not making a match last Season."

"That was by choice, Louise. If I had wished for an offer I could've showed two gentlemen that I can think of off the top of my head who would've furthered their acquaintance with me, but it was not what I wanted." In fact, Mary had done everything in her power to thwart suitors. One could not give her heart to a man who was only interested in what you brought to the marriage. That was not who Mary was. She wanted to be able to converse with the man she married, to be on equal footing within their home. If she could not have such outside the walls of her house, then she would damn well have it within it.

"And now you wish the duke to further his acquaintance?" Louise searched her gaze, a small frown upon her brow.

Mary shrugged. "I don't know what I want from the duke, another kiss would be nice," she said, teasing Louise a little. "He's different from anyone I've ever met before I suppose. He doesn't ridicule me for my likes and he actually talks to me, no one ever really talks to you in London or listens for that matter. The gentlemen make out they do, but they really do not."

"And the duke does?" Louise asked, grinning.

Mary nodded. "He does, and it doesn't hurt that his kisses are very nice too." Left her aching in places she didn't even know could ache. She wanted to feel that again.

"You're too wild, Mary." Her friend shook her head, an amused smirk across her lips. "Whatever will your family do with you?"

Mary laughed. "Nothing or perhaps they could lock me up in a convent abroad I suppose, but Papa would never allow that. As much as they may despair at my independent ideas and hobbies, they would never break my heart by punishing me for them."

"That is true." Louise nodded toward the door. "The duke has arrived."

She cast a glance in his direction and watched as he entered with her brother by his side. The two made a striking pair. The duke with his dark hair and coloring and her brother who was all blond and angelic. Both had reputations about London however, the duke more than anyone. A gentleman every debutante wanted and yet none had managed to turn his gaze.

Until now…

He met her stare across the room as they made their way into the throng of guests and the place behind her breast fluttered. Mary watched as he stood beside her brother, quiet and watchful of the room, her more than most, and she couldn't help but wonder what if. What if she was the one to turn the duke's gaze to her and only her. Forever.

Would he make her give up her love of freedom, her desire to do as she wished whenever she chose, her hobbies outside the ballroom. Would he be like so many of the gentlemen of the *ton* who only saw their wives as trophies to be admired, exalted and boasted about, but never anything else.

The thought left her cold and she twisted the

mistletoe in her fingers, wondering if she should simply stop teasing the duke and leave him well alone. As it was, the kiss she bestowed on him only yesterday in the drawing room had been a risk, and had her parents or brother walked in and seen her actions the duke would already be her husband. The kiss on the terrace was worse with the ball taking place right beside them. But surely a gentleman who took an interest as he did was not so backward in thinking. Surely he would not wish her to change.

"He appears to watch you a great deal, Mary."

Mary turned and threw the piece of mistletoe into the fire behind them, before sitting on the settee before the hearth. She smiled at Louise. "He's simply watching to make sure Lord Weston does not try and court me. Do not read into his attention any more than that."

"I think you may be wrong about that," Louise said, sitting also. Mary fidgeted with her gown and fought not to look in his direction. An impossibility almost.

Mary set out to enjoy the night of impromptu dancing some of the guests took part in, supper, games and cards. Her mother had ordered made her favorite desserts of lemon cake and ices. Her father wore his silly Christmas hat that had little elves sewn onto it and her mother's festive gown was the deepest shade of red with small sprigs of holly sewed about the hems.

It was times like these with her family that she loved the most, and her eyes smarted that if she married, it would no longer just be the four of them. She would leave to spend such times with her new husband. The gentleman might choose to spend Christmas alone or with his own family. Everything would change.

Out the corner of her eye she watched as the duke sat in a seat across from her and Louise. He crossed his long legs, leaning back in the chair and waited. It reminded Mary of a lion before it pounced on its prey.

The heat of his gaze bore into her until she couldn't take it any longer and she looked at him. He glanced at her with an air of boredom and heat rose on her cheeks at the memory of their time on the terrace. She swallowed, hoping he'd assume the fire had made her warm and not him.

"Did you know that you're sitting under a sprig of mistletoe, Lady Mary?"

Mary looked up to see a row of holly and mistletoe had been strung across the room's ceiling directly above where she sat. She cringed. "I did not," she said in a tone that she hoped conveyed boredom and not hope. Louise chuckled and tried to mask it with a cough.

"I'm going to talk to your mama for a moment. I'll be back soon, Mary," she said, standing and leaving her alone with the duke.

Mary fidgeted with her hands in her lap, her attention snapping back to the duke. His eyes ran over her person and she shivered at the heat that banked in his gaze. Desire rushed through her, hot and impatient and she closed her eyes a moment to gain some semblance of control. She shouldn't want to kiss him again, but little else had occupied her mind since they'd done it last. She was turning into a veritable wanton.

How could she ever remain a spinster, a wallflower if she hankered for his touch, his mouth on hers and everything else that he could give her?

"Lord Weston isn't sitting with me, so why are you, your grace?" she asked.

He leaned forward, running a hand over his jaw. He looked up at her and a piece of his hair fell across his eye. It made him look even more wicked than normal and her stomach fluttered. "That, Lady Mary, I have been asking myself and I cannot fathom as to why."

She raised her brow, having not expected him to be so honest. The way he was looking at her, as if she were the tastiest morsel in the room made her question her priorities. She licked her lips, wondering yet again if he would be the type of man who'd ask his wife to change who she was for the sake of the title, of what was expected by the *ton*.

Mary couldn't abide by such a life if that was what he wished. Not that the duke was looking to marry her, but from the hunger she read in his eyes, he was certainly after something.

"Really?" Mary cast a glance about the room, seeing that they were quite alone. "I think I do."

He leaned back in his chair, a grin on his delectable lips that she wanted him to ravish her with. "Do tell," he said, matter of fact.

Never one not to be honest or talk bluntly she studied him a moment. "I think you're here because you want to be. I think you're here because you want to kiss me again," she whispered. "And I think you're here because you are trying to work out why that is the case."

His eyes narrowed, his features cooling a little at her words. "While I will admit that your kiss was very…enjoyable, I'm merely here to keep Lord Weston from approaching you. The cad can find someone else to ruin, it won't be you."

But maybe it'll be you instead… Mary bit her lip, a part of her wanting Lord Weston to enter, to court and make a fuss of her, if only to set off the duke's ire. "If I married Lord Weston I'd always live near my childhood home. I could continue on as I always have in Derbyshire. His lordship could come and go as he pleases and so too could I." Mary leaned forward, knowing she was giving him a little glimpse of her assets. "Perhaps you ought to leave so he can continue his courtship of me. I'm not immune to staying in Derbyshire."

All lies, she was totally immune to Lord Weston's charms, certainly after she saw what he was doing with Lady Hectorville and after she'd kissed the man who sat across from her. The duke's gaze darkened further, and she schooled her features, not wanting him to know she could read him like a book.

CHAPTER 10

D ale took a calming breath, not sure if he wanted to shake a little sense into the maddening chit or kiss her senseless. Both, he assumed would do equally well. He'd promised Peter he would keep Mary out of Lord Weston's clutches, but it was another thing entirely to keep her out of his own.

True, she drove him mad, vexed him often with her sharp tongue, and kissed like she'd been taking part in such actions for years, not days. The memory of her in his embrace haunted him nightly, and he'd taken his gentle-manly needs into his own hands. Literally.

He cleared his throat. "You do not need to make any hasty decisions; you have next Season still to attend." Dale drank in the vision of her. The moment he'd seen her tonight, her golden silk gown and emerald necklace gave her a festive air, and his gut had clenched at the beauty she was.

How had he not seen it under all those ribbons and bows. He could only fathom that she'd done all that she could to remain invisible when in Town. That was no longer the case. No gentleman in attendance was unaware of Lady Mary's presence, and the admiring glances, the attention she'd had bestowed on her these past days was proof of that.

Next year she would find a gentleman who suited her and she would marry him.

The thought left him cold.

"If I made my decision now, I would not have to attend London next year. I could stay in Derbyshire." She picked up her glass of wine that sat on a small table beside her chair and took a sip. She met his eyes over the rim of the glass, and he could read the amusement in her green orbs.

What are you playing at minx…?

"And now that you've taught me how to kiss, what sort of passions I would like in a husband, Lord Weston may be open to my eligibility. Lady Hectorville is after all a lot older than himself. I think I'm more suited to him in age."

Anger simmered in Dale's blood and he fisted his hands in his lap. "You would kiss Lord Weston if given the opportunity?"

"Of course," Lady Mary said, shrugging one delicate shoulder. "I kissed you, did I not? I'm three and twenty, more than old enough to know a little of what is to come should I marry. And I must admit that I find kissing very…" she pursed her lips and his body hardened. "Nice."

Dale ground his teeth, having heard enough of Mary kissing anyone she deemed suitable. "Just because Lord Weston is your neighbor here does not make him a suitable candidate. I will not allow you to throw yourself at him."

She stood, and he sat forward as she strode toward him, walked past and ran her hand up his lapels to his shoulder. His body roared with annoyance. She had not agreed to his terms. To her brother's wishes. "You cannot stop me, your grace."

The hell he couldn't. He stood and stormed after her. He followed her into a nearby corridor that ran off the library, it was unlit and the bare wooden floors gave rise to it only being used by servants.

"I will tell your brother what you're playing at, so I can stop you, Lady Mary."

She rounded on him, pushing him hard up against the wall. He stared at her a moment, not quite believing she'd manhandled him in such a way, before all thought fled from his mind when he realized her hand was running down his chest to run across his stomach.

He lay his head back against the wall, watching her take her fill of his body, wishing that her hand would delve lower and wrap about his aching cock.

"Should I tell my brother what you did to me over the terrace railing, your grace? How you made me ache. How you made me crave things I don't even understand? If I'm willing to throw myself at Lord Weston it all could be laid at your door?"

"How so?" he rasped, his voice laced in agony.

"Because," she said, her hand running about his waist to drop lower and cover one cheek of his arse, squeezing it a little. Her lips were just a breath away from his. She smelled of wine and spices. Dale kept his hands locked at his side knowing that if he placed them on her, there would be no turning back with what he wanted to do with her.

"At night the pleasure you wrought inside of me is all that I think about. I want to have that again, and if Lord Weston marries me, then I can have that and everything else as well. My life here as it's always been."

"You do not need to marry to find pleasure." Dale cursed his words, but he could not regret saying them. He wanted her. Wanted to taste and kiss every morsel of her body. Wanted her to shatter under his ministrations.

"And just as you instructed me in the art of kissing, you'll instruct me in that art as well?"

"Hell yes," he said, slamming his mouth against hers. She gasped, and kissed him back with as much fire, as much need as his own. His body was aflame, hot and wanting. He broke the kiss, ignoring her moan of displeasure and looked about. Seeing a door nearby, he pulled her toward it, opening it to find a storeroom housing linen.

Dale yanked her inside, closing the door and snipping the lock.

Before he'd turned back to her, she'd clasped his face and pulled him in for a kiss. A small part of him thought that she'd vexed him on purpose, brought on such a reaction from him. But right at this moment, he didn't care. All he cared for was that she was in his arms and his to have.

He backed her up toward a small table and lifting her quickly he sat her atop it. For a moment he watched her, both of their breathing was ragged, her breasts rising and falling with each intake of air. In the meagerly lit room, her golden gown was a beacon. Her leg idly swung, her silk slipper falling to the floor and he bit back a groan, knowing what he was about to do to her could never be undone.

Dale kneeled, slipping her other foot free of her shoe. He ran his hand up her long, soft stockinged leg reaching up until he felt the ribbon about her garter. Untying it, he slipped one and then the other off her leg, unable to stop himself from leaning forward and kissing her inner thigh, her knee, her sweet, delicate ankle.

Her fingers spiked through his hair, and he looked up, meeting her gaze. Her eyes were wide, hungry, her face flushed with anticipation and perhaps a little discomfiture.

She had no reason to be so. He'd never do anything to hurt or embarrass her.

He gathered the hem of her gown and slowly slid it up her legs and prayed she would not stop him.

MARY SHOOK ALL OVER, her body thrumming with expectation and wonder over what the duke was about to do to her. She had goaded and teased him into acting out in such a way, but the idea she could find pleasure without losing her innocence was an opportunity she would never pass up.

He pushed her legs apart, leaving her vulnerable, and causing her to lean back on her hands. Heat bloomed on her cheeks but she could not look away, for she was mesmerized by what he was doing to her. He bestowed an open mouth kiss on her inner thigh, hot and wet. The action was so private, a ministration that she'd never thought a man would ever do to a woman. Mary gasped, biting her lip, uncertain of what he meant to do from this point on.

"Lie back," he commanded, his voice a gravelly purr. The duke stood and pushed her to lay flat on the table. A stack of linens lay beneath her head and she gasped as cool air kissed higher on her leg, before her gown pooled at her waist.

His large hands slid over her abdomen, her thighs, before pushing her legs further apart. His hot breath above her most private of places warmed her, and then he was there, his mouth, his tongue, teasing, flicking and kissing her as he had against her mouth.

Mary reached down, clasping his hair, holding him to her and pushing away the little voice that shouted at her to stop. That this was not appropriate or becoming for a lady. But she no longer cared. All she cared was that his mouth was on her and whatever he was doing to her felt so perfectly delicious.

He clasped the underside of her legs and lifted them to sit on his shoulders. Pushing forward, he flicked her with his tongue, before she felt him run a finger down over her core, teasing her entrance.

Mary moaned having never felt anything so wickedly good before in her life.

"You taste so damn sweet," he said, meeting her gaze as he pressed one finger slowly into her.

She bit her lip, wanting to scream at the pleasure of his touch. Instead she clenched around his finger, milking it and wishing there was another part of him that could fill and inflame her.

He teased her relentlessly for some minutes. It was all too much, but not enough. And then she was there, a pinnacle worth the climb and one she wanted to fall from again and again.

She gasped as pleasure coursed through her, and all the while the duke did not let up. He continued to pull and tease every last drop of bliss from her he could. Her muscles felt spent and weak and she sighed, smiling a little as he stood and helped right her gown, her stockings and the silk slippers that had fallen onto the floor.

"You look positively ravished."

Mary sat up, leaning on her elbows. "And you, your grace look like you're in pain." She sat all the way up, flattening out her gown and checking that her hair was reasonably tidy. Running a hand over his jaw, she touched his lips, heat coursing through her with the knowledge of what they could do to her.

She shook her head. "I had no idea that a man's mouth could be so very clever."

He smiled, chuckling and stepping between her legs, his hardened member hard up against her own sex. She clutched at his lapels, fire coursing through her once again.

"You might be surprised just how very clever I am." He kissed her and she could taste her own tartness. Such a thing should revolt her, but instead, she drank him in, loving the fact that he'd held no such remorse in bringing her pleasure while leaving her a maid.

She broke the kiss. "Tell me how I can please you."

His nostrils flared and he stepped back, severing the contact. "It is enough that you did this evening. We need not do any more."

He walked to the door and opened it a little, looking out into the hall. "There is no one about. You should return to the parlor or head to your room. I shall make an appearance and then retire myself."

Mary shuffled off the folding table, checking that the linens behind her were as they had been when they entered the room. She came up to him, trying to gauge what he was thinking. What he thought of her and what they'd done. "Even with what happened in here tonight I do not want you to think that I expect anything from you. Marriage is not an institution that I want unless I'm certain I've chosen correctly, so please do not allow any gentlemanly honor to raise its head and insist that you make an honest woman of me."

Something flickered in his eyes, relief, regret, that she couldn't tell. He leaned down, kissing her lips and the action felt almost final. Like he was drawing a line beneath them and finishing the little liaison in his life.

"I'm glad you do not expect such a thing, Lady Mary, for as you know I also do not wish to be saddled with a wife, not for some time yet. I do not wish to give you false hope of something more even though I should after what I just did to you."

She shivered at the reminder, her body wanting more of him. At least in this respect. "Then we're in agreement," she said, tapping his cheek with the palm of her hand before moving past him and leaving him in the linen closet. Mary started toward her room, not wanting to face anyone, and feeling as though they had both lost a sweet opportunity that was not offered to everyone in life.

Making her room, she entered and shut the door, stifling a yelp when she found Louise sitting on the chair before the fire. "Oh, you're back. I wondered where you got off to. Your mama was looking for you and I said I'd come and check on you thinking you'd be in your room. But you were not." Louise threw her a penetrating stare. "Where were you, Mary?"

Heat flamed her cheeks and for a moment she fought to come up with an idea that would quell her friend's suspicions. But at Louise's knowing stare, she knew it was pointless. Louise had always been able to read her like a book.

"I was with the Duke of Carlton. In a linen closet. Alone."

Louise's eyes flared in alarm, her mouth gaping like a fish out of water. "And were you talking to the duke in this closet?"

Mary sat across from her, pulling her legs up beneath her gown. "Oh yes we talked a great deal. He in fact used his mouth a lot." Heat infused her face at the memory of his wicked mouth that even now her body craved to feel again.

"Be careful, Mary," Louise said, her tone serious. "Or you'll end up married before the New Year, nevertheless the next Season. I didn't think you wanted a husband at all. Too stifling and controlling for your nature."

All true, husbands had always brought forth an idea of selfish, lazy obnoxious beings who would tell her what to do and when. What to wear and how to act. And yet, the duke had not dismissed her lifestyle, or thought it was unbecoming of a woman. Perhaps the duke, as high and mighty as he was, was in fact not so very stuffy after all. He could perchance be different from all the rest.

"I'm still a maid. There was no indiscretion, Louise, so please stop looking at me so shocked." Well, there was rather a nice one, but nothing that could ruin her since no one knew of it. Some things should remain private, and her rendezvous with the duke was one of them.

"You spoke of marriage with the duke?"

"Well, actually he brought it up, but only to remind me of the fact that he was not looking for a bride any more than I was looking for a groom. So we're quite in agreement on that score."

The thought left a hollow ache beneath her breast. She liked him, more than anyone else before and they were friends. Intimate ones at that.

But would he suit as a husband? Would he allow her to be who she was? Certainly now that she knew what a man could do for a woman, taking a husband wasn't so foreign to her. The duke certainly had been the first man to ever inspire desire within her, and so she would not discount him too soon, even after what they'd both said downstairs.

She shivered, thinking of his touch, his wicked kisses over her body. Perhaps being married would not be so much of a chore after all. Not if they were all like the Duke of Carlton. And not if she were to continue on as she'd always had when not under the condescending gaze of the *ton*.

CHAPTER 11

D ale lay in his bed staring up at the ceiling, the dark winter night as chilled as his own respectability. He should not have touched Mary. Not one strand on her pretty dark-haired head.

His cock stirred at the thought of her beneath him, writhing and grinding herself against his mouth and he groaned. Damn it. He shut his eyes, willing the torturous memory away, and yet it did not. If anything, it became more vivid, tempting him to leave the room, stride to hers and finish what they'd started.

He'd not traveled to Derbyshire to marry a country chit who was too independent and bossy for his nature. He'd always pictured a nice docile woman by his side when the time came, a blonde goddess with angelic features. The harridan that slept only a few doors from his was the antithesis of all that he'd pictured.

And damn she tempted him. More than any had before.

Dale sighed, his body taut with unsated desire. He forced himself to stay where he was, not to move and seek her out. To show her more of what a man and woman could do together without compromising her maidenhead.

A slither of light burst into the room as his door opened, before it was closed just as quick. The snip of the lock had him sitting up.

"Who's there?" he asked, trying to focus his eyes on the figure that moved slowly toward his bed.

He inwardly groaned when he recognized who was present. "You need to leave, Margaret. There is nothing in this bed for you."

She came up onto the mattress, a pouty expression on her lips that made her look absurd and a little desperate. "Come Carlton. Let me love you as you like." Her hand slid over his cock and he pushed her hand away, hating the fact that his body roared for release. But he didn't want Margaret beneath him. He wanted the maddening miss who slept down the hall.

Dale pushed away from her, getting off the bed. He clasped her upper arm, pulling her toward the door. "Out. Before someone sees you in here. What we had is long past and I'm sure there are other gentlemen present at this house party who'll welcome you into their beds."

She glared at him, all seduction gone. "You used to be amusing." He unlocked the door, ushering her out. At her little squeak, he looked up and met the shocked gaze of Mary.

❦

MARY TOOK a couple of steps backward almost stumbling. "I'm sorry. I'm just on my way downstairs. I left the book I was reading in the library earlier today," she babbled, moving past them, pulling her robe closer about her and ignoring Lady Hectorville's giggle and whispered conversation with the duke about being caught.

What the duke said in reply was lost to Mary as she headed downstairs. That she was actually heading to the duke's room when he'd escorted Lady Hectorville from his company was not what she'd expected to see. Grateful she had been saved from her own foolhardiness she headed toward the library. She went into the library and picked up the first book she could find, an old tome on gardening in England's northern lands.

Mary took a moment to calm her heart. She blinked, breathed in a deep breath to try and halt the tears that blurred her vision. This was why she was not suited to be the wife of any gentleman. They were unfaithful, rotten to the core; people who wanted all and everything without a care as to whom they might hurt in their pursuit of pleasure and vice.

The duke could have at least waited a day before stooping so low to invite her ladyship into his bed. "Bastard," she mumbled. That she'd only parted from his company hours before, that he'd had his hands and mouth on her person the same day as her ladyship left a sour taste in her mouth and a dull ache behind her breast.

The door to the library opened and the duke came in, looking about the darkened space searching for her. Mary didn't move from her place beside the door, not in the mood to help his cause in finding her in any possible manner.

He turned and spied her, shutting the door with a snap. "Mary, let me explain."

She moved away from him, pulling her robe tighter about herself as if to protect her heart. "What I saw was more than self-explanatory, your grace."

He strode over to her, his tall, imposing frame dwarfing

her against the bookshelf. "I did not sleep with Lady Hectorville. She came to my room and I told her to leave. What you witnessed was my ousting of her."

Mary looked up into his eyes and in the moonlight saw the determination there to make her believe him. He was a renowned rogue, rumored in London to have many lovers. Finding him in such a compromising position at a house party would not be out of character, but there was something in his tone that gave her pause. Stopped her from accusing him of being a liar.

"Why should I believe you?" she asked, needing him to tell her that she was wrong in her assumptions and he was being honest. "I've heard the rumors about you and Lady Hectorville. That she was once your lover."

"That was a mistake that I made one night when I was in my cups. I have not made the error again. What you saw just now was me kicking her from my room."

"So you forget often what you do when you're drunk. Shows a certain type of fickleness of character, your grace." She shook her head, hating the fact she'd allowed herself to think that there could be a possibility with him. A future. The duke was no different than every other gentleman in the *ton*. Only out for what they could get, whether it be women or blunt. To be married to a man, allow herself to care for someone who might simply imbibe too much one evening and sleep with someone else was not to be borne. She certainly could not stomach such an insult.

His grace sighed, looking up at the ceiling a moment before meeting her gaze. "I was not married, Mary. The tryst hurt no one. When I marry, I will be true to my wife. *Always*."

Mary crossed her arms over her chest, her stomach in knots over what to believe. What she saw or what the duke was telling her. She had gone to his room after tossing and turning in bed thinking of him, wanting to see him again, be with him and see what else he could show her.

Scandalous behavior and not so different from what the duke and many of their set did every night in London during the Season. She held no hope of marrying the man, so to be so offended and upset seemed a silly reaction to have.

That's because you do hold a little hope the duke will ask for your hand…because you care.

Mary pushed the thought aside, dismissing it. "You don't owe me an explanation, your grace. We're not betrothed."

The muscle in his jaw clenched as he stepped toward her. "I need to explain. You need to understand."

"What?" she asked, meeting his gaze. "What do I need to understand?"

He stepped closer still, his warm, muscled body warming her blood. "You need to understand that the only woman I want in my bed is you."

Mary swallowed, clasping the book against her chest as if it were some lifesaving apparatus. Did his grace really mean that?

He glanced down at the tome in her hand. "Where were you off to really? I would be surprised if your reading desires had turned to gardening in the northern climes of a sudden."

She bit her lip, the need to flee, to save herself rode hard on her heels and yet she could not move away. "I find gardening very interesting and engaging." What on earth was she saying!

"Liar," he whispered, leaning down and clasping her cheeks.

Mary nodded. "Yes. That too."

He took her lips in a searing kiss, lifting her quickly to place her on the bookcase shelf behind her.

"You've been haunting my dreams and waking moments, Mary. Only *you*."

That was said with such an edge of frustration she believed him, and something improper inside of her thrilled. His height placed him directly at her core and she melted into his arms. All thoughts of Lady Hectorville fled from her mind, of his roguish ways in Town, all of it. The moment he touched her she knew it was right. What she wanted.

His hand slid down to grapple with the hem of her nightgown, the cool night air kissing her legs as he pushed it to pool at her waist. And this time, she would get what she wanted. Him.

DALE TRIED to rein in his overwhelming need for the woman in his arms, but he could not. And if he were honest with himself, unless she said to stop, he'd do all and anything that she wanted.

"Tell me again," she murmured, a sensual, secretive smile about her lips.

He ground against her core, the memory of her sweet lips making him as hard as stone. "I want you and no one else."

Her fingers spiked through his hair, pulling him close. "Yes." Her whispered word snapped the thin thread that he walked along, the one all gentlemen should to keep them from despoiling virginal women set on husbands. Mary might not be interested in husband hunting right at this moment, but her family certainly was and that in itself should give him pause.

But it did not.

The house was deadly quiet, the falling snow outside masking any exterior sounds, and all he could hear was them. A melody that drove him to part her legs, to tease her flesh with his fingers before fumbling with the front of his pants.

Their movements were desperate, quick and full of need. Her fingers clawed into his shoulders, her body slick and hot, ready and willing for what was to come. Dale kissed her with a fervor that left him breathless, he'd never been so desperate to sheathe himself within a woman before, to lose himself and forget everything that impacted his life.

It was simply Mary and him. No-one else and that was enough.

She begged him, her raspy, seductive tone whispering against his lips and he kissed her, deep and sure as he thrust within her. She stilled in his arms and he held himself motionless a moment, waiting for her to adjust to his size.

"I'm sorry," he said, kissing her cheek, her chin and neck, reaching down to run a hand over her breast and sliding her puckered nipple between his thumb and forefinger. She relaxed in his arms, her hands pulling at him in silent want, and he slowly eased out, before thrusting back within her again.

She moaned his name, an elixir that banked a fire burning within him. He took her, laid claim to her body, the slap of skin hitting skin the only sound in the room. Mary didn't shy away from the ferocious way they came together. Being a maid, they should be on the softness of sheets and bedding, taking his sweet time to teach her how to love, to move and take pleasure. Not this way, hard up against a wooden bookcase, sneaking about in the quiet of the night. Part of him registered the shame of taking her so and he cringed.

"Dale," she gasped, her legs high against his hips. She watched him as he pumped relentlessly into her hot core until at last she lay her head back against the cupboard and let go.

He smothered her cry of release with a kiss, her tight core milking him of his own pleasure. Dale slumped against her, their breathing ragged and his ability to move, to pull out of her and set them to rights lost on him a moment.

Her legs went limp and he pulled back, helping her off the bookcase and to stand. Righting her nightgown and his own breeches which shamefully he'd not even removed, had simply ripped open at the front. He pulled her into a kiss, needing to hold her in his arms, to taste her sweetness on his lips.

The door flew open and they pulled apart as if they'd been burned. Dale steeled himself as the furious Peter and Lord Lancaster stared at him, murder most clearly on their mind.

Dale glanced behind his lordship to the stairs leading to the first floor and didn't miss Lady Hectorville turning toward her room, a self-satisfied smirk on her face.

"You had better have a good explanation as to why you're both down in the library in the middle of the night alone, and why I find you kissing my daughter, Carlton."

Mary snatched up the book on the nearby shelf, holding it against her breast as if it would somehow protect her. No amount of armor would protect them for what was to come.

"I wanted to read and so came down to the library to fetch a book. His grace was helping me decide."

Dale cleared his throat as both Peter and Lord Lancaster threw disbelieving looks at Mary.

The need to protect her roared inside of him and he found himself saying, "Actually, I have asked Mary to be my wife and she's agreed."

Mary let out a little yelp, but he didn't look at her. His lordship gaped at him, and Peter glared. "What have you done to my sister, Carlton?"

He'd never heard his friend speak to him with such deadly ire before, and he clamped his jaw shut. He wasn't a fool and he certainly wasn't going to tell anyone that he'd just shagged Mary within an inch of her life, and damn well enjoyed every delectable moment of it. The thought of marrying her should fill him with regret, with fear and yet it did not. She might test him at times, question his decisions, but surely, she would know how to conform to the role that was required of her as his wife. That he was a duke and she would need to be a true and elegant duchess. Perform her duties and not cause any trouble.

"Nothing, Peter," Mary said. She turned to him, clasping his arm. "Your grace, you do not need to offer simply because we were caught in the library together. A kiss is not such an offence that marriage is the outcome."

He took her hand, wrapping it into his, squeezing it a little when he noticed hers was shaking. "We will be married four weeks from now. The banns may be called. We'll marry here in the drawing room with only close family and friends. Are you in agreement, Lord Lancaster?"

Mary stared up at him, her eyes wide and filled with shock.

"Say yes," he said when she continued to stare at him as if he'd sprouted two heads. "Yes, Mary. Say it," he urged.

Mary turned to her father. "May I have a moment with his grace, please, Papa? I need to speak to him about his proposal."

"Absolutely not," her brother interjected, slicing a finger through the air. "I think you've been alone quite enough already this evening."

Her father pursed his lips thinking over her request. "You may speak to the duke, but we shall be present. We will afford you a little privacy by going to stand before the fire."

Mary waited for her father and brother to move away, before she turned back to Dale, not quite sure how he could seem so calm and in control of himself. She was beyond confused and her heart seemed to be beating louder than a drum in her ears. "Why me, your grace?"

"What do you mean, why me?" He glanced at her clearly confused. "After what just happened, I thought you might be a little relieved rather than questioning my declaration."

Mary frowned, not wanting anyone to marry her out

of obligation. "You know that I wanted to marry someone who, if at all possible, I loved. A man that would allow me to continue in the same vein in which I live now. To remain in the country instead of in Town. You, your grace cannot be that man."

He cleared his throat, and stood taller like a soldier as if he were about to go into battle. "I like you, I think that we will do well enough together. As for how you live, you must understand there will be limitations of course. I'm a duke, when you marry me you'll be a duchess. Your place will be at my side, having said that," he said at her gasp, "that does not mean that we'll always be in Town. We shall return to Carlton Hall regularly, and certainly often enough to sate your desire for the outdoors."

Mary stared at him a moment, lost for words. A week in Town was too much. London had always made her feel out of place. It was simply not who she was. If he forced her, their marriage would not be a happy one. "But that's not what I want. I don't want to be in London most of the time. I want to marry a man who suits me and my character, my likes and dislikes. You do not."

"We do suit. We suited very well not half an hour ago," he whispered.

At his scandalous reminder heat shot across her skin. "Hush, my father will hear. And you know that is not what I mean. If I have to marry, I want to marry a man who prefers the country to Town. You do not and your standing within the *ton* would mean that I would have to be by your side all the time. Never mind the fact that you do not want a wife. I fail to believe that all of a sudden you've had an epiphany and now want a wife."

"I have not had an epiphany, I'm merely doing what is right and you will marry me, Lady Mary. There is no choice. I think you understand as well as anyone the possible repercussions of our meeting earlier tonight."

Oh yes, she understood very well all the repercussions of what had transpired between them. Of being forced into a marriage neither of them wanted, and the possibility that she might fall pregnant. "I'm too opinionated for you. If we were to marry, you would soon tire of me not wishing to follow you to London. I don't want to quarrel with you."

He blanched at the mention of such a thing, and ran a hand through his hair, leaving it on end. "We shall not quarrel if you behave like a duchess, the well-bred young woman that you are, we will get along well enough."

She raised her brows. "I'm not one to be told what to do, your grace." She took a step away, crossing her arms across her chest. "I will not marry you."

"You have no choice."

Mary swallowed the bile that rose in her throat. The thought of being a social matriarch, of hosting and giving balls and soirées left her dizzy with dread. She could not do it. "Everyone has a choice."

Dale turned back toward his lordship and Peter. "It is agreed. One month, my lord, and Lady Mary will be the new Duchess of Carlton."

Her father burst into a smile, clapping his hands. Her brother, however, stared at the duke with deadly ire.

"Congratulations, your grace. Mary darling." Her father shook Dale's hand and pulled Mary into an embrace.

"I wish to talk to the duke," Peter said, not using the duke's given name. An oddity, for Mary had only ever known her brother to use the duke's given name while at home these past weeks.

Her father readily agreed. "Of course. No doubt you

wish to have a toast celebrating the newly engaged couple." He pulled Mary toward the hall. "Come, Mary. Tell me of your wishes for your wedding day." Mary glanced over her shoulder meeting Dale's gaze as they left, so much still left unsaid between them. Did he believe she would not marry him or did he truly think them engaged?

Her father walked her upstairs, discussing how happy this news would make her mother and her throat tightened with panic. This was exactly the situation in which she did not want to find herself and for all the duke's gentleman-like honor, it was not needed here. Not yet at least.

Her father stopped at her bedroom door. "We shall tell your mother together tomorrow. Now," he said, opening her door and ushering her inside. "Off to bed, my dear. The next few weeks will be busy indeed and you need your rest."

Mary stared at the door as it closed. Had they all lost their minds? What about what she wanted, what the duke wanted, what he really wanted. It was not her he really wanted, she was certain of that.

If there was one thing she disliked it was being managed, and she'd been utterly managed this evening. She stomped her foot, and growled at the door. It wasn't to be borne and she would not be marrying anyone unless he loved her enough to allow her to be who she was. *Always*. And it did not escape her that if he had offered a word of love…of some gesture, she would have said yes. The ache in her heart bloomed to encompass her entire body. How could she really consent to marry a man she feared she had fallen so much in love with…but he only *liked* her?

DALE TURNED BACK to Peter after losing sight of Mary and her father. She was shocked, there was no doubt, and probably felt a little managed by him as well. In time he hoped she would thaw to the idea. He was not the type of man to hold anyone back from being who they were, and he would not start now with his wife. Only in society would he expect Mary to abide by society's line.

She would have to be by his side when he went to London, for either the Season or when Parliament resumed, but when they were not obligated to be in Town, the idea of being carefree, home on his estate with Mary made him eager for the first time in as long as he could remember to go home.

He walked over to the decanter of whisky pouring both himself and Peter a glass. He held it out to his friend who followed him and placed it on the sideboard when he didn't venture to take it. "Say it," he said to Peter when he merely stood before him, glaring.

"How could you," Peter said, pointing a finger in his direction and stabbing it at him as if he wished it were a blade. "Did you ruin her? Could you not, out of respect for our friendship, not leave my sister alone. Do you not have enough women to warm your bed that you had to take an innocent, your best friend's sibling?"

Dale raised his chin, hating that Peter's words were true. All of them. He was a cad. Known about London for his many lovers, his wayward nights on the town. But Dale also could admit to himself that his lifestyle no longer satisfied. He was sick of it, weary of keeping up an appearance when in truth his desires had shifted.

Having Mary tonight had been the moment he realized she made him feel complete. Satisfied beyond measure. A niggling of it had occurred when in the linen closet, but being with her fully this evening had proven the point. As much as he'd railed about marriage, he was simply railing against the institution because he'd not found the right woman.

His parents' marriage had been a disaster because there were no feelings between them, other than annoyance and regret. He liked Mary at least, and she was an earl's daughter, not wholly wild at heart. That he'd ruined her came into play. She could be carrying his child, and that alone forced his hand into offering marriage.

"I will be faithful to Mary. You have my word on that. I like your sister very much and her exuberance. She will keep me on my toes." And it would be no hardship to have the little hellion in his bed at night.

Peter threw him a disbelieving look. "I find that hard to believe. You may have been one of my best friends, but should you hurt my sister in any way, I will make you pay."

"I shall not hurt her. On the contrary, I shall try and make her happy." Try and ensure that their home life was a happy one. A peaceful, calm place that they would never bicker in.

"You dislike confrontation, and Mary is the embodiment of all that. She is not a woman to be managed and if you try and force her you will find your marriage one of regret."

The pit of his gut clenched at the thought of having an unhappy marriage. Mary was independent and opinionated. A slither of doubt entered his mind that he'd been hasty in acting the gentleman. But then, being caught kissing after he'd shagged her forced his hand in any case.

"I know you, Carlton, and I know how you suffered in your parents' home. I do not want to find my sister has entered a similar fate as that of your mother."

Dale clenched his jaw. The insinuation from his friend hurt and he took a couple of moments to cool his temper.

"I would never abuse Mary or any woman. How could you think I would?"

"I do not think you would, but she's my sister. My concern stands with her."

Dale stared at Peter as he stormed from the room. Damn it, he didn't want them to fall out over this. He'd broken Peter's trust to be sure, but he would do all that he could to make Mary happy. He might not love her, but many marriages had started out on less solid foundations and survived.

He drank down his whisky and then not wanting to waste the second glass that sat untouched on the sideboard, he drank that down too. All would be well, he was sure of it, and in time he would prove to Mary, Peter, everyone that their misgivings on the match were unfounded.

CHAPTER 13

One month later

Mary stared at herself in the mirror in her bedroom, a bride staring back at her. She took in the dark locks pulled into line by many pins and a pretty veil that sat over the top of her curls, lying softly over her silk and embroidered light blue gown.

After her marriage today she would be the Duchess of Carlton. She stared at herself, her eyes too large it would seem, a frightened tinge to their appearance.

Her stomach roiled at the thought of marrying the duke. She'd not seen him these past four weeks. He'd left Christmas Day after their betrothal announcement stating he needed to return to London to prepare for their marriage and to notify his many estates that they would visit each one during their honeymoon.

She clasped her hands, trying to ignore the excited chatter of her mama and Louise who were in the room with her.

"Mother, I need to see the duke. At once," she said, her voice but a whisper.

"What was that, my darling?" Her mama came over to her, her brow furrowed in concern.

"I need to speak with Dale. Before I marry him. I need to speak with him alone. I will not attend downstairs until I do."

Louise and her mama glanced at each other, a question in both their eyes. Mary took a calming breath, knowing it would not appear well that she was asking for such a thing, but she needed to speak with Dale. Needed to know before she took her vows that he would not expect her to be the perfect duchess that she could never be.

"I will go fetch him," her mama said. Louise came over and clasped her hand, squeezing it a little before too, leaving her alone. Mary went and sat on her bed, waiting for Dale. The heavy, determined footfalls sounded in the hall outside her door and her stomach fluttered knowing she'd see him again.

Her door opened and then he was there. The perfect, magnificent Duke of Carlton that made women's heads turn at every event. If she had to marry at all she could never share him, and to think that their marriage could end as so many *ton* marriages did, with disillusioned couples that tolerated each other but little else would not do for her.

She had never wanted to marry, but to marry without some sort of affection, without some sort of promise that he wouldn't box her into the life of a proper, respectable, biddable wife was no life at all. She'd rather be ruined than suffer such a fate.

DALE REMEMBERED to breathe as he looked upon Mary, whom oddly he'd missed the last month while away in Town. She was so beautiful, so different from the ribbon-and-lace wallflower that he'd met prior to Christmas.

The woman who sat before him was poised, elegant, a true duchess, but the glint of independence, or rebellion flickered in her green eyes and gave him pause.

"You look beautiful Mary," he said, coming over to her. She stood, meeting his gaze with an unflinching strength that he admired. "You wanted to see me?"

She clasped her hands before her, biting her lip and his body hardened at the sight. He'd missed her, not just her lively conversations and blunt, to the point opinions, but also he'd missed being with her. Alone.

"I wanted to talk to you about us. About what you expect from me as your wife."

Dale sat on the bed, pulling her down to do the same. He took her hand, unable to stop himself from rubbing his thumb across the inside of her wrist. His ministrations brought a delightful flush to her cheeks and all he wanted to do was to kiss her. To take her into his arms and prove to her, that whatever concerns she might have about them, they were not warranted.

Over the past month he'd reflected a lot on his life, on his parents' marriage. One thing was clear above all else. He was not his father, and Mary was not his mother. They had entered the marriage with no affection and as the years went by, their discontentment, their dislike of each other had turned toxic.

He was not that type of man. He would never be that kind of weak person who took out their frustrations, their rage on others.

"Go on. State your terms." He schooled his features,

willing to give her anything that she wished so long as she was his by the end of the day.

She looked down at their entwined hands, her brow furrowed. "You know my character. You know that I'm independent and opinionated, and also a bit of a blue-stocking. After having been caught in a compromising situation with you and seeing that there was no other option for us to marry, I do think that we'll do well enough as any other couple setting out on this marriage journey. But," she said, pausing.

He lifted her chin, needing to see her eyes. "But what, Mary?" he asked.

Her tongue darted out and licked her lips and Dale fought to concentrate on the conversation at hand. He was totally besotted by a woman that in truth he hardly knew. He wondered at the emotions roiling throughout him, what they meant before pushing them away to listen to what she had to say.

"But I will not change who I am to suit your friends, your title or your expectations of what you may think a duchess should be like. If I see or hear something that I think is cruel, or untrue I will seek to repair the error. I will not like people to further your standing in the *ton*, and I will not stop my hobbies. Any of them, even climbing rocky outcrops that I do most summers."

He bit back a bemused smile. She was perfect. "Is there anything else?" he asked, his tone severe.

Her eyes flared, but instead of crumbling under his supposed ire, she lifted her chin, her determination to get what she wanted overriding her fear of his opinion. "I will not share you, your grace. Not with anyone. Ever. If I ever heard word that you've been unfaithful to me, our marriage will be at an end. I may not be able to divorce you, but that is exactly what will happen without all the legalities of it. If I'm to be your wife, it is my bed and only my bed that you'll find yourself in. If you're unable to promise me my wishes, I will not marry you today."

THE DUKE STARED AT HER, his face giving little away as to what he was thinking. His hand still held hers, his thumb making her insides quake with remembering how they were together when alone. How very clever his hands were when on her person.

She took a calming breath, waiting for him to speak. How had all her hopes ended up being tied to a man she knew very little beyond a month ago?

"They are a lot of stipulations." He stood, walking a few steps from her. His back was rigid, proud and Mary knew what she asked was a lot. Possibly too much for a man of his rank and power to allow. But she could not give herself over to anyone unless they allowed her to be who she was. A rough and tumble girl from Derbyshire who didn't play by the rules, and never wanted to.

"But I find myself at liberty to agree to your terms. I should not expect anything less from my duchess," he said, turning toward her, a wicked grin on his lips.

Mary let out a relieved sigh, standing and throwing herself into his arms. His arms came about her, strong and fierce and within a moment she found herself kissing him. Their lips entwined, his hands over her back, her bottom and then one thigh as he lifted her up against his heat.

She moaned, kissing him with a fierceness that left her breathless, very much looking forward to tonight when they were alone. The idea frightened and exhilarated her at the same time. Whatever the duke evoked in her was new and absolutely wonderful.

"Do you really mean it?" she asked, pulling back and wrapping her arms about his neck.

He nodded, his eyes dark with unsated need. "Oh yes, I mean it. I did not think I wanted a duchess, nor one that I knew would push and pull me in all directions, but that was until I found you. I will never hurt you. I shall never dishonor you. You have my word on that."

Mary smiled, her eyes smarting with tears. "I suppose we should go downstairs and get married then, your grace."

He lowered her to the ground, kissing her softly once more. A kiss that seemed filled with a promise of forever. "I suppose we should."

He stepped to her side, holding out his arm. "Shall we, Lady Mary?" he asked, the proper gentleman and duke once more.

Mary threaded hers arm through his, a rightness settling over her like a balm. "We shall."

EPILOGUE

Spring 1801 - The Season

M ary stood beside her husband whose hand lay gently on the arch of her back. His thumb brushed slowly back and forth, and she smiled, knowing he was teasing her on purpose.

"Behave," she said, smiling up at him.

He grinned back. "I do not know what you're talking about."

She shook her head, watching her friend Louise take part in a country dance, the first of many now that they were back in Town. It was bittersweet for Mary, as Louise would soon be off to York and no longer her companion. She would miss her friend dearly.

Mary watched with growing concern as Louise looked less than pleased to be in the arms of Lord Lindhurst. "She's not enjoying herself. She looks positively bored."

The duke cast a curious glance in Louise's direction, his lips thinning in agreement. "So it would seem." He paused, turning to look at Mary. "Are you sure she wants to go to York. You have stressed that she's more than welcome to stay with us, have you not?"

Mary frowned, knowing it was what Louise wanted. "I will talk to her when we return home. Maybe I can convince her to stay."

The duke nodded, pulling her closer, his arm slipping about her waist to lay across the small bundle of life that grew within her belly. Their child. Just the thought of having a son or daughter left her overjoyed, and now that she was married to Dale, pregnant and utterly happy, she could not imagine her life any other way.

Dale had been true to his word. He'd taken her to all his estates during their wedding trip and she had explored his lands, ice fished when weather permitted and anything else that took her fancy. Not once had he tried to cut her wings, and now a new adventure grew within her, a lifetime of surprises and happy moments to come.

She could not wait.

"What are you thinking about?" he asked, meeting her eyes. "You have the oddest look upon your face."

Mary covered his hand on her waist with her own. "I'm just thinking about how happy I am. How happy you make me. This is terribly gauche of me, but I'm glad we were caught in the library that night. I thought what I had before was all that I wanted, but it was not. I was deluding myself."

He kissed her temple, ignoring the startled glances thrown their way at such a public show of affection. "Have I told you that I'm also glad of that night. Not simply because it was so very pleasurable," he whispered against her ear, making her chuckle. "But because it meant that I won you. I adore you," he said, tipping up her chin to look at him.

Mary stared at him a moment, having never heard him say such a sentimental thing before. "You do?"

He nodded, his eyes darkening in hunger. "I think it's been quite obvious for a few months now, and I'm sure the *ton* knows as well that the Duke of Carlton has fallen in love with his wallflower bride."

Mary bit her lip, her eyes blurring with unshed tears. "You love me?" To hear him say such things made her heart want to burst from her chest. Relief poured through her, thankful that she was not the only one to suffer such a fate.

"I do. I think in fact that I fell in love with you the first moment I saw you in that ridiculous dress with all those ribbons and bows. You were the most adorable, unfortunate being, that how could one not possibly fall in love with such a woman."

She smacked his hand playfully before clasping it. "I suppose if we're being honest with each other I should tell you too, that I find myself of similar emotions to you, your grace?"

He looked at her skeptically. "Surely you can do better than that, duchess."

She turned into his arms, wrapping her hands about his neck. The duke held her close, unafraid to scandalize the *ton* that the Duke and Duchess of Carlton were being too forward in public. Mary played with the hair on his nape, watching him as he waited. "I love you too," she said, leaning up further and kissing him. "I think I fell in love with you the moment I felt your hard, delicious abdomen beneath my hands in the conservatory. How could a woman be immune to such a being?"

"You are truly too bold, duchess, but never change. Promise me you'll never stop being you."

Mary leaned up once again. "I can promise you that,"

she said, kissing him again, this time not stopping even when the gasps and some whistles from the gathered throng told them they should. Mary had never been one to conform to Society's rules, and she wasn't about to start now.

A KISS IN SPRING

Kiss the Wallflower, Book 3

A broken carriage wheel at the base of the Scottish highlands is the last thing Sophie Grant needs on her trip to Scotland. Determined to make the most of her stay in the quaint village of Moy, she discovers some delightful attractions, including the Laird Mackintosh, who lives nearby.

Upon an invitation to the Laird's home, Sophie is thrust into a world of decadence, privilege, and wealth—everything she never had. Laird Mackintosh is tempting and beguiling with his scandalously hot kisses. However, Sophie knows he's hiding something—something that could change everything.

Brice Mackintosh is torn between his family's expectations, and his newfound feelings for Sophie. What started out as a game, a distraction before he fills his obligations is turning into more. But when the truth surfaces, Brice worries that he may lose the only woman he's ever loved.

CHAPTER 1

Highlands Scotland 1805

Sophie Grant dozed halfway between asleep and awake as the carriage continued on north, heading toward a small fishing village near the Isle of Skye. She'd never been to Scotland before and after this arduous journey, she doubted she'd ever go again.

How far away could this little seaside village be? Even so, they'd been traveling for what felt like months, but was in fact only weeks. Granted, they had stopped most nights, and during some breaks, had extended the journey to take in the local attractions or simply to rest both themselves, their driver and the horses.

She settled back into the squabs, luxuriating in the plush velvet seats and highly polished equipage. At least her little sojourn was more comfortable than taking the post. Her new brother-in-law, the Marquess Graham had insisted she use one of his carriages and had sent both a coachman and manservant to ensure her and her maid's safety.

So far they had very little to complain about, except the never-ending road or that the farther north they traveled the colder it seemed to get.

Sophie had thought spring in Scotland would be warmer than this, but apparently not.

A loud crack sounded and the carriage lurched frighteningly to one side. Sophie slipped off the seat and landed with a thump on the floor, her maid, sleeping on the opposite seat came crashing down on top of her and supplying Sophie with an elbow to the temple.

Distantly she could hear the coachman and manservant talking outdoors before the door swung open and the driver was there, taking in their disheveled appearance.

"Are you hurt, Miss Sophie, Miss May?" he asked, reaching in to help her maid climb off Sophie and regain her footing.

Sophie untangled herself from her dress and managed to slide toward the door and then step out onto the uneven, pothole-filled dirt road.

"Well, I think we can at least say why our wheel has broken in two." Sophie glanced at the sad wooden wheel lying beside the carriage, several spikes missing completely, possibly on the road behind them before the wheel collapsed under the carriage's weight.

"We're not far from the town Moy. I can leave you here with Thomas and go and fetch a new vehicle or we can all walk to town and I'll return later to pick up Thomas and collect your belongings."

"We'll walk with you, Peter. If you're happy to wait here with the carriage, Thomas?" Sophie asked, not wanting him to stay here alone if he did not feel comfortable.

"I'm armed, Miss Sophie. I'll wait here until Peter

returns. Town is not so far away, I can see smoke from some chimneys already."

Sophie looked north up the road and true enough, there were little swirls of smoke floating up in the air behind a small rise in the road. "Oh, we're not far at all." She reached into the carriage and looked for her reticule. Finding it on the floor, she picked it up and turned back to their little group. "Shall we?"

The walk into the village took no longer than half an hour and soon enough they were walking past the few cottages the village sported. A small sign pronounced the town to be Moy. A few of the locals came out to stare and some welcomed them with a friendly smile or wave.

"Do you think there is an inn in town, Miss Sophie? That carriage wheel will take some days to repair," her maid, Gretel asked, looking about the town with a less-than-pleased visage.

Sophie took account of the sleepy village, fear that there would be no inn washed over her. "I hope so. We need to secure rooms for some days and wait out the repairs. We're in no rush after all, and the carriage being Lord Graham's, I'd prefer to wait for it to be fixed than leave it here. But there doesn't seem to be a lot of people living here."

"I'm sure all will work out, Miss Sophie. Do not worry," Peter said, throwing her an easy smile.

They came to a crossroad and thankfully spied what looked like the local inn. It was made of stone and a thatch roof. A carriage sat parked to the side, and a young stable lad placed luggage at its back.

Sophie hoped that it was a place travelers could stay, or they would need to leave Marquess Graham's carriage here and travel on without it. If there was a carriage they could procure, in any case.

Peter led the way into the taproom, which had some men seated at the bar drinking ale. A barman with a long, graying beard came up to them and leaned upon the counter. "What can I help ye with?" he asked, taking each of them in before turning back to Peter.

"We're after two rooms if you have them available. Our carriage has broken a wheel outside of town and I'll need a cart to collect our luggage, if you please."

The barman rubbed his bearded jaw. "Ach, we can help ye with that to be sure, but I only have one room left, we're not officially an inn, but we can help ye out since our guests overnight are leaving as we speak. If you're willing, sir, I can put you up in the stables on a cot."

Peter nodded. "That will be fine. We'll need two cots as I have left a manservant with the carriage."

The barman stood, and Sophie found herself looking up at the towering gentleman. He was as tall as he was wide, his fiery-red hair and stature perfect for the position he held. "No trouble, sir, that can be arranged." He bellowed out for a woman named Bridget and within a minute a young woman bustled into the room, her hair askew and her apron covered in cooking stains. She smiled at each of them and Sophie smiled back.

"Show these ladies upstairs and have Alfie set up two cots in the stable. We'll also be needing the cart hitched."

"Of course, Father," she said, opening a small door in the bar and coming out to them. "If ye will follow me, my ladies. I'll show ye to your room."

"We'll be in the stable, Miss Sophie. I'll have Thomas bring in your luggage when we return with it."

"Thank you, Peter." Sophie followed the young woman up a narrow flight of stairs, stepping to the side when another young woman carrying a bucket and dressed in similar clothing to Bridget passed them on their way down.

They made their way along a passageway before coming to a room at the very end. The young woman unlocked the door with a key and swung it wide open.

"Here is ye room, my ladies. I'll have hot water and linens brought up straightaway. There is a private parlor downstairs if ye do not wish to eat in your lodgings, but ye do have a small table and two chairs if ye wish to."

Sophie walked into the room, taking in the double bed that looked clean and inviting. The curtains were new and there were flowers on a small table. A fire burned in the grate and the room was warm and welcoming.

"This is lovely," she said, stripping off her shawl and throwing it on the bed along with her reticule. "For an inn that doesn't trade in accommodation, it is very well-kept and presentable."

The young woman blushed at the compliment and her chin rose slightly with pride. "Aye, we're very lucky. The inn is owned by our local laird Brice Mackintosh but run by my father. His sister is responsible for the recent refurbishment of this room. 'Tis the only one we have since the building is so small. The few patrons we get here always appreciate a clean bed and good meal."

"That they do," Gretel said, sliding back the curtain to look outside. "May we order an early dinner? We've been traveling all day and I have to admit to being quite famished."

"Of course," the young woman said. "We're serving roast chicken and beef stew this evening, which do you prefer?"

At the mention of food Sophie's stomach rumbled. "I'll have the stew please, and a pot of tea if possible."

"I'll have the same, thank you," Gretel said, pulling off her shawl and laying it on a chair by the fire.

The young woman bobbed a quick curtsy and started for the door. "I'll be back shortly, my lady."

"You may call me Miss Grant."

"Aye, of course. I shall return, Miss Grant." The door closed behind the young woman and Sophie stripped off her gloves, placing them on the mantel as she warmed herself before the fire.

"What a lovely inn and so accommodating. Certainly a much more pleasant place than some of the English ones we've stayed in."

Gretel nodded, coming to sit at the small table. She pulled off her gloves before yawning. "I'm dreadfully tired. A nice meal will be just what we need, along with a good night's rest."

The warmth from the fire slowly penetrated Sophie's bones and she shut her eyes, reveling in being warm and out of the jarring carriage. "I think we'll be here for several days. Perhaps there is a carriage-maker in the town who can repair the wheel, but I'm doubtful. I should say it will have to be brought up with the post from London."

"But that could take weeks," Gretel said, her eyes wide with alarm. "Although the lodgings are very comfortable, whatever will we do for all that time? Is there anything about to look at? I think I could count on one hand how many cottages were here."

Sophie walked to the window and stared out at the street, spotting a blacksmith and a small shop of some kind, but from where she stood she couldn't make it out.

"We'll ask tomorrow what there is to see and do here. I'm sure we can pass the time well enough, and anyway, we've been on the road for so long, a little break from travel will do us good."

Gretel nodded. "I'm sure you're right."

A light knock sounded on the door before it opened and Bridget entered, carrying a tray of tea and biscuits, along with a small bowl of cream and jam. She placed it down on the table. "The tea has just been poured, so perhaps let it sit for a little while before taking a cup."

"Thank you, it looks delicious."

"I'll bring dinner up in about ten minutes. Cook is just finishing it up now."

Sophie smiled at her, seating herself at the table. "Thank you, that is very good of you."

"You're welcome, Miss Grant."

When they were alone once again, Gretel went about putting cream and jam onto the biscuits along with preparing the tea for them to drink. They sat in silence for a time as they ate and enjoyed the refreshing drink, both lost in their thoughts.

"The young woman said that the inn is owned by the local laird and his sister. Perhaps we can visit with them. I've never met a Scottish laird before. He may live in a castle," Sophie teased. "I know how much you enjoy old houses."

Gretel nodded as she took a rather large bite of her biscuit. "I've always thought that Scottish lairds lived in castles, so I would expect nothing else," she mumbled.

Sophie chuckled. "I think I understood what you said, but really, Gretel, maybe smaller bites in the future."

Gretel smiled, her eyes bright with laughter. "Of course," she mumbled yet again.

Sophie poured herself another cup of tea. Being stuck in this sleepy but quaint town would surely be diverting enough to while away their time until the carriage was repaired. The landscape alone was beautiful, the forest and surrounding rugged hills drew the eye and beckoned one to explore. Maybe if they hired a local guide, they could picnic at a location the locals enjoyed.

Yes, they could have ended up stranded in much worse locations than Moy and they would make the best of their time while they were here.

CHAPTER 2

The following morning after breaking their fast in their small room, Sophie made her way outside with Gretel, walking into an inn yard that housed their carriage, a few horses and little else. "Come, we'll walk through the town and see what we can find." Maybe the shop she'd seen sold pastries. She'd always been fond of sweets, although she rarely had them as a child. There were never enough funds for such treats. But now that she had the means, she and Gretel often enjoyed sugary pastries in front of the fire before bed.

They passed very few people on the street. She supposed because the town was not so very far from Inverness, it was only logical that travelers continued on and broke their journey there. They too would have done the same had the carriage wheel not decided to break off.

The air was fresh and she pulled her shawl closer about her shoulders. She supposed she really ought to start wearing her coat as they traveled farther north.

She spied their driver speaking to the local blacksmith, no doubt about their wheel, but the man's constant shaking of his head didn't bode well for them to be out and back on the road traveling toward Skye sooner rather than later.

They came to the shop she'd seen yesterday and she was pleased to see they sold not only food but houseware and linens. Sophie stared in through the shop windows at the few items they displayed there. Her mouth watered at the sight of a queen and seed cake. She glanced through the glass and felt her eyes widen at the sight of a tall, quite imposing figure who stood at the counter. He had his back to her, the strong, straight lines beneath his shirt revealing to all what a lovely, lean and muscular figure he had beneath that thin article of clothing.

But it was his kilt, made of a green, woven wool within a darker green pattern that had her biting her lip. She'd never seen a highlander before, but that was certainly what he was. Straight from the mythical legends this area was famous for.

His hair was long for a man and large curls that looked wind-kissed or mussed from bed sport sat about his shoulders. She grinned at her own imagining of how his hair was so unkept, but still it did not stop her from wanting to run her fingers through the coppery locks.

She clenched her hands at her sides, reminding her she was wearing her kid-leather gloves and would not be able to feel him even if she were to be so bold. Not that she would, but he was nice to look at in any case.

"Are we going to go inside, Miss Sophie?" Gretel asked, shuffling on her feet and rubbing her arms to warm them. "I'm freezing. I don't know how we'll survive going farther north. Even this far up in Scotland is cold enough."

Sophie nodded distractedly, her attention fixed on the Scot being served by a young woman with a white apron over her pink, woolen gown. "Yes, of course."

They entered and a little bell dinged above them.

Sophie glanced up at the brass bell before looking back toward the counter and the breath in her lungs held. She felt her mouth pop open with an intake of much-needed air as the green, hard stare of the highlander took his fill of her.

Gretel cleared her throat at her back and Sophie remembered to step forward, moving toward the counter and trying with all the willpower ever afforded to her to keep her attention on the pastries she intended to purchase.

Her cheeks burned and she could feel his gaze tracing over her, before he turned back to the serving girl. "How much do I owe ye, Rhona?"

His voice was deep, smooth like liquid chocolate, and the shiver that ran up her spine had nothing to do with the frigid air in this part of the world.

Sophie glanced toward where he stood and watched as the serving girl leaned over the counter, her ample advantages in full view of anyone standing in the store. "Two farthings please, Laird Mackintosh."

Laird? The highlander reached into his sporran and passed the woman some coin.

"Thank ye, Rhona. I'll see ye next week."

The young woman tittered and Sophie bit back a smile at her infatuation with the man, not that Sophie could blame her. He was not at all what she was expecting to find this far north in the wild Scottish highlands.

He turned toward Sophie and caught her eye and for a moment she could not look away. His compelling eyes drew her in and she turned, following his progress as he made his way out the door, before striding past the shop front windows and disappearing up the street.

"He's a fine laird, if ever there was one," the young woman behind the counter sighed to an older lady who'd come to stand beside her. The elder shushed her and Sophie stepped up to the counter, ensuring she was served by the younger girl.

"May I order two queen cakes and a loaf of bread with seeds on top, please?" she asked. They were quite alone now, Gretel waiting patiently behind her and the older woman in the store serving another customer.

"Of course ye can." She busied herself packing up the pastries, wrapping them in wax paper.

"Did I hear you say that the gentleman that you just served was a laird?" Sophie met the woman's widened eyes and pinkened cheeks and smiled. "He looks very friendly," she continued, hoping to gain some information.

"Oh, aye, it was and he's a Scottish earl as well. He lives in Moy Castle half a mile northeast from here, not far from the banks of Loch Moy. He often comes into town to enjoy my mama's cooking. Honey biscuits are his favorite."

He had a sweet tooth, but then, so did she so she could not fault him on that. Not that she was looking to find fault with the man in any case. It was simply a little odd that a man of his size and stature, who looked like a Scottish warlord, would come into a bakery and buy sweets. She smiled, handing over her payment and taking the small parcel from the shopgirl.

"Thank you. Have a good day," Sophie said.

"You too, my lady," the young woman called out as they left.

They made their way outside, and Sophie took in the small village and the large, rocky outcrops of the highlands that dwarfed the town in the background. It was certainly an idyllic location, but even now in the middle of spring the air was chilly, the ground still damp underfoot.

They walked along the road for a time, looking at the many cottages, some that reminded Sophie of the village that she grew up in. It did not take them long to come to the edge of town where nothing but forest and a waterway greeted them.

"There is a bridge and what looks like a path leading up the hill, Miss Sophie. Shall we explore a little?"

The day was still young after all, they had a little food with them now, and they had their woolen cloaks. Sophie nodded, seeing no reason why they could not.

"Yes, perhaps it'll lead up to a lookout over the town." They had little else to do to fill the time before the carriage was repaired and Sophie was not ready to go back to their room at the inn just yet. A little fresh air and exercise would do them good.

They walked for a time in silence, both lost in their own thoughts. Every now and then Gretel or Sophie would point out a splendid view, or a plant that caught their eye.

The wind whipped at Sophie's hair and she pulled her shawl up over her head to keep it from blinding her. "The wind is picking up, Gretel. We should probably head back soon."

Gretel stopped, pointing ahead of her. "We're almost there, just a little farther."

The hill they climbed was steeper than Sophie first thought, and the breath in her lungs burned as she continued to climb. The ground underfoot was rocky in parts, and slippery in others and nerves pooled in her stomach that perhaps their morning walk was beginning to look like a bad idea.

With that thought, her foot landed on a plant that hid a stone. It slipped out from under her and she toppled forward, coming down onto the ground and slamming into a boulder. An acrid taste entered her mouth when she bit her tongue. Sophie sat up, her vision swimming a little.

"Miss Sophie!" Gretel said, running to her as best she

could and kneeling before her. Her friend fumbled in her pocket and brought out a handkerchief, pushing it against her forehead.

Sophie hissed in a breath at the sting of her friend's touch. "Ouch, that hurts."

"You're bleeding. You hit your head and you're bleeding more than you should be."

Sophie swiped at her cheek, glanced down, and gasped at the amount of blood on her fichu and gown. "Oh my Lord, I'm going to bleed to death."

Gretel bit back a smile, pushing harder against her wound. "While I do not think it is as bad as all that, I do think I should fetch help to carry you down. I don't want you to faint and hit your pretty head again."

Sophie glanced at Gretel. It was just like her friend to try to make a small joke in the middle of a disaster. She sighed. "Fine. I'll sit here if you think it's best, but I'm sure I could make it." She looked down the path that they had walked. It was an awfully long way back down.

"I'll be back as fast as I can. Do not move," Gretel said, and then she was gone.

Sophie watched her disappear down the side of the hill before she was out of sight. She pressed against the wound on her forehead, dabbing at it a little to see if it was still bleeding. A light thumping started at her temples and she shuffled over to a large boulder and tried to protect herself from the wind.

How long she sat there she did not know, but as the hours passed and the afternoon grew darker and colder, she slipped into sleep on the craggy ground, heedless that her gown was growing ever more damp by the minute.

Brice Mackintosh had better things to do than rescue women who were foolhardy enough to walk up hills during this time of year. The ground was damp and slippery and the lass was lucky she'd not broken anything else other than that thick head of hers.

After having been waved down by a young woman running from the bridge that led to the summer lookout over the town, she'd then gone on to explain that her mistress had fallen and needed help down the hill.

Brice looked at the sleeping woman. The once-white handkerchief she'd been using to press against her head wound was lying in the mud and her wound gaped, the congealed blood seeping slowly down her forehead.

He cringed. The injury would need stitching and that in itself alleviated some of his anger at being waylaid. He kneeled beside her, reaching out to shake her shoulder. "Miss. Wake up, miss…" He shook her shoulder a little more and this time her eyes fluttered open.

Her lashes were long and dark, and yet her hair was sun-kissed. Whatever hairstyle she'd had this morning had long ago fallen out.

He stared at her as she sat up, reaching out and taking her hand to help her. She clutched at her head and he cringed when she did. "I'm Brice Mackintosh. I'm going to carry ye down to the town. Will ye let me, lass?" he asked.

She glanced at him, confusion in her gaze, but she nodded, trying to stand.

Brice stood and, reaching down, swooped her into his arms and started back toward the village. Her arms went about his neck and she gave out a sweet little yelp at his manhandling. She smelled of lavender soap and her hair even better, like wild berries and fruit.

The wind blew it into his face, and he fought to keep it out the way as he made his way down the hill. She would be tall, he could tell, and carrying her against his chest put into focus how very womanly she was. Her bottom hit his stomach and his hand sat just beneath her breast as he carried her—both locations on her person that felt ample and lush.

He frowned, reminding himself that being here, helping this lass would make him late for the dinner party he was holding for his potential future wife. His sister would accuse him of being late because she believed him to be indifferent to Elspeth. A truth that even he acknowledged even though he'd never tell his sister such a thing. He glanced down at the lass and caught her studying him.

"How are you doing down there?" He took in her wound. It still wept, but had at least stopped bleeding. As for her appearance, it was disheveled to say the least. Half her face sported dry blood, and her golden locks too were a little stained and clumped from the wound.

"Your friend said you're staying at the inn. I'll have a doctor sent straightaway over to you when we return."

"Thank you," she said, speaking at last. She frowned up at him, studying him as if he were an oddity. "Are you the laird I saw in the shop earlier today?"

Realization struck him and he stumbled a little. That was where he'd seen her before! As per usual, his daily walk and honey biscuit purchase had today been a little less banal that it normally was. And it was because of this lass in his arms. "Aye."

He'd heard the door to the shop open, but it wasn't until he'd glanced to see who had stepped inside that his body had stilled at the sight of her. She was all golden beauty. Her eyes so wide and blue that they would make even the sky envious. He'd stared at her, unable to look away before he'd realized his mistake and had turned back to Rhona to finish being served.

In Moy there were few women who looked like the one in his arms and it had merely been a shock to see anyone. She was a Sassenach as well, and not worth his time.

He was to marry a Scottish lass, Elspeth Brodie in fact. A woman who was as robust and capable as anyone he knew. The fact that she'd never raised one ounce of attraction in him was beside the point.

Many marriages were based on friendship and they were friends…most of the time.

Finally they made the bridge that separated the walk up the hill and the town. Her friend stood waiting for them, a deep frown on her brow as she worked her hands before her in worry.

Brice sent her a comforting smile, trying to put her at ease. The young woman visibly relaxed upon spying them.

"You're very strong. There are few who would be able to carry me all this way and without even puffing." She studied him and he refused to meet her gaze lest she see just how very fascinating he found her.

"I work. I should imagine you know very little of the trade." She stiffened in his arms and he inwardly cringed. There was no need to be so curt and opinionated about the lass in his arms. For all he knew she did work, although her fine clothing and hands that were soft against his neck told him otherwise.

She was no trouble to carry, in fact, she weighed very little, although her close proximity did give way to thoughts that he should not be having, not with this lass at least. Brice reminded himself that he was expected to marry Elspeth. A woman who was native to this land and wouldn't fall over on the craggy mountaintops and cut her head open like this lass.

He came up to her friend and helped the woman in his

arms stand. "I'll help ye to the inn and then fetch the doctor. He'll have ye fixed up soon enough."

Brice took her arm, helping her forward. "Thank you again for assisting me. My name is Sophie Grant, by the way." She stopped and held out her hand.

He stared at it a moment before reaching down, clasping it and bowing over it a little. Something in his gut twisted watching her and he turned back toward the inn. He needed to get her back and settled. There was much to do at home, what with the dinner this evening. His sister would no doubt be flustered and bossing everyone about since he wasn't there to keep her in check.

Not that he ever could.

"I'm Brice Mackintosh," he said at length, nodding to the few locals who glanced their way and stopped to watch what their laird was doing with a bloodied woman.

He supposed the sight didn't place him in a favorable light, but what could he do under the circumstances? He could not have left her there. The drop in temperature alone overnight would've taken her life, not to mention it wasn't his nature to turn from people in need.

They made the inn and Brice, with the aid of the tavern staff, helped Miss Grant to her room, her friend fussing to ensure hot water and linens were brought up straightaway.

Their room was the only one available for guests, and Brice glanced about, spying the large leather traveling cases.

He helped Miss Grant to the chair before the fire, ensuring she was sitting before he stepped back. "I'll have a doctor sent immediately. I wish ye well, Miss Grant."

She glanced up at him. Was that a flicker of disappointment in her gaze? Surely not. He was imagining things now?

The other woman came over to him, taking his hand and squeezing it. "Thank you ever so much, my lord. We're so very appreciative of your help. I do not know what I would've done had you not stopped."

Brice backed toward the door. "Think nothing of it, lass. Yer friend will be better soon enough."

She smiled, following him, before shutting the door quietly behind him as he made his way down the passage. At the tavern, he stopped to greet John Oates, a tenant of his before heading outdoors.

A man bustled up to him, his fine clothing and pale skin gave him the air of an Englishman. He sighed. What was it today with the English needing a Scot's help?

"My lord, I don't know how to thank you enough for the help with Miss Grant." The man clasped his hand, shaking it vigorously. "I was out, you see. Our carriage is broken and being repaired and I did not know Miss Grant had been injured. I do not know what I would've said to her sister had something happened to her." The man worked his cap in his hand and Brice waved his thanks aside. "I was more than willing to help. Ye have no reason to worry. She's safe and sound in her room now."

The man sighed, nodding. "Thank you. I shall let my master know of your kindness. It will not be forgotten."

Brice frowned at the mention of his employer. "Master?"

"Oh yes, Miss Grant is the sister-in-law to the Marquess Graham."

For a moment Brice couldn't think of anything to say. She was nobility, or at least, related to English peers.

If that was the case, what in the hell had a woman of rank—even if only by marriage—been doing walking around the wilds of the Scottish highlands without a manservant? Or for that matter, staying at an inn with only a woman servant in her room?

Moy Inn may be quiet and the only accommodation in town, but it was far from safe for an unprotected woman. There were many riffraff who passed through and could've assaulted or stolen from them.

"Dinna let her wander around Moy alone, 'tis not safe for her or her servant." Who, no doubt, the other young woman fussing about Miss Grant's skirts was.

"Of course, my lord. Thank you."

Brice left then, striding to the doctor's residence only some houses away and paying for his services to the young woman. He then started back to where he'd left his horse. By the time he hoisted himself into the saddle, drizzle had settled in over the town and with it a decided chill to the air. He pulled part of his kilt over his shoulders and pushed his horse into a trot, needing to get back home sooner rather than later.

He had a dinner to host for his possible future wife. He sighed at the thought. He supposed he'd have to start courting Elspeth Brodie soon. The obligation held little desire for him. The image of Miss Sophie Grant flashed before his eyes and he let himself remember her soft, curvy flesh against his. The smell of lavender and fruits of all things sweet and succulent.

Pity his future was not so alluring to his palate.

CHAPTER 3

Sophie woke with only the slightest headache the following day. The doctor had come, and forced her to endure two stitches up high on her forehead, which she would never forgive him for. The pain of having a needle threaded through skin was not to ever be borne again and Sophie had promised herself no more hillside walks. From now on she would keep to flat, dry ground. Not steep, rocky, damp ground that was abundant in these parts.

"Would you be up to having breakfast in the parlor downstairs, Miss Sophie? The day has dawned very bright and the room gets the lovely morning sun."

Sophie slipped on her slippers. She walked to the window and looked out over the street. Again the town was a hive of activity and just as Gretel said, the day looked much more congenial to outings than it did yesterday.

"Yes, I feel well enough." She checked the bandage on her head. "I'll have to wear my jockey bonnet to cover the bandage. If I tip it a little over my brow and to one side, I don't think anyone will see the injury." She picked up her hat and sat it over her hair, tying it simply at the back of her head.

"I think that'll work well, miss." Gretel checked her over and, clasping her shawl and handing it to her, she opened the door. "Shall we?"

They enjoyed a lovely breakfast of toast and kippers, along with a nice hot pot of tea. The cook had even placed some bacon and eggs on the platter.

A little while later, Sophie slumped back in the chair, not able to eat another bite. "Shall we go for a walk?"

Gretel glanced at her, shock etched onto her face. "Do you think that's wise after yesterday?"

Sophie laughed. She supposed her friend had a point. Yesterday had not been either of their best moments. "I want to go look at the little river that runs behind this town. We'll not go far, I promise. Will you join me?"

Gretel nodded, standing. "Of course, there isn't much else for us to do."

Unfortunately that was true. Sophie stood, and they started out of the inn, heading toward the river. For some hours they walked along the banks, sitting when they needed a break, and talking to the few locals who were fishing at certain locations along the way.

"I must admit that this town really is quite lovely, even if it is terribly small."

Gretel nodded. They sat along the bank in long grass, simply watching the clouds pass over the highlands in the distance.

"You must send word to Miss Anderson. She'll be expecting you in a few days and she may worry when we don't arrive."

Sophie nodded. "I shall pen a letter tonight to her and we'll send it with the morning post. I should not think we will be here too much longer in any case. Peter said they were able to get a wheel from Inverness."

"Miss Grant! Hello! Miss Grant is that you?"

Sophie turned at the female voice calling to her, or hollering would be a better term. From the direction they had walked came a young woman, dressed in a tartan skirt and white shirt, her shawl was wool and her hair was a simple plait at her back. She smiled and waved and for a moment Sophie was unsure what to do. Should she wave back to the strange woman who obviously knew her name, or wait and see?

She stood, brushing down her gown and decided that the lady looked harmless enough. What with her wide smile and bright eyes, she was obviously no threat.

She came up to them, panting heavily, and she clasped her midriff, smiling at them and yet unable to speak due to her exhaustion.

"Are you well?" Sophie asked when after a moment the woman still had not caught her breath.

"Apologies, Miss Grant," she said, panting. "I've been trying to catch up to ye. You walk very fast for a Sassenach."

Sophie raised her brow. For an Englishwoman she walked fast? She didn't know whether to be proud or offended by the remark. "Can I help you with something?"

The woman nodded. "Aye, I'm Elizabeth Mackintosh, Laird Mackintosh's sister. I think ye met my brother yesterday."

The lady reached out and took Sophie's hand, shaking it with vigor. "It's very nice to meet you. Was there something wrong, or is there something you need?" she asked, unsure why the woman was tracking them down.

Elizabeth chuckled, pushing back a lock of hair that had fallen over her face. The laird's sister was just as handsome as her brother, except her hair was a fiery red, which Sophie could well agree suited the woman's exuberance and zest for life.

"Oh nay, nothing to worry about. My brother informed me ye were from London and the Marquess Graham's sister-in-law. I know the marquess well. He's a mutual friend of the family I stayed with during my coming out many years ago. Knowing this, I coudna allow ye to stay a moment longer at the inn. Ye must come and stay with us at Moy Castle."

Sophie glanced at Gretel, who in turn stared bright-eyed at Elizabeth. The thought of staying with the laird of the area was tempting, and not only because the accommodations would be a little more roomy and comfortable, but also quiet. The inn was terribly noisy to all hours of the night. The few locals who did live in the village seemed quite in love with the taproom. "We would not wish to intrude."

"Och, 'tis not an intrusion at all. We have ample room and plenty to keep ye occupied. I understand yer carriage is being repaired?" Elizabeth Mackintosh shrugged. "I see no reason why ye shoulda come and stay."

Sophie looked to Gretel and with a small nod, she came to a decision. "Very well, thank you, Miss Mackintosh. We'd be delighted to be your guests."

THE FOLLOWING DAY SOPHIE, with the help of a servant, stepped out of the carriage that the laird had sent to collect them in Moy. She glanced up at the castle structure, a large, square tower sitting pride and center. The details about the roof were ornate and gothic in appearance and to Sophie did not represent what she'd always assumed a clan stronghold would look like.

Not that Scotland was allowed to have clans, such as they were hundreds of years ago. Even so, the families that had survived Culloden still bore the names, the independence and pride of their people.

Elizabeth bustled out of the hall, coming over to them. "So glad you're here, and just in time for lunch. Come, I'll show ye to yer rooms so ye may freshen up before we eat."

They made their way indoors and Sophie felt her eyes grow wide at the size of the home. The entrance housed a library to one side and another room of equal mass on the other. Settees, a piano and other opulent furniture littered the space and oozed history and a well-used home.

Elizabeth started up the central staircase that was large and imposing like the house itself, its dark oak drew the eye and all but shouted wealth and power in these lands.

She followed Miss Mackintosh upstairs to the second floor. Turning right, Elizabeth strode down a long hall. "In there is the smaller drawing room, and if you follow me down the second passage," she said, turning yet again, "here you'll find the guest bedrooms. I also sleep in the farthest room down the hall here as it's a corner room and has great views over the park from both windows. My brother occupies the other wing. I'll show ye that tomorrow."

"Where shall I stay, Miss Mackintosh?" Gretel asked, her eyes as wide as Sophie felt hers were. The home was even larger than the marquess and her sister Louise's country estate. One could possibly become lost in all the rooms and corridors.

"There is a little adjoining chamber with a bed, side table and closet in through here for you," Elizabeth said. "You may order your meals in here or join the servants below stairs. I've instructed the housekeeper either will be acceptable. Her name is Mrs. Kenny."

"Thank you," Gretel said, seemingly pleased with her accommodations.

"Dinner is at eight sharp and we always dine in the great hall. That is downstairs," Elizabeth said, looking over the room before starting toward the door. "Once you're settled, please come down to have luncheon. We're having a simple buffet today, so no need to feel ye have to be there straightaway for serving."

"Thank you," Sophie said, turning to Gretel as Elizabeth closed the door behind her, leaving them alone.

"This house is out of a dream. The Mackintoshes must be very rich indeed," Gretel said, walking into her room, her voice muffled.

Sophie turned, taking in what was to be her space. Again, all dark woods, rich Aubusson rugs, windows that ran from floor to ceiling. The view of the lands drew her eye and Sophie looked out onto the park. She could well understand why Elizabeth wanted a room with two windows overlooking such a landscape.

Large elm and oak trees spotted the lands, native grasses were left to grow wild and there was only the smallest area of lawn that surrounded the house itself before giving way to nature. Movement caught Sophie's eye and she spied a stag, munching on the undergrowth, perfectly content. She could well understand that. With the view from here, her room was far and beyond better than the inn's.

Sophie turned and sat on the window ledge. An imposing fireplace, opposite the bed, dominating the other side of the room. Even from where she was, she could feel the warmth emanating from it.

"I think we'll be very comfortable here."

Gretel bustled over to her. "Come, Miss Sophie, I'll get you ready for luncheon, fix up your hair to hide your wound, and then you best head downstairs. I'll unpack our things while you're gone and have my lunch in here today. That way I'll have you organized for this evening's entertainments, whatever they may be."

Sophie nodded, sitting at the dressing table while Gretel went about fixing her pinned hair and ensuring her gown was suitable for lunch.

How things had changed. Only a few years ago she was living in the small village of Sandbach with her aunt and brother. Louise away working as a lady's maid, and now she was a marchioness. Beyond happy and in love with her husband and taking care of her and Stephen as she'd always had.

To be in the Laird Mackintosh's home as a guest was simply too fantastical to imagine, and yet, here she was. Louise had made her promise to behave and enjoy her time away from London and this was certainly a lot of fun.

She just hoped the other house guests were as welcoming as Elizabeth Mackintosh had been.

"There, all done, Miss Sophie."

Sophie glanced at herself in the mirror. Her morning gown of rose pink was the height of fashion in London and because they did not have far to travel out to the hall this morning, she'd forgone wearing a traveling gown.

At least by doing so she was ready to dine. "Thank you, Gretel. I shall see you after lunch." She took a calming breath, the pit of her stomach twisting at the thought of seeing the laird once again.

To see if he was as handsome as her mind told her he was or if she'd simply hit her head so hard that it had left her confused and muddled of mind.

CHAPTER 4

B rice sat at the head of the table and spooned mouthful after mouthful of food as he tried to hasten his departure from lunch. His sister sat quiet, a small smile playing about her lips and his eyes narrowed. What was she up to?

His attention snapped to the end of the table where Elspeth Brodie, his intended if his family had their way, sat and ate. Her expression was blank, displeased even. Was there something wrong with the food? "Is the food not to yer liking, Elspeth?" he asked, catching her eye and throwing her a small smile.

She looked back at him as if he were an inanimate object not worth her time. "Nay, the broth is too salty for my palate. Ye should have a word with yer cook. It seems she's inadequate."

Brice nodded, even though he had no intention of talking to Mrs. Ross. She was one of the best in the area, and made the most delicious-tasting kippers anyone north of the border. She wouldn't be going anywhere.

He spooned more broth into his mouth. The thought

of meals such as these for the rest of his life, of a wife who disliked his cook and his home if he were to guess, didn't raise too much excitement in his blood. Why his parents had wished for such a union was beyond him. Just because one was friends with another clan did not mean such unions were necessary. He stirred his broth. But he knew the reason why. Debts must be paid and even if the fiscal ones were long over, the moral one still remained.

The door to the hall opened and every muscle in his body seized at the sight of the woman who strode into the room. He gaped at her, spoon partway to his mouth as she started toward Elizabeth.

His sister stood, gesturing to a chair beside her. "Everyone, this is Sophie Grant from London. She's the sister-in-law of Marquess Graham. Sophie, this is our neighbor and friend Miss Elspeth Brodie and of course my brother whom you met yesterday."

Elspeth took in Sophie's appearance and smiled, sitting up and paying a little more attention to what was going on about her. Brice watched his intended for a moment, wondering why Sophie would spark such a reaction, certainly nothing else had.

Sophie glanced at him, her tentative smile slipping a little. He schooled his features to one of disinterest. "Welcome, Miss Grant. I can only gather from your appearance here this afternoon that my sister has invited ye to stay?"

Miss Grant glanced at Elizabeth and he knew his sister had not told her that he knew nothing of their coming here. "Rest easy, Miss Grant, ye're more than welcome."

He sighed, not sure how he was going to go about the house now with her under its roof. She was beyond beautiful, and even the little cut on her forehead that her maid had tried to mask with her hairstyle didn't detract from the fact that he liked what he saw.

Brice stood, going to the server for more food, needing to distract himself. All would be well. He'd be polite, show her about the grounds and be friendly. Just because she was one of the most handsome people he'd met did not mean that they would get along as well. Not to mention Elspeth was here with the full knowledge that if he should ask she was to say yes to his proposal.

He slumped back in his chair, his appetite gone. For a time he pushed the bacon and fried egg about his plate and let the conversation about him continue without his input, until he heard Sophie's sweet voice and his gaze was pulled away from his food.

"What did you think of the house, Miss Grant?" Elspeth asked. Brice glanced at her, having not heard such interest in her tone for all the years he'd known her.

"Very well, Miss Brodie. The house is beautiful and the grounds are marvelous. I said to my maid before coming down that even Luke and Louise would be envious."

Pride filled him at her words and he found his lips twitching.

"Do you really? I always thought Moy Castle quite cold and masculine. 'Tis too grand for my blood and that of our Scottish ancestors too I believe."

Brice stared nonplussed at Elspeth. The woman was daft, just like both her parents.

"Ye disagree, Miss Grant," Elspeth stated matter-of-fact.

"I do," Sophie said, taking a sip of her wine. "It is no secret that I along with my siblings grew up with very little. We are not nobility, even though my sister has married into that sphere. A house like this, grand, old, full of history and family memories is something I know naught of. We lived in a cottage growing up in a small village in northern England.

"My aunt took us in after our parents died, and even though she loved us, we were never really a family after that. At least not one that was together until Louise married the marquess. I would've loved to have grown up in a home like this. A residence that has seen generations of my blood before. A sanctuary that could never be taken away from you. A place you'd always have as home."

Brice started when his sister clapped, nodding at her words. "I agree, Miss Grant," she said. "Moy Castle has been here hundreds of years and will be for hundreds more. 'Tis a shame that others are not so fortunate."

"Well, we'll see what ye think of the castle after a cold winter. The rooms I grant ye are warm, but 'tis a dreary, dark place. If ye're ever in Brodie land, ye must come to call, Miss Grant. Ye're more than welcome at my home."

Miss Grant smiled at Elspeth and his gut clenched. If the house was so dark and dreary as per Elspeth's opinion, then a smile from Miss Grant surely made it brighter.

"I would like that, thank you. Maybe on our return to London I shall call."

"Och, aye, that's right. Brice did mention that ye were not staying in the area long. Ye have a friend in Scotland that ye were traveling to see."

"I do. We went to the same school in Sandbach for a time before her family moved back to Skye. Her father is a tenant farmer for a laird up there."

Brice continued to eat, but didn't engage himself in the conversation. Miss Grant, for all her high connections now, certainly came from nothing, but her continual relationship with those whom she knew before her family's elevation was a credit to her. So many people forget who they were once they become something better, in his opinion at least.

"Now, I think that is enough questions for Miss Grant. She's here to enjoy herself and not be hounded by you lot." His sister turned to Miss Grant. "If ye like, this afternoon my brother has to oversee some of the tenant farms here. Would ye like to join him?"

Her gaze snapped to his and with little choice thanks to his meddling sister, he said, "Ye're more than welcome, Miss Grant. It shoudna take too long and 'tis a nice enough day for a ride."

She studied him a moment, her teeth working her bottom lip as she decided what to do. Brice couldn't tear his gaze from her mouth and all thoughts filled his mind of how soft her lips may be.

"If you're sure," she said at length, her words uncertain.

Brice pushed up from his seat, striding toward the door. "'Tis fine, Miss Grant. I'll meet ye at the front foyer in an hour." Brice strode from the room, heading toward his own to change. He would have a word with his meddling sister who wanted him to act the host and tour guide it would seem. He wasn't laird for amusement's sake, he had work to do, people to attend. Running about the lands and showing a Sassenach his home wasn't one of them.

When he returned he would have a stern word with Elizabeth and ensure she kept her busybody self out of his business. And keep the delectable, sweet and alluring Miss Grant away from him also.

❦

AN HOUR LATER, they met in the foyer and with very few words spoken, the laird made his way toward a large stone building near the rear of the house. The stables were a long, rectangular-shaped structure with multiple stalls, all of them filled with both working horses and pleasure mounts.

"Ye may ride Elizabeth's horse. She's a placid mare, and will no throw ye.'"

Sophie walked up to the stall he pointed to, crooning as the mare made her way over to her and placed her soft velvety nose into Sophie's gloved palm. "What a sweetie you are," she said, leaning over and kissing her horse's nose.

"Can ye ride?" he asked, stopping to stare at her.

Sophie frowned, not liking his tone or the fact that just because they had been poor did not mean they could not ride a horse. Which, in truth, neither she nor Stephen could when Louise had first married the marquess, but Luke had put an end to that and taught them both very well.

"The marquess taught me. I'm sure I'll be able to keep up." She raised her brow at him and he turned his back to her, yelling out orders to a nearby stable hand to saddle her mount.

Sophie stepped back and kept out of everyone's way as they readied the horses. Her mare was a pretty brown and had the sweetest eyes. She glanced at the laird, watching as he busied himself with his horse, the corded muscles on his arms visible even under his shirt. He wasn't wearing his kilt today. Instead he was wearing a shirt, greatcoat, tan trews and boots.

Heat prickled her skin as her eyes took their fill of him. She'd never seen such a handsome man before, certainly in London the gentlemen whom Louise had introduced her to were nothing like this Scottish one.

The men in London seemed like boys compared to this man.

"Are ye ready, lass?"

She jumped at his curt question, meeting his gaze. One

eyebrow was raised and she nodded, trying to ignore the fact that he'd caught her staring at his person.

"Of course." A stableman led her mare up to her and, using the mounting block beside the stall door, hoisted herself up into the leather saddle.

The laird didn't wait for her, simply pushed his horse into a trot, leaving her to scramble behind to catch up. It was little use, as soon as his larger, more powerful mount made it outside, he pushed him into a canter and Sophie pulled up her mare, watching him.

What was he doing? Was he taking her for a ride to see some tenant farms or being a total ass and leaving her behind to get lost?

She pushed her mount into a walk. If he did not want her to come with him he only need say. Did the man have no manners? She rode for a few minutes on the grounds near the estate and never far enough that she could not see the house through the trees.

The sound of thumping hooves echoed in the woods and she continued on, wanting to ignore the Scottish buffoon since he found it so very easy to ignore her.

He appeared through the trees, his brow furrowed in a deep scowl. "What are ye doing, lass? Ye're supposed to be following me."

Sophie walked her mare over to his, stopping before him. "You took off so fast that I wasn't quick enough to see where you went. If you did not wish for me to accompany you, you only had to say. I would've been quite content to stay at the house."

He rubbed his jaw, the action bringing her attention to his mouth. Damn it, she didn't need to see how very lovely his mouth was, even when pulled into a disapproving frown.

"Ye said you could ride. Are ye a liar?"

Sophie sighed. "Oh no, I can ride, but I will not chase you like a little puppy. A gentleman would wait for his partner before taking off ahead of her as if the devil himself was on his heels."

He looked away from her, mumbling something she could not make out. Although the word *devil* and *was chasing him* she did hear. "I never said I was a gentleman." His eyes snapped to hers. She swallowed, his penetrating stare doing odd things to her belly.

"I have other obligations today other than the tenant farms. I dinna need to be held up by an Englishwoman who canna ride."

Sophie glared. How dare he? "I think I shall return to the house. I do not wish to intrude on your time and be a burden." She swallowed hard the lump in her throat at his rudeness. What was wrong with the man? That he didn't like her was obvious and the thought of staying another night under his roof wasn't to be borne.

He pointed into the trees. "The house is that way. Good day to ye, Miss Grant."

She didn't bother to reply, simply turned her horse back toward the house and left. On her return to the stables she spied her coachman. "Peter, any word on the wheel and when it will be ready? I do wish to leave here as soon as possible."

Her coachman doffed his cap. "Yes, Miss Grant. The wheel will be no more than five days away. We'll be on our way soon enough."

"Thank you," she said, starting back toward the house. She made her room, slumping onto her bed. Gretel came in, bustling toward her.

"What are you doing back so soon? I thought you were out on a ride with the laird?"

The reminder made her fist her hands and punch the

bed on either side of her. "The man is an oaf. He left me behind and then tried to say that I couldn't ride and keep up." She sat up, staring at nothing in particular. "We cannot leave soon enough. I fear our appearance here at his house is not what he wished."

Gretel came and stood before her, taking her hand. "It'll be alright, Miss Sophie. You know that Miss Mackintosh welcomes you here, and so you are her guest. Just ignore the laird. Like you said," Gretel remarked, going over to the fire and throwing on a couple of peat logs on to burn. "We'll be gone soon and all of the time here will be quickly forgotten."

If only he were that easy to forget. With his striking profile, his muscular frame and a face that would make even Lord Byron jealous it would not be an easy feat. To ignore his barbs and not react, a trait she was known to do, would not be the easiest thing in the world.

Sophie had always gotten along well with most people, so for the laird to be so very prickly left her discombobulated. "I think I'm going to have to talk to the laird to ensure our stay here is not against his will. It's his home, after all. I would hate to intrude."

"I'm sure he'll be back from the tenant farms soon. He spends most of the afternoons in the study downstairs."

Sophie glanced at Gretel, who busied herself cleaning up her combs and brushes on her dressing table. "How do you know that about the laird?" Something akin to jealousy shot through her at the thought of her friend knowing more about the man than she did. Why it would bother her so? She had not one clue and she didn't want to delve into those particulars right at this moment.

"Oh, the housekeeper Mrs. Kenny said. Like clockwork apparently the laird arrives at his study and doesn't leave until late in the afternoon, just in time to prepare for dinner."

Relief flowed through her that Gretel wasn't watching his every move. She shuffled off the bed, disgusted at her own thoughts. Gretel may be her servant, but she was also her friend. "I'm going to go for a walk about the house. Explore a little. I shall not be long."

Sophie walked into the corridor and started toward the passageway that led to the staircase. The house was enormous and she couldn't help but wonder that when the laird's sister married and left, what he would do with all this space.

But then she supposed, he too would be married and possibly filling the rooms with children.

She strolled through the smaller drawing room and into a little antechamber that overlooked the front yard. The sound of horses' hooves pulled her gaze to the window and she watched as the laird jumped down from his mount, handing his horse to a waiting stableman.

His long, purposeful strides to the house kept her attention on him and heat pricked her skin at the sight. She lifted her gaze to look out over the grounds, vexed at her own stupidity.

She was attracted to him. That was what was wrong with her. Even with his coarseness and overpowering ways, there was something about him that drew her to him.

Sophie had not thought she was the type of woman who enjoyed rakes, but here she was...enjoying this one quite a lot. Or at least, enjoying the view of him, not so much when he opened his mouth.

Moving away from the window, she made her way through an upstairs sitting room, past a stairway that went up in the tower that sat central to the home. She passed another staircase leading downstairs and then came to a long passage.

The walls were lined with family portraits and there was a long Aubusson runner that ran the length of the parquetry floor.

Sophie strolled slowly, looking at each of the family portraits of the laird's ancestors. All of them looked stern, but there was something about their eyes that was kind. The children always appeared happy and carefree and she couldn't help but wonder if any of them were of the current Laird Mackintosh.

At the end of the passage stood another window and Sophie glanced outdoors, seeing that this vista was simply too perfect for words.

"What are ye doing in this part of the house?"

Sophie let out a little squeak at the stern question. She'd not heard him join her. She turned, glancing up at the highlander who embodied everything that every young debutante in London dreamed of.

Herself included. His hair was mussed from his ride, his clothing mud-splattered and damp, and she'd never seen a more handsome gentleman even when at the finest balls in London.

"I was looking around, my lord. I promise I won't steal anything," she said, a little more sternly that what was required. She pushed past him. She didn't have to stay in this part of the house. There were still many places left to explore, including the tower. The laird could keep his little secluded wing all to himself.

He clasped her arm and then dropped it just as quickly. "I dinna mean to offend ye, lass. But ye shouldn't be in this part of the house. 'Tis not seemly."

She scoffed at his use of the word as she tried to stifle a smile. "Seemly?" At the voicing of the word she chuckled. "I do apologize. I shall leave. I would hate for your reputation to be ruined."

"Are ye laughing at me?" he asked, stepping toward her.

The urge to flee rode hard on her heels, but she didn't move. Something told her that if she did he would follow close on her heels. Not an unwelcome thought, unfortunately. Maybe she ought to run.

"A little, but I promise my amusement is only limited to your words, not anything else."

"So ye dinna find me amusing? I thought after our morning that ye would think me nothing but an ass."

Sophie did chuckle then, taking a breath and relaxing a little. "Oh, I did find you one of those, but if you show me about your tower I may forgive you your ungentlemanly manners."

He stared at her a moment, and his dark, hooded eyes that ran over her person sent a delicious shiver across her skin. Sophie fought not to fidget at his inspection of her. Instead she held his gaze, not willing to let him know just how very nervous he made her.

"Very well, I'll show ye the tower. Come," he said, striding past her and back toward the staircase. Sophie took in his back, her gaze sliding over his bottom. Trews really were lovely fitting pants for men.

She hastened after him, his steps long and quick, eating up the distance to where the tower door sat open. He made the entrance and she followed. The tower was of stone construction and smelled a little musty. Goosebumps pricked on her skin at the temperature change and she followed him up the stone stairs that were worn down by hundreds of years of footsteps.

"How amazing to know that your ancestors all walked these very rooms, each and every step that we walk on they too have placed their feet."

He nodded. "I know, it has always been a fascination with me too. The house is old, with many stories to tell."

"If only it would speak," she said, meeting his gaze.

He smiled, the first one she'd seen and the first one she had pulled forth. She sighed. How was the man more handsome than anyone she'd ever met before? And why did he have to live so very far away from her home in London? Far away from her family?

"Come, the view from the top is remarkable."

The view from where Sophie stood was pretty impressive as well, she mused.

CHAPTER 5

B rice counted each stone step leading up to the top of the tower. Anything to keep himself distracted from the woman who followed him.

Miss Grant was a diversion that he didn't need to endure right at the moment, not when he was on the cusp of offering marriage to Elspeth. A union between the Mackintosh and Brodie clans had been long desired—both their parents, may his rest in peace, had wanted the union. He could not ignore his father's last dying wish.

Determined to ignore the unearthly pull he had toward the lass, he turned his mind onto his responsibilities for tomorrow. He had planned to go hunting, possibly even stay out at the lodge for a night or two. The idea of being away from home no longer tempted him as much as it should.

He could guess as to why.

"Just a few more steps and we'll be at the top." He cast a glance over his shoulder and her eyes flicked up to meet his. His step faltered and he cursed himself a fool for not concentrating. He'd break his neck soon and then where would he be?

"I'm glad. I do not think that I've climbed up a tower this steep before or with this many steps. How many are there?"

"One hundred and eighty if ye're counting from the first floor up. The steepness of them makes it feel like there are more than there are."

She chuckled and his skin prickled. He liked the sound of her genuine, throaty laugh. He'd like to hear it more often.

"I suppose it would."

He came to a door at the top of the stairs and, pushing it, held it open for Miss Grant. She stepped past him, and he took the opportunity to admire her up close. He really needed to get a command on himself. She was not for him. She was for some London fop who lived in England and within an easy distance to her siblings. No English lass wanted to move to the highlands of Scotland. No sane one anyway.

The wind was strong this afternoon and a small smile played about his lips as he watched her battle with her hair and try to take in the view before them at the same time. It was a pointless exercise as the wind had already won this war.

Her golden locks whipped about her shoulders and face, giving her the air of country lass, without care or vanity. He liked what he saw.

"'Tis beautiful is it not?"

She glanced at him, nodding once. "It is the most beautiful country and I'm looking forward to seeing more of it."

He looked out over the grounds, forcing himself to glance away from Sophie. "I suppose ye're referring to yer friend ye're visiting in the highlands. Where does she reside?"

"Jean resides near the Isle of Skye. I've not been there before, but she writes that it has the most delightful walks if one enjoys the sea and forest."

"I've been to Skye. Ye'll enjoy yer time there if it's one of a recreational kind." To live there and earn a living from farming was not an easy occupation. The life was hard, fickle, and the seasons, harsher farther north, made farming difficult. "Is Miss Jean in service?"

She frowned, stepping up to the turret and looking out over the courtyard below. "She works as a tutor, but her mother has been ill and so she's been home for several months. Jean and I became friends at school in Sandbach." Sophie turned to him, smiling. "She reminds me of you actually."

He raised his brow, surprised at such a thing. "How so?" he found himself asking, wanting to know more about her and her life. And more importantly how a woman could be similar to him.

"First and foremost I suppose it's the Scottish burr and then the hair, although yours is a darker shade of red, more burnt copper, Jean has fiery-red locks." She stepped closer to him, reaching up to touch a strand, running it through her fingers.

He stared at her, having never been touched by a woman he hardly knew, at least in such a forward manner. Whether she knew what she was doing was improper or not, her touch caused his heart to beat loudly in his ears. There was little chance he'd remind her of her inappropriateness and have her move away.

An overwhelming urge to reach out and clasp her about her small waist and hoist her hard up against his body assailed him and he clamped his hands firmly at his sides. He would not allow temptation to sway him from what both the Mackintosh and Brodie clans desired. Elspeth would suit him well enough. Give him the bairns both families needed to ensure the family lines continued. Keep everyone happy.

All except for him…

He pushed the thought aside. He would be happy enough, especially when he had a son or daughter. To hold his own bairns would make a marriage to a woman he respected and liked, but did not love, endurable.

She let go of his hair, dismissing him and walking toward the other side of the tower. "I've always been very jealous of people who have unusual hair colors. My hair is plain and common."

"There is nothing common about ye." The moment the words left his mouth he wanted to rip them back. And the delight that crossed her features at his words made him realize his mistake. He didn't need to flatter her. He only ever need be polite. She would never be anything to him. His fate was sealed. That her sister had married into nobility also sealed her fate to a point. Even if she did not know it, her sister would expect her to marry well. Into the London sphere in which they circulated and to a man of equal standing to that of the marquess. She would not want her sister to marry beneath her.

"Thank you, my lord. How very nice of you to say." She looked at him as if she could see his statement left him uneasy and found this amusing.

He gestured toward the view, wanting to change the subject. "If ye look here ye can see Loch Moy through the trees. We swim there when the weather permits."

"I've not swam in years," she said, her disappointed tone pulling at something behind his ribs. "Not since I was a child at least."

He didn't like the idea of her missing out on the simple things that made life worth living. Swimming, laughing, playing. All of those things that he'd adored as a child, and still partook in at times as an adult. "'Tis spring, mayhap we'll get a day while ye're here that'll permit me to take ye down to the loch."

"Really?" Her eyes brightened and she smiled. "I'd like that very much," she said as she continued to take in the view. "Although I have nothing to wear."

He cleared his throat, the imagery of her wearing very little or nothing at all while swimming tortured his mind. Miss Grant was a beautiful woman, with a body that would make Venus jealous. God save him, but a part of him had offered just so he could enjoy seeing her wet and at his mercy.

He was going to hell.

"Elizabeth has attire that will fit ye well enough, but as I said, we'll have to wait and see if the weather permits. It may be the case that ye'll be back to yer travels before we can go."

"That would be a shame." She glanced up at him, her dark-blue orbs glinting with mirth. "I should like to swim with you."

Heat prickled his skin and he turned abruptly, needing to move, to get away from the temptation that Miss Grant offered. Why she affected him so he could not understand. Perhaps it was because he could not have her. And damn it all to hell, he wanted her. Just one taste. One stolen moment would satisfy him for the many years that loomed before him. But alas, he knew that he could not act on his desires. He was destined for a marriage that would be as cold as a highland winter where there would be no swimming in spring or stolen kisses. Where there would be nothing at all except duty.

ஓண்

THE FOLLOWING day Sophie smiled as Gretel handed her a swimming outfit that Elizabeth had loaned her. She strode to the window, throwing up the sash and feeling the temperature of the air. It was decidedly chill and she sighed, disappointed that today would not be the day the laird took her swimming.

She went about her morning routine, bathing and dressing in one of the new gowns Louise had purchased for her before traveling to Scotland.

The breakfast room was empty upon her arrival and she looked at the clock on the mantel. Had she slept in? "Has everyone breakfasted before me?" she asked as a footman set a plate of ham and toast before her, along with a cup of tea. She added a dash of milk.

"Miss Mackintosh and Miss Brodie have requested trays in their room this morning as the laird has traveled to Inverness for the day."

"Oh," was all she managed. The day was simply getting worse and worse.

Why she longed to see the laird again she could not fathom, not after how he'd treated her on the horse ride the other day. But in the tower yesterday she couldn't help but think she'd glimpsed a part of him he didn't often show, and she liked what she saw.

He wasn't so disapproving and cold. Quite the opposite. In fact, he seemed genuinely interested in her past and wanted to take her swimming.

The idea of being in the water with him, having him touch her, left her skin to prickle with expectation.

She shivered at the idea of his hands sliding over her flesh, of holding her in strong, capable hands. Sophie glanced out the window, willing the weather to be warmer tomorrow so she might feel exactly what she wanted.

Him.

She took a sip of tea, sighing at the sweet, rejuvenating tonic. She wanted to ensure that the truce that had sprouted between them continued, and the laird didn't revert back to the cold, cutting self he was the other day. He was much preferable this way, and with time perhaps he would tell her a little about himself, just as she had.

The day passed in a reasonable manner. After breakfast she'd gone to the library and picked out a book on the Scottish clans, wanting to know more about his people and the culture.

Sophie had then looked about the first floor, walking through the great hall that was a room stuck in a time past. With a great hearth at one end and the dais that sported six chairs before it at the other, she could imagine the lairds of old sitting before their subjects, eating hearty meals and listening to music and clan gossip.

Rows of tables sat within the hall. In years past the stone would've been covered in rushes, wolfhounds would have skulked about the clansmen's legs, men and women living under the patronage of the Mackintosh laird, eating and enjoying their time within the fold.

Sophie sat in a large, leather wingback chair set before a large bank of windows overlooking the grounds. She flicked through the book on clans, taking in the different tartans and the boundaries to each clan's lands.

"'Tis good to see ye taking an interest in the clans, lass." Brice leaned over her chair, pointing out the Mackintosh clan's land. "We've been here centuries and God willing we'll be here hundreds of years more."

"I've always found history interesting and Scottish history is full of clan wars, wars against England. Culloden comes to mind." She turned in the chair and met his gaze. "Did your clan suffer any losses at Culloden?"

"Aye," he said, a small frown marring his otherwise perfect brow. "Too many, but alas, 'tis a war the Scots were determined to have and so as with any war, good men are lost."

She turned back to the book, closing it. "I've been looking about your house, learning all its different corridors and staircases. Did you know you have seven staircases throughout the house?"

He sat down across from her, grinning, and she couldn't look away from his disheveled auburn hair or the wicked amusement that glowed in his eyes. "Actually, we have ten, two are servants' staircases."

Sophie chuckled. "Ten? If two are servants' stairs, that makes nine. Where is the tenth staircase?"

"Oh aye, there is a dungeon staircase. Did ye not find that today on yer travels?"

The thought sent a shiver across her skin and she shook her head. "No, I did not, but it sounds fascinating." He didn't further elaborate and Sophie wondered if she should ask him to show her. A little forward some would say, but the idea of seeing a dungeon, something she'd never seen before was too much of a temptation to pass up.

"Will you show me?"

He stood, holding out his hand. Sophie took it, and the moment her hand touched his a shock of awareness ran up her arm. His hand was warm and large and she couldn't help but think of how those very capable hands could hold her close, keep her from harm. "Of course, I'll show ye."

BRICE MADE their way down to the cellars, which led farther into the two dungeons the castle boasted. They were made during the construction of the house, but very little information remained on who was held there or why.

As a child he'd played down here often, never finding it scary, damp or ominous. Elizabeth on the other hand refused to come down here, stating the rooms were haunted by a dark-cloaked monk.

The small, narrow tunnel leading down to the dungeon was made of rough rock. An old rush lamp sat just where the cellar lights dissipated, and using flint, Brice lit the rush, bathing the area in light.

He bit back a smile when he felt Sophie clasp the back of his coat, holding him for support.

"Are ye alright, lass? Not afraid are ye?"

"My holding on to you is not obvious enough that I'm terrified?" She chuckled and her laugh, both self-deprecating and soft, did odd things to his body, made him feel things he shouldn't. Made him want things he couldn't have.

"There is nothing down here to be scared of. I promise ye that."

They came into the first of three chambers. Brice lifted the rush lamp and showed Sophie the walls. Even after the hundreds of years, they still sported chains and bolts hammered into the rock. The walls were damp, water oozing from the surface. "It would not have been the nicest place for people to be kept."

She stepped around him and looked about the space. She clasped her arms before her, rubbing them. "It's cold in here. Do you not feel like someone is watching us?"

Brice shrugged, glancing about also, anything to keep him from staring at the sweet Sassenach before him. "I dinna feel anything, but Elizabeth refuses to come down here too, so mayhap there are spirits still lingering, waiting to be freed."

Right at that moment, the rush lamp blew out and darkness enfolded them. Brice stood there a moment, the hair on the back of his nape standing upright. No such thing had ever occurred before. He gasped as Sophie threw herself against him, her arms holding his waist in an unyielding grip, her head huddled against his chest.

He wrapped his arms about her and turned her toward where he knew the tunnel entrance was. "I'll take ye back upstairs," he said, her muffled reply unintelligible against his chest.

He held her tight, probably closer than he needed to, but he liked the way she felt in his arms. Holding out his hand he came to the wall and worked his way across until he felt the tunnel entrance. They walked slowly and Brice kept his hand above him to ensure he didn't let a low, over-hanging rock hit him or Sophie.

"I do not think I'll come back down here again," she said, just as the light from the cellar started to penetrate the space.

Brice had to admit to feeling a little relief at making it back. He'd never had a candle or the rush lamp go out on him just as it did back then, and even he could admit to feeling a little unsettled by it.

"'Tis all well now, Miss Grant. I'll not let any harm come to ye."

She pulled him to a stop, glancing up at him. Unable to keep his attention anywhere but on the woman in his arms he met her gaze.

His stomach clenched as she studied him, her face still a little ashen from her fright. He pushed a lock of hair away from her face, slipping it behind her ear.

An overwhelming need assailed him to pull her close,

lean down and kiss those delectable lips that were slightly apart and plump, ripe for the picking.

"Here ye are, I've been looking all over the house for ye."

Sophie wrenched out of his arms and inwardly cursed the arrival of his sister. Elizabeth had an uncanny ability to turn up at the least unwelcome times.

"I was showing Miss Grant the dungeons. We lost our lighting and I was assisting Miss Grant toward the light." What on earth was he saying? He shut his mouth with a snap before anything else absurd came spilling out.

"Really?" His sister glanced between them and he recognized that stare well. She was summing him up, wondering what really was going on.

He clasped his hands behind his back lest he wrench Miss Grant back beside him. He'd wanted to kiss her, had been seconds away of doing exactly that. Perhaps he ought to thank his sister for interrupting them when she did. There was something about Miss Grant that made Brice realize that one taste of her would never be enough.

"We've served tea in the drawing room upstairs. Come, Sophie, we'll walk up together. Elspeth will join us there."

Brice watched them go, waiting a few minutes before he followed them up the cellar stairs. What had he been thinking? The reminder that Elspeth waited for his proposal sent shame spiraling through his blood.

He owed it to his parents to fulfill their most-cherished wish. God knows he'd been difficult enough with all other things in his life while they were alive. He at least ought to do this one thing for them, even though it was too late to make amends for being a difficult child.

Brice made for the library, wanting solitude and time to think. He needed a plan that would keep his hands off

Miss Grant while also gaining enough courage to ask Elspeth for her hand in marriage.

Neither option was appealing. He shut the library door and made his way over to his decanter of whiskey instead. A drink first, then everything else that he was to do would come next.

CHAPTER 6

Sophie watched the laird during dinner that evening, wondering if she'd imagined that he was going to kiss her earlier today. He'd certainly had a wolfish look about him as he leaned toward her before his sister interrupted them.

All afternoon she'd been edgy, annoyed and fidgety that they had been interrupted. That in itself was vexing as the laird had not been the kindest to her when she'd first arrived here, but perhaps it was just his way. The day they were to go riding he'd been busy and she had been thrown into his care.

Whereas today he'd offered to take her down to the dungeons. He'd had spare time to spend with her. His property was vast, it was possible that his coldness toward her the other day had been simply because he'd not had time to mind her.

She shivered as she remembered his hands, clasping her firmly about the waist, holding her fast before him. It had taken all her willpower not to lean into his touch when he'd placed her hair behind her ear.

She swallowed, reaching out to take a sip of wine. She glanced at him and found him watching her. His gaze took in her face and dipped over her body and Sophie's breath caught in her lungs. With each inspection over her person she swore she could feel it as if he were touching her himself.

She'd had men look at her so in London, certainly after her sister had married the marquess and placed her higher in society. That her brother-in-law had bestowed on both her and her brother a modest inheritance also helped.

But with the way the Laird of Mackintosh drank her in, as if she were the sweetest honey to swallow, a thrumming ache formed low in her belly and she couldn't help but wonder what it would be like to be taken in his arms, kissed within an inch of her life.

How delectable that would be.

Her skin heated, but she would not look away from him. If he were trying to scare her away, or warn her off with his heated gaze, he'd mistaken her character for a woman who could not hold her own. She was a Grant, not a woman to be toyed with or assumed to be weak simply because she was female. If he would look at her so boldly, then she would in turn take her fill and take a portrait of him in her mind for the many years to come when hundreds of miles separated them and they went on with their busy lives.

Elizabeth cleared her throat and only then did his lordship look away.

"I was thinking since the weather has been so lovely that we may picnic at the Viking ruins tomorrow. Would ye like that, Sophie?"

To visit Viking ruins sounded simply wonderful and she nodded. "I would love to see them. I understand that the Scots have a lot of ancestry to thank the Vikings for."

Elizabeth smiled, spooning some soup into her mouth. "We do. If ye have not noticed my brother is obscenely tall and walks about as if he should have a sword in his hand."

Sophie chuckled and his lordship scoffed. "Who says I dinna have a sword, sister?"

The idea of seeing him wield one was not an image she needed to imagine. She was already picturing him too perfectly as it was. Even so, to explore outside the house, see a little of the Scotland she wanted to before their carriage broke down sounded like a wonderful day out.

৩৯৩

The carriage ride to the ruins was of short duration and it wasn't long before servants set up a small table and chairs along with food and wine.

The ruins were located in a heavily wooded area near a small river that apparently ran into Loch Moy. "The Vikings would use waterways to transport their goods, and travel."

She glanced up at the laird, having not heard him come up behind her. His voice ran over her like a soothing balm and she couldn't think of a more pleasant way to pass the time than to listen to his Scottish brogue.

"Will you show me about?"

He glanced toward where Elspeth and Elizabeth sat at the table, having tea and biscuits. "Aye, of course. This way." He gestured for her to precede him and she went ahead.

They walked on in silence for a time before his lordship said, "I must admit that I've never met a woman like ye, Miss Grant. Ye're not what I expected when ye arrived at Moy castle."

"Really?" she asked, curious to know what he thought of her. "What did you think I'd be like?"

"Spoiled. A London debutante who was used to getting her own way and would look down on anyone she deemed beneath her."

Sophie raised her brow, halting her steps. "You do not have a very high opinion of the English, then." She continued on and felt more than heard that he was close on her heels. "I suppose because I'm not spoiled and have known menial chores in my life that I'm not like that. Not that I do not enjoy having servants now, I must admit I loathed having to wash my own clothes, but no, I would never look down on anyone for their situation in life. I know my future would have been vastly different had my sister not married a marquess."

"I'm very glad that yer sister did marry the marquess."

Again she stopped and turned to face him, settling her gaze on his. They were hidden from view here within the trees. Through the foliage about them she could make out the stone ruins of the Viking location. "Why do you say that?"

Their eyes met and held. Her heart beat like a drum in her ears, and if she were of a more delicate constitution her knees may have given out on her in that moment. He was devilishly handsome and oh so tempting.

"We would not have met had she not."

She smiled, pleased he would think such a thing and say it aloud to her. "We may have still met, but I doubt your sister would've invited me to stay." A sad truth when one was beneath another due to wealth and rank. How many people missed marrying their soul mate due to being married off to other people that family and society thought appropriate?

She would never do such a thing. If she fell in love

with an innkeeper or farmer she would marry him and enjoy her life and love. She would even leave London and her family if it meant living with the man who made her heart flutter. Even if that meant leaving her family whom she'd only just been reunited with after all the years apart.

"If she had not invited ye, I would have I'm sure."

She raised her brow. "Really? You did not seem too fond of me accompanying you the other day horse riding. Are you certain you would've invited me to stay?"

He ran a hand over his jaw, looking up at the sky as if it would help him explain himself that day before looking at her. "I apologize for leaving ye behind and being so rude." He frowned and she wondered what was going through his mind. "I acted appallingly and I hope ye forgive me."

"I will think about it," she said, turning toward the ruins. Her booted foot caught a stick and Sophie toppled forward, the ground coming up fast to meet her nose. Strong, capable arms wrapped about her waist and stopped her fall.

He wrenched her back against his chest and she sighed, the hardness of him against her back warmed places in her body no lady should know could be warmed.

She turned in his arms, determined to thank him and move away but her feet wouldn't budge from their spot. Her blood pumped loud and fast in her ears and she watched, enthralled, as he leaned down and, finally, kissed her.

His mouth covered hers and her mind whirred at the softness of his lips. For a man who was all brawn and muscle, hard about the edges, his lips were soft, supple and sending her wits to spiral.

Sophie leaned up on her tiptoes and kissed him back,

not willing to miss out on such a situation in life that had never been afforded to her before.

His hands tightened about her waist, slid about her back and pulled her close. Her nipples ached and through her thin muslin gown she prayed he could not feel what he was doing to her body. He broke the kiss, staring at her as if she'd grown two heads.

"I suppose this is where you tell me you're sorry for kissing me and that it won't happen again," she said, breathless.

His lips twitched. "Nay, lass. This is where I tell ye that now that I've tasted yer sweet lips, I'll be doing it again."

ॐ

BRICE TOOK HER LIPS AGAIN, heedless of who may come upon them. At this point he did not care who saw them kissing. He liked the lass, she was kind, intelligent and unlike anyone he'd ever known. Certainly he'd never met a Sassenach like her.

He pulled her close, her warmth and scent of lilies intoxicating his senses and making his head spin. Her kiss, untutored at first, followed his lead and he edged his tongue slowly into her mouth, inwardly crowing when she made a delectable mewling sound of pleasure.

"Ye're so sweet, lass," he said between kisses, holding her close and dipping his head yet again. She met his desire for her with that of her own and he growled when she tentatively pressed her tongue to his.

"Yes, lass, that's it." He wanted her to try, to tempt and tease him as much as he was trying to tempt her. It had been so long since he'd wanted a woman in such a way. Certainly a good few months since he'd bedded a lass. Such a courtship was a night of pleasure and little else. A woman who understood he wasn't looking for a wife any more than she was looking for a husband.

But the lass in his arms now, untouched and perfect in so many ways, was not for him. The reminder ought to have made him wrench away, apologize and leave her just as she'd said earlier, but he didn't. If anything it made him to want to take all and everything she offered him. To be with her as long as she would stay at Moy.

She pulled back, breaking the kiss and immediately he missed having her in his arms. Sophie stared up at him with something akin to awe and he knew deep down, to part from her, have her leave when her carriage was repaired, would be hard.

Hard to watch and hard to allow.

Her hand fluttered up to touch her lips, now red and a little swollen from his touch. "I've never been kissed like that before."

Damn it all to Hades, he'd never kissed anyone like that before either. Certainly not with the simmering emotion he felt coursing through his veins. He liked this lass and that in itself was more telling than anything. To spend more time with her would only mean he'd become more attached, less likely to let her go.

He could not walk that path, no matter how tempting it was to go against everything he'd promised his parents. Elspeth was to be his wife. Not an English lass that, due to no fault of her own, ended up in his town.

"Did ye like my kiss?" he couldn't help but ask. He was a glutton for punishment.

She nodded, her eyes glazed in wonder. "I did." She stepped against him, taking his hand. "While I do not know what such a kiss means, if anything or nothing, I will tell you this. While I'm here at Moy, and a guest in your home, if you feel the inclination to kiss me in such a way again, I'm more than open to it."

He chuckled, unable not to. "'Tis a fine idea, lass. I'm in agreement of yer proposal."

"Very good. Now, shall you show me the ruins?"

"Come," he said, leading them toward the old fort. "There is much to see."

Sophie found herself staring at the laird on and off during the remainder of the day. Within a few minutes of stepping into the old Viking ruins, they were joined by Elizabeth and Elspeth, who both had childhood stories of playing within the grounds, of fascinating finds, like swords and coins, along with what they thought the different buildings and areas that spread out through the wooded area were used for.

The day was long but enjoyable, and Sophie had to admit that she felt quite at home here so far north in Scotland and so very far away from her family.

While she tried to take everything in about the ancient site, her mind kept wandering to the kiss she'd shared with the laird. What did it mean? Was he going to start courting her? Did he see her as a possible candidate for a wife?

She had very little experience with such matters. Her life in Sandbach had been closeted, her aunt venturing out very little unless it had something to do with their church.

When she had left Cheshire for London and to live with Louise, although she'd stepped out in Society at times, nothing like what just occurred with the laird had ever happened to her in Town.

If he did wish to marry her, make her his wife, Moy was a very long way from her family and she'd only just gotten them back. They had been separated from Louise since their older sister was only eight years of age. Sophie wasn't sure she was ready to part from her yet, or certainly part from her when the Scottish highlands were so very far away.

She sat at the small table set up for their luncheon and dismissed the fanciful thoughts. The laird had simply kissed her. To read anything more into the act would be silly and she would be foolish to believe that from one kiss one could decide to spend the rest of their lives with that person.

She was sure there were plenty of people in London who kissed and did not expect a marriage proposal the very next day.

"What do you think of the lemon pie, Sophie?" Elizabeth asked, biting into her own portion.

Sophie glanced down at her plate, having forgotten the food sitting untouched before her. She forked a piece of the pie and placed it in her mouth. "It's very good," she said, between chews.

Laughter caught her attention and she looked over to where the laird was walking with Elspeth. Elspeth was laughing at something the laird had said, and she was smiling up at him. It was the first time she'd seen Elspeth react in any way toward the laird. Sometimes when his lordship tried to engage her in conversation, Elspeth looked bored and disinterested at best. "Elspeth looks very pretty today," Sophie said, watching the two and ignoring the bite of jealousy that assailed her.

Elizabeth looked to where her brother was walking. "Yes, she does. We've been friends since infancy and our parents were the best of friends."

"She's spent a great deal of time here from what she said earlier." Sophie did not understand why she needed to know these things, but something inside her chilled at the sight of the laird with another woman. A Scottish, eligible woman.

"We all grew up together practically, either here or Elspeth's home Brodie Hall."

She watched as the couple walked, arms linked, toward the river that ran past where they were picnicking. "And Elspeth has not married?"

Elizabeth popped a piece of fruit into her mouth and shook her head. "Nay, she's never been inclined as far as I know. Although an heiress and set to inherit her father's holdings, she'd be a catch for anyone."

Even the Laird Mackintosh…

The words were unspoken, but they hung in the air all the same. A warning of sorts assailed her that perhaps the laird wasn't looking at her for a wife at all, but the Scottish lass he'd grown up with and already cared for.

Sophie turned in her chair and glanced in a different direction, not wanting to think such a thing. The laird wouldn't kiss her and be setting his cap for someone else. He wouldn't do that. Scottish or English, he was a gentleman and to court two women at once would not be gentlemanly behavior.

The thought was little comfort for she knew very well that gentlemen did such a thing all the time and she'd be a simpleton indeed to think this one was any different.

CHAPTER 7

L ater that night Sophie sat at the desk in her room and penned a letter to Louise. She had never been one not to be honest and open and so she told her sister of her growing feelings for the laird Mackintosh.

She threw her quill down on the desk, a sense of impatience overcoming her. Sophie looked out the window and stared at her reflection instead of the outdoors, the daylight giving way to night. The house had been abed for hours, even her maid Gretel was long asleep, but it eluded Sophie. Her mind would not settle after her kiss this afternoon or the laird's marked attention toward Elspeth not long after.

She picked up her glass of water and found it empty. Her stomach rumbled and she sighed. There was no use in trying to sleep unless she had a little bite to eat and drink.

Sophie wrapped a shawl about her shoulders and, picking up a candle from atop the mantel, she made her way to the door and the servants' stairs that came out near the kitchen on the first floor.

She made the kitchen with little trouble, and with the

stove still simmering with coals, the room was warm and smelled of flour and baked meat. She walked along the table, lifting up some linens to see what food lay beneath and found some bread from dinner that evening.

She sat on a stool, pulled the plate toward her, and started to eat. The aroma of yeast filled her senses and she sighed in pleasure as her stomach stopped protesting its hunger.

"Are ye alright, Miss Grant? I was making my way upstairs when I saw ye come out of the servants' stairs."

Sophie jumped at the sound of the laird's voice and she chewed quickly, needing to swallow before she spoke. "I hope you do not mind me coming in here at this late hour. I was writing a letter to my sister and I found myself a little hungry."

He came into the room, wearing nothing but trews and a shirt, which scandalously was not tucked into his pants. There was no cravat, a smooth, tanned chest peeked out from his untied top and his hair looked mussed as if he'd run his hand through it too many times.

Her stomach clenched, all hunger deserted her for another hunger altogether. She stared at him, taking her fill and not quite believing that he'd kissed her. After their little slip in etiquette, he'd kept a polite distance for the remainder of the afternoon, never cold or aloof, but he was certainly watchful for what he said or did.

But now, here in the small, warm room, her body longed to be in his arms again and she couldn't help but hope that he wanted to kiss her again too.

"Ye are more than welcome to whatever ye want, whenever ye want, lass." He walked over to a nearby cupboard and pulled out a bottle of wine. "Cook always keeps a well-aged red in here. I'll have a drink with ye and then escort ye back upstairs."

Sophie smiled, watching as he sat down opposite her across the table. He poured two glasses, sliding her drink across to her. She picked it up and drank deeply, parched after eating the bread and taking her fill of him.

"The bread is good, is it not? 'Tis one of my favorite dishes on a cold winter's night."

"It's very filling and fresh."

He reached over and she started as he wiped off what she imagined was a little crumb from her cheek. Her heart thumped loudly in her ears when he didn't immediately move away, and instead cupped her cheek in his hand.

"Ye're so beautiful, lass. I dinna know how I'm going to stay away from ye."

Sophie swallowed, having never heard such a sweet thing in her life. She stood and moved about the table to come to stand before him. He turned in his chair to face her and she reached up, smoothing out the small line that marred his forehead.

"You're not what I expected to find in the highlands either. You're quite a surprise, Laird Mackintosh."

He reached up and hugged her loosely about her back. "Call me Brice, please. I think after this afternoon we're past formal forms of address."

Her face heated a little at his reminder of what they'd done. "Will you call me Sophie?"

His mouth lifted in a small grin and her nerves skittered across her skin. "Aye. Sophie," he said, in a heavy brogue. "I can call ye that."

"I like the sound of my name on your lips," she whispered, stepping between his legs and coming up hard against him. His arms tightened about her back, his large hands splaying across her spine. It felt right. That she was in the right place for the first time in her life.

"I like the sound of yer name on my lips as well," he said, before he leaned up and kissed her.

Sophie met him halfway, having wanted to kiss him since the afternoon. The moment their lips touched, the agitation, the restlessness that had plagued her the whole night dissipated and everything was right in the world.

The kiss was everything and more. His mouth coaxed and tempted her, made her feel things she'd not known were possible between two people. His lips were soft, moved over hers like silk, his tongue tempting and warm against her own.

She met his kiss with her own, wanting to show him she too could tease and explore. His hand slid up her spine, sending a delicious shiver to course across her skin before he clasped her nape, turning her slightly to deepen the kiss.

Sophie clutched about his neck for purchase as the kiss turned from sweet and slow to something completely oppo-site. No longer did he tease and tempt her, the kiss now took on a life of its own. He kissed her hard, deepening the embrace and taking control of where the kiss was going.

Sophie's knees gave way and his arm clasped tight about her back, hoisting her onto his lap. She went will-ingly. How could she not? To be kissed in such a way made her mind blank, and she didn't wish to be good. Not right now in any case. She'd been well-behaved all her life. One scandalous kiss in a kitchen in the middle of the night would not hurt.

She didn't know when she'd get another opportunity for such a treat. Maybe with her husband if she was fortu-nate enough to marry a man like the laird who made her burn, made her mind constantly busy with thoughts of him.

"You're so sweet, lass. Ye make my teeth ache."

She pulled back, running a hand across his stubbled

jaw. "Mine too," she said, seeing no reason not to be honest. He did make her long for more stolen kisses, for nights such as these that would never end.

Even if that meant that her time in England with her family, a family that had only recently been reunited, would be separated again by hundreds of miles.

He kissed her again, slower this time before he pulled back and helped her to stand. "I'll escort ye back to yer room. 'Tis late and the house can sometimes be hard to move through when the candles have all been doused."

Sophie checked that her dressing gown and shawl were still covering her before she allowed him to escort her from the room.

He took her hand, his large palm encasing hers as he led her from the kitchen. How was it that a simple touch of hands could discombobulate her so?

She glanced up at his profile, strong and rugged, a perfectly straight nose and cutting cheekbones. A devastatingly handsome man and one who made her stomach clench. Would he ever lose control with her? Would there be more kisses? Oh, how she hoped there would be.

Tonight, however, was not the night. The gentleman that he was, he escorted her to her room and simply bowed before leaving her staring after him. She watched as he strode back up the corridor, heading toward his own part of the house.

She sighed. "I hope I find a husband like you," she whispered into the dark. To live a life beside a man that excited, challenged and tempted her were what dreams were made of. Her sister had been so fortunate, maybe she would be as well.

In London no one had ever tempted her as much as Brice did, but that did not mean they were not out there. She simply needed to give it more time.

"Are you coming in, Miss Sophie?" Gretel asked, from inside the room.

"Oh yes, thank you," Sophie said, pulling off her shawl as she came inside and set it down on a nearby settee.

"Was that Laird Mackintosh I saw leaving down the hall?" Gretel asked, picking up the shawl and placing it over the back of a nearby chair.

Sophie went over to her bed, climbing in under the covers. "I went to the kitchens for some food. I'm sorry that I woke you. You may go back to bed now."

"May I speak plainly?" Gretel asked, standing at the end of Sophie's bed and ignoring Sophie's vague answer.

Sophie didn't like the sound of such a thing, but they had been friends for so long that she would not deny Gretel her opinion. Whatever it may be. Some women of nobility would never allow a maid to speak such, but that was not who Sophie was, or who she wanted to be. "If you like."

Gretel nodded. "Take care with the laird, miss. The staff here seem adamant that his lordship will marry the Scottish lass Elspeth and before the year is out. If that is the case, please take care if he happens to escort you back to your room in future."

Elspeth. Sophie frowned, having wondered the same thing, but having never heard this desire spoken aloud by anyone. "I'm sure you're mistaken," she said, her voice unsure even to her own ears. She played with her blankets, smoothing them out over her legs. "He's not injured me in any way, but should he be engaged to someone else, I'm sure he would be honest and tell me. We're friends, you see, and I can promise you the laird is not a deceiving man."

Gretel took in her words before moving back over to where the door to her adjoining room stood. "Even so, guard your heart. I do not wish to see you hurt. One never knows what the future holds."

"Goodnight, Gretel," Sophie said, putting an end to the conversation. The laird would not deceive her so. If he was intended elsewhere he would not kiss her with such passion. He would not kiss her at all.

She smiled at the memory of their interlude only minutes before and fell asleep dreaming of when she could do it again.

CHAPTER 8

T he following morning Sophie came downstairs and
found her driver kicking his heels in the foyer. "Good
morning, Peter. Are you after me for something?" she
asked, coming to stand before him.

"Miss Sophie, good morning. Yes, the wheel for the
carriage arrived yesterday from Inverness and has been
repaired. We can continue with our journey tomorrow if
you wish."

Footsteps sounded on the parquetry floor and she
turned to see Brice striding purposefully toward her. She
bit her lip, and blinked at his kilt and shirt, his only articles
of clothing. Heat rushed to her cheeks and she turned
back to Peter only to see him contemplating her and the
laird.

"Is there something the matter, lass?" Brice asked,
coming to a stop beside her.

She shook her head. "No, nothing." She glanced up at
him, her stomach summersaulting at being near him again.
Her fingers itched to reach out and wrap about his waist,
pull him close so he may kiss her again.

Sophie shook her head, dismissing the fanciful thought. She really did need to get a hold of her emotions.

"My carriage is repaired. Peter was just saying we may continue on with our journey tomorrow."

His smile slipped before he schooled his features. "We shall send word this afternoon regarding Miss Grant's travel arrangements." Brice clasped her hand and pulled her toward his study. "If ye'll excuse us."

Sophie didn't have the opportunity to say thank you to her servant before she was whisked into the laird's office where the door was shut, the snip of the lock loud in the empty, sizeable room.

"What are you doing, Brice? With the way you just acted, I'm not sure what my driver will think."

He walked over and then leaned up against his desk, watching her, his dark, hooded gaze pinning her on the spot. She fought not to fidget, although why she felt as if she were about to be scolded she had no idea.

"I dinna care what yer driver may think or anyone else. What I wish to know is if ye are going to be leaving me tomorrow?"

Leaving me? Sophie came up to him and uncrossed his arms covering his chest, placing them about her back. "Are we welcome to stay for a few more days then, my lord?"

He threw her a half smile, his grip about her waist increasing and making her belly clench. "Aye, ye're more than welcome. If fact, I'd love for ye to be a guest here for some weeks. Mayhap write to yer friend in the highlands and ask her to travel here to see ye. She'd be more than welcome also."

"Really? You'd do that for me?"

He leaned forward, brushing her lips with his. "Aye, I'd do that and more if it meant that I could keep ye here for a little while longer."

Sophie would love to have her friend come and stay and she would write her today and ask if she'd come. "I will ask her to stay, although I'm not certain she'll be able to. She helps her parents with the family income, but I will ask in any case."

He let her go and walked over to the fire and threw a log into the grate, watching the flames lick the wood. Sophie stayed where she was, unsure what was going through Brice's mind.

"Is everything well, Brice?"

He glanced at her and she wondered if it was regret that she glimpsed in his eyes. "'Tis a sweet sound hearing my name on yer lips, lass. Yes," he said, turning to face her. "All is well. The fact that yer carriage is ready has me wondering when ye will be leaving these parts. To continue on with yer travels either to the highlands or back to London."

Sophie came over near Brice and sat on a settee. "If Jean comes here, then after her stay I'll return to London. I received a letter only yesterday from Louise and she and Stephen miss me dreadfully, or so she says."

"Ye are close with yer siblings then?"

"Even though we were separated for many years, or at least Stephen and I were from Louise, we've always tried to stay close. Now that I have Louise back in my life, I do find I miss her dreadfully as well. I'm not ashamed to admit that I cannot wait to see them again."

He ran a hand over his jaw before that same hand ran through his hair, leaving it on end. "So our time with ye is limited. 'Tis a sad day that we'll have to bid ye farewell from our land."

"Even a Sassenach?" she teased, grinning.

He chuckled, coming to sit beside her, pulling her into

the crook of his arm. "Aye, even an English lass such as yerself."

Some hours later Brice sat at his desk and went over the ledgers from his steward, yet his mind refused to concentrate. His thoughts kept straying to Sophie, who right at this moment was somewhere in his house, somewhere he was not.

His every waking hour he wanted to be near her, watch and admire how her pretty little hips shifted with each step. How her long, blonde locks caught the highland sun and glistened like ripe wheat.

The idea that her time here was limited left a hollowness inside. He wasn't fool enough to not know that he did not want her to go anywhere. Yet he could not ask her to stay either.

His path in life was set many years ago and Elspeth and her family were expecting a proposal in the coming months. He could not let them down, even if Elspeth seemed far from inclined to have him as her husband.

The lass had many times stated her desire to remain a spinster and had he not promised his parents he'd marry the lass, he'd be loath to disappoint Elspeth and take away her dream.

A knock at his door startled him from his reflections and he yelled *enter* more abruptly than was probably necessary.

His good friend Angus Campbell glanced about the threshold, smiling. "Brice, how are ye, my friend? 'Tis been an age since I've seen ye darken my threshold. I thought I'd come and darken yers instead."

Brice stood, gesturing him to enter. "Angus, 'tis good to

see ye. More than ye know. Come," he said, walking about the desk to pour two whiskeys. "Sit and have a drink with me. I'm in need of advice."

Angus glanced at him as if he'd lost his mind, which Brice was starting to think he had. "Is something wrong? 'Tis not like ye to ask for help."

That was true, he very rarely asked for anything and yet, right now, Angus was the only person he could trust and confide in. He was his friend of many years, and both held confidences for the other that would never be told. Angus would listen and help steer him through this obstacle course called Sophie Grant.

He handed Angus a whiskey and sat back down. "What brings ye to these parts in any case? Ye're a long way from home."

"Aye." Angus nodded, taking a sip. "My sister has had a bairn and I'm on my way to see them at Avoch. If ye remember she married a landowner up there two years past."

"I remember it well. 'Twas a grand celebration that night. I'm glad yer sister is happily settled. How is Aberdeen?"

"The same." Angus studied him a moment before he said, "But I can see ye have something on yer mind. Out with it, man."

Brice sighed, leaning back in his chair, running a hand over his face. He'd never asked for such advice before and to do so now was out of character and foreign to him. "I dinna know what to do about a lass."

Angus raised his brow. "Are ye feeling well? Never would I ever thought to hear those words uttered from a Mackintosh's mouth."

Brice stared up at the ceiling in the hope that it may give him some divine insight into what he should do.

"There is a woman here. Staying as a guest of my sister's. 'Tis a long story, but she came to stay after injuring herself in town. She's bonny."

A slow smile formed on Angus's lips. "How bonny?"

"She's the bonniest lass I've ever met and my troubles have now doubled because I canna keep my hands off her."

Angus did chuckle then, smiling fully. "Have ye tupped her?"

"Nay, she's the Marquess Graham's sister-in-law. To tup her would mean I'd have to marry her and ye know that I'm all but promised to Elspeth."

Angus rolled his eyes. "No matter what ye promised yer parents, or hers for that matter, I'll be surprised if Elspeth marries anyone. I've always thought she found men quite the bore, whereas women she seems more than happy to be around."

Brice narrowed his eyes, having never really taken much notice how Elspeth behaved around men, but now that his friend mentioned it, she did seem more inclined to converse with the female sex. Maybe she did not like men at all.

"'Tis not just my parents who expected a match. Elspeth's parents do too, and ye know they still believe we owe them our land due to that blasted loan Father took out from them before I was born. If everyone who wished for such a union were no longer living I wouldn't worry so much about the promise, but they are. I'd be letting them down if I dinna align the Mackintosh and Brodie clans together."

"That, my friend, is a load of horse dung. Elspeth's parents may long for whatever they like, but the debt has been paid, and why would ye not want yer daughter to marry with affection? Ye dinna have to do what anyone says. Ye're a Mackintosh, a laird. Ye may marry whomever ye want."

"A Mackintosh never goes back on their word, and I gave my word to my parents."

His friend threw him a consoling look before he said, "I understand, I do, but marriage is a lifelong commitment. Ye dinna want to be stuck with the wrong lass forever and a day. Marriage is nae supposed to be an endless cycle of torture."

Brice chuckled, glad of his friend's arrival and his words of wisdom, which all made sense, but still, he would need to think on what to do. He'd never broken his word to anyone before and to start doing so now for a woman that in all reality he hardly knew was foolish. In the coming weeks he would see how things went, and then make a decision at the end of it.

"Tell me ye are staying. We'll be having dinner soon. I'd love for ye to meet my guest."

Angus finished off his drink, placing the crystal glass down on his desk. "Now that I know of yer struggles ye'll not be getting rid of me, not for one night at least. I need to meet this English lass of yers and see what all the fuss is about."

Relief poured through him like a balm that his friend would be here, tonight at least, to support him. "Ye'll like her, Angus and then ye will be as confused as I am."

"Probably," his friend said, finishing his drink. "Now, where am I sleeping? I need to change before dinner."

⚬⚬⚬

AT DINNER that evening Brice sat at the head of the table and watched with growing annoyance as Angus and Sophie chatted to one another.

340

His sister had placed them together, and even though Brice trusted his friend with his life and everything else, the sight of him laughing, engaged, and enjoying the evening with his lass left a sour taste in his mouth.

He pushed about the roast potatoes on his plate, glancing up every now and then to see that they still spoke about all subjects, some of which even he had not discussed yet with her.

Elspeth on the other hand was reading some book that she tried to conceal under a napkin. Elizabeth, like him, looked a little put out by Angus talking to Sophie and he narrowed his eyes, wondering if his sister held some feelings toward his friend.

Angus would be a good match for his sister and he knew him well enough to know that he would treat his sibling well. But knowing his friend as well as he did, he did not expect him to marry for some time yet. He enjoyed his bachelorhood too much.

He took a sip of wine, nodding to a waiting footman that the sweet course could be served. The pudding that was placed before him did little to lift his mood, even if it was one of his favorite dishes.

Sophie thanked the servant and glanced up the table toward him and a right hook to his stomach would've had less impact.

Her lips lifted into a knowing smile and he could not look away. The urge to go to her, wrap her up in his arms and kiss her to distraction overwhelmed him and he shook himself to remind himself they were in public.

There would be nothing of the sort, not unless she sought him out again or he came across her somewhere in the house when she was alone. It was one major advantage of having a house like this. One could get lost or remain lost so no one could interrupt or intrude on one's day.

He winked at her and smiled as a deep flush rose on her cheeks, making her even more beautiful to look at. His sister's clearing of her throat brought his attention to her and her pointed stare and raised brow was proof enough she'd caught him.

Brice turned back to his meal, eating his pudding with more zest than was necessary. There was nothing so bad that he'd done other than kiss the lass. Nothing wrong with him teasing her a little at the dining table either, even if his sister seemed overly shocked by his actions.

Who was he kidding? He was skating on thin ice and playing with fire at the same time. And yet, he could not remember a time when he'd enjoyed fire and ice so much in his life.

CHAPTER 9

The following day dawned warm and without a gust of wind to mar the beautiful spring weather. Yesterday after dinner Sophie had written to her friend Jean, inviting her to come and stay, and she hoped more than expected her to come. They were a family who worked for their living and times could sometimes be hard. A sojourn south to simply do nothing other than visit friends was not usual for them and so she didn't think she would be able to come.

Sophie sat outside on the lawn that her room over-looked. The grounds were vast and from here she could see down into a valley that looked to have a small stream running through it. Placing her book beside her, she started to navigate the small decline, wanting to explore more of this marvelous estate.

She couldn't imagine growing up in such surrounds. The village of Sandbach had been small, quaint, but not a lot happened. As for the small cottage her aunt had owned, it had been three bedrooms, a kitchen and drawing room. All modest and little, but comfortable. Her aunt had been a proud woman and had tried her hardest to give them a little luxury while they grew up.

When she'd moved into her sister's London home with the marquess she'd not really understood the divide between the rich and poor. But she did now. The divide was monumental and at times, when they drove through the streets of London, looking out on the poor begging for food or work, she wondered if it would ever be breached.

When she returned to Town she would join a charity and try to give help to those she could. She had been fortunate, had been able to step out of a life of servitude, which she was destined for, into a life of a woman who could choose her future, a husband. So many were not so fortunate.

The walk through the trees down to the small river was cooler than up on the lawn and she pulled her shawl closer about her shoulders. The dappled sunlight lit her way and a crack of a stick made her pause, only to see a deer a few feet away looking at her as if surprised she'd impinged on his solitude.

Sophie continued on working her way through the ferns and undergrowth that had been allowed to grow wild this far away from the house.

The tinkling sound of flowing water met her ears and she pushed through the thick foliage and came to the side of the river. She stifled a gasp and stepped back behind a fern, hoping that Brice had not seen her, for she had certainly seen him, all of him in his naked glory.

Heat infused her face and she lifted her hand, patting her cheek in the hopes of bringing its temperature down. Unable to resist, she peered through the bushes again, watching as he dipped into the water, before coming up again, the water slithering over every ounce of muscle that his body sported.

And there was a lot of muscle, all of it flexing and tightening with each of his movements as he wrung out his hair.

"Do ye like what ye see, lass?"

Sophie gasped, slapping a hand over her mouth. She glanced up at the heavens, wishing right at that moment that she was anywhere but here. She'd been caught ogling him like a little strumpet instead of turning about and heading back toward the house, which is what she should have done the moment she'd intruded on his privacy.

Oh dear Lord in heaven, how would she ever face him again?

She turned around, giving him her back, although she was sure he could not see her well enough to know she'd granted him that modicum of privacy. "I do apologize. I did not know you were here. I should have made my presence known."

She cringed again at being caught. What did he think of her?

"Dinna fret, lass. I dinna mind ye looking. Ye may look as much as ye like."

Sophie bit her lip, counting to five in the hopes that she would not turn around and take her fill some more. He was too tempting for his own good and he damn well knew it.

"Somehow I do not believe that would be appropriate, my lord."

His replying chuckle made her shiver and she shut her eyes, reveling in it a moment. "And our little trysts over the last few days have been appropriate? No one is here and we're hidden from view from the house. What does it matter if ye look at me while we talk?"

Sophie took a calming breath and called his bluff. She turned, stepping through the undergrowth and leaned against a nearby tree watching him. "Happy? I'm looking at you now, my lord."

"Brice, please," he said, walking toward her in the water. The action drew her attention down to his abdomen and the sharp V that delved into the water. She'd never seen a man so naked before and her mind swirled with the idea that he was as naked beneath the water as he was above it.

"Do not come any closer, Brice. Our kissing behind closed doors is one thing, but if you step out of that water and I find you're as naked as I fear you are, that is quite another scenario altogether."

He threw her a mischievous grin and she shook her head. He was impossible! His hands ran along the water's surface and she was envious of them, wanting them upon her body instead.

"Aye, I'm as naked as a babe." He winked and she let out an exasperated sigh. "If you dinna want me to join ye there, why do ye not join me in here? The day is warm, and I'm sure ye have a shift on. That will do. 'Tis what my sister swims in when she partakes in the activity."

Could she go for a swim? She glanced behind her and just as Brice said, the house was hidden from view, and therefore eyes. It had been so many years since she'd swam and here was her chance. Not only that, here was her chance to swim with Brice. She could not turn him down.

She turned back to face him, before reaching up and unbuttoning the top of her gown. "Turn about and let me get undressed."

BRICE SWORE, a cold shiver running down his spine with the knowledge that he'd baited Sophie into coming into the water with him.

How the bloody hell would he keep his hands off the lass? The mere thought of her wet, practically naked and near him in the water was enough to make him hard as rock.

If he were a gentleman he would have ignored her presence, finished his swim and left, but he could not. He could not stop himself from talking to her, of asking her to join him. He was a veritable cad.

Should his sister or Elspeth catch them swimming together, scantily dressed and alone, his plans to merge the Mackintosh and Brodie clans would be a dream buried with his parents.

The idea that the lass slowly changing behind him, the sound of clothing being laid over small bushes and slippers being kicked off was also a dream he could not ignore.

He wanted her. Not just here and now, but in his bed tonight, and every night she had left in Scotland. The realization ought to shock sense into him, but it did not. It merely threw images of Sophie into his mind, her hair mussed from their lovemaking, her wide blue orbs sleepy with satisfaction.

Brice fisted his hands at his sides. How the hell was he going to keep his hands off her?

Water sloshed behind him, and he did not turn to look until he was sure her body was fully submerged. "Can I look at ye now, lass?"

"Yes, if you want."

Oh yes, he damn well wanted to... He turned, watching as she walked out a little deeper. The linens from her shift bubbled up from behind her and he caught a glimpse of her upper thigh. The blood in his veins turned molten and he refused to leave the spot on which he stood.

I will not touch her. I will not touch her. I will not touch her.

She laughed, ducking under the water and coming up before him. "Are you not going to swim with me? We can race to the other side if you like."

A race. Perfect. Just the thing to keep his mind and hands off the woman who was driving him to distraction.

"On my count, ready, set..." He dived forward, not waiting to say go and heard her protestations before concentrating on swimming to the other side of the river. It was only a small distance and not deep enough that he could not touch. He made the other side with little effort and turned to see her beside him. "How did ye make it so fast?"

He'd not thought she would keep up. He was a strong swimmer and she was a lass after all. More delicate and unused to such strenuous exercise.

"I swam. I will admit that I think you won, but only just. She stood facing him, her face a little flushed from effort. His heart turned in his chest and he reached for her, unable to keep away.

He tried. God damn it he tried to remain aloof, to not get attached, but it was impossible. She was simply lovely and after years of living in such a secluded location, away from society, his life already mapped out, it was nice to have a little change in his home. Not that his sister and Elspeth were dull, but that they had all grown up together, they were all, including himself, set in their ways and living a life where nothing happened.

A tiresome life if he were honest.

He hoisted her up against his chest. A growl ripped from him as she lifted her legs to wrap about his waist. She didn't shy away from his nakedness, and he didn't hide it from her either. She would only have to glance down and she would see how very much he enjoyed having her in his arms.

"Is this my prize, Laird?" she asked, her voice a whispery purr that made him burn.

She didn't move or undulate against him and, blast it, he wanted her to. He wanted her to seduce him so he didn't feel like the veritable cad who stole the innocence away from the English lass. A woman who was not for him.

What do ye want, lass? The words formed in his mind and he stood still and silent waiting for her to say anything else. He would not ask her, he could not. If he should utter those words and she say *him* there would be no turning back. No denying himself.

He held his body rigid, not willing to let her move or remove herself from his hold. His breath came quick, his heart beating loud in his ears as she slowly closed the space between them and kissed him.

"You may not answer my question, Brice, but I know the answer anyway." She kissed him again, hard and deep, and he didn't try to stop her, didn't push her away, set her down in the water and tell her to leave. That they should not do this.

They were going to do this and he was going to damn well enjoy every minute of it.

He kissed her back, devoured her mouth and clasped the nape of her neck, moving her to his will. Her body slid against his, fitted him like a glove and he groaned when her sex, separated from him by the thinnest of material, pushed against his engorged cock.

It would take little effort to rip up her shift, grab his shaft and slide into her hot, willing body. She gasped against his mouth and he took the opportunity to slide his tongue against hers, loving that she in turn followed his lead and did the same back.

"Ye're so beautiful, Sophie," he whispered against her lips. She threw him a small, seductive smile that would make any man fall to his knees and kissed him back.

The sound of women's voices floated through the trees and he stilled, before tearing Sophie off his body and placing her before him in the water, hoping his body would shield her from view.

"What is it?" she whispered, staring up at him with eyes wide with concern and still hazy with desire.

He pushed down his want of her and mouthed, "People."

She ducked a little in the water and he turned his head as his sister and Elspeth came to stand on the opposite side of the bank.

The shocked gasp from Elspeth reached him and he was glad to see she had turned around. His sister, however, stared at him with annoyance, her arms crossed over her chest.

"If ye had not forgotten today is my day for the river. Ye may finish yer swim and go," she said, raising one brow.

Brice fought to work out what he could do so no one was ruined here today. Not Sophie's future and not his own with Elspeth. Not that they were engaged, but still, she was who was expected to become the next Lady Mackintosh.

"I only just arrived, Elizabeth. I'll come get ye when I return to the house so ye may come down for a swim." He gave them his back again, hoping that Sophie could not be seen. "I'm naked, so 'tis best if ye leave me be."

Elspeth muttered under her breath and started off, or he assumed she walked off since the sound of leaf litter under feet could be heard. His sister, however, did not move. He cursed the stubborn lass. She was a Mackintosh to the bone.

"I dinna want to swim when the day cools, so I suggest ye get yerself out of the river and home within the next half hour. We'll be in the upstairs drawing room when ye want to let us know that ye're finished."

"Right ye are, lass," he said, not willing to argue with her a moment longer. He just needed her to leave so Sophie could return to the house unharmed and still as innocent as she arrived. He glanced down at her and found her eyes fixed on his manhood that was still painfully aroused and bobbing before her in the water.

Heat rushed his face and he covered himself, having never been more ashamed of himself in his life. What was he doing?! How could he treat her with so little respect? He ought to be horsewhipped.

Her hands came out of the water and covered his, pulling them away. With just one touch he was back to where he started before they were interrupted and he cursed the fact he'd let her do anything to him, let her ogle and touch him to her heart's content if that is what she wished.

He was going to hell, if he were not there already.

CHAPTER 10

Sophie reached out and pulled Brice's hands away, wanting to see what it was that had pressed against her sex.

She was not aware of what men's manhood should look like or what size they came in, but something told her Brice was well-endowed and he knew it. That he knew how to make her want him and to forget all the principles she'd been brought up to follow and adhere to was another matter altogether.

His manhood bobbed in the water, just beneath the surface, but she could see it, its hardness and length. Sophie reached out, running a finger over the tip, sliding it down toward the base. His manhood jumped and she glanced up, her stomach fluttering at the heated, intense stare he bestowed upon her.

She watched him and she clasped her hand about his shaft. She stroked his length and he gasped through clenched teeth. "Did I hurt you?" she asked, releasing him.

He reached out and took her hand, placing it back on his body. "Nay. The opposite, lass."

She bit her lip, touching him again, now taking her time in exploring. The male sex was a curious thing. Hard as steel and yet as soft as velvet. The thought of this long, thick shaft going into her made her legs clench both in fear and need. Obviously such a thing was normal and he would fit. It was what was done after all in marriage and there was no reason they would not work just as well.

His hand came over hers and showed her what to do, to tighten her hold and increase her pace. His stomach muscles clenched and she reached out with her other hand and ran her fingers over his chiseled abdomen.

"We need to stop, lass," he said, his eyes holding hers as she continued to touch him.

Never in her life had she wanted anyone with the need that coursed through her blood right at that moment. She wanted him. Wanted him to lay claim to her. To carry her out of this water, lay her on the bed of grass along the river bank and do wicked, naughty things to her.

"Stop, Sophie," he said, in no way reaching for her hand to stop her. She did not want to either. In fact, had they not been interrupted by his sister and Elspeth she would've allowed him to take her in the water.

His hand came over hers and pulled her away and he stepped back. She glanced up at him and read the determined set of his jaw and knew he'd not let her touch him again. Not here at least.

"I canna let you continue what we're doing. 'Tis not right. Ye need to return to the house before I rip yer innocence from ye without a second thought or care."

The voicing of his wish only made the possibility more alluring, but he was right. Elizabeth and Elspeth would be back here soon and she needed to return to the house before they were caught. It would not do anyone any good to be compromised and she did not want her sister or brother traveling to Scotland to call Brice out for his conduct.

She stood, not caring that her shift had turned transparent or that he could see every curve, every asset of her body. "I will see you at dinner." Sophie dove back toward the opposite side of the river and swam toward where she'd left her clothes. Thankfully Elizabeth and Elspeth had not seen them when they had come down for their swim.

She dressed quickly and left, taking one last glance at Brice through the trees before she disappeared. He stood where she left him, hands clenched at his sides and head bowed. Whatever was he thinking? Or better yet, maybe he ought to stop thinking so much and simply feel. If there was one thing that Sophie was certain of after today, he was right for her. The only man who had ever stirred her heart, mind and body.

Sophie made her way through the trees, sticking to their cover for as long as she could before heading back indoors via the servants' entrance and then stairs lest she run into Elizabeth and have to explain her wet underclothing.

Coming to the upstairs hall, she checked to ensure no one was about and headed for her room. Gretel was there to meet her, and she sighed, a displeased frown creasing her brow when she spied her dishabille.

"I apologize for the state of my clothing. I went for a swim."

Gretel helped her undress, *tsk tsking* as she peeled the layers of clothing off her.

"It's a warm day. Miss Elizabeth came by to see if you wanted to swim with them, but they've only just left so I can only assume you swam alone. That's not safe, Miss Sophie."

Sophie glanced down at her slippers, now ruined from their trek to the river and back. "The river wasn't deep. It was perfectly safe," she lied, not wanting Gretel to know or imagine what happened while she was there. The delectable touches, the kiss that swept her off her feet, the man who'd captured her attention, body and soul.

"I should imagine you're looking forward to returning home after our travels. With the carriage now repaired, we're free to leave for Moy whenever you're ready."

Sophie nodded, lifting her arms as Gretel pulled her shift up over her head. "I've actually invited Jean to come here for a visit. We're not due back in Town for some weeks yet, and with the incident with the carriage I fear our traveling to Skye may not be possible. There is simply not enough time. But Jean may come here for a week or two and then we shall part ways from here."

Gretel laid her wet clothing over her arm, assessing her in the same way Louise did when she was trying to figure out a puzzle. Namely her.

"You've grown attached to the laird," Gretel said, sighing. "I knew you would. The moment you both saw each other I knew there would be trouble."

Sophie frowned, reaching over to her bed and picking up her dressing gown. "And so what if I have grown attached to him. He's eligible, and so am I. There is nothing wrong with that."

"No, there isn't, but do not forget he lives in the middle of nowhere. You swore when you left Sandbach that you would never move to another little hamlet with fewer than one hundred people living in it. I don't mean to speak out of turn, but there are only two people living here plus a handful of servants. I fear if you marry the laird you'll be bored within a week. Not to mention you've only just got back your sister. Have you forgotten you promised her to marry and live close to her in England so you'll never be apart again?"

Sophie slumped onto the bed, having not forgotten, but merely ignoring her own promises. It was true, the laird did live high up in Scotland. Mackintosh land was closer to Inverness than it was to London.

Of course she'd wanted to marry and be close to her sister, but surely Louise would understand that if she loved her husband, she would be happy for her, wherever she was in the world.

"You make me sound fickle. Scotland is beautiful and I should love to live here if that is what my future holds. But a stolen kiss does not equal marriage. You're getting ahead of yourself and above your station."

Gretel raised her brow. "Oh no, you're not going to pull that high-and-mighty stance with me, Sophie Grant. We were equal once and do not forget that I hold the position your sister did before she married the marquess. You've been my oldest friend before nobility got in the way and I'll speak plainly and honestly with you always."

Sophie stood, coming over to Gretel and hugging her. "I'm sorry. I did not mean what I said. I'm just so confused. Brice makes me so muddled that I do not know what I should do."

Gretel pulled her over to the settee and sat beside her. "Please take care, that's all I ask. And do not make any hasty decisions until you've spoken to your family. I like the laird, I do. His sister and their friend also, but heed what I told you some days ago. There is a rumor that he's to wed Miss Elspeth. Promise me that you'll ask him before anything else passes between you. I do not want to see you hurt, that's all."

Sophie clasped Gretel's hands, squeezing them a little. "I will ask him. I promise." A shiver rocked her body and she huddled into the robe. "Please ring for a bath. I'm quite chilled all of a sudden."

Gretel stood, ringing the bell beside the fireplace. "Of course. I'll get your things ready."

Sophie watched her disappear into her dressing room and she frowned. Gretel was right. She needed to be wary. What did she really know of the laird or his plans for his future? Nothing really. And why was Elspeth here? Of course, they were allied clans, and just like the English they had house parties and stayed at each other's estates, but was her being here because of what Gretel had said before?

Was Elspeth expecting a proposal of marriage?

She shivered at the thought and stood, going to the fire to warm herself. The idea of Brice married to someone else, of taking her in his arms just as he took her today made her stomach twist in knots and left a sour taste in her mouth.

No matter the answer, she needed to find out the truth and then she would know what to do.

Then she would decide if he were worth risking her reputation, gambling her heart and leaving her family behind.

CHAPTER 11

The following evening Sophie sat in the great hall after dinner, warming herself before the fire after a cold change had blown in through the day.

The house, no matter its mammoth size was warm and welcoming and she watched the flames as they licked the wood and turned it slowly to ash.

She'd not seen Brice all day and he'd been absent from dinner the night before. Sophie wasn't certain what to make of it. Was he avoiding her, or after Gretel's words yesterday, was she reading into situations and circumstances more than she ought?

Elspeth too was still in residence and twice today it had been on Sophie's tongue to try to gauge why she was a guest here. Was there an understanding between the families?

A shadow passed over her and she glanced up to see Brice standing before her, his trews damp, his boots mud-splattered.

She glanced at him, not moving, and he stared back and all thoughts of leaving him alone, of not touching him again, flew right out of her mind. He closed the space between them, wrenched her out of her seat and kissed her.

Hard.

Sophie melted against him, wrapping her arms about his waist. She kissed him back with as much passion as she could summon. Heedless of where they were or who could walk in on them at any moment, the kiss went on, her body aching for things no well-bred young lady ought to want.

He clasped her chin and tilted her head to kiss her deep. She moaned when he stepped into her, pushing his hardness against her stomach.

"I missed ye today," he said, breaking the kiss.

She took a calming breath, nodding. "I missed you too."

He shook his head, scowling. "I canna stay away from ye. I've tried. I canna do it."

Sophie licked her lips, unable to hide the pleasure his words brought forth. Her body felt as though it were on fire, alive and burning for the man before her.

"I want you too," she said, having never uttered anything so scandalous or truthful to a man before in her life. Brice was a laird, a gentleman, he would not hide anything from her. Gretel was wrong. The rumors were wrong.

"When can we be alone?" she asked, wanting him to say now. Follow me and we'll be alone right now.

He glanced behind himself and stepped back. "I will not ruin ye, Sophie. No matter how tempting ye are or how much I want ye in my bed."

She shivered at the thought. Now that she'd seen him naked, to picture him above her on a soft bed, his strong, muscled body pinning her down made her body ache. "And if I want you to? What then?"

He sighed, running a hand through his hair. A muscle worked in his jaw before he said, "Dinna tempt me, lass. I'm drawing every ounce of honor I have not to take ye whenever I see ye about the house. Ye're literally driving me mad."

She grinned, the fact that she drove him to distraction was a welcome reprieve for he drove her mad as well. "It's my choice, is it not? What if I choose you?"

He reached out, running a hand across her cheek, one finger trailing across her lips before he let it fall to his side. "Ye cannot."

Sophie raised her brow. "We'll see about that."

"See about what?" Elspeth asked, coming into the room, a book held against her chest.

Sophie didn't move, but she could not say the same about Brice. He started at the sound of Elspeth's voice and couldn't look more guilty if he tried. She smiled at Elspeth before taking her seat again. "We thought we may take a ride tomorrow, if the weather turns back to being pleasant. I was merely saying we'll have to see about it."

Elspeth nodded, glancing out the window before seating herself beside Sophie and opening her book. "I'll not be riding. Have ye forgotten that Mama will be arriving tomorrow, Brice? She'll want to see ye, of course."

Brice's face paled before he smiled. "Nay, of course I had not forgotten. We can ride after yer mother arrives if ye do wish to come. She normally travels in the morning in any case."

"Hmm, yes, she does," Elspeth said, her tone disinterested and bored. "But no, I shall stay here. Thank ye for the invitation though."

Brice bowed, inching back toward the door. "I'll see ye at dinner," he said to them both. Sophie leaned back in the settee, wondering why he was a little unsettled by the news of Elspeth's mother's arrival. Maybe there was an understanding between them. But how could she ask such a question without looking like a woman who was seeking her own proposal?

It was such a private thing to query about that she would have to figure out another way to ask in a round-about way. Elspeth chuckled at something in her book and Sophie glanced at the young woman. She was pretty in her own way, her red hair long and curly, bringing out the green in her eyes. But there was something about her that didn't fit with Brice. They were friends, that she had no doubt, but there was no spark, no desire. Not like when she was around him.

Just the thought of having him near her made her shiver and ache with need. His voice gave her lascivious ideas, and as for his wicked mouth and hands, well, she would never tire of those on her body.

None of that would matter if he was going to marry someone else. As for that institution, Sophie wasn't certain she wanted to live so very far away from her family should he ask. There were many obstacles to work through should they align their families. If only he lived in London, then he would never be rid of her and the choice to marry him would be as easy as breathing.

🐉

BRICE STOOD out in front of his home, Elspeth at his side, her arm linked with his as her mother's carriage rolled down the drive and before the castle doors.

Elspeth had taken after her father in looks and mannerisms and was the opposite to what her mother was like. In the woman's youth she'd been a reputed beauty that even his own father had courted before his beloved mama had won his heart.

A footman opened the carriage door and Brice helped her down and kissed her cheek. "Welcome, Lady Brodie. 'Tis good to have ye here with us again."

She slapped his chest playfully, turning to her daughter. "Enough with the Lady Brodie, Brice. Ye know my name is Margaret."

He smiled as she kissed her daughter, before they headed indoors, chatting to themselves. He followed behind into the great hall where they had set up a small repast for lunch before they headed out on their afternoon ride.

Sophie and Elizabeth were already in the hall and he couldn't help the small twitch of his lips at seeing her again. Every time he saw her something in his chest tightened and he was starting to think for the very first time in his life he'd fallen for a lass.

And not just any lass, but an English one at that. She watched him, her wide, blue eyes glistening with amusement and knowledge that only they shared. A mutual understanding of enjoyment, of attraction.

For he certainly felt that for the lass. To the point where he'd tell his family and Elspeth's to go to Hades so he could have the one woman who made him burn.

"This is Miss Sophie Grant, Mama. She's the Marquess Graham's sister-in-law. She's staying here from London."

Sophie curtsied and smiled at Margaret. Lady Brodie's demeanor changed within an instant, cooled and became more aloof than he'd ever seen before.

"Miss Grant. How fortuitous that you are here. I understand from my daughter's letters that you'll be leaving us soon, heading farther into the highlands, I understand."

"Ah, not any more, my lady. I fell over on my first day here in the village and injured myself. The laird and Miss Elizabeth were kind enough to allow me to stay here while I recovered, but the delay has stopped me from being able to visit my friend in Skye. I do hope however that she can travel here for a stay."

Margaret laughed, a tinkling sound that oozed conde-scension. "The guest is now inviting other guests to stay." She turned to Brice, her smile brittle. "Has the Laird of Mackintosh been taken in, I wonder."

His sister glanced at him wide-eyed and he counted to five before replying lest he set one of his family's oldest friends back in her carriage and send her on her way. "'Twas my idea to invite Miss Grant's friend to stay. We're loath to see her leave and wished to prolong her visit her as much as we could."

Sophie threw him a thankful smile as Elizabeth clasped her hand.

"Shall we have some tea?" he asked, wanting to change the subject.

"I think a whiskey will do me better," Margaret said, her tone cold. She sat on a nearby chair and glanced at them all as if she were the matriarch here. "Miss Grant, yer sister married very well. When I heard of yer particu-lars I wrote to my friend in London. She informed me yer elder sister was a lady's maid and now here ye are, a guest at an earl's home. Ye must be well-pleased."

"Mama," Elspeth said. Her mother gave Elspeth a quelling glance and she sat, her lips thinning in concern.

"I'm very pleased for her, my lady. She married the man she loved, which can never be a fault."

Margaret raised her brow. "Ach, but does the marquess

love her in return? 'Tis all very well to love one's husband, but these London marriages are never happy ones. Too much diversion, too many temptations. I'm very well-pleased that we live where we do. Ye may keep yer town life, Miss Grant. 'Tis not for a Scot."

"I for one enjoyed London when I traveled there," Elizabeth said, taking Sophie and seating her on a settee a little distance away from Lady Brodie. A fortunate thing since the woman had released her claws and was wanting to scratch Sophie's eyes out from the looks of it.

"I agree, Elizabeth. I think London would do me very well should I travel there." He winked at Sophie and she smiled at him. Once again it was as if the sun came out and warmed his soul. There was no use for it, he was besotted with her and now he had to figure out what the hell he was going to do about it.

"You are both more than welcome at the marquess's home in London or Ashby House, which is in Kent, should you ever visit us."

"And here ye are yet again, Miss Grant. Inviting people to homes that are not yer own."

"Lady Brodie, that is unkind. Ye will apologize to Miss Grant," he said, his tone brooking no argument.

Her ladyship's mouth puckered up as if she'd eaten something sour. Brice held her gaze, not willing to have Sophie insulted through no fault of her own. She could not help who her sister married, and he was sure from the way Sophie spoke of her siblings that they were very close, and any friend of Sophie's was a friend of theirs.

He frowned. Had Lady Brodie sensed his and Sophie's connection? She'd certainly fixated on Sophie from the moment she arrived. Had Elspeth written to her ladyship of her concerns? The horror on Elspeth's face right now after her mother's atrocious behavior would make one think not.

"I apologize, Miss Grant. Ye must make allowances for my blunt tongue. 'Tis a Scottish habit I never grew out of." Lady Margaret stood. "Come, Brice, there are things to discuss."

She started for the door and Brice bowed before following the harridan out into the corridor. Something told him the things to discuss were exactly the things he wanted to avoid.

CHAPTER 12

"What is the meaning of this lass being here and the looks that ye both keep throwing each other? I'll not have it, Brice. Ye're to wed Elspeth and ye know it. 'Tis what ye agreed to before yer parents died."

Brice sat behind his desk, hating that what she said was all true and cursing himself for the bloody fool he was in having promised such a thing when under stress from his parents' illnesses.

"Ye know that I care for Elspeth and should she agree, of course I'll marry her, but the marriage will not be one of affection. Not in the way that a marriage should be. Is that what ye want for yer daughter? Dinna ye want her to marry the man she loves, not merely respects?" Certainly after being with Sophie, he couldn't think of anything worse than marrying a woman he did not desire every minute of every day and respect her opinion. Sophie was both delectable and intelligent, enjoyable to be around. She was certainly no simpering miss who would make his teeth ache from clenching.

"Bollocks. Elspeth cares for ye a great deal and should ye turn yer head her way ye'd see that. Ye need to send the English lass home and ye need to do it soon before she starts to get ideas into her head that ye are going to offer her marriage. Dinna think I've forgotten why ye have this grand home still in yer hands. 'Tis because of the Brodies and their blunt."

"And the loan has been paid back in full with interest, need I remind ye." He loathed that his parents had asked for help, and yet at the same time he was grateful still to have Mackintosh Castle in the family.

"Agreements were made as well as money passing between hands that day. Dinna forget yer promise, Brice. Yer parents would roll over in their graves should they know ye were playing with a Sassenach."

He rubbed a hand over his jaw, the thought of Sophie going back to London haunted him. For her to be courted and admired, married to someone else made the blood in his veins chill. He glanced out the window, anywhere but at lady Brodie and her all-seeing eyes and viperish mouth.

"Her carriage is repaired and she is healed from her injury. I'm certain that Miss Grant will not be with us for too much longer." Bile rose in his throat at his words. How would he ever send her away? To watch her carriage roll down the drive, out of his life forever made him want to punch something. Hard.

"Good, for I would hate to see a young Scottish lord such as yerself throw away yer future happiness on a Sassenach. Marriage to my daughter, as both her and yer parents wished is best for this area and our clans. We must keep the Scottish bloods in the highlands pure. 'Tis a good match with Elspeth," she said, her tone cajoling. "Ye'll see. In time ye'll learn to love her."

Brice didn't want to learn to do anything, certainly not how to love someone. What a cold, unfeeling marriage he would have if that were the case.

Damn his idiot younger self for promising such a thing to his parents. It would be a mistake he would live with for the rest of his life.

Lady Brodie stood, starting toward the door like a warrior facing battle.

"Lady Brodie," he called out, halting her steps. She turned, facing him. "Dinna be rude to Miss Grant again. Ye may hail from Clan Brodie, which has been our closest ally for hundreds of years, but I'll not have any guest under my roof shamed simply because she's walked into a situation not of her making." He gave her ladyship a pointed stare. "Do ye understand?"

She gave one sharp nod. "Understood, so long as ye understand as well."

"I do," he said, watching the door close behind her ladyship and close on any hope he harbored that his future could be different than what had been planned.

SOPHIE SECLUDED herself up on the tower roof with the book on Scottish clans and looked at who Clan Mackintosh had married over the years. All she could find were other clan names, and information. It seemed Clan Mackintosh only married Scots and never the English, never a Sassenach from over the border.

She placed it down on the small blanket she sat upon and glanced out over the lands. Lady Brodie hated her. It was an undisputed fact and no matter how much Elizabeth and Elspeth tried to dismiss her notion, Sophie knew it to be true.

But why?

That was the question she was asking herself. Why would anyone take an instant dislike of someone unless they were threatened by them? She brought her knees up against her chest and leaned on them. Maybe what Gretel had been saying was true. The two families were meant to join through the marriage of Brice and Elspeth.

Not that that made any sense, for Elspeth showed very little interest in Brice, she showed Sophie more notice than him. Brice certainly liked the woman, but there was no chemistry between the two. Not that she'd ever seen.

She sighed. She would have to talk to Brice and listen to what he said. She should not have been kissing him if he were betrothed to another. Not that she thought that he was. He would not act so shamelessly.

"I've been looking all over the house for ye, lass. Are ye all right? I'm sorry about Lady Brodie. She can be hard toward strangers and, well, English ones more than most."

Sophie glanced at him, not moving from her position. "She doesn't like me, which is fine."

Ask him Sophie. Ask him now.

But how could she ask him something so personal? She shut her eyes, willing herself to be strong.

Brice came and sat beside her, leaning back against the stone wall. "The last week that ye have been here has been one of the best weeks of my life. I'll miss ye when ye go."

Go? So he expected her to leave still. She could not ask him now what was between him and Elspeth. How could she when he certainly saw no future with her?

Pain tore through her chest at the thought of leaving him. Of returning home and not seeing his wickedly handsome and teasing face across the table each morning where he'd wink and grin and make her smile.

"I will miss you too." She would not lie. She would

miss him. Terribly so. "I think it's best that I leave as soon as the letter from Jean arrives. I have doubts that she'll come, but I hope you won't mind if she does."

He shook his head, reaching out to take her hand. His warm, gloveless fingers ran over her flesh and shot goose-bumps across her skin. "Nay, ye are both welcome, for as long as ye like."

If only that were true... Sophie sat back and stared at nothing in particular, her mind a whirr of thoughts of wants and means.

He clasped her jaw and turned her to face him. She lost herself in the dark-green depths of his eyes full of longing that she too could acknowledge. Not willing to leave without experiencing what it would be like to have someone whom you loved, Sophie closed the space between them and kissed him.

It was a gamble, a risk, but she could not leave without having this just once more.

He met her halfway, taking her lips in a kiss that made her toes curl in her silk slippers. She reached up, clasping his shoulders and kissed him back with as much passion as he. His lips moved across hers, took and played with her mouth until she did not know what to do or what she wanted.

Well, she knew what she wanted. She wanted Brice.

He broke the kiss, standing and pulling her up with him. He didn't say a word and she did not ask him, for deep down she knew where he was going. They climbed back down the tower stairs, entered the passage that ran along his side of the house and walked toward his chambers.

Nerves fluttered in her stomach and she clasped her abdomen, unsure suddenly if she were ready for this. He stopped at the door and turned to face her. Sophie read the question in his eyes and determination straightened her spine. She reached past him and opened the door, swinging it wide before pushing against his chest and walking him backward into the room.

She shut the door and turned the lock. Tamping down her nervousness, she twisted around and gave him her back. "Can you help me with my ties?"

A light brush of his lips against her shoulder and she reached behind, clasping his face. "Clothes first, my lord, then you may kiss me again."

He chuckled, a low gravelly sound and she knew she'd never tire of him. Never not want him.

His nimble fingers made short work of her ties, pushing her gown to pool at her feet before her shift, stockings and slippers all followed soon after. Her body shook as she turned to face him, naked as the day she was born and so ready to be with the man before her.

The man she loved.

Sophie reached up and slipped his cravat loose, throwing it to the floor with her gown. She allowed her hands to drop over his chest and abdomen, taking pains to enjoy every facet of his body. His breathing was ragged as she pulled his shirt out of his breeches, sliding it up over his head to visually enjoy him as much as she physically could.

She devoured him, taking in every delectable thing about his chest, the small smattering of hair, his flat stomach and bulging pants.

Sophie bit her lip when she looked at the size of his manhood. He seemed even larger than he did in the lake and trepidation skittered down her spine that they may not fit.

"Damn it all to hell." He swooped her up in his arms,

closing the gap to the bed in only a few strides. She let out a little squeak when he threw her on the bed and she bounced once before he came down over her, pushing her into the thick, warm bedding.

"The way ye look at me. 'Tis too much." He kissed her, stopping her from replying. Sophie took the opportunity to show him instead of saying just how much he affected her as well. How he was too much and not enough. That she would never have enough of him.

Their lips took a life of their own, both seeking, taking and teasing the other. Somewhere in the back of her mind a warning voice urged caution, but she could not. If she were to leave, then she would have this once. Lay with the man she loved. It would sustain her for the rest of her days and whatever future she had before her.

Her fingers skimmed down his smooth back, running over his bottom before reaching between them and undoing the buttons on the front. He moaned, urging her to touch him. He needn't. She wanted to touch the hard yet velvety skin of his manhood.

She clasped him firmly and rolled her thumb across the top of his phallus. He pushed into her hold and she grinned. To have him at her mercy was a heady thing.

He threw her a wicked grin and kissed her before setting little bites down her neck, her chest, paying homage to each of her nipples. His tongue slid against the puckered flesh and little electrical shots pulsated to her core. Sophie writhed beneath him, pushing her body into him, silently begging for him to take her.

"Soon, love," he whispered against her stomach, kissing her lower still until the warmth of his breath fluttered across her mons. She stilled at the ministration.

"What are you doing?" she hissed, trying to sit up a little.

He pushed her back down, pinching one of her nipples and making her gasp. "Tasting ye."

Sophie wasn't sure what he meant, but when his tongue slid across her flesh in the most private of her places, his words became perfectly clear and not for anything would she stop him. For his clever mouth once again driving her to distraction.

❧

BRICE DIDN'T KNOW how he had allowed a kiss to lead them here, but now that he had Sophie in his bed, he'd never let her go. Not for family duty or expectation, not even for his clansmen. Somewhere along the way, he'd fallen in love with the lass and there was no going back now.

He tasted her with his tongue, teased her flesh until she was writhing in his hands, her fingers spiking through his hair and holding him right where she liked.

He liked it too. He teased her, pulled her close to her release and then took it away, inwardly enjoying himself immensely and wanting to prolong their time together. He didn't want to go back to the real world. He wanted to stay here forever. In Sophie's arms and in bed.

"Please, Brice." His name was but a gasp and he came back up over her, using his hand to tease her sensitive flesh. "Do ye like me touching ye here, lass?"

He slid one finger into her wet heat and she gasped, closing her legs about his arms.

"Yes," she breathed. "Please, I want you."

The words were precisely what he wanted to hear. He moved his hips to between her legs, guiding himself into her. She opened for him like a flower before the sun. He moaned as he slid into her, breaking her maidenhead, careful not to hurt her too much.

"I dinna want to hurt ye, lass." He paused, giving her time to accommodate him.

She stared up at him, her eyes clouded with lust. "It's not too bad. Please do not stop."

Brice took his time before he sheathed himself fully. She was warm, and so damn tight. His balls ached for release.

"Ye are so beautiful, lass."

She reached up, pulling him down and taking his lips. He thrust into her and she moaned against his mouth, making his cock rock hard. He tupped her fast, pinning her down. The need to see her come apart in his arms, to shatter before him was his whole focus.

Her legs came up about his hips, one sliding over his back and he clasped her thigh, pushing deeper still, harder. She allowed him take his fill as he brought her ever closer to release.

She thrashed under him, helping him to ride her and he'd fought not to lose himself. Her fingers scratched down his back, her core tightening even more about his cock.

"Come for me. Fuck, lass, come," he demanded, his need overwhelming him.

She gasped his name and he kissed her, masking her sounds as she contracted about his cock, spiking his own orgasm and milking him for all he had.

He slumped beside her after a time, both their breathing ragged. Brice rubbed a hand over his brow, feeling the light sheen of sweat there. "Are ye alright, lass? I wasn't too rough?"

She rolled over, coming to lie in the crook of his arm. He glanced down at her and his heart thumped loud in his chest. She was all softness, sweetness that he never wanted to part from. "No. You were perfect."

No. *She* was perfect and he was a perfect bastard for taking her innocence. But what was the problem with that when she would be his wife? He would not let her go. Not now. No matter what Clan Brodie thought on the matter.

CHAPTER 13

The following morning Sophie floated about her room, her mind whirring with thoughts about Brice, of what he'd done to her yesterday afternoon and how they'd secluded themselves away, oblivious if they were missed or caught.

Her sister would skin her alive should she know what she'd done, but what was a little scandal when one was in love? And if anything was proven to her yesterday it was that she was in love with Laird Mackintosh.

She took a calming breath as her stomach fluttered with the acknowledgment of such a fact. Soon she would join the family for breakfast and see him again. After their actions she could not see any other possibility for them but to be married. Not that she'd lain with him to force his hand, but surely one could not say such sweet things, touch with such reverence and not care. Not want that person in their life always.

Sophie dabbed a little bit of rosemary on her neck and stood, taking one last look at herself in the mirror. "I will see you before luncheon, Gretel," she said, watching as

Gretel came out of the dressing room with two of her gowns in her hands.

"Have a good morning," her friend said, sitting before the fire with what looked like needle and thread.

"I will." Sophie started down the long hallway, excitement thrumming through her. She didn't come across anyone on her way to the dining room, but upon entering it she knew something was wrong.

Elizabeth sat staring at her brother, her face ashen and Elspeth did not look much better. As for Lady Brodie she was blotchy and red. Sophie's steps halted. Was her ladyship angry or upset? When she turned, she knew what she was.

She was furious.

"Good morning," she said, continuing into the room and hoping she'd misread the situation.

"Is it true, Sophie?" Elspeth asked, tears brimming in her eyes.

Sophie looked to Elizabeth and then Brice for clarification. Brice looked to Elspeth, sighing. "I've already told ye the truth. No need to ask Sophie about it."

"Miss Grant, need I remind ye, young man," Lady Brodie said, her voice cold and hard.

Sophie folded her hands in her lap, unsure if everyone had found out what they were up to yesterday, or if Brice had declared something that she wasn't aware of.

"Was this yer plan all the time?" Elspeth asked, her eyes now as hard as her mother's. "To come here and land yerself a rich husband? Were there not enough Englishmen in England falling at yer feet that ye had to throw yerself at my betrothed?"

Sophie gasped, looking to Brice. "You are engaged?" The room spun and she clasped the chair, hoping she'd not topple off.

"I'm not engaged, Sophie," he said, turning back to Lady Brodie. "I never proposed to Elspeth."

"Posh," her ladyship snapped back. "It was expected. Wanted by both clans and ye dare come here this morning and tell me after our discussion yesterday that ye've changed yer mind. I'll not have it, and nor will I let ye make a mockery of our family name or our child."

Sophie looked to Elizabeth and the sadness she read in her friend's eyes gave her pause. The union between Brice and Elspeth was expected all this time, and he'd dallied with her and she'd let him.

She cringed, shame washing through her. "I did not know," she said, her eyes burning all of a sudden.

"Sophie, 'tis an old desire of my parents and Elspeth's too that was made when they were ill."

"Dinna ye be forgetting that Clan Brodie saved this stronghold financially so ye may inherit. What a way to thank yer friends. Throw a beautiful, strong Scottish woman out with the pig scraps for an English whore."

"Do not insult Miss Grant again, Lady Brodie or I'll be kicking yer ass out with the pig scraps as well," he roared.

Sophie jumped in her chair, unable to comprehend what had happened. The day had started off so beautifully and now? Now it was what nightmares were made of.

"May I see you in your office, my lord?" she asked, standing and glad that her legs didn't buckle under her. She fled the room, further insults flying at her back from Lady Brodie and the sound of Elizabeth's voice consoling her ladyship and Elspeth.

Sophie made the laird's office and went and stood beside the roaring fire, her body shivered and felt chilled to the bone.

Brice followed her, shutting the door as he strode in. "Sophie, I'm sorry. I dinna think they'd take my declaration to marry ye this morning so hard. Ye didn't deserve such treatment."

Sophie shook her head, not able to comprehend how he thought any of this was tolerable. "Did you allow the Brodie clan to think that you would offer for their daughter and only changed your mind when I came here?"

He glanced down at the floor, his inability to meet her gaze telling. "'Tis difficult to understand. There may have been a hope between the families, but I never offered marriage to Elspeth. I want to marry ye, Sophie," he said, finally looking at her. "I want ye."

"You only want me because your mind is still addled from yesterday. Had I not fallen over in Moy and hurt myself, and then been offered hospitality here, would you have married Elspeth?"

He ran a hand over his jaw, taking his time in answering her. "There is a possibility that would have occurred, aye."

Sophie shook her head, ice running through her veins. What a fool she'd been. She'd risked so much, had trusted him and this is what was happening all the time. "You bastard. How could you? How could you chase me, allow me to think there may be a future between us when all the time you were planning on offering to Elspeth?"

He reached for her and she slapped his hands away. "When? When did you decide that it was me that you wanted, and don't you dare lie to me, Brice."

A muscle ticked in his jaw before he said, "Yesterday."

Bile rose in Sophie's throat and she clasped her stomach, scared she was going to cast up her accounts all over his highly polished wood floor. He came to her, taking her hand and she pushed him away, stumbling toward the door.

"You decided you wanted me," she said rounding on

him. "After you'd had your way with me. What was I to you, some plaything? A little English diversion before you settled down with your Scottish lass? Or did I merely meet with your exalted bedding standard and Elspeth did not? If you tell me that you had similar relations with her I fear my actions will not be my own."

He held out a hand, placating her. "Nay, never, Sophie. I would not do that. Please understand, I did not think I'd meet anyone like ye. I canna think of anyone I want to spend the rest of my life with more than ye."

Sophie stared at him, and damn it, a small part of her wanted to believe what he said. That duty was his only path forward until she had arrived and he'd fallen for her. But never had he talked of the future, only that he would miss her when she left. Surely had he planned for them to be together he would have spoken of dreams, of a future with them here in Scotland. But he had not. He'd not mentioned the word love at all.

She was a fool.

"I do not believe you. You're not who I thought you were. I'm going back to my room to pack. I'll be leaving today."

"Sophie, no, please." He strode over to her, taking her hands. "Please believe me. I dinna mean to hurt you or Elspeth." He shook his head, seemingly struggling to find the right words. "I did not know that I would meet a lass that would make me question my word, my promise to my parents."

She pulled out of his grasp and started for the door. "But you did hurt me, didn't you, and your promise to your parents was broken the moment you first kissed me, so I do not want to hear such excuses." Sophie shut the door behind her, her legs felt heavy and unstable, and using the staircase bannister she slowly made her way back to her room.

The house about her blurred with unshed tears and she bit the inside of her cheek to stop herself from crying before the few servants she passed.

However would she face Louise? However would she face her future husband, whomever he may be now that she was ruined? No one would have her now. A little chiding voice beat against her ear, telling her what a fool she was, a silly country miss who had stepped into a world she wasn't prepared for and had lost.

And the voice was right and so too Gretel. Too blinded by her feelings for the laird, she could not see or hear what was happening right before her. That he had played them both and she'd lost the game.

Damn Scots. She would never trust another.

CHAPTER 14

Spring ended and so too did summer in the highlands and the first snows of the season had started to fall and stick. It would be a cold winter this year, a hard winter. Not that he expected anything else. He deserved to be isolated, cold and lonely, especially after what had occurred in the spring when Sophie had been a guest here.

The thought of her, as usual, sent pain to coil in the vicinity of his heart. He leaned back in his chair, shutting his eyes, wanting to picture her as they were the day before she'd left. Warm in his arms, gazing at him with such adoration and trust that he'd never want for another.

He shook his head. He'd made a right mess of things and true to her word she'd packed up the day after he'd taken her to his bed and hightailed it back to London. Her friend had written stating she could not come, which was fortunate as Sophie had left in any case, and he would not have known what to say to the woman had she arrived.

A light knock sounded at his door and his sister peeped around the threshold. "May I come in?"

He gestured for her to enter, sitting up to lean over his

desk. "Of course. What is it ye wanted to talk to me about, Elizabeth?"

She held a missive in her hand. Her demeanor, the worry lines about her eyes made him pause. "What is it, lass? Has there been bad news?"

Elizbeth worked her bottom lip and he was about to expire before she said, "I dinna want to tell ye before, but I've been corresponding with Sophie the whole time she has been back in England. I've had news today from her."

Everything in his body came to life at the sound of her name aloud. Elizabeth had not mentioned Sophie to him, not since the day she had left. "What does she write?"

Does she ask of me? Is she well? Is she happy?

"She's betrothed to be married."

"The hell she is." He surged to his feet, sending his chair backward to crack on the mahogany floor. "To whom?"

"Does it matter?" Elizabeth said, watching him warily. "Ye let her go."

He gaped at his sibling, having never heard her say something to him like that before, cutting and condescending as if Sophie's leaving was his fault.

Well, aye, it was his fault, but he had tried to get her to stay. To believe what he was saying. He'd been a fool, a blind idiot, but he would have married her. Would have loved her had she only given him a chance.

"Ye let her believe that ye never loved her. Did ye tell her before she left or did ye allow her to return to England thinking ye'd ruined her without a shadow of shame upon yer soul?"

Brice stilled at Elizabeth's words. "Ye knew?" He strode to the window, ripping the curtains back to see outside.

"Of course I knew ye'd ruined her. She all but glowed the morning she walked into the breakfast room and before

Lady Brodie tanned yer hide, ye too looked like a cat who'd licked the cream." Elizabeth shook her head at him, her eyes hard with annoyance. "Ye need to fix this problem before it's too late."

He nodded absently, his mind running through everything that he needed to accomplish to get to London by the fastest means possible. "I never told her. She was so angry that I did not think it would make a difference. I was wrong." He turned to face his sister. "I won't let Sophie marry anyone else, not unless that anyone is me."

Elizabeth stood and joined him at the windows. She smiled, another thing he'd not seen for some months. His sister had been angry at him and consequently given him the silent treatment ever since Sophie and Elspeth had departed.

He'd thought Elizabeth had blamed him for Elspeth running away to the continent to travel abroad, but he couldn't help but wonder if Elspeth had been more than pleased by the turn of events. Not initially, but certainly when her lady's maid had mentioned such a trip abroad, she'd been only too willing to travel with her.

Lady Brodie however had promised retribution, but really there was little she could do other than become a rival clan. Clan Mackintosh no longer owed anyone anything, and no one would be calling in a favor on him in the forthcoming future.

He was free to travel to London and get his lass back. And that was exactly what he was going to do. "Wish me luck," he said, kissing Elizabeth on the cheek and heading for the door.

"Good luck, brother."

He ignored her parting comment that he would need it.

CHAPTER 15

London

Sophie wrung her hands before her as she paced in her bedroom. Today she would marry Mr. Mathew Fitzgerald, a childhood friend from Sandbach who was training to be a barrister, and a man who did not evoke one ounce of desire in her, no matter how much he tried with his kisses.

He had come up to Town, wanting to visit Stephen whom he'd not seen for some years and they had been thrown together. Heartsick and missing Brice, Sophie had perhaps shown more notice than she really felt toward the gentleman, and within a month he'd proposed and shockingly she'd said yes.

"Why did I do such a thing?" she said aloud in her room to no one. She was alone, wanting to have the few hours before she gave herself to a man who was suffocating in his attention toward her, that had only become worse after she'd agreed to be his wife. "This is a disaster."

Her vision blurred and she swiped up her handkerchief from her dressing table, dabbing at her cheeks. Damn Brice and damn Clan Brodie and everyone who thought that the laird of Mackintosh would make a great match to a woman whose only asset was that she was Scottish.

They certainly did not love each other, but then he'd never told her that he loved her either so her point was moot.

She missed him.

Sophie slumped on the bed, fighting the need to curl into a ball and never go anywhere ever again. She'd written to Elizabeth, part in hope that she would give news of her impending nuptials to Brice. But today was her wedding day, and she'd not heard back from Elizabeth or seen her fiery-red Scot since the day she left.

He did not care.

She supposed Brice would be married now to Elspeth. She ought to thank Elizabeth for not telling her such news for to read it in black and white that Brice would never be hers would've been a heartbreak she could not have faced.

But she did have to face it. He was gone and she was about to marry a man who loved her, or at least, liked her very much.

A commotion downstairs sounded and she stood, going to the door and opening it. Yelling sounded from the foyer and Sophie stilled when the very distinct and very demanding Scottish burr reached her ears.

Brice!

She shut her mouth with a snap, unsure whether she should go and see what he wanted or hide. What was he doing here? Did he come to wish her well, to apologize and show that marriage to other people was the right course? Was Elspeth with him?

Her fingers clenched the handle, but her feet refused to move. Not that they had to for Brice appeared at the top of the stairs and, looking about to see which way to go, spied her.

"Sophie," he said, the sound of her name on his lips was like a balm over a festering wound.

"Brice. What are you doing here?" she asked, coming out into the corridor to meet him. He took her hands, glancing behind him. Her brother-in-law came into view at the top of the stairs, yelling out to Brice.

Brice wrenched her back into her room, the snick of the lock putting an end to Luke interrupting them.

"Sophie, let me in and I'll escort Laird Mackintosh outside."

"I'd like to see him try," Brice said, his voice brooking no argument.

Sophie sighed. "It's okay, my lord. I will speak to Laird Mackintosh. I will be down shortly."

There was a small delay before the muffled sound of Luke's voice met her ears. "Very well. I'll be in the library with Louise when you're ready."

She turned back to Brice, unable to stop herself from taking in all his grandeur. He looked travel-weary, his clothes dusty and rumpled. His hair was longer and he'd not bothered to tie it back and so it sat upon his shoulders, the red, fiery locks making her want to run her hands through it, pull him toward her and kiss him.

She'd missed him so much.

Sophie stepped back, needing space to think straight. He had a way of discombobulating her. "Why are you here, Brice? Should you not be in Scotland with your wife?"

He reared back at her words. "I dinna have a wife, lass, not yet at least. Did Elizabeth not tell ye what happened after ye left?"

He wasn't married? Hope and despair ran through her at the declaration. He wasn't married, but she was to be soon and so it was too late.

Wasn't it?

"Elizabeth never mentioned you at all." Not that she'd wanted to hear of his marriage, of where they had traveled for their honeymoon. Just the thought of Brice lying with another woman made her head ache. For weeks after leaving Scotland she'd had nightmares of such a scene, of him kissing Elspeth and consummating the marriage. Of stealing kisses such as he had with her, but instead of Sophie in the dreams, it had been Elspeth, her mother's mocking voice whispering in her ear that she was nothing but common English nonsense.

"I dinna marry Elspeth. In fact, I asked them to leave the same day ye departed for London." He reached for her and she edged away. If he touched her, she'd be lost and she had Mathew to marry. A good man who was right now getting ready in another part of the marquess's home. Brice and his distraction were not needed.

"I should have come after ye, to tell ye how sorry I am. I'll admit, I should never had dallied with ye, stolen kisses that were not for me, but the day that I found ye on the tower I'd made up my mind to marry ye, lass. I want ye to marry me still." His eyes beseeched her and her heart beat loud in her ears. "I love ye, Sassenach. You're the only lass I want beside me for the rest of my days, however many that will be."

Sophie swiped at her cheek, biting the inside of her lip to distract herself from all the wonderful things he was saying. "You should have told me what your family expected of you. Had you just said that it wasn't what you wanted, all those stolen kisses would not have felt like lies."

"I'm sorry, lass. I was stupid."

"You were, but then you are a man…"

He grinned, that devilishly handsome smile, and she knew the fight was lost. She loved him. Loved him still. Senseless, obstinate Scot that he was. "I never said I was an angel, lass, but one kiss from ye, one look, and there was no way that I was going to let ye go. Tell me ye'll marry me." He stepped before her, and this time she didn't step away when he reached to hold her.

She sighed at being back in his arms. It was like coming home. Perfect and right in every way. "I'm marrying Mr. Fitzgerald today," she stated, wanting him to grovel for just a little longer.

"No ye are not. Ye're going to marry me instead. Say yes."

Sophie raised her brow. "We have a whole wedding planned today. Guests will be arriving soon. Why, Mathew is only a few doors away getting ready." She gestured to herself. "If you haven't noticed I'm in a wedding gown."

He glanced down at the blue silk gown with overlaying lace and his gaze darkened. "Say yes, Sophie, to my question. I'll not be taking no for an answer. Ye know ye love me as much as I love ye. If ye marry whatever his name is ye'll regret it and I'll have to force ye to have a lifelong affair with me. Now, ye dinna want to do that, do ye?"

No she did not want to do that, and although she would hurt Mathew she knew that to marry him would hurt him more in the long term. "You love me, do you?"

His lips twitched and she reached up, wrapping her arms about his neck, needing to touch him, to be reassured that he was here, alive and well and for her. "Ye know I do. I would never have taken ye to my bed had I not meant for ye to be my wife. I was a fool not to follow ye to London, but I thought that I had lost ye. I convinced myself that the time we'd spent together had been too short for ye to fall in love with me as much as I was in love with ye."

She shook her head, weary of it all and a little sad that they'd wasted so many months wallowing in their own grief of losing each other. "How very wrong you were." Sophie could no longer wait, she leaned forward and brushed her lips against his. His hands tightened about her back and she settled against him. "I missed you too. So very much."

"And?" he asked, meeting her gaze. "Is there anything else that ye need to be telling me?"

She chuckled, supposing there was. "I love you too. I think a little part of me fell for you the moment you scooped me up in your arms on that hillside in Moy."

"Ye were very sweet in my arms, lass. I knew right then that I was in trouble and then when ye arrived at my home, I could not see straight for wanting ye. 'Tis not something I'd ever experienced before, but now that I have, 'tis a need that I'm not willing to live without."

"Neither am I," she said, kissing him fully. They came together, the kiss turning molten, and after months of being apart there would be no separating them again. Her responsibilities, her wedding flew from her thoughts as only Brice occupied her mind. They tumbled onto the bed and his deft fingers made fast work of her gown, sliding it up her hips to pool at her waist.

Sophie welcomed him, wanting him more with every minute of every day. He sat back and ripped off her pantalettes, her stockings, leaving her bare to his inspection. He watched her, his gaze dark and brimming with need and love.

She should have recognized it before she fled from

Scotland for the way he was looking at her now was the same as he'd looked at her the day she had given herself to him. She'd given him her heart that day and it would seem so had he.

He kissed her, drugging her with his touch and she could not get enough. She wanted more, so much more. Sophie pushed on his shoulder until he understood and rolled onto his back. He brought her with him, and she straddled him.

She gingerly moved to take Brice into her, not sure if being with him in this way was even possible.

He shut his eyes, a whisper of a moan slipping past his lips. "That's it, lass. Take everything from me."

Sophie leaned against his chest and moved again until she found a sweet rhythm. He felt larger this way, filling and inflaming her beyond anything she'd thought possible. She would never get tired of this for it was simply heaven and to have Brice's heart made it even more perfect.

Somewhere, deep inside, he teased her closer to the peak she longed to experience again. He sat up, holding her shoulders and helping her come down on him harder. "Brice," she gasped as her body shattered around him, spiking tremor after tremor of sweet release to course through her body. She rode him, took what he gave her and kissed him as he spent within her.

Their coming together was quick and frenzied and for a few minutes they stayed as they were, waiting for their breaths and hearts to settle.

"Ye'll marry me and no one else, lass. Are we in agreement?"

She nodded, unable to form words right at that moment. She ran her hands over his cheeks, enjoying the coarse stubble that peppered his jaw. "I have to tell

Mathew that I'll not be marrying him. Will ye come with me?"

His jaw hardened and his gaze cooled a little at the mention of her betrothed. "Aye. I'll come with ye. I'll not be letting ye out of my sight again."

Sophie grinned at his protectiveness or jealousy, both she would presume. "Good, because I'll not be letting you out of my sight either."

She started when a loud, insistent knock banged on her door. "Sophie, what the hell is going on in there?" her betrothed yelled, banging again and rattling the handle.

Brice glared at the door. "Come, lass, no time like the present to tell everyone under this roof that ye're mine and I'm yers and nothing, not even a Mr. whatever his name is from wherever will change that fact."

CHAPTER 16

B rice stood at the side of the ballroom as his bride danced with her brother. The Marquess Graham and Louise stood next to him, talking of their impending trip to Scotland to see them once the Season ended.

They were leaving for home tomorrow and he could not wait to have Sophie back in Scotland. The only sadness to this day was that his sister had not been here to see him marry the woman he loved. But Elizabeth had practically pushed him out the door to go get her back, and so he knew she'd forgive him eventually.

"My sister is glowing, Brice. You make her happy." Louise glanced at him, smiling, and he smiled back, pleased to know he had the marquess's and marchioness's approval. After his hasty arrival last month, and his declaration on the day of Sophie's wedding that she'd not be marrying anyone other than him, he was glad he'd not done too much damage to his relationship with Sophie's family. Once they saw how happy she was, they had relented and forgiven him and then proceeded with untold enthusiasm to help organize a new wedding. One each party involved was passionate about.

"I try, my lady," he said, knowing that he'd try damn hard. At times he thought that maybe he was too eager to please, and yet he would not change. He loved her, so very much, and wanted nothing but her happiness.

The minuet came to an end and Sophie walked back over to them on her brother's arm, their laughter and her pleasure at being in their company making his lips twitch. His heart clenched and he marveled at the fact that he could adore someone as much as he adored Sophie.

His wife…

"My waltz, I believe," he said, taking her hand and kissing it. Her gaze met his and he read the need, the devotion he saw there. He knew the look well as he sported it always when about her.

She chuckled, taking his arm. "That would be my pleasure, husband."

He guided her onto the dance floor, pulling her into his arms closer than he ought. Not that he cared what the matrons of the *ton* thought of his actions. He'd hold her as close as he damn well pleased and tonight especially. It was their wedding ball that they'd wanted to hold instead of a breakfast.

"Happy?" he asked, pulling her into a spin as the music started and the dance commenced.

"Always," she said, her hand lightly playing with the tartan over his shoulder. "You look so handsome today. My very own highlander."

He stopped dancing, and, leaning down, kissed her fully, not stopping even when startled gasps and muffled laughter sounded from about the room. "And you, my dearest wife, are my very own Sassenach."

She grinned up at him, laughter in her eyes. "Not a Sassenach anymore. I'm a Scot now. Forever."

Aye, forevermore…

EPILOGUE

Sophie made it to the top of the hillside that she'd tumbled on two years past. She stared out over Moy and the highlands, including their own home Moy Castle, which she could just make out in the distance. "I have made it," she declared. "Two years after trying to climb this mountain, I have conquered it."

Brice came up behind her, pulling her against his chest. She wiggled into his hold, liking his warmth and strength at her back. "I would debate the term mountain, but even so, try not to fall over, lass. I'll be loath to carry ye back down again."

She turned, slapping his arm. "Tease. You enjoyed every minute of it the last time."

He grinned. "Aye, I did. In fact, it drove me mad that ye were in my arms, but ye weren't mine. Ye have a very delectable bottom, did ye know?"

"I know. You tell me often." She linked her arm in his and pulled him over to a small outcrop of rocks, before taking a seat. "I wanted to come here because this is the first place we met."

He joined her, sitting down and taking her hand, idly playing with her fingers. "Aye, it was. I canna thank your brother-in-law's carriage enough that the wheel decided to come off and strand ye here. Had it not, we would never have met."

"Hmm," Sophie said. "I think we're destined to meet our soul mates, and that no matter what, fate will play a hand and join the couples somehow. That carriage wheel was always going to come off here and we were always going to meet and you were always going to fall madly in love with me."

"I canna disagree with that last statement. 'Tis very true." He leaned over, kissing her quickly.

Sophie clasped her stomach, nerves flittering in her belly. "I wanted to bring you here today because there is something I want to tell you."

He glanced at her, a small frown marring his brow. "Are ye alright, lass? Is there something bothering ye?"

"No, nothing like that," she said, waving his concerns away. "I wanted to be here when I told you that I'm going to have your baby. You're going to be a father."

Brice stared at Sophie, words failing him. After two years of marriage he'd started to worry that a bairn of their own was not going to happen, and he'd accepted that fact. He loved Sophie more than anything in the world, including a child that did not exist and he'd never fret over something that he could not control.

Her words sent his mind reeling and the ground shifted under his feet a moment. "Ye are?" he managed to croak out, a lump wedged firmly in his throat.

"I am." She nodded. "The doctor confirmed it for me

when I went to town yesterday and so today you find us here, where we met and where two will soon be three."

He clasped her face, kissing her and pulling her into a fierce hug. "Oh Sophie, I dinna know what to say, other than I'm shocked, ecstatic." He pulled back, wiping the tears that spilled down her cheeks.

"You're happy then?" she asked.

He laughed, hugging her yet again. "God damn it, aye. I love ye, lass," he said, kissing her. She chuckled when he didn't stop.

"I love you too," she said, squealing when he stood quickly and swooped her up in his arms. "What are you doing?"

He started for the path and the way back down toward the village. "Carrying ye. I'll not have my pregnant wife overexerting herself and so I'll carry ye back down."

She threw him a bemused look. "If you wish. I enjoyed my little ride in your arms last time we were here. I'm more than willing to do it again."

He stopped to kiss her hard. "I enjoyed it too, lass." And he'd spend the rest of his life showing her just how much.

Dear Reader,

Thank you for taking the time to read *Kiss the Wallflower box set, books 1-3*! I hope you enjoyed the stories.

I'm forever grateful to my readers, so if you're able, I would appreciate an honest review of *Kiss the Wallflower Books 1-3*. As they say, feed an author, leave a review! You can contact me at tamaragillauthor@gmail.com or sign up to my newsletter to keep up with my writing news.

If you'd like to learn about book four in my Kiss the Wallflower series, To Fall For a Kiss, please read on. I have included the prologue for your reading pleasure.

Tamara Gill

TO FALL FOR A KISS

Lady Clara Quinton is loved and admired by all. She has no enemies—excluding Mr. Stephen Grant. After an atrocious encounter with Stephen during her first season, Clara vowed to never befriend him or any member of his family. But when Mr. Grant saves her in Covent Garden from a relentless and lively admirer, Clara falters in her promise.

Disliking everything about the social sphere he now graces—including Lady Clara—Stephen wants nothing more than to steer clear of the indulged and impolite woman. Her contempt of him and his family has been made known all over the town. However, after coming to her aid one night in London, the vowed enemies come to a truce.

. . .

Now, a landlord at the property adjacent to her country estate, a storm leaves him stranded at the duke's home. Uncovering Lady Clara's secrets and vulnerabilities changes the way he sees the privileged woman. Will this newfound knowledge force him to see her through different and admiring eyes? And will Clara see there is more to Stephen than his lack of noble birth...

PROLOGUE

Covent Garden, London Season, 1809

Lady Clara Quinton, only daughter to the Duke of Law, gingerly backed up against an old elm tree, the laughter and sounds of gaiety beyond the garden hedge mocking her for the silly mistake she'd made. The tree bark bit into her gown and she cringed when Lord Peel would not give her space to move away.

Walking off with Viscount Peel had not been her most intelligent notion after he insisted she see a folly he was fond of. After her acquiescence, her evening had deteriorated further. If she happened to get herself out of this situation it would be the last time she'd come to Covent Garden and certainly the last time she had anything to do with his lordship.

"Please move away, my lord. You're too close."

He threw her a mocking glance, his teeth bright white under the moonlit night. His mouth reeked of spirits and she turned away, looking for anyone who may rescue her. What did he think he was going to do to her? Or get away with, the stupid man? "My lord, I must insist. My father is expecting me back at our carriage."

"Come now, Clara, we've been playing this pretty dance for years. Surely it's time for you to bestow me a kiss. I will not tell a soul. I promise."

She glanced at him. Lord Peel was a handsome man, all charm, tall, and with an abundance of friends and wealth and yet, the dance he spoke of mainly consisted of her trying to get away from him. There was something about the gentleman that made her skin crawl as if worms were slithering over her.

He'd taken an immediate like to her on the night of her debut several years ago, and she'd not been able to remove him from her side since, no matter how much she tried to show little favor to any of the men who paid her court. She was six and twenty and sole heir to her father's many estates. She wanted for nothing, and with so many other things occupying her mind of late, a husband did not fit in with her plans at present.

If she were to marry she would have to leave her father, and she could not do that. Not now when he was so very ill and in all honesty, there had been no one who had sparked her interest, not since Marquess Graham during her coming out year before he up and married a servant. Clara would be lying if she had not felt slighted and confused by his choice.

"If you should try and kiss me, my lord, I shall tell my father of your conduct. I can promise you that. Now move." She pushed at his shoulders and she may as well have been pushing against a log of wood. He didn't budge, simply leaned in closer, clasping her chin and squashing her farther into the tree trunk. She cringed at the pain he induced.

"Do not make me force you, Clara." His voice dropped to a deep whisper full of menace.

Fear rippled through her and she shivered, glancing beyond his shoulder. Should she scream? To do so would court scandal. People would come scrambling to her aid, and she would be left having to explain why she was alone with Lord Peel in the first place. Especially if they did not have an understanding. Clara could not put her father through such gossip. He had enough on his shoulders without her worrying him with her own mistakes.

"You're a brute. How dare you treat me like this?" She tried to move away once again and as quick as a flash he grabbed her, wresting her to the ground. She did scream then, but with his chest over her face her cry for help was muffled.

Clara pushed at him as he tried to kiss her, his hands hard and rough against her face. "Stop," she said, "please stop."

He merely laughed, the sound mocking, and then in an instant he was gone. For a moment she remained on the ground, trying to figure out what had happened and then she saw him. Mr. Grant, or Stephen Grant, the Marquess Graham's brother-in-law and a man she'd promised to loathe forever and a day. He stood over Lord Peel, his face a mixture of horror and fury. Somewhere in the commotion Mr. Grant must have punched Lord Peel, for he was holding his jaw and there was a small amount of blood on his lip.

Clara scrambled to her feet, wiping at her gown and removing the grass and garden debris from her dress as best she could. Mr. Grant came to her, clasping her shoulders and giving her a little shake. "Are you injured? Did he hurt you at all?"

Clara glanced at Lord Peel as he gained his feet. He

glared at Mr. Grant as he too wiped garden debris from his clothing and righted his superfine coat.

"You may leave, Mr. Grant. You're not welcome to intrude in a private conversation I'm having with Lady Clara."

"Private? Mauling someone on the ground is not what I'd consider a conversation, my lord. I heard her shout for assistance. I hardly think the conversation was one of Lady Clara's liking."

Clara moved over toward Mr. Grant when Lord Peel took a menacing step in her direction. An odd thing for her to do as she had never been friends with the man and to seek his protection now went against everything within her. But if she were to remain at Lord Peel's mercy, she would choose Mr. Grant of course. He had two sisters after all, and from what she'd seen over the years he loved them dearly. He would not allow any harm to come to her. Mr. Grant reached out a hand and shuffled her behind him, backing her toward where her father would be waiting with the carriage.

Lord Peel's eyes blazed with anger. "Of course it was to her liking. We're courting, you fool."

She gasped, stepping forward, but Mr. Grant clasped her about the waist and held her back. "How dare you, my lord?" she stated even as Mr. Grant restrained her. "I never once asked for you to pursue me and I never gave you any indication that I wanted you to."

Lord Peel glared at her. Mr. Grant turned her back toward the opening in the hedge where they had entered the small, private space and pushed her on. "Go, Lady Clara. I shall speak to his lordship. I can watch from here to ensure you reach your carriage, which if I'm not mistaken your father is waiting beside and looking for you."

Clara clasped Mr. Grant's hands, squeezing them. "I cannot thank you enough. You have proven to be the best kind of man for coming to the aid of a woman you may not be inclined to help under normal circumstances. I thank you for it."

He threw her a puzzled glance. "Should anyone bellow for help and I hear it, of course I will come. Now go, Lady Clara. The time apart from your guests has been long enough."

Clara nodded, turning and walking away. She reached up and fixed her hair, hoping it did not look as out of place as it felt. As she walked back toward the revelers, a little of her fear slipped away knowing Mr. Grant watched her. She glanced over her shoulder, and true to his word, Mr. Grant continued to survey her progress and ensure she arrived back at her carriage safely.

A shiver of awareness slid over her skin, completely opposite to what she experienced each time she was in the presence of Lord Peel. She'd always disliked Mr. Grant and his siblings, one of whom married Marquess Graham, her own suitor during her first Season and the man she thought she would marry. He did not offer for her hand, choosing to marry a lady's maid instead.

"There you are, my dear. I've been looking for you."

She reached up and kissed her father's cheek, her legs of a sudden feeling as if they would not hold her for too much longer. "Shall we go, Papa?" she said, taking his arm and guiding him toward the carriage. The coachman bowed before opening the door for them.

"Yes, let us go, my dear. I've had quite enough time in the gardens and watching the *ton* at play."

Clara stepped up into the carriage and sank down on the padded velvet seats, relief pouring through her that no one other than Mr. Grant had come upon her and his lordship in the garden, or the position that they'd been found.

Heat rushed over her cheeks and she picked up the folded blanket on her seat and settled it about her father's legs as the carriage lurched forward. Anything to distract her from the memory of it.

"Shall we ring for tea and play a game of chess when we arrive home, Papa? It may be a nice way to end the evening just us two together."

Her father glanced at her, a little blank and unsure. "I think I shall retire, my dear. It's been a tiring evening."

"Very well," she said, swallowing the lump in her throat that wedged there each and every time she was around her parent. She knew the reason he no longer liked to play chess, cards or even the piano, at which he'd once been proficient, was because he'd forgotten how. His mind over the last two years had slowly disremembered many things, even some of the servants who had been with them since she was a girl.

Unbeknownst to her father Clara had sought out an opinion with their family doctor and he'd agreed that her father had become more forgetful and vague, and that it may be a permanent affliction.

She sighed. The fact that there was little she could do to help him regain his memory saddened her and as much as she tried to remind him of things, an awful realization that one day he'd forget her had lodged in her brain and would not dissipate.

What would happen after that? Would he still be as healthy as he was now, but with no memory, or would whatever this disease that ailed his mind affect his body as well.

The idea was not to be borne. He was all she had left.

"Maybe tomorrow, Papa, after breakfast perhaps."

He smiled at her, and she grinned back. "Maybe, my dear, or you could ask your mother. I know how very fond of chess she is."

Clara nodded, blinking and looking out the carriage window so he would not see her upset. If only she could ask her mama, who'd been dead these past ten years.

❦

STEPHEN STOOD between Lord Peel and the man's exit at his back in the gardens. The moment he'd strode into the small, private area and seen a flash of pink muslin and a gentleman forcing a woman into kissing him a veil of red had descended over his eyes and he'd not known how he'd stopped himself from pummeling the man into pulp.

"You will leave Lady Clara alone or I shall speak to her father of what I witnessed this evening. Do you understand, my lord?"

Peel chuckled, the sound mocking and full of an arrogance that Stephen was well aware of with this gentleman. He was also aware that he'd once been married and that his wife had fallen ill not long after their marriage. Of course, upon the young woman's death, Peel had played the widower very well, and had enjoyed the copious amount of money that his young wife had left him, or so Marquess Graham had told him one evening when Stephen had noticed his marked attention toward Lady Clara. A woman who seemed to show little interest in the gentleman trying to court her.

Lord Peel tapped a finger against his chin. "I forget... Do I need to listen to you? What is your name... Mr. Grant, isn't it? Son of nobody."

Stephen fisted his hands at his sides, reminding himself that to break the fellow's nose would not do him or his sisters any good now that they were part of the sphere this mongrel resided within. He'd already hit him once, to bloody him up too much would not do.

"You are correct. I'm Mr. Stephen Grant of Nobody of Great Import, but I will say this… You're no one of import either if the rumors about you and your conduct are to be believed."

Lord Peel's face mottled red and Stephen was glad his words struck a chord in the bastard. He needed to hear some truths and to know that his marked attention toward women, his inability to grasp that he saw them as nothing but playthings for his enjoyment had been noted and talked about. He pushed past Stephen and he let him go, not wanting to waste another moment of his time on such a nob.

The gentleman's retreating footsteps halted. "Lady Clara will be my wife. I will be speaking to her father soon about my proposal and I will have her. I am a viscount. It is only right that Lady Clara marry a man such as myself, so if you look to her as a possible candidate as your wife, you'll be sadly mistaken. Move on and marry a tavern wench, that'll suit your status better. A duke's daughter is not for you."

Stephen glared at the man's back as he disappeared into the throng of revelers still dancing and enjoying their night in Covent Garden. "Yes, well, Lord Peel, she's not for you either and I'll be damned if I'll let you have her."

LEAGUE OF UNWEDDABLE GENTLEMEN SERIES AVAILABLE NOW!

Fall into my latest series, where the heroines have to fight for what they want, both regarding their life and love. And where the heroes may be unweddable to begin with, that is until they meet the women who'll change their fate. The League of Unweddable Gentlemen series is available now!

LEAGUE OF UNWEDDABLE GENTLEMEN

ALSO BY TAMARA GILL

Wicked Widows Series
TO DREAM OF YOU

League of Unweddable Gentlemen Series
TEMPT ME, YOUR GRACE
HELLION AT HEART
DARE TO BE SCANDALOUS
TO BE WICKED WITH YOU
KISS ME DUKE

Kiss the Wallflower series
A MIDSUMMER KISS
A KISS AT MISTLETOE
A KISS IN SPRING
TO FALL FOR A KISS
KISS THE WALLFLOWER - BOOKS 1-3 BUNDLE

Lords of London Series
TO BEDEVIL A DUKE
TO MADDEN A MARQUESS
TO TEMPT AN EARL
TO VEX A VISCOUNT
TO DARE A DUCHESS
TO MARRY A MARCHIONESS
LORDS OF LONDON - BOOKS 1-3 BUNDLE

LORDS OF LONDON - BOOKS 4-6 BUNDLE

To Marry a Rogue Series
ONLY AN EARL WILL DO
ONLY A DUKE WILL DO
ONLY A VISCOUNT WILL DO

A Time Traveler's Highland Love Series
TO CONQUER A SCOT
TO SAVE A SAVAGE SCOT

Time Travel Romance
DEFIANT SURRENDER
A STOLEN SEASON

Scandalous London Series
A GENTLEMAN'S PROMISE
A CAPTAIN'S ORDER
A MARRIAGE MADE IN MAYFAIR
SCANDALOUS LONDON - BOOKS 1-3 BUNDLE

High Seas & High Stakes Series
HIS LADY SMUGGLER
HER GENTLEMAN PIRATE
HIGH SEAS & HIGH STAKES - BOOKS 1-2 BUNDLE

Daughters Of The Gods Series
BANISHED-GUARDIAN-FALLEN
DAUGHTERS OF THE GODS - BOOKS 1-3 BUNDLE

Stand Alone Books

TO SIN WITH SCANDAL

OUTLAWS

ABOUT THE AUTHOR

Tamara Gill is an Australian author who grew up in an old mining town in country South Australia, where her love of history was founded. So much so, she made her darling husband travel to the UK for their honeymoon, where she dragged him from one historical monument and castle to another.

A mother of three, her two little gentlemen in the making, a future lady (she hopes) and a part-time job keep her busy in the real world, but whenever she gets a moment's peace she loves to write romance novels in an array of genres, including regency, medieval and time travel.

www.tamaragill.com
tamaragillauthor@gmail.com